Hilda's Home
A Story of Woman's Emancipation

by

Rosa Graul

Double9
BOOKS

Hilda's Home
A Story of Woman's Emancipation
by Rosa Graul

ISBN: 978-93-62201-36-2

Published by

DOUBLE 9 BOOKS

2/13-B, Ansari Road
Daryaganj, New Delhi – 110002
info@double9books.com
www.double9books.com
Tel. 011-40042856

ABOUT THE AUTHOR

Rosa Graul, a pioneering voice in literature, penned the compelling masterpiece "Hilda's Home: A Story of Woman's Emancipation," which stands as a beacon of empowerment and enlightenment. Through her insightful narrative, Graul unveils the journey of Hilda, a woman determined to break free from the constraints of societal norms and carve her path towards emancipation. In "Hilda's Home," Graul masterfully explores the complexities of womanhood and the quest for autonomy in a patriarchal society. Set against the backdrop of the late 19th century, Hilda's journey unfolds as a poignant tale of resilience, courage, and self-discovery. As Hilda navigates the challenges and obstacles in her path, Graul delves deep into the intricacies of human emotions and societal expectations, shedding light on the struggles faced by women seeking liberation and self-fulfillment. With unwavering determination, Hilda challenges conventional notions of femininity and asserts her right to independence and agency. Through her evocative prose and vivid characterizations, Graul invites readers to embark on a transformative journey alongside Hilda, where the pursuit of freedom becomes a rallying cry for all women striving for equality and empowerment. "Hilda's Home" stands as a testament to Graul's literary genius and her unwavering commitment to championing the cause of women's emancipation.

CONTENTS

CHAPTER I

"And I may hope? You will not give me a decided no for answer?"

The time was a lovely June evening. The moon was at its full, wrapping everything in a silvery haze, while the air was laden with the sweet perfume of roses and of new-mown hay. The scene was the lawn of a beautiful suburban home on the outskirts of the city of Harrisburg. Under the swaying branches of the silver maples that lined the carriage drive leading to the house could be seen a maiden and youth walking slowly back and forth, his fair head bent slightly forward, anxiously awaiting the answer from the trembling lips. The flash of the dark eye and the heightened color of her usually pale face gave evidence of a tempest within. Then slowly the dark eyes were raised to the blue ones above them, and slowly came the answer,

"I do not know!"

"You do not know?" He repeated the words as slowly, surprise struggling in the tone of his voice as he spoke.

"Imelda, surely you know if you love me, if you 2are able to grant my heart's desire?" Saying which, he caught her hand in his and drew her out of the shadows into the bright light of the full moon.

"Look at me, Imelda, and tell me what you mean! Can it be that I have been deceived in you? I believed you loved me. I thought I had often read the proof of a tender emotion in your eyes; and now you tell me you do not know."

Deep feeling quivered in every cadence of his voice. He was terribly excited, terribly in earnest; so much was easy to see.

The smile that for a moment played about her lips was a sad one. Softly and clearly the words fell from them.

"You have not misunderstood me. I do love you, O, so much, but—" The sentence remained unfinished. With a low, happy cry he gathered her in his arms. His silken mustache swept her cheek, his lips closed firmly over hers. For a moment all else was forgotten; their souls blended in that kiss—a draught fraught with divinest love. It was bliss, ecstacy, such as only those are able to enjoy who are possessed of a pure mind. For a few moments the girl gave herself up to the enjoyment of blissful consciousness. Then with a determined effort she freed herself from his embrace, laid her soft hand upon his shoulder and, standing with her head slightly thrown back, said: "But—I do not know if I can marry you."

Surprise showed plainly in his every feature. "You love me, and do not know if you can marry me! Imelda, you are an enigma. I cannot understand you. What can you possibly mean?"

A sigh escaped the parted lips. "I mean, my Norman,"—laying a hand on either of his cheeks—"I mean that I would fain keep my lover! I am afraid of a husband. Husbands are not lovers."

The surprised look upon his face intensified until it became perfectly blank. "Husbands are not lovers? Child, who put such notions into your head? As husband and wife, when we are such, then will be the time of the perfect blending of our love—you mine and I thine. Imelda, now that I know the sweet boon of your love is mine, I want to realize it in its fullness. You must grant me the consummation of it."

Again she was folded in his arms, pillowed upon his breast, while his cheek rested against hers. She felt the increase of his passion in the kisses he pressed upon her lips. His breath mingled with hers. She felt and heard the mighty throbs of his heart, while his love for her seemed almost to overpower him. She felt her blood in a feverish glow as it pulsed through her veins; it was heaven, but—a shudder suddenly shook her frame, she whispered, hurriedly, intensely: "No! No! No! I can not, can not marry you. I am afraid!"

With a mighty effort conquering the tumult of his emotions, but still holding her closely pressed, he could only articulate, "But why? Why should you be afraid when I love you, oh, so dearly? I want you for my own, my precious one—my very own, where never the breath of another man can touch you; where you will be mine forever more."

"And when the time comes that this feverish love-fire of yours shall have burned itself out, when you begin to tire of me,—always me—what then will I do with my intense love nature? a nature to which love is life and without which I cannot live. What then, Norman, will become of me?" She lay back in his arms and again holding his face between her hands she asked the question with a fierce intensity that left her voice a mere husky whisper,—"Norman, Norman, what then will become of me?"

Norman Carlton was more than surprised; he was fast becoming puzzled. There was every evidence that the girl he was holding in his arms bore him a deep-rooted love, but that she should, at the outset,—at the very moment of the meeting and blending of these two intense natures, that at such a time there should arise in her heart a fear of the future,—fear that a time might come when his love for her might not be the same, did not at all accord with the knowledge he, until now, possessed of the feminine nature.

Woman, as he had found her, was only too willing to believe all the love rhapsodies of man. If he but offered her marriage he was always held by the gentler sex to be the soul of honor. And really, thought he, what greater honor could man confer upon woman than marriage? To make her his wife, to give her his name! Yet here was a woman who with the intensity of a perfectly healthy and normal endowment, bore him a love which only such an one could give, and yet—and yet withheld the trust that he, until now, had found inseparable from the love of woman.

She seemed to be possessed of a doubt that his love would be a lasting one, in the face of the fact of his having just made her an offer of marriage,— using the argument, against all his passionate wooing, that love would not last. He had heard, but had read little, of the doctrines that were at this time being agitated in society, of marriage being a failure; that there was no true happiness in domestic life, etc., etc. Could it be possible that this girl, who had wound herself with the most tender coils about his heart, had imbibed such heresies? He hoped not! The love he bore her was a pure love, and a pure love only he must have in return, and could a love that he had heard termed "free love,"—such as he understood the term, be a pure one? She loved, and yet refused marriage. She clung to the lover and repelled the idea of a husband. What could it mean! It was beyond Norman Carlton's conception of pure womanhood.

He was indeed the soul of honor. He held all womankind in high esteem. He revered his mother, and held his sister as one to look up to. His highest conception of happiness was the mutual love of the sexes, the consummation of which meant marriage. His idea of home, and of home life was something exalted, while his ideal of a wife was a thing to be held apart from all the world. She should be his to care for, to make smooth the rough paths of her life, to protect and guard her. She should be the mother of his children. He felt, he knew his love would be as lasting as the hills. Why then should she fear? With conflicting emotions he gently clasped her hands while he sought to read what was hidden within the depths of those brown wells of light.

Gently, softly, he spoke: "Why should my girl doubt the strength, the durability, of my love? Does not intuition tell her it will be safe to trust me?"

"Aye, I do trust you, Norman. I would willingly place my hand in yours and follow you to the end of the world. With your love to lean on I would wander with you to some isolated spot where there was no one else to see the whole year round, and be happy, O, so happy, and yet— —"

"And yet what?"

"How do you know that this love will last? How is it possible to speak for the future? How can you, or I, or anyone, control the fates that have or may have, other affinities in store for us? How can we know—O, Norman, how can we know? Believe me, I do not doubt your love. I know its precious boon is mine, but the future is dark, and I fear to trust myself to its unknown mysteries." And sobbing she sank upon his breast.

Here was indeed an enigma. Would he be able to solve it? Willing to enjoy the present but fearing to trust the future. This queer girl was conjuring up dread, though often heard-of facts, but in his case utter impossibilities. Trembling for the love that at present so surely was hers, lest by some dread possibility in the future she might lose it, yet dreading, fearing to enter that indissoluble marriage tie thereby securing unto herself for life the object of her love. Long the lovers wandered up and down the shady walk. That their love was mutual, that there was a natural affinity between their souls, that both possessed that in their make-up which was necessary for the completion of the other, was apparent, yet while he longed and plead for that closer tie called marriage, in order to perfect their relations, she shrank from it as from some dread abyss.

"Let us be happy just as we are," she pleaded. "We can walk and talk, kiss and sing, and be unutterably happy when we are together. Please, please do not let us speak of marriage. I almost hate the mere mention of it. I have seen so much of the misery it contains. Of all the married people I have known, after the first few months or perhaps the first year, generally after the first babe has come, they have 7drifted apart,—they do not miss one another when separated, and I know of but very few cases indeed where happiness reigned queen in their homes. I have known many happy lovers who found, after entering into the matrimonial state, that they had made a sad, a very sad mistake. They did not realize what they had expected. I do not want to think that such would be our case, but I cannot conquer the fear of it. Let me be happy in the knowledge that your perfect love is mine in the present hour. I have no fear of losing you. I feel, I know, that I am as necessary to you as you are to me."

And with that he had to be content, for the time being at least. She was his by all the bonds of affinity that nature had established between them. He felt that she was pure and good, although he knew next to nothing of her past life. The handsome home that lay just in front of them, whose beautiful grounds, bathed in the silvery sheen of moonlight, was but a temporary home, for this queenly girl. Her position in it was only that of a menial. Its pretty sparkling mistress had brought her home with her from a visit to that western metropolis, Chicago, "A friend of my school days," she had said. "An orphan in straitened circumstances." So she had entered its stately portals as a companion to its mistress, a nursing governess to two pretty little girls of four and six years.

As Alice Westcot was a favorite in society, and as her husband, Lawrence Westcot, was a man of prominence, this obscure western beauty, although appearing in a somewhat lowly position, was, with a certain hesitancy, but withal rather graciously, received. To be sure, society was careful not to make too much of her—that is, the lady portion of it. O, woman! how cruel you can be to your sister woman. Dainty lips curled while fair delicate hands drew more closely dainty skirts when this unknown queenly girl drew nigh. It is only fair to say that she was not treated thus by all women—society women. Now and then true worth was found under the butterfly exterior. Women could say nothing against her, even if they would say nothing for her. Men doffed their hats, while their admiring eyes followed the fair form. But there was something in her bearing and manner that commanded their respect. As yet no man had dared to address her in anything but a respectful tone.

But little cared Imelda for the haughtiness of the one or the admiration of the other. Pretty, lively Mrs. Westcot treated her more like a sister and friend than a menial, and often in the seclusion of her chamber, where she could lay aside the mask of conventionality, the bright little woman had made a confidant of Imelda. Then all the life, all the smiles and animation, would disappear. The blue eyes would fill with tears, and the trembling lips confess such tales of woe as would blanch the roses on the health-glowing cheeks of the horrified girl, while the lips of the listener would answer: "Again! Again has marriage proven a failure! Is it ever, oh! is it ever, anything else?" Her lips would quiver, the dark eyes would fill with unshed tears as a fair face, a sunny smile, and eyes which seemed pure wells of truth, arose before her mental vision. Then she would question, "Are all men alike? Is it ever and always the fate of woman to be the slave of men?"

Norman Carlton was a friend and visitor of the Westcots, and as Imelda ever moved freely about the house, it was not long until they met. Both frank and pure in heart and mind, both worshipers at nature's shrine, it was not strange they should be attracted. Indeed, it would have been strange had it not so been. They loved. But Imelda's past had been freighted with so many dark experiences and observations of married misery, of married woes, that she felt no desire to bring her sweet love dream to a sudden end—to deal it a death blow by placing upon it the seal of marriage.

"If you knew, you would understand," she said in answer to his wondering gaze.

"And may I not know?"

"Some time, Norman, some time, but not yet awhile, not yet. Tonight let me be happy, boundlessly happy."

So they walked up and down under the silver maples until the hours waned. The moon had changed her position, and the brightly lighted windows were fading into darkness. Thus reminded of the flight of time, they parted—she to seek her snowy draped chamber and dream of what the dark future might perchance have in store for her. Sunny, golden dreams they were, to judge by the happy smile that lingered on the lips where yet his kisses lay warm, while again a thought of those darker times that lay hidden in the past, would break in upon the sweet present and like a somber cloud overcast the heaven's blue, so would she feel a gloom cast over her young happiness. Shivering she disrobed and sought her couch, that she might, in sweet slumber, forget the world and its woes, and thus continue her waking dreams of him who constituted her heaven.

And Norman? With his head bared to the cool air, he watched the graceful form flit across the lawn and disappear within the house. Then, murmuring, "You are a mystery, my sweet queen, but, for all that, my pure love. Whatever it may be that makes you differ from other women I know that none but pure emotions can stir that fair bosom. Good night, my winsome love! Good night! Whatever the sad experience may have been that has seemingly destroyed your faith in man, I mean to win it back. I mean to prove to you clearly that at least one man is worthy the unbounded trust of one pure woman."

A little while longer he stood, until a light, flashing from one of the upper windows, told him that Imelda had entered her room, and was probably preparing to retire. Again his "Good night" was wafted upon the air in a love-laden whisper, and then his firm tread could be heard receding in the distance as he wended his way quickly under the whispering silvery maples.

CHAPTER II

What of Imelda's past? What were the dark forbidding shadows that threatened to overcast her future?

Nothing unusual; interwoven only with a story such as has darkened many another young girl's life. The history of one woman's life, the threads of which were woven so closely with hers as to hold her to those past memories as in a net in whose meshes no loophole had been left. Imelda's mother, just such a bright, beautiful and queenly girl as she herself now was, had wrecked her life upon the rock upon which thousands daily, hourly are wrecked. Of what this rock consisted we shall see as our story proceeds.

Nellie Dunbar was the child of poverty. She was one of eight children, whose parents probably could not have taken proper care of one. So, instead of giving Nellie that which every child has the right to demand of those who take upon themselves the responsibility of ushering children into existence, viz: a thorough education to develop their mental capacities; proper care of their young bodies to enable them to become full rounded women and men; careful, tender nurture of both body and soul—instead of giving Nellie and her numerous brothers and sisters all this it was only in their very young days—days when the minds of children should be free and unburdened of care save childhood's plays, that they were able to send them to school at all. While yet of very tender age, when toys and books should have been their only care, these were laid away upon the shelf and their young strength pressed into the much needed work of helping to support the family.

Oh, ye parents of the millions! Do you ever think of the wrongs daily and hourly perpetrated upon the children, those mites of humanity whose advent into the world you yourselves are directly responsible for; upon whose unborn souls you place a curse that is to work out its woes in the coming ages—children who with all their unfitness are to become in turn, the parents of the race?

Nellie found work in a cloak factory, and, as she sat day by day bending above her machine she often almost cursed the fate that made her a working girl; only she had been taught that such thoughts were impious. That it was a good and all-wise "God" who had mapped out her life, and that it would be wicked to be anything but thankful.

But Nellie's heart was rebellious. Not always could she quell the longings that would well up therein. So when one day a handsome, dark-haired, dark-eyed man found this beautiful uncultured bird she fell an easy victim. It was the old, old story over again, of a trusting maiden's love and of man's selfish appetite. Not that he was a greater villain than men are wont to be, but men, like the bee, are used to sip the honey from every fair flower hereon they may happen to alight. He knew he would be envied the possession of the love, the favor, of this beautiful creature, by all of his friends, while the possession itself would be unalloyed bliss to him.

But a time came when his plaything tired the man of fashion and culture. He would have dropped it, but he had reckoned without his host. Maddened by the sneers and innuendoes of her hitherto companions and by the insults of men, all the latent devil that lies hidden and veiled within the heart of many a loving woman, was aroused. Having managed to purloin from her brother's pocket a shining little toy and hiding it within her heaving bosom, she sought her betrayer's side. With burning cheeks she demanded of him to do her justice.

He would have tried again to soothe her fiery blood with honeyed words, but they had lost their power. Her faith in him had been destroyed; never again could she trust him. He sought to allay her fears with fair promises; he would marry her, if she would wait a few days; he wished to arrange his affairs; he would prepare a home for her.

The young girl's eyes flashed ominously as she answered: "No! I will not wait. Now! instantly, do I want my due."

Herbert Ellwood began to grow impatient. He was tired of the scene. Curbing his temper, however, he again made answer: "This evening, then, I promise to be with you although you are very foolish not to wait a few days longer, until I should have had prepared a home to take you to."

She looked like a lovely fury as she stamped her foot in rising anger. "Now!" she cried. "Now, within the hour! I cannot, I will not trust you one moment longer."

The hot blood mounted to his white forehead,—Did this pretty fool think that she could command him?—him who had always been the darling of fair women?—him who needed but to hold out his hand to find it eagerly clasped by any of a dozen fair ones? Scorn curled his lip, and the habitual gentleness from his manner suddenly fled.

"Enough," he cried.—"I am tired of this. Go home and wait until I come."

With this he turned his back upon her, making it very plain to her that he considered the obnoxious interview at an end. But the demon in the girl's heart was now fully aroused. With a quick step she had reached his side. Despair and anger gave her strength. By one quick movement she whirled him round when he found flashing in his eyes the shining barrel of a revolver.

"I will avenge my honor on the spot, here and now,—wipe out my shame in your blood if you delay an instant longer to do me the justice I demand."

She spoke the words in a tragic manner. She had worked herself into a frenzy, and Herbert felt it was dangerous to longer trifle with her—that she was capable of executing her threat. So he submitted to the inevitable. With a sigh he donned his coat and hat and hailing a hack they were quickly driven to the nearest minister's whose son and daughter witnessed the ceremony.

Through it all Nellie's cheeks were the color of blood; her eyes gleamed like living coals. When all was over, her overwrought nerves gave way. Breaking into a fit of hysterical weeping, she sank at her unwilling bridegroom's feet. Frightened and shamed he gathered her in his arms, carried more than led her from the bewildered minister's presence into the waiting hack.

He was at a loss where to take her. He could not take her to his bachelor apartments. He feared to take her to her mother in the condition she was in, knowing only too well that the ignorant woman would not hesitate to heap abuse upon her daughter's head when she knew all. So, after a few moment's consideration, he named some distant hotel to the waiting hack driver, where, upon their arrival, he procured rooms and saw that she was properly cared for.

It was long ere she became quiet. The unhappy girl walked the room, backward and forward, while a storm of sobs shook her form. For a time Ellwood feared insanity would claim her. He was not at heart a bad man, and such an ending to this day's work would have been most unwelcome to him. He had been living merely to enjoy himself, as a certain class of young men are in the habit of doing, though it be at the expense of some other member of the human family, probably not stopping to think, not realizing, what the cost may be to that other. He had fallen desperately in love with Nellie's fair face and, had she loved him "more wisely," as the saying is, it is likely he himself would have proposed marriage. But his fever having cooled somewhat he recognized only too well the fact that they two were not mated; that true happiness could never spring from such an union.

But—well, things had taken a different course. Full well he knew that he had wronged the beautiful but uncultured girl. He was now called upon to make reparation, and marriage had set its seal with its "until death do us part," upon them.

As remarked before, he was not a villain. Now that the deed was done it took him but a short time to make up his mind to abide the consequences, be they what they might. He knew they were unsuited to each other; that they had very little in common, but he knew that she was beautiful. He would never need to be ashamed of her appearance. He had had the benefit of a splendid education. He had a lucrative position, and by casting overboard many of his old habits and associates he thought they might be able to get along. Then, too, she was used to work. She knew and understood the value of money; surely with her experience in life she would be able to manage— would understand the art of housewifery.

Alas, he did not know, did not understand how this having been used to work all her life caused her to hate work. As he had been lavish with her—spending his money freely when in her society, the idea had taken deep root in her brain that he was wealthy; whereas he had only that which his position—bookkeeper, secured him. She had denied and stinted herself so long that now she meant to enjoy.

It was not an easy matter for the young man to be true to his resolves and do what he considered his duty by her. If, in those first hours when her grief had been at its greatest, he had folded her to his heart with real affection, instead of forcing himself to every caress—to hide the deep disappointment in his inmost heart—may be he might yet have reawakened the love that through deceit had turned to Dead Sea fruit upon her lips. Or, if she with womanly tenderness had coaxed his ebbing love into new life, things might have been different. But, as it was, the hour wherein she had found herself compelled to force him to comply with her demands and make her his wife, in that hour her love for him had died—died for all time.

Had she been a woman cultured and refined she would have scorned him; that lacking, she was simply indifferent. She no longer cared for that which once had constituted her heaven, but, on the contrary, was inclined now to a desire to get even with him, as the saying is. It was not a great soul that Nellie was the possessor of. A poor but pretty—nay, a beautiful girl, born under circumstances such as children of her are usually born under, surrounded and reared in the same manner, what could you expect?

And Herbert Ellwood? Ah! he felt more keenly. The sowing of the wild oats that young men are unhappily supposed to have a right to sow, and even ought to sow, according to the views of some—had only for a time threatened to stifle that which was good and true in his nature; and bitterly in his after-life did he rue the sowing.

After having made up his mind that there was now but one proper course for him to pursue, that course he meant to pursue. Days passed on. He soon found that to harvest his crop of wild oats was not so easy or so pleasant as the sowing had been. Nellie's temper was the rock upon which all his good resolves stranded. He would have taught her many things that would have had a tendency not only to make her a polished lady but which would have been of daily, almost hourly use to her, but she mistakenly argued that as she had been good enough in the past to while away the time with, pretty enough to cause him to fall in love with her, she was good and pretty enough now as his wife, just as she was. She did not understand that it was ever so much more difficult for a wife to attract and hold a husband, even in those few cases where love rules supreme in the home of the married couple, than it is for a bright and sparkling young girl to win a lover.

But time sped on; the months passed by and then came the hour when the cause of this most unhappy union was ushered into existence—a little brown eyed babe. The fair Imelda was born. For a while it seemed as if the young couple would return to the love of their earlier days. The advent of the little creature was something wherein they had a common interest. But as Nellie grew stronger her attention was all taken up by baby, who proved a charming dimpled darling, cooing and laughing in the faces of both parents alike.

But the young mother never was the old self again. The charming girl soon developed into a fretful discontented woman. The man that found life such a disappointment gave all his love to his baby daughter and it was not long until the baby screamed and struggled at his approach. Perched upon his shoulder, her tiny hands buried in his clustering curls, she would babble and crow with delight. For the time Herbert Ellwood would be happy, but even this sight—a sight that would have melted most young mothers' hearts with pride and happiness, was only another bone of contention between them. Squabbles and quarrels were of daily occurrence.

Nellie was irritable and dissatisfied. Her health was failing her. Herbert was tired and disgusted with his unpleasant home, and began to spend his evenings away from it. In consequence many lonely hours fell to Nellie's lot. Often her pillow would be wet with tears. She was unhappy and knew not the reason. She laid the blame at Herbert's door; whereas he, poor fellow, had done all in his power to bring things to a different issue. He had miserably failed.

But neither knew the reason why. Both failed to understand that as they had ceased to attract, as they had scarcely so much as a single thought in common, they should long ago have parted. They were falling in with that most abominable practice of modern times and of modern marriage,—to "make the best of" what contained *absolutely no best!*—as their union was miserably barren of all good qualities. Each was conscious of a dull aching void, with no understanding as to how it could be filled.

Time passed on, and other babies came,—unwelcome, unwished for mites of humanity that sprang from the germ of a father's passion, gestated by a mother with a feeling of repugnance amounting almost to hate. What mattered it that in the hour of birth each new comer was caught lovingly to the mother's breast, when in that moment of mortal agony the wellspring of her love had been touched. No amount of *later* love could undo the mischief done *before its advent*.

Some of these babes were ill-natured and puny from their birth, born only to pine away and die, racking again the mother's heart. Two others, a boy and a girl, grew to be the torment of the household and the bane of their mother's life. And still the babies came, and oh! so close, one upon the other, until the poor mother thought life was a burden too great to be borne.

Such a flood of anger and hate towards the father and husband, would sweep over her heart as the knowledge of each conception was forced upon her! At such moments she felt as though she could kill him.

Reader, can you read between the lines? Can you see the hidden skeleton in this miserable home? Do you understand how it all could have been avoided? Herbert Ellwood, as stated before, was not a bad man. Instead, he possessed many noble qualities. But he was a child of modern society. He was a husband, possessed of a wife. He had always been what the world calls true to that wife. He was possessed of health, strength and passion. Is it necessary to say more? The story is a plain one, and an old one. The thinking reader will find little difficulty in discerning that theirs was the curse of modern marriage life.

CHAPTER III

Such had been the early life of Imelda Ellwood. Surely not the best of environments for the development of a young character, but, singularly enough, Imelda's was so sweet and pure a nature that in spite of all the close contact with impure elements she remained thus pure and sweet. But early she became disgusted with home life, measuring all to which the name applied by the standard she had known. Even as a child she was wont to say: "I will never marry." Home to her meant the elements of war. Her brother Frank, just fifteen months younger than herself, and sister Cora again only sixteen months younger than Frank, were the torments of her life. Frank's teasing propensities were so great that he was utterly reckless as to his methods of indulging them, so he succeeded in making those around him miserable. If Imelda had a new book, he was sure to damage it in some way. If she had a new article of clothing, he would ridicule it until the very sight of it became hateful to her. If she made an engagement to go somewhere and he became aware of the fact he would contrive to make it impossible for her to keep it, or at least to detain her so long that she was robbed of the greater part of the pleasure she had expected to derive from it.

Cora was tantalizing, obstinate and contradictory; always opposed to everything that Imelda wished. Sometimes she felt that she almost hated them. Added to this her mother cast a heavy burden upon the tender shoulders of the young girl. Almost always with a babe in her arms, or expecting one, she let her shafts of ill-temper play upon her eldest daughter. Often it seemed there was a certain bitterness and vengefulness directed against Imelda as the author of all her troubles — it having been her expected coming that caused the consummation of this most unhappy marriage. Conscious of having in some way incurred the ill-will of her mother, but unconscious as to the *how*, Imelda often wept bitter tears at the unjust treatment she received at the hands of her who should have been the child's best friend. In this case it was the father who proved himself such. Early these two found in each other a comfort and help such as is rarely known between father and daughter.

To her he imparted all the knowledge that should have been the mother's care, and although the little Imelda saw but little of the inside of a schoolroom, she grew up a really fine scholar.

After having instructed her in all the rudimentary branches, he taught her the classics. He taught her elocution, music,—instrumental and vocal, book-keeping, shorthand, etc. Next, German and French.

Herbert Ellwood was a scholar, and he made a scholar of his daughter. She was eager to learn, and it was a pleasure for him to teach her. Even this proved a bone of contention in that home,—a home which was as unlike what a home should be as could well be imagined. Her mother grumbled over the wasted time, poring over books when there was so much work to be done. Cora turned up her saucy nose and said, doubtless the time was coming when she would have to humbly bow to Madame Doctor, or Lawyer So and So, or Professor of some University; while Frank thought more likely she was getting ready to catch some "big beau," and maybe become "My Lady" to some rich foreigner, some great Lord, or something of that sort. Imelda had by this time, to a certain extent, become callous to such taunts, and quietly went her way, performing obnoxious duties that were waiting to be done, with no one else to do them.

But as the years went by changes came. First; the greatest and most lamentable of them all, was the death of her father.

For years past he had been ailing, and the time came when he was unable to work. At first he brought his books home in the evening, and with the assistance of his faithful child strove to complete the task he found himself unable to cope with alone, and, by working hours after he had been compelled to lay aside his pen Imelda was able to finish his work for him. But the time came at last that he was unable to do anything. He could no longer go to his daily labor. All day long he would sit near his open window and watch the busy turmoil in the streets below. Then he become too weak even for that; so he lay upon the bed watching his beloved child, and wondering what she would do when he was gone. His wife and other children did not seem to worry him. His thoughts were all concentrated upon Imelda, and Imelda's heart almost broke as she watched the thin white face grow thinner and whiter day by day. Now and then the thin emaciated frame would be convulsed with a fit of coughing that would leave him perfectly exhausted. Tenderly she would smooth his pillows, would hold a cooling drink to his lips, then with a firm hand she would smooth his brow until under her gentle, soothing influence he would fall into a light slumber.

Then Imelda would glide away from his bedside, and, if possible, seek her own room for awhile, where she could relieve her overcharged heart of the load that was suffocating her. Tears would flow and ease would come. Although her mother had in her early childhood taught her to pray, Imelda never now thought of seeking aid or relief in prayer. She had long been a skeptic. She had seen the dark side only of life, and she often wondered if life held any brightness for her? How often had she asked without receiving an answer: "Why must my young life be so different from that of other girls?"

Just at present the fear of losing her beloved father was paramount to everything else, and while she felt as though an iron hand was clutching at her throat she watched and saw his life slowly ebbing away, and, at the close of a calm, balmy autumn day he quietly fell asleep, never again to awaken, and on the 18th of October, Imelda's seventeenth birthday, he was laid away to rest within the tree-shaded cemetery.

After that, Imelda had more duties to perform, heavier burdens to bear. Contrary to what might have been expected, her mother refused to be comforted, and became even more fretful and irritable than before. Imelda moved about calm, pale and tearless, but with oh! such an aching weary heart. But never a word passed her pale lips—for who would have understood that ceaseless pain—and for which she was reproached as being heartless and unfeeling.

Although Herbert Ellwood had always been able to command fair wages, there had been nothing laid aside for a rainy day. His wife never had been what is known as a good housewife. She believed in taking the things the gods provide and let the morrow take care of itself. So when he was no longer able to follow his daily occupation, they were without means. His long and lingering illness had plunged them heavily into debt, the burden of which rested solely on Imelda's slender shoulders. And—they must live! Both sisters found work behind the counters of a dry goods emporium. Cora grumbling and daily declaring that it was a shame, and that she was determined to make a change as soon as a chance offered. Frank too, was told that it was time he placed his shoulder to the wheel, as the combined efforts of two girls were hardly sufficient to support a family of five, for there was another little girl of two years: "Baby Nellie" she was called. But Frank would put his hands in his pockets, whistle the latest air he had heard at some low "variety show," bestow a kick upon the frolicking kitten, make a grimace at baby Nellie and walk out as unconcerned as though there were no such thing in the world as the worry and trouble of procuring food for hungry mouths and clothes for freezing backs, or paying rent to keep a miserable roof over their heads. Imelda's face would perhaps grow a shade paler and the trembling lips compress more tightly, but farther than that she gave no sign. From her mother it would generally bring forth a flood of tears.

Imelda would feel as though a cold hand was clutching at her throat as she watched her mother. Poor mother! What had life brought to her? It had been one long succession of trials, sorrow and woes without the ability to cope with them. Once, and only once, Imelda ventured to gently wind her arm about her. With an impatient movement the poor woman had brushed it aside, accompanied with an irritable, "Don't!" After that Imelda never ventured to approach her again. Her sensitive spirit had been deeply wounded, but she also knew that her mother could not by any possibility understand her. So she tried hard not to bear her any ill will. She eagerly sought for every excuse she could think of for the mother whose life she knew had been made up more of thorns than roses.

So, the weeks and months went by in a weary routine, but bringing with them new troubles and fresh sorrows. Frank, who had persistently refused to put his hands to any kind of work, had idled away his time with companions who were wholly as bad if not worse than himself. Under the leadership of one more bold than the rest they had for some time been perpetrating deeds of petty larceny until they were caught in the act. The most of them were arrested and a term of work house stared them in the face. Frank, however, with one other succeeded in absconding. This was the news that was brought home to the despairing mother and grief-stricken sister. Never again had the poor mother seen or heard aught of him. They knew that he possessed a passionate love for the water and they felt sure that he had gone to sea.

And yet another trouble awaited them. Cora, who was now sixteen years of age, and who gave promise of beauty in the future, though as yet undeveloped, had formed the acquaintance of a graceless scamp, fair of face, with but the possession of a decidedly insipid smile—a brainless fop with an oily tongue. The willful girl had been meeting him for some time before Imelda became conscious of the fact. Long and earnestly did she strive to reason with the refractory sister, pointing out to her the many defects of this very objectionable lover.

But Cora had always been obstinate, and the years had brought no change in this respect. In plain words, she told Imelda to mind her own business. A short time after she disappeared—leaving a note stating she had "gone to live with one with whom she could have a little peace," as she expressed it.

For some time the mother and sister were unable to trace her whereabouts, but one evening, some six weeks later, Imelda had an errand to another portion of the city. Returning about ten o'clock she hailed a car and presently found herself seated opposite her runaway sister, and with her the partner of her flight. To judge from the manner of both there was little happiness or love or *peace* between the couple. Even to an ordinary observer it would have been apparent from the sulky and extremely careless outward appearance of the two that Cora's love dream had been cut very short.

After the first shock Imelda conquered her fear of risking an altercation in so public a place and seated herself at Cora's side. There was something in the defiant attitude of the girl that caused her heart to stand still with a nameless dread, but she forced herself to speak.

"Cora," she said, "are you married?" Cora paled, and in her companion's eye was a wicked flash. A hesitating "Yes," fell from the lips of the wayward sister. Intuitively Imelda felt that she was telling a falsehood, and her heart sank within her. She understood that the willful girl was leading a life of deliberate shame. Only a short time until she would be cast off, and then— —?

Imelda could not bear to contemplate the "then!" With a sound like rushing waters in her ears, she arose from her seat and staggered toward the entrance of the car. She must get away from the near presence of the twain, out into the open air. She felt that she must suffocate in there. How she reached home she never knew, but *that* night sleep was a stranger to her eyes. The next day she went about her work a trifle paler, her footsteps a trifle slower. While her mother fretted over the child that could leave her in such a fashion without one thought of the pain she was inflicting on loving hearts, she never heeded the drooping gait and the pained expression upon the face of her eldest child.

The winter had come and gone, and come again and the watchful eye of Imelda detected that the mother's step was slower. The tall figure was slightly bent and an unnameable something about her struck terror to the daughter's heart. She drooped and faded day by day, and the much tired girl knew that darker days were coming. Often on coming home in the evening she would find her mother lying on the bed, not asleep, but broken down, without ambition enough to lift the weary head from the pillow; little Nellie crying bitterly with cold and hunger, or perhaps the poor baby had sobbed itself to sleep upon the floor while its mother seemed to have lost all interest in what was going on around her.

Imelda moaned in despair. She was needed oh, so much at home. The ailing, wasted form of her mother appealed so strongly to her aching heart for the care there was no one to bestow. The baby felt like ice as she pressed the tiny thing to her heaving bosom. But how could they live if she remained at home? Only what her tender hands were able to earn did they have to keep the wolf from the door. And if she ceased to work? What then?

Imelda knew and felt that darker days were coming, darker than she had yet known, and her impotence to ward them off almost drove her to despair. But the time came when she felt that she could no longer remain away from the bedside of the dying mother, come what would. To make matters still worse little Nellie had contracted a severe cold, and many sleepless nights fell to her share walking to and fro, from the bedside of the sick woman to that of the ailing child. One by one all the little comforts and luxuries of former days were parted with. Pretty trinkets her father had given her and which, therefore were of great value to her, were all sacrificed.

In the early spring the change came. The baby had been unusually feverish for several days while the mother was sinking fast. The night was bitter cold and Imelda knew she must not sleep. Both patients were nearing their end. Folding her shawl more closely around her shoulders to be more comfortable, she prepared for her long and dreary vigil. Never a word did the mother speak, breathing heavily in a dull stupor. Toward midnight she moved uneasily. Imelda bending over her saw her lips move. She bent lower and caught the whispered words, "Frank, Cora." That was all.

The wayward ones, who had taken their mother's life with them, to them the last breath was given. Nellie and Imelda were with her. It was the absent wayward ones that had left a void. When the morning dawned, it was to find the weary woman at rest; the woman whose life had been one long mistake. The baby moaned. Imelda lifted her to her knee, and as the sun sent its first rays through the dim window pane the fluttering breath left the little purple lips, and Imelda was alone—alone with her dead!

CHAPTER IV

After the body of her mother had been laid away, by the side of that of her dead husband, with the youngest of eight children clasped in her arms, Imelda changed her home to a little attic room. When all was over she returned to the store where she had now been employed three years.

In the early days of her engagement there she had become acquainted with a bright cheery little girl, Alice Day by name, with whom she had become fast friends, although a greater contrast one could scarcely imagine than existed between the personalities of the two girls. The one, small, bright, saucy, sparkling; the other, tall, stately, sad. Although Alice did not have that high order of intelligence that Imelda was the possessor of, yet she was so purely child-like and frank, that they at once attracted each other; each supplying to the other that which she did not possess. Their friendship, however, was of short duration. Pretty Alice had a lover, a traveling salesman at the time, whose home was in the east. He was about to establish a business of his own and so would no longer have opportunities of seeing his little lady-love; a state of affairs that did not meet the approval of either the young gentleman in question or that of the fair Alice. So he proposed to take her with him as his wife.

Alice was married and Imelda saw no more of her friend. Now and then a letter came and she knew that the husband was prospering; that Alice lived in a beautiful home, and that two sweet babies, girl babies, had come to make music in that stately home.

About the time that Alice left the store to become a wife another girl found employment with the same firm; a tall, stately girl whom to describe would be extremely difficult. Fair as a lily, ruddy as a rose, with a bearing almost haughty. One moment a laughing, rollicking sprite, the next if some unlucky individual dared to address her with a freedom she thought uncalled for her blue eyes would emit such scornful flashes that you almost felt their scorching heat. The color would rise in her cheeks until they were stained a dark hue; her lips would be compressed so firmly that they appeared almost white.

Sometimes it appeared as though two distinct and separate spirits inhabited the body of this girl, so utterly would the different moods change her from one to the other. We might go still farther, and say there were three spirits. Three in one, for there was still another phase of her character. In the first, she was the rollicking, teasing, mirth-provoking sprite, the next, she was soft, melting, a child of dreams, and in the last a proud, scornful, haughty woman. Talented and gifted by nature, her character was as yet unformed. Future events would determine which phase would predominate.

Such was Margaret Leland when first Imelda knew her. The two girls were soon strongly attached to each other. Margaret was very sympathetic and Imelda was in need of sympathy. Misery loves company, it is said. So when Imelda one evening told her the story of her life, with all its trials and shadows,—which revelation was made after the death of her father, Margaret reciprocated by giving a history that was fully as sad as her own. Interwoven with her life were just as bitter tears, and if Margaret had not stood above an open grave her life had nevertheless been overshadowed by such tragic events that it took all the innate pride of her nature to enable her to hold up her head. Probably to this very cause was due the fact that she sometimes let this pride carry her to extremes.

It was on a fine summer evening not long before wayward Cora had deserted them that Imelda and Margaret had been walking together and found a seat in beautiful Lincoln Park. Imelda had just finished relating her story, omitting nothing of the mistakes that had been so fatal to the happiness of her parents. "I cannot understand," she concluded, "why it was they were so utterly unhappy. It often appeared to me that my mother almost hated my father, although he was far above her mentally, possessed of remarkable intelligence, having had the benefit of an education so thorough that often I have wondered how a match so unsuited was ever made. I have never known my father to be really unkind, although often impatient, as my mother could be very trying. However, I have often sought to excuse her for that; her health for years had not been of the best and the babies would come oh, so close! Poor mother! I suppose almost any woman would have broken down under it."

"I should think so," replied Margaret's low sweet voice. "Only think! eight children in how many years?"

"Fifteen," answered Imelda, "and you must remember, too, she had three miscarriages in that time. Yes, it was too much. Do you know," she continued musingly, "that the thought often comes to me, that while lover's love must be great, it is not great enough, not strong enough to withstand the storm of married woes. I have never had a lover, but have often dreamed of lover's joys. But tell me, where do you see lovers among married people?"

"Married lovers are indeed a rare sight," Margaret answered, "and," she continued, startling the ear of the listening Imelda, "love certainly is a beautiful dream. I know of what I am speaking, for it has come to me, e'en that; but *'marriage is a failure,'* and, as I think now, I do not believe I shall ever trust myself to its deceiving, cruel fetters."

"Then what will you do?"

"Remain as I am, free as the birds of the air. No man shall ever say to me, 'thou shalt' or 'thou shalt not'!"

Imelda stared at her friend in open-eyed wonder.

"What then will become of your love?" she asked.

Margaret's lips trembled as a sigh escaped them. "Ah, Love, sweet entrancing Love! Imelda, he is a fickle boy; promising you heavenly bliss to entice you into his meshes. They sound so fair, these promises, so bewitching in the rosy hue he weaves about them, until — —"

"Until what?"

"Until you permit his alluring voice to entice you into those rose-woven and satin-covered fetters called marriage bonds. Then, in a most tantalizing manner, after all loopholes of escape have been closed, he takes his departure with mocking laughter and leaves you only the blackness of despair. Your weak hands are not powerful enough to hold him with all the man-made laws of the land. He comes to us all unsought, in rose-strewn dreams. If you would retain his blissful presence you must meet him full of trust and confidence. Fetter this laughing, happy boy and he will slip from between your clinging, clutching fingers. In spite of yourself he is gone. You are alone, bound to a loathsome corpse. Never again will the sweet little cajoler walk by your side, in the old form, to soothe your aching heart with his warm perfumed breath. And if ever, in very pity for you, he shall make the attempt to draw near in another form, to warm your frozen heart, you are forced by the cruel laws of a cruel society with your own trembling hands to murder him.

"Marry? No! I may enjoy a lover's love, may mount with him to realms of bliss, and when the time comes that we have outgrown each other, the time when one may be mounting too fast for the other to keep up, as when one becomes a weight, clogging the footsteps of the other, then at least, no unnatural fetters will have bound us. We can still follow our own sweet wills, and should Love again with his winsome wiles approach me with his golden dreams, I shall then be free to clasp him in my embrace. I may once again be happy in the sunshine he is sure to bring with him, and shed around him."

Awestruck Imelda listened. Margaret's cheeks were glowing with excitement. Her eyes shone with a splendor Imelda had never noted there before, while the look in them seemed far-away. Where were her thoughts? What visions floated before her mind? Was it the lover she spoke of, with whom she was mounting to unknown heights of bliss, or was she looking into the far-away future where he was the same, and yet not the same? When Love shall have taken upon himself a different guise than he at present wears? Who knows? Imelda listened spellbound to this dreaming girl, almost fearing to break the silence that ensued.

"Margaret, who taught you that? Where did you learn to hold such views of love and marriage?"

Almost instantly the entranced look faded from the face of the beautiful blonde. That most holy glow gave way to a sickly pallor. The lips quivered like those of a grieved child, and the eyes filled with tears.

"Experience," she faltered.

"Experience? You?"

"Yes, Imelda. Listen. I will now tell you the story of *my* life. Or, more properly speaking, that of my mother; but which has nevertheless influenced mine to such an extent that all my life, I suppose, the results of it must walk by my side, follow me wherever I go. To begin with, my mother has been what the world calls 'a divorced woman'."

"Divorced!" Imelda exclaimed in a startled manner.

"Yes, divorced! Married at the tender age of sixteen, she thought all that was needed to make earth a heaven was the complete union with the man she loved. A few week's she lived in a fool's paradise. She was young, inexperienced, with character undeveloped, else even in that short time she must have seen and understood the innate coarseness of the man who was her husband, whom she had promised to love, honor and *obey*, and who is my——father! In a very short time it dawned upon her that they had no tastes whatever in common. A brutal coarseness soon became manifest that caused her to shrink at his every touch. He soon came to understand this and it roused the very devil in him. He delighted in torturing her in every conceivable way. He did not even stop at blows."

"*Blows!* Oh,—" gasped Imelda. A bitter smile for a moment curled Margaret's lips, and then she proceeded:

"And that man is my father. Oh, why must I say it!" It cost her a great struggle to proceed. Imelda asked her to refrain, but Margaret insisted that she must tell her all, saying, "I would have to tell you some time that we may fully understand each other," and in a few moments she continued:

"The thought of separation never entered her mind in those days. She worked; a slave could scarcely have been more driven. A slave! Can it be possible there ever has been a worse slave than my mother was? And then the babies came. All through the time of gestation she had to work, to perform the hardest labor, and often my——father would come home intoxicated and, if it was possible for him to descend a step lower than was his wont, that was the time. I myself know little or nothing of those days, but my mother has made me her confidante, and every word she has told me is engraven on my heart. Oh, how she must have suffered in those awful, awful times! She was helpless under his brute power, and the relations that should only be the expression of a pure and holy love, that should, in my opinion, be fraught with divinest bliss, became to her the tortures of hell. Many a night sleep was a stranger to her eyes, and, other nights again, sleep came only after her pillow had been drenched with tears. Under such circumstances her children were born. Is it any wonder that the world is filled with criminals and idiots?

"How it was ever possible for me to be what I am is more than I can comprehend. I know I am far from perfect. I am terribly self-willed and can never bear being crossed. My mother was proud and self-willed also, and though she learned to hate and loathe the man whom according to law she was in duty bound to love, and though she suffered untold agonies I think her pride, her self-respect, would never permit her to stoop to anything that would degrade her, if we except the fact that she was forced to live in marriage with a man who was in every way a brute. It is to this pride and self-respect, I think, that I owe it that I am able to lay claim to a higher and better nature than it could otherwise have been possible for me to possess.

"Oh, the disgust that I feel when I hear matters pertaining to sex made light of. These relations to my mind are something sacred and pure. But the sensual man who believes that woman was made for his use only—the man who commits continual outrages upon the woman who is legally bound to him, upon her who bears the name of wife—such men defile the air with their very breath.

"If under such circumstances a woman in her own soul, through her superior mind, can create and hold a world of her own, making it possible to ward off many evils that would naturally be the inheritance of her children, what may she not do under conditions that are favorable? Thus I think it was that mother stood above my father as the stars are above the earth.

"But I have deviated. The years passed, and three times she had become a mother. Always for a short time after the advent of a little one my father seemed to show some marks of humanity, treating mother with some show of kindness, but not for long. It would soon wear away and when the trying season of gestation was upon her again he would be tenfold worse. My mother thinks the reason for this was that during those seasons she was more averse than ever to sex relations, which relations on his part meant neither more nor less than debauchery of what should have been an act personifying and realizing holy love. She would shrink from his touch as from a reptile. Not being able to understand her, as he was not possessed of a single refined instinct, it had the effect to infuriate him.

"Seven years my mother led this life. Her first born, a boy, died when he was a little more than a year old. Then I was born. After that came another boy. When Osmond was two years old and I four, my mother one day, with both of us left my father's house forever. During the last year or two matters had been growing worse and still worse, until finally they had become unendurable.

"My mother being a well-developed woman and possessing strong attractive powers would unconsciously draw the passing glances of men wherever she might chance to be. In spite of all she had been compelled to pass through, feeling was not yet dead within her. An intelligent and attractive man always had the power to move her to animation and life. This, again, my father could not understand, and to his many other faults was added that of an insane jealousy. It was the last straw that broke the camel's back. Having been subjected to his indignities until she was able to bear them no longer she resolved to submit to no more. So one wet, cold evening in the early autumn she returned to her childhood's home."

CHAPTER V

"But if my mother thought she was now freed from her husband's persecutions she was soon to be undeceived. He dared not enter her father's home but when the shades of evening came she soon found it was not safe to step outside of the house as she never knew the moment that he, like some uncanny apparition, would suddenly appear before her, and soon he succeeded in making her so nervous that she was almost afraid of her own shadow.

"Added to this trouble was the necessity of procuring work, for my grandfather was not blest with any surplus of this world's goods. It was with him as with so many thousands of others, weary work from early morn until late at night, in order to make both ends meet. The feeding of three new boarders and the procuring of proper clothing for them was a matter of no small importance.

"So having treated herself to several weeks of rest my mother most seriously began to think of suitable employment, and one day began the weary search for work. Many were the disappointments met with ere that search was successful. But at length the tiresome tramp was ended. She had answered an advertisement for chambermaid at a hotel and been engaged. Little enough did it promise to bring her. It was the best, however, she was at that time able to do. Having had no educational advantages no very large field was open to her, and the need at hand was pressing.

But her trials, it seems, had only begun. It soon leaked out that my mother was a woman with that obnoxious appellation a 'grass widow.' She was young yet, only twenty-three, and libertines, both young and old, thought her their rightful prey. But her proud spirit rose to the emergency. None ever ventured to accost her a second time with undue familiarity. It was a severe strain upon her, nevertheless, and she had not been very strong of late. Soon the effects of this strain became apparent, and often she feared she must utterly break down. All that winter she was under a doctor's treatment, who would insist she must have rest, absolute rest, or he would not answer for the consequences.

"But how could she rest? She had her two children besides herself to clothe, and she could not bear to think of being an added burden to her father's family. So she only more firmly compressed her lips and bravely worked on.

"No doubt she would have rallied more quickly but for the incessant fear she was in of meeting my father. He shadowed and dogged her footsteps. He threatened to steal her children. He circulated the vilest reports about her and well nigh succeeded in ruining her reputation. When she appeared upon the streets or in any public place she imagined she could feel the stare of every man she met. All this had much to do in keeping her poor in health and spirits.

"But as time passed her unusually strong nature began to assert itself. Being freed from the curse of sex slavery her nerves became stronger. The dark circles under her eyes disappeared. By and by she began to gain strength in spite of the doctor's assertion that she could not do so without positive rest. But the knowledge of having her every footstep dogged, her every action watched, was a constant horror to her, and she often wished— if it were not for her children,—that she were at rest in the grave.

"But at twenty-three it is not so easy to die. The young pulsing blood courses with too much strength and warmth in the youthful veins. So she lived and grew strong, and by and by youth more fully asserted itself. She again took an interest in life and her cheerful ringing laugh could now sometimes again be heard, making glad the hearts of her children and friends.

"But yet another trial awaited her. My father was getting tired of single-blessedness. At different times he had sent messengers to my mother to ascertain when she intended returning to her home and duties. To all such she made the answer—'Never!' So, just two years from the date she had left him, he entered suit for divorce.

"I cannot understand how that man's blood flows in my veins. Of all the despicable means imaginable none were omitted to gall her sensitive nature. He dragged her fair name through all the mire and filth known to the divorce court. She was tortured with numberless disgusting questions, such as I think no one has the right to ask, even though holding the highest office in the land. The loathsome secrets of her chamber of horrors were dragged into the light of day, for the court must know *why* a woman *dared* to desire to leave her husband.

"The offensive questions that were asked her, and even more offensive remarks made in an 'aside' by the prosecuting attorney, stung her to the quick. Her white and trembling lips refused to answer but still the torture went on. They must lash the quivering bleeding heart until she was on the verge of insanity.

"Then the daily press took up the refrain. My father, of course, was the wronged party. The man always is. Nothing of his inhuman treatment appeared in their columns, but a blazoning of all the lies and slanders he had in his maliciousness hurled at her defenseless head. Oh, the sneers and the scoffing! I wonder how she ever lived through it.

"I understood nothing of all this at the time, but since I have become old enough to understand, my mother herself has told me all the dark story, and I never get done wondering how she ever was able to bear it. Methinks if it had been *me* there would have been murder in my soul. I really believe if a man would subject me to such insults and abuses I could in my righteous anger plunge a knife into his black heart!"

"Margaret! Margaret!" gasped Imelda, "how can you talk so?"

Margaret had arisen and stood with clenched teeth and hands. Her lips compressed and eyes flashing, a picture of towering wrath. Then suddenly breaking down she burst into a storm of uncontrollable grief and tears. Imelda rose, and gently placing an arm about the weeping girl sought to draw her to her side.

"Come, sit here," she said, "and compose yourself. Remember all this has long since past, and——remember also——he was your father!"

"*My father!*" With ineffable scorn were these words uttered. "To my everlasting shame and sorrow, be it said, he *was* my father, but do you think that that fact would deter me from denouncing him as the monster he is? And you can say it is all long since past! Oh, Imelda, Imelda, in this *one* instance,—my mother's case,—is in the past, but oh! in how many thousand cases is it not true today? It is *now*, that those horrible deeds are being perpetrated. Oh, thou *holy* '*sacred*' thing called *marriage*! How many sweet, pure temples of womanhood you are daily, hourly defiling, by the unrestrained lust hidden under thy protecting shelter. O, that I could proclaim it over the world; O, that I could reach the innermost recesses of every pure woman's and every trusting maiden's heart. Beware, oh! beware the serpent's sting. How long, oh, how long has the burden, the blame of the *downfall* of man been placed upon the slender shoulders of woman, while man stands smiling by, gloating to see how easily the burden is kept there by that horrible bug-bear custom. As it has been customary for her to bear it it is supposed she always must bear it.

"Man sets up one standard of morals for woman and another for himself. She, according to his idea of the term 'pure,' must keep herself *pure*, undefiled, untouched. That means, to strangle nature's desires, nature's voice and nature's longings until some man who has been letting his passion run riot, desecrating nature's gifts until what remains is but a wreck and mockery of true manhood, comes to claim her in her inexperience. Then, in thousands of cases he drives her to insanity or to an early grave, with his insatiable lust.

"Marry! I would not marry for all the wealth that is yet hidden within the bowels of the earth. I will never, never, permit myself to become a piece of property, wherewith some one man may do as he wills. I intend to remain sole owner of my person."

Imelda was awed by the storm of passion that shook the stately form of her friend. Her words seemed metallic shafts of a "white heat," entering her sensitive soul. Could it be possible that man under his smooth outward seeming, could be such a monster? Surely, surely such are only exceptions, rare exceptions, never the rule. Her pure soul revolted at the horrible accusations to which Margaret had just given utterance. And, perhaps, this horror was intensified by hearing such accusations drop from the lips of a girl whom she had always regarded as the impersonation of maidenly purity.

And was not this girl pure? Yes; one look into that face, shining with a glory almost unearthly, was sufficient assurance of that. But were those accusations true? Again the conviction forced itself upon Imelda that, so far as Margaret herself was concerned, those lips were certainly not expressing a falsehood. But where, where had she learned to speak in this manner? She spoke of the sweetness of love and the bondage of marriage in the same breath. How could she speak of the desirability of the one without the sanction of the other? They must go hand in hand, and bear the risks attending such association. There was no other way.

These thoughts passed rapidly through Imelda's mind; faster far than it takes to trace them. Believing she might have misunderstood her friend she could not but give speech to the doubts that were agitating her.

"Margaret! Margaret!" said Imelda, "calm yourself. Your words and manner are so strange; I am unable to comprehend them. How can you speak thus of marriage and yet welcome love? Surely I have not been mistaken in you when I thought you a pure woman. You could not mean to make holy love illicit, and desecrate it by removing the holiest of all holy sanctions, marriage?"

Margaret's sweet excited face underwent a change. The color faded slowly, leaving it purest white. The firmly closed lips trembled; the fireflash in the eyes died out; slowly the tears gathered in them until the great pearly drops rolled down over the white cheeks, splashing upon her tightly clasped hands. A sad look overspread the expressive face as she said:

"My Imelda, have I shocked you? When you have been observing married people, married life and all the consequences attending it, as long and as closely as I have been, you will see as clearly as I now do that of all things imperfect under the sun, *marriage* is the *most* imperfect."

"But what would you do?" again questioned Imelda.

An added sadness seemed to settle upon Margaret's face as she answered:

"Nothing, nothing at present. My mind is in a tumult seeking to break through the cobwebs and mists that are beclouding it. I often think, think, think, until my brain reels and then find myself no farther than at the beginning."

"But you were telling me, or giving me to understand that you have a lover. I cannot understand how you, with the withering contempt in which you hold man, could ever fall in love."

Like a gleam of sunshine a smile flitted over Margaret's face. "O, Imelda! I am only human, and a child of nature, and nature demands, you know, the attraction of the sexes, and Wilbur Wallace is a man *above* the average."

"You love him?"

"I love him."

"But then— —how— —" stammered Imelda, not knowing how to shape her question as to how Margaret's views of marriage would meet those of the young lover in question.

Margaret smiled. She understood what Imelda would ask.

"*He has not asked me to be his wife.* He does not wish it. He loves me too well to place me in a bondage, the chains of which might wear my life away. He would take me as I am, cherish me as something holy, lead me where I am weak, but teach me to be strong."

"And you are going to accept this offer? or— —probably have accepted it!" came in broken accents from Imelda's stiffening lips.

But Margaret slowly shook her head. "I do not know, my dear, I do not know. Here is where the cobwebs and mists keep everything enshrouded in such utter darkness that I cannot see. O, that they would either clear away, that I might see, or that I were daring enough to explore the darkness and daring enough to take the risks I might incur. But here I stall. Wilbur understands, and patiently waits. I know he is trustworthy but I have not the courage."

"And it is this lover of yours that has been poisoning your soul with such radical ideas? O, Margaret, beware! you know the old adage men are deceivers ever, and I would not have my Margaret among the lost."

Margaret turned and looked at Imelda as if a sudden thought had struck her. "I will say no more," she said; "but I would have you know *him*, my lover. Will you promise to meet me here next Sunday afternoon at two? I will then take you where you will meet many radicals, and Wilbur Wallace among the rest. There will be a lecture, the subject being, 'Modern Radical Reform.' A very interesting discussion is expected. Will you come, Imelda?"

Imelda's sweet dark eyes were filled with a troubled look, but the searching glance with which she scanned the face of her friend could detect nothing but the utmost purity and truth.

"I will come," she said.

CHAPTER VI

Just as the city clocks were striking the hour of two Imelda neared the seat that the two girls had occupied a few evenings previous. Margaret was already awaiting her and a bright smile lit up her countenance when she espied her friend.

"On time, Imelda. I am glad. I feared you might have changed your mind, as I had not seen you at the store for several days. I thought something might have happened to prevent your coming, or that possibly I might have frightened you."

"Mother has not been feeling well. That explains my absence. As to changing my mind, I had given you my promise. Do you not know me sufficiently well by this time to know that I never willingly break it?"

"Forgive me, dear," said Margaret, as she drew her arm through Imelda's. "I did not mean to imply you were fickle-minded, as some girls often are, but you will admit that our conversation of a few evenings ago would be a stronger test than most girls would prove equal to. But" (looking at her watch) "we will have to walk rapidly if we would be on time. I never like to enter after the meeting has been opened; it always creates more or less of a disturbance."

The girls walked briskly to the car, then rode about thirty minutes when another five minutes walk brought them to their destination. The little hall was already well filled, and as Margaret led the way up the aisle, she was greeted with smiles and nods from all sides. It was apparent that she was well known and it was at once observed that she was accompanied by a stranger. Many were the admiring glances bestowed upon the beautiful girl. However, there was not long time for conjecturing who she might be, as a rap upon the desk soon called the meeting to order. A tall, dark man of perhaps thirty years had arisen. Imelda thought she had rarely, if ever, seen such piercing black eyes, which accompanied by a dark, heavy moustache, gave the speaker a somewhat fierce appearance, as in a clear, strong voice he began:

"Friends! Comrades! I am highly pleased to see so many here upon this occasion, when we hope to be able to offer you a by no means common treat.

The lecturer is one well known in radical circles,—a woman who by her undaunted courage and brilliant intellect has won for herself an honored name. This is a time when many reforms are discussed and agitated. Many are openly avowing their faith and belief in this or that reform, while many more not so daring do not openly join themselves with radical movements. In their inmost hearts, however, they are with us, while others again as yet are 'on the fence,' their hearts torn with doubt, their understanding still clouded with the mists of superstition and prejudice. But as they are more or less earnest seekers of truth, these mists will clear away and they will be enabled to see things in their true light. Not much more than ten years ago the word 'socialism' evoked from the average man and woman only a smile of contempt. Those who were pleased to apply that cognomen to themselves were looked upon as a species of mild lunatic. Anarchy was regarded with a still stronger aversion (as indeed it yet is). The general impression of this class of people was that they were lazy, even to filthiness. It was believed by a great many that the most severe punishment that could be inflicted upon an anarchist was to condemn him to a bath (laughter.) He was considered a dangerous individual, as he was supposed to be one who would not hesitate to knock a fellow workingman down and force him to share his hard earned wages. It was believed he was ever ready to blow out the brains of some other individual who happened to be possessed of a little more than himself of this wicked world's goods, and was considered at best a dangerous lunatic. But today? Even our worst enemies are forced to respect us (applause). We know they fear us. Not in the sense they once did, but they fear our influence upon the working class, the so-called bone and sinew of the American nation.

"There are many other reforms. Each and all have their advocates showing that the people are awakening out of their deep lethargic sleep and are beginning to think. Not least among these reforms, is the reform in matters pertaining to sex. The thinking men and women of today no longer can close their eyes to the fact that the vices and immoralities of the masses, as well as those of the so-called better classes, are spreading in a manner truly appalling. But worst of all, and attended by the worst possible results, is the sex slavery of the married woman. To discuss these reforms in their varied phases is what of the head. Her figure was too slight, her face too pale, her features too irregular to lay any claims to beauty, but as she opened her lips and began calmly to speak she at once claimed the full attention of her audience. Having arranged her discourse in a careful manner, it was utterly impossible to misunderstand her meaning, and as she gradually warmed to her subject the tired look faded from the large, intelligent gray eyes, her cheeks became slightly flushed, the fair brows seemed irradiated with a luminous glory.

Soon Imelda seemed spellbound as she listened to the clear bell-like voice that conjured up picture after picture before the mind's eye. The speaker painted the contrast between the very wealthy and the very poor. On the one hand rolling and rioting in luxury, on the other wallowing in filth; the sinful idleness of the one, the lavish toil of the other.

"If you will follow me," she said, "I will lead you to the homes of poverty, of toil, of subjection, of vice and of crime, and again to where the so-called refined elements dwell. Together we will search for the truth, together lift the veil and seek for the inward cause of the outward effect.

"In the abode of poverty we find a pale and emaciated woman bending over her sewing at a late hour of the night. The wintry winds howl and the has brought us here today. Before doing so, however, we will listen to the discourse about to be delivered by the able lecturer, Althea Wood. I now have the pleasure of introducing to you Miss Wood."

Here the slender, black-robed figure of a woman arose and moved to the side of the speaker, greeting the assemblage with a slight and graceful inclination window sashes creak! The fire in the stove has burnt out. Her fingers stiffen as the hours speed on. Upon a pallet in the corner lies outstretched the figure of a man. From time to time a low moan escapes the pallid lips. Beside him lie the forms of two children, pale, wan and emaciated.

"Why all this? Because in the days of health and strength, when he received wages that were something more than a mere pittance, confident that he would always be able to provide for those he loved, this man had been neglectful of the future. They had lived comfortably and enjoyed life.

"But by and by, because of over-production in commodities there had come long months of enforced idleness. Then, because of privation and mental anxiety this man had fallen a victim to that dread disease, consumption.

"And now, although and because, on every street, magazines of clothing were overflowing, so that there was scarcely room to store any more, this poor woman must wearily toil by the midnight lamp to increase the already superabundant supply of clothing. Although and because the granaries were filled to bursting, she and hers must go hungry. Although and because the market is overstocked with coal this poor family must shiver with cold through the long wintry nights. Although and because the millionaire and his family cannot find means or ways to spend the millions wrung from the sweat of the weary toilers, is this heart-rending suffering of the poor.

"Lightly as we entered we depart from this abode of woe. We try the next door. This time it is a woman's form that lies outstretched upon a miserable pallet. Several small children, scantily clad are playing upon the bare floor. A young girl stands at the window, looking out at the fast-falling snow. In her hand she holds on open letter. She is fair to look upon. Decked with the world's riches men would rave over her. But what are the emotions stirring this young heart? Her mother, brothers and sisters are starving. All her scanty earnings cannot supply the sick mother the needed medicines and the family with necessary food and clothing.

"Just one year ago the husband and father had been brought to this then cheerful home, crushed almost out of the semblance of humanity, by the accidental falling of timbers carelessly piled by his fellow workman. 'The firm should be held responsible,' had been a frequent comment by those who knew of the occurrence; but the victim was buried, and soon the matter was forgotten by all except the bereaved family.

"Again it was a case of improvidence; of happy content. The husband and father had lavished his love and his earnings upon his wife and children. They had lived and enjoyed life, without thought of a 'rainy day,' and now they were destitute.

"The letter in the girl's hand shows her a way out. She has but to give her hand in marriage to their landlord, upon every lineament of whose face is written 'hard, hard.' But he is rich, and if she would barter her youth and beauty for his hoary head and his money, he would to see to it that a good doctor should be at once provided for the mother and also that the wants of the little ones should be cared for. If no—they owed him six months rent, and on the morrow they would be forced to seek another roof to cover their heads and bodies from the wintry weather. And thus the cold, hard alternative was presented to this inexperienced girl, this rosebud just opening to the sunshine of life, with its dreams of love and happiness—the cold hard alternative of sacrificing herself in a loveless marriage or of seeing her sick mother and young sisters and brothers turned out into the pitiless storm. Stern poverty bade her smother her dream of conjugal bliss on the altar of duty to mother, sisters and brothers.

"Another picture: Again sickness in the abode of poverty. One beautiful sister bending over the dying form of another,—dying for want of care, want of medicine, want of food. A high fever is racking the prostrate form and the despairing sister knows that if the sufferer does not soon receive the needed relief she will be beyond its need. No work—and if she had work she could not leave the sick one, as there is no one else to care for her. Where to get the money to bring relief—aye, to save life!—is the question staring her in the face, awaiting answer.

"There is a way by which the money may be procured, and there is a pain in the look of the well sister that far exceeds that on the features of the unconscious sufferer. It marks every line of the fair face; it settles deep about the compressed lips.

"As the night shadows deepen she grasps a light wrap and throws it over her head. She bends, kisses the burning lips with her own icy ones and with a gasping sigh goes forth into the chill dark night. Not far does she go till she leans against a lamp post, as if for support. The wind blows her scanty skirts about her but she does not heed. The minutes pass by until a half hour has sped, when a man comes along, walking with a rapid step. He is buttoned up to his chin in a great fur-lined overcoat. As he nears her she holds out one cold, stiffening hand, as if asking for charity, but no sound passes her lips. He stops and looks at her. She sees he is young, but the look in his eye makes her flesh creep. She flings the covering from her head, showing a face of exquisite beauty. The act has caused all her wealth of glossy raven hair to fall over her shoulders.

"Ah! she was an exquisite tempting morsel, but what mattered it for her! She was but the child of poverty. When she returned to the bedside of the sick sister, an hour later, there was an unnatural light in the dark eye, a hectic flush on the otherwise pale face. But the trembling hands held *gold*; she could now procure the sorely needed help for the sufferer.

"And why is all this? Because of man-made laws; because of 'tyranny of the dead;' because of the dictates of society; because of the iron rules of state and church; because of helpless poverty in chains of submission to accursed monopoly.

CHAPTER VII

"Now walk with me a few blocks onward. A different portion of the city is reached. Here are carriages filled with ladies dressed in velvets and furs. Their dainty persons adorned with flashing jewels. They throng the operas, concerts, reception rooms, while faultlessly attired swains hang upon their every word. Their life is one round of seeming pleasure. Daily and nightly emotions, aspirations, good and true and pure, are recklessly trodden under foot. Fair hands are sold while hearts are crushed. The highest bidder is sure to win the stake. They take the yellow gold their fair bodies have bought them and with it deck the casket whose contents are one mass of corruption. The smiling lips hide the starving aching heart.

"And whence comes the gold for which this daily barter of souls take place? Coined from the life blood of the poor. Every cup of the intoxicating wine of life they lift to their lips is seasoned with the sweat, the life blood of the toiling masses. Sighs are woven into the glittering meshes of their silken robes. Crystallized tears are the pearls the seamstress has sewn into the glittering folds as she plied her needle in the dead of night.

"And the fawning swains? The lady whose dower is the most golden is the favored one. The oily tongues daily, hourly, fabricate the smooth falsehoods. They swear love eternal, and for the time being make martyrs of themselves to worship at the golden shrine. What matters it that he has led a life that would lay low the silver head of a fond mother; a life that would paralyze a proud and loving sister's heart; that would blanch the confiding maiden's cheek,—could they but know. But they do not know, and so the sensualist transmits the germ of poison and disease to the coming generation.

"Women accept such moral and physical wrecks of humanity, with hollow skulls added to their other numerous imperfections, and in nine cases out of ten the women are just as shallow brained as the men they accept. While the man of fashion is seen at the gambling table, at the racecourse and in the drinking saloons, flirting with gaudily dressed girls, the woman of fashion discusses the latest style of party dress, counting on her finger-tips how many masculine hearts have been laid at her feet, and, in order to kill time, pores over the latest novel.

"And from this seed, sown in such reckless fashion, the coming generations are to grow. What is to furnish genius to those unborn generations? Whence is to come the soulful man and woman? How is purity to thrive in an atmosphere of poison and corruption?

"When we enter the realm of the law and look into the records of crime, we find the account simply appalling. When we read the number of divorces granted, and the vaster number applied for and not granted, we wonder whether there are any left who still honestly advocate wedlock. Read the pleas upon which those divorces have been granted and they will show you that so long as loveless marriages are entered into, so long as men and women are mismated, just so long will the marriage bond mean a galling bondage; and so long as such marriages are entered into and children begotten from them; so long as the prospective mother sees in the coming child only an added burden; so long as this child is undesigned and undesired; and so long as the gestating mother suffers for and craves what are impossibilities to her, just so long will there be crimes and records of crimes; just so long will prisons be filled with criminals.

"What is the most numerous of the reasons that form the pleas for divorce? 'Illicit love'! In spite of all laws; in spite of the iron hand of custom, in spite of the trampling underfoot of all the tender passions known to the human heart, that heart demands and will have its rights. What matters it if society has cased it in outward fetters that are supposed to confine it to prescribed limits. When nature demands its rights this casing becomes too small; the fetters too weak to bind. The frail, weak human heart expands and swells until its bonds burst and like a caged bird regaining its freedom, the heart seeks its mate in the free wild wood to follow nature's law. The divine law of freedom is written deep within the human heart. No matter how deeply it is encrusted under the ice of mercenary motives; no matter how firmly clutched by social custom, when love comes knocking for admittance all, everything, must give way before his all-conquering power. Bar and double bar the doors, but 'Love still laughs at locksmiths,' and 'Love will find a way where wolves fear to prey.'

"O, Love! love! love! How thy holy, thy soul-redeeming power has been defamed! Unholy passion, that burns and sears with vice the hearts of men, has oft been mistaken for that holy flame. Love, sacred love will elevate, will cleanse from all impurities, will awake ambition, will be an incentive to noble deeds, to a noble life. But passion alone enervates, disgusts, wears out both body and soul; it drags down its votaries to groveling depths.

"But how seldom do mothers teach their children the difference between the two? The smiling mother gives her innocent daughter to a hoary head and a seared heart if there is but a golden covering to them. A 'splendid match'—from a worldly view—is all that is needed. But the sequel too often shows how splendid the match has been. Only when the heart is still in death does it no longer throb with pain and sickening dread at the touch of him who should have thrilled her whole being with exquisite happiness. How many are able to read aright the story in the still white face?

"Go visit the homes of the dead and see there the number of graves that entomb the forms of youthful wives and mothers. Go enter the abodes of the insane and count the rows of staring eyes proclaiming a living death,— all caused by the barter of sex life. Go through the length and breadth of the land and see the signs of heart-break; the pitiful misery that is the lot of mankind, and all caused by 'Man's inhumanity to man,' and especially man's inhumanity to woman.

"Go where you will, into lordly mansions of the rich, into the hovels of the lowly poor, and see the subjection of woman unto man. He rides roughshod over her most sacred and tender ideals. Every hope in the once bounding heart has been crushed. Her fate is to please her 'lord and master,'—to keep *his* home for *him*; to entertain *his* guests; to bear *his* children; to rear them for *him* to dispose of as *he* may see fit—thus forcing her to bring into the world a race of slaves, a race degenerated by having implanted in the heart of the unborn child all the evil passions that naturally rankle in the breast of woman so enslaved and outraged.

"The soul is unthought of in this reproduction, which merely takes place to satisfy the animal in man. The desire, the inclinations of the mother, are not considered. To cater to the passions of man, to be the mother of undesired children is her *natural* sphere in life. She must thank God that she has been selected thus to be the instrument to perpetuate the race. Home, sweet home, has been sung until it echoes and re-echoes throughout the land, but to millions of women it has been simply a prison, a hellish prison.

"The church, 'the man of God,' its instrument, stands upon one side. On the other side stands the state. In case the church is not strong enough to control woman, the state holds up to her aching eyes the terrors of the 'law of the land.'

"Oh, the path of woman is a straight and narrow one! Woe unto her if she dares to depart therefrom. And yet you wonder how it is that criminals throng the land; that there are so many that will not respect the rights of others. Did anyone ever respect any rights of the mother that bore them? Why; she *had* no rights! Then how could any one respect them? Bound by man-made law and church superstition from her infancy her fate is linked fast with that of the working class. She and they must alike be kept in subjection.

"O, workingmen, O ye toilers, ye producers! O womankind! mothers of coming generations, awake, arise, and hand in hand, break the bonds that enthrall you, that enslave you, body and soul. Refuse to longer be any man's slave. Assert your rights. Clamor for your freedom, and rest not until you have obtained it.

"It is impossible that in squalor and filth, purity should be gestated. Assert your freedom, O women! Demand it, clamor for it, fight for it! Never for one moment cease to struggle for it. Be united in your efforts, hand in hand, shoulder to shoulder, and the day is sure to come when victory shall be yours."

"I am afraid," the speaker went on, — "I am afraid I have been telling you more of the evils that need reform than of the methods of securing that reform; and, while I am radical in the extreme, yet I condemn not one single method or idea that may help to bring about one single reform, be it ever so small. 'Rome was not built in a day,' and the world will not be reformed in a day, or a week, or a month, or a year. But as the days and weeks and months and years speed by, each reform will furnish its aid in bringing about the much desired result. Everyone who is working for reform, or in other words, working for humanity's best welfare, no matter in what line it may be, is doing his or her share of the work, and will doubtless receive the full credit that is due them. Only this I would add, while everyone is riding his or her own hobby, I would look beneath this mass of corruption and unearth the underlying cause. To lay the ax to the root is what must be done in order to fell the giant, and to be able to do this we want freedom, *freedom, freedom*! No more laws to bind our thoughts and shackle our hands. We want to be free, to let the hearts within our bosoms beat as they will; free to follow the dictates of our normal desires; free to extricate ourselves from the old and customary when we recognize it as evil; free to let our souls soar into the regions above the clouds; free to enter the upper chambers of the mind; free to tear down the structure of rottenness that enables the few to drain the life blood of the millions and to coin it into shining gold wherewith to perpetuate their power. Free to use our own inheritance, the grand gifts of nature.

"O thou glorious, O thou great, grand, redeeming 'Liberty'! Thou shalt yet wave over this beautiful world the banner of holy brotherly love! Thou shalt yet secure to us this much needed freedom. Thou shalt yet see its fruits in the coming generation of a new-born people, — when poverty, hunger and misery will be unknown! When crime will be a forgotten word; when the rule of the church, like that of the state, will be a thing no longer remembered; when prisons will be swept from the face of the earth; when justice, glory-crowned, at the right shall stand; when charity no longer has a place, since her vocation shall be ended; when the awaiting of unborn humanity will be regarded the coming of a joyous event, and when disease shall have succumbed to the master hand of science, death no longer a dreaded monster, but a friend that comes only as a result of nature, to claim those that have lived their glorious life to the end, and who fain would resign that hold upon it in exchange for the peaceful rest that follows the well-performed labor of the day.

"O, friends and comrades! to hasten that day I ask you to join the band that but yesterday was small indeed, but which today has swelled to such size as to alarm those that would place their feet upon your necks, and which will continue to swell more rapidly day by day until the down-trodden will arise as one man to demand their natural birth right."

With glowing cheeks and sparkling eyes the speaker took her seat amid deafening applause.

CHAPTER VIII

A long drawn sigh flattered from the trembling lips of Imelda while Margaret's face glowed with excitement equaled only by that of the speaker. When the excitement which followed had abated somewhat, the presiding officer rose and again his strong, clear, but pleasant, voice was heard. Almost instantly the profoundest quiet reigned. His handsome face had caught something of the general excitement and he carelessly threw back the black locks that clustered about the open brow.

"Friends and comrades," said he. "You have listened to the discourse of a noble woman, on a most important subject. A noble woman, because she dares to assert her womanhood; dares to assert the *I*. She dares to fly in the face of custom, in the face of power. She dares to point out where evils lie hidden. Dares to show you where the curse of poverty stalks; where its birth place is, side by side with that of vice and crime. She has pointed out glorious possibilities for those who may dare in the present to provide a way to secure the rightful inheritance of the many. And to judge by the applause you have accorded to her you have rightly understood and justly appreciated her. But notwithstanding this appreciation we know that not all our friends agree with our lecturer, and so, in accord with our custom we will now hear what others have to say. We invite you, one and all, to take part in this debate, and let us know what your views are. 'Free discussion' is our motto at these meetings.—"

The chairman resumed his seat and an expectant hush fell upon the assemblage. One, two minutes passed; then arose a gentleman upon whom the snows of many winters had fallen, to judge by hair and beard, but whose general appearance otherwise did not show old age. His business-like, "Mr. Chairman," had a pleasant sound, while general attention was now directed toward him.

"Ladies and gentlemen," he began, "courtesy would at any time demand of me that I treat ladies with the greatest respect, yet the lady who today has entertained us, and who has given us the benefit of her intelligence and knowledge of humanity, has not told us all the causes of the trouble. I must pay her the compliment to say that she understands how to handle her subject. I too have observed many instances of despairing young girls who sacrifice themselves by selling themselves for life, or for an hour, in order to obtain the means wherewith to make brighter the declining pathway of some loved one. I have known cases wherein the betrayed, outraged maiden had given her trusting love in vain, and was then driven to seek an untimely grave. In the homes of the wealthy it is a well known fact that love seldom enters. With environments which ought to bless the unborn generations decay and degeneracy is even more marked than among the poorer classes, since among the latter love does often take by the hand the maiden and lover to join them together, and, for a while at least, hovers over the pair. Often one child, and sometimes more, is the result of loving union. But where only sordid gain is the object of marriage the fruits must of necessity be of an inferior order. To my mind, this evil, this marriage evil, is the worst of all evils. Instead of the home being the birth place and cradle of love and truth and peace, it is the hot-bed, the breeding place of vice. The unwelcome child incarnates the germs of disease, of vice and crime. The dissatisfied mother implants in her offspring abnormal desires and passions because her own desires have been dwarfed and disregarded. Thus the enslaved mother sows the seeds of tyranny in her child. It matters not if such a home be one of plenty or want. One breeds the roue, the other the criminal of the future. I only wish to state here that so long as the people bow to an 'unknown God'; a God who is supposed to rule somewhere up among the stars, in a place called heaven; a God who will punish those who have been truer to nature than to the impossible teachings of the church, by burning them in everlasting fire, and so long as the people sustain a state or government that holds them in bondage; a state to which they must pay tribute for every privilege they enjoy, even unto the privilege of choosing a mate; so long as the credulous people pay tribute to the parasites called politicians who fasten themselves wherever they can find a foothold, just so long must we continue to endure the evils portrayed by the last speaker. So long as labor is a slave to capital, so long as the workingman is but an irresponsible part of the machinery that produces wealth for the few, just so long will woman be a slave to man, and just so long will children be a curse instead of a blessing, and just so long will crime and disease stalk abroad. The workingman must first strike for and gain his freedom. Then the emancipation of woman will follow. I have nothing farther to say."

Amid appreciative applause the man of many winters resumed his seat. Next arose a man with snapping black eyes and jetty hair who with cutting sarcasm dissected the lecture, telling his hearers that in ninety-nine cases out of a hundred all the poverty, the ill-luck, was due to the man or woman's own fault. "The working people," said he, "as a class, are lazy; they are extravagant; they are vicious. They would rather spend their leisure time in saloons, swilling beer and poor whiskey, and in playing cards, than with their families at home; they would rather lounge and loaf upon street corners than do an honest day's work; they would rather follow a course that would lead them to steal, and even murder, and thereby get them into the penitentiary where they would be only too well treated. If it were not for the church who with her gentle and peace-diffusing influence keeps the working classes in a measure content, and under control, there would be no telling to what deeds of outrage the ignorant, licentious masses of people would go. Take away the influence of religion and what would be the result? Without fear of a god or devil, like a brutal horde of wild beasts with nothing to restrain them, they would fall to murdering and plundering everything and everyone that stood in their way, regardless of consequences, just so they could satisfy their ungovernable appetites."

The only thing this man could think of that could be done was to make more laws; laws more stringent and binding. Then enforce them to the letter.

"We speak of loose morals," said he. "Could there be anything more loose than the ideas of marriage that are fast becoming popular? There are almost as many divorces petitioned for and granted as marriages entered into. Divorces are too easily obtained. The laws are too lax. If such were not the case people would be more careful in entering the holy portals of marriage. But there are so few that any longer consider marriage as something holy that it is becoming a menace to the country. Again I ask for more laws. Let them be stringent and let them be rigidly enforced. Let those that are forming such contracts and entering into the bonds of marriage, understand that it is for life, that there is no escaping the consequences, and then people will get along better."

CHAPTER IX

There was not much applause this time, when the speaker resumed his seat. Some few laughed, but here and there, as you cast your eye over the audience, you could see compressed lips and flushed cheeks. But as the platform was a free one, where everyone was invited to freely speak his convictions, no one attempted to interrupt the speaker, although many felt the hot blood of indignation mount to their cheeks.

Almost immediately upon his resuming his seat a woman rose, and, upon addressing the chairman, had the right to speak accorded her. A woman probably forty years of age, but looking nearer thirty. A woman who in her youth might have been handsome and who was yet passably fair. Of figure she was tall and well developed. The light brown hair was combed back so as to leave the low brow free and uncovered. The blue eyes were sparkling with a light that was not caused by a sense of pleasure. The finely curved lips were quivering with suppressed emotions as she fearlessly walked forward and faced the audience.

"Friends! Comrades!" she began, with a voice both clear and strong. "It is not often that I feel myself called upon to make any remarks at these meetings. My sentiments generally are so clearly expressed and so well defended by those who are better able to treat the subjects that as a rule are under discussion here, that I find more pleasure and benefit in listening to others than in taking part in discussion. But this afternoon I feel impelled to make a few remarks, hoping that you will bear with me if I am not able to express myself quite as concisely and correctly as I might wish. I do not wish to find fault with our lecturer in regard to what she has said, but—if it could be called a fault—with what she did not say. Although she has painted you pictures most dismal and saddening I can assure you the half, nay, the one tenth has not been told. Methinks there are some things that she has too lightly touched upon, and which our friend, Mr. Roland, has somewhat more plainly pictured. The 'looseness' that Mr. Warden so much deplores in divorce laws does not exist. In fact these laws are so stringent as to place the possibility of obtaining a divorce beyond the reach of the poor. Divorce laws, like all other laws, are for the special benefit of the moneyed class. They can avail themselves of divorce if they see fit, and that they do see fit rather often is quite evident. And for once I must give the privileged class credit for something. Notwithstanding Mr. Warden's lament that divorces are so easily obtained I claim there is nothing more difficult. The most excruciating torture that it is possible to inflict upon a sensitive and refined woman is to drag her into our modern courtroom and subject her to the quizzing process of shameless lawyers, who ply her with numberless questions that cut to the quick the sensitive heart and lacerate it as though some diabolical machine filled with knives of all shapes and sizes were making mince-meat of it. These lawyers luxuriate in cruelly delving in these wounded and bleeding hearts so that it takes a woman of tremendous courage to willingly undergo this dissecting operation, and therefore comparatively few seek the redress of the law. It drags forth, into a foul atmosphere, the most sacred treasures, and defiles them with the vileness that so often is found in the precincts of the law. It hurls a woman from her pinnacle of respected womanhood into the depths of disgrace. It prohibits her from the companionship of the good and pure. It ostracises her from what is called 'good society,' it points the finger of scorn at the child that calls her 'mother.' If that child be a boy there is a chance for it to win its way in the world, but if it be a girl then hard will it be for her to gain a foothold upon the steep and rugged pathway she will have to climb.

"How can a sensitive, womanly woman desire to confront a room filled with coarse, unsympathizing men and relate to them the stories of her woe? How can she tell of tears shed in the dead of night; of how her sacred womanhood has been abused; of how her outraged person is forced to submit to his loathsome touch? Broken down, suffering from oft-repeated child-bearing, tired unto death with her manifold duties, sick in soul as well as in body, I say how can she tell all this, with all those strange leering faces about her? She would rather go on suffering until death comes to her release, or perhaps her overburdened brain gives way, while the world wonders: 'What could have been the reason? She had such a good, industrious, sober husband, who has always so handsomely provided for her every want, and such a nice large family of children growing up around her. How could she have been else than happy?'

"They really cannot understand what could have caused her brain to give way. Aside from this, not everywhere is it possible to obtain a divorce for such reasons as I have just mentioned. In some states if she is not treated to blows, neglected with her children to such an extent that cruel want speaks from the hollow eyes and sunken cheeks, she will be told she has no just cause for complaint, and should go home submissively to her liege lord and master, thankful for the home provided for her, and should bow her head in humility to the great and all-wise God who has made all things well.

"O, it is a noble sphere that has been marked out for woman—marked for her by her owner, her lord, her master! Why cannot she be content, why cannot she be satisfied? Aye, satisfied! O, if she could only be aroused to universal dissatisfaction, there would be hope for her emancipation in the near future.

"Our friend, Mr. Roland, has made the remark that in order to free woman, man, the workingman, must first be freed,—the economic conditions must first undergo a universal change. Then why, in freedom's name, is woman's cause not more frequently urged as an argument to that end? O, that woman herself would only awake to a sense of her condition! O, sisters, awake! Hasten the advent of the coming day that proclaims your freedom from the tyranny of man, by aiding him to obtain the rights that are justly his. Lend your aid in freeing man from the thralldom of state and monopoly, and ever bear in mind that the same blow which shatters your brother's fetters will also free you. That which insures his freedom and independence will do the same for you. For when the day comes in which justice reigns, she can no longer stand with blindfolded eyes while woman's life is fettered."

As the speaker ceased, and the applause burst forth, Imelda bent her head near Margaret, whose cheeks glowed like twin roses.

"Who is she?" she asked, and Margaret in answer whispered:

"My mother!"

CHAPTER X

For an instant Imelda was startled. She had never seen Mrs. Leland and had pictured to herself a different woman; but as she looked again she could see the likeness between mother and daughter, and there crept into her heart a thought of her own mother, and she contrasted the weary, fretful, listless woman with this mother of her friend, who, after the life of trials and sorrows that had been hers, had arisen in such splendid self-confidence; who had burst the chains that bound her; who now dared to hurl such scathing truths, like firebrands into a magazine of powder, as it were, ready to stand by the result the explosion must bring forth. She began to understand the source whence her young friend received her strength of character.

Mrs. Leland's words, even more than those of the lecturer, burned into her heart as her thoughts wandered to her almost worshiped father, now sleeping under the ground. Over her tortured heart crept a fear that possibly even he had not been to that fretful, oft-times unjust mother, all that he might have been. There might have been pitfalls carefully hidden from her sight—for her mother never made a confidante of her child. But she knew of the inharmonious life that had been theirs. She could not remember ever having caught sight of the holy flame of love between them. And yet—the babes had come. She knew the mother had not desired them. She felt dazed. Her head swam, as these thoughts coursed through it in much less time than it takes to trace them here.

But again someone was speaking, and again the horrors of married life were pictured. How woman is sold! Woman has no outlet for her overcharged feelings save in tempestuous temper and tears. Generally, in time, the temper is subdued and the tears alone remain, and the world wonders why woman so soon loses her attractive powers; why the sparkling girl overflowing with magnetism turns so soon into the pale, weary, hollow-eyed woman who finds life's happiness turned to Dead Sea fruit upon her lips.

As Imelda listened she felt as though a cold hand were clutching at her throat. The world seemed slipping from beneath her feet. Then another rose and in his turn spoke of the holiness of marriage, of the holiness of the church, of the holiness of the state. Like hollow mockery the words echoed and re-echoed in Imelda's ears. What could be holy now after she had seen the evil withdrawn and the sickening truth exposed to view. Like one in a dream she listened and wondered that any one could still be sincere in uttering such words as in all good faith this man seemed to speak. It seemed as if, all in a moment, where had heretofore appeared rose-strewn paths, she now saw only pitfalls whose yawning depths were ready to engulf those who foolishly set their feet upon the treacherous edge. Still, as in a daze, she realized that the speaker was done, that once more Althea Wood was speaking. The clear, sweet voice resounded through the room.

"My friends," she said, "it would be indeed difficult to express the pleasure I have felt listening to the discussion this afternoon. Nor can I express how thankful I am that my cause has been so warmly championed, notwithstanding the efforts of those who cannot as yet see this question in the new light in which it is viewed by many of you. I agree with those of my friends who claim that this vexed question does not receive the attention that it deserves. It is sad and pitiful, but true, that the average man and woman are so unwilling to hear this subject discussed that it requires a great effort to speak of it. They may be willing to pick up a book that treats on this subject, and, screened in the seclusion of a private room, try to digest the writer's ideas, but under the fire of other eyes to hear from the lecturer's lips these tabooed subjects is quite another thing. So long, however, as sex is considered impure, something for which the human race should blush, just so long will it be not only a difficult but painful subject for lecturers to discuss. The consciousness that we would probably be misunderstood is unpleasant.

"O, that I might live to see the hour when this beautiful earth shall be freed from the crushing fetters of custom; from the deadly poison of superstition and prejudice; from the grinding heel of monopoly,—to see a race of men and women enlightened, liberated, self-reliant, free. Not an enforced freedom, keeping them ever on their guard, fearing the lurking enemy in the entrenchments, back of the bulwarks of authority and the fortifications of avarice and low desires. No! the time for such hypocrisy will then have vanished. We shall then hail the time when a race of freemen shall exist because of the universal demand for and recognition of it. The race will have become purified in the fires of truth, love and justice. When it shall have risen to the height where it will have attained the full knowledge of its worth; where and when it shall have demanded its rightful birthright, the right to own itself; the right to the product of its toil; the right to recognize truth wherever it is found.

"Just so soon as you make that demand, earnestly and sincerely, your right will have come to you. Begin with recognizing the great truth that you are an individual, that you are rightfully sole owner of your own mind, of your own brain capacity. Let no outside influence enthrall you; break your chains, set your mind at liberty, and it will soon work out the salvation of the body. When once you can see that there are fetters the desire to break them will come; the effort to break them will follow the desire.

"Before I close I will say to my Christian critics that if there were not so many laws there would not be so much of the ignorance of which they now complain. Laws and customs keep the masses in the old ruts, destroying the strength wherewith they otherwise could elevate themselves to nobler heights. To the everlasting disgrace of the church it must be said that its influence keeps the deluded masses in their benumbed condition, content to spend their miserable lives in abject slavery. Pitiable is the fact, but cruelly true, that many of them desire nothing more ennobling than to seek oblivion of their troubles in the depths of the intoxicating bowl.

"But Freethought is not the cause of this desire. Her mission is to break the fetters that bind man's mind; to sweep away the cobwebs and mists of superstition; to slay the tyrant prejudice that bars the entrance to the new and the true.

"When the truths of science shall have been mastered by the law-ridden and priest-ridden people, when they shall have obtained the right to own themselves, then with the disappearance of ignorance will also disappear vice and crime. My heart aches at sight of this poor, deluded, cheated people, daily robbed more and more by laws that were made for none but slaves to obey. The rich man makes them and of course never expects to come in contact with them otherwise than to inflict them upon those who produce his wealth. Love needs no fetters. Nothing binds human hearts but Love.

"So, once again I urge you to awake; to come to a realization of your own thralldom, and then in turn to help others to awake to a consciousness of this yoke of slavery borne by you all. Then the world will move onward; will move rapidly toward that millennium that is to be the realization of evoluted humanity."

CHAPTER XI

As the meeting was dismissed, all in a moment the earnest truth-seekers were transformed into a social assemblage. Hearty handshaking abounded and equally hearty laughter was heard upon all sides. For several minutes it seemed to Imelda that she had been forgotten by her friend who had been joined by the chairman of the afternoon, but she had more than enough to occupy her mind in observing the scene before her, and reviewing the two hours she had just passed through. Many and conflicting were her emotions. Every word, almost, that had been spoken had sunk deep into her heart and she again experienced all the sensations of surprise and indignation she had felt, the mere memory of which almost caused her heart to stand still and chill the blood in her veins. Never in all the years of her young life had she dreamed of such dark depths of hopeless woe.

Just then a hand lightly touched her arm and she heard Margaret's sweet voice:

"Imelda, my dear friend, permit me to introduce to you another friend, Mr. Wallace."

Imelda suddenly found herself confronted by the chairman of the meeting. The interruption was opportune, as it recalled her to herself. Wilbur Wallace's darkly bronzed face was all aglow. A happy light shone from the dark eyes and the clear strong voice had a ring in it that could have been caused only by something very pleasant. The next moment Imelda's hand was folded in his strong clasp while the words: "I consider myself fortunate in meeting Miss Ellwood here this afternoon," most pleasantly struck her ear, and he continued: "I very much hope that the pleasure may be often renewed." Imelda felt the icy clutch slowly being removed that had been holding her enthralled; a more life-like smile lit up her face as she replied:

"The pleasure will be mutual, I assure you."

"Then we may hope to see you here again?"

"Why not?" she asked. "I have heard much this afternoon which, although not pleasant in itself, was both new and interesting, and I have no doubt I shall be able to learn much here which would be impossible for me to learn elsewhere. While the facts, as they have been shown here today, are almost impossible to believe, yet if true, it is time I knew something about them. But I cannot see the remedy; how do you propose to alleviate, or rather to banish such evils?"

Imelda's dark eyes looked questioningly into the now serious face of Wilbur Wallace, whose answer promptly came.

"The solution of that problem will, no doubt, be the work of future years, albeit much can at the present time, and also in the near future, be done to make the way clear. 'Making the way clear' is what we trying to do. This is a meeting place for thinkers—free thinkers, all of them, and no matter what their ideas of God, of the church, may be, they all have come to the conclusion that there is something wrong somewhere, and that church and state bear a large share of the blame, is plainly to be seen. The so-greatly despised 'anarchist' is, I think, more largely represented than others." There was a quick uplifting of the brow of the young girl at the mention of the word 'anarchist.'

"I do not understand," she said. "The colors wherewith I have seen the name painted are not very attractive. If I have had a mistaken impression I would like to have my error corrected." At this moment the old gentleman, Mr. Roland, accompanied by Miss Wood, stepped up to the little group.

"What matter of importance is being discussed here with so much interest?" broke in his pleasant voice. "I must confess to a desire to join with you, but first permit me." Here followed the necessary introductions, then Wilbur Wallace spoke.

"Miss Ellwood being a stranger to our circle, is also a stranger to the ideas usually discussed here. Consequently she finds them not unmixed with a certain amount of gruesomeness."

"And what particular idea, or object, or fact, is it that fills you thus with unpleasant feelings?" asked Mr. Roland of Imelda.

"I think almost everything that I have heard spoken of here today. If all I have heard here today be true, every young girl would be justified in shrinking from marriage as she would from the brink of a dark abyss."

"That is well expressed," said Miss Wood; "and if we could but impress that idea upon the mind of every woman there would soon be a new state of affairs. When woman learns the true worth of herself she will insist on the right to dispose of herself as she will see fit, and not as she is commanded to do by the arbitrary laws of a society that is man-made."

For a few moments Imelda was lost in thought, then her dark eyes flashed upward.

"I understand that if woman could be successful she would be able to enjoy a glorious freedom. But would not this very freedom have some very undesirable results? Undesirable as a large family of children may be to the majority of women, as it most inevitably dooms them to a life of drudgery, yet under circumstances of unlimited freedom, such as you advocate, how long would it be until the race would begin to dwindle away? For many women, as I know them, would prefer not to be mothers at all, and very few of them would wish for a large family. We all know that the life of the infant is but a tender plant that sometimes does not long survive the hour of its birth. Do you think such a state of things would be desirable?"

"My dear Miss Ellwood," Mr. Roland replied, "the idea of the extinction of the race would indeed not be pleasant to contemplate, but the perfect freedom of woman would naturally overcome the very dangers you fear. The desired and gladly welcomed child will of necessity be superior to that which is undesired and unwelcome. When a prospective mother is filled with thoughts of that coming event she lives during that period only for the well being of that mite of humanity. She will seek to observe, to study, the laws of nature to their fullest extent, and being in the possession of sexual freedom will soon learn to understand these glorious laws. So children will be born into the world in a more normal and healthy state than is now the case, and the result will be fewer little graves. Then again woman will develop mentally and she will bestow upon her unborn babe a legacy of brain power that at present, under our corrupt social system, is an utter impossibility. So even though there would not be so many undesired unfortunate beings called into life the quality would be so vastly superior that the loss in quantity would be anything but loss, — rather gain."

"I agree with you," Imelda said, "but here the question arises, How will woman be enabled to gain this freedom that is to bring about so many desirable results?"

Young Wallace made answer:

"Woman's awakening to the consciousness that it is needful will be the cornerstone upon which her freedom will be built, but she will need the help and support of outward influence. So long as man is the slave of 'the almighty dollar,' so long will woman be the slave of man, because in the present state of society she is dependent on man for her maintenance. The economic battle goes hand in hand with that for woman's rights. Man needs woman's aid in this battle for the rights of humanity, and the blow that shatters the shackles of wage-slavery will also break the chains that hold her sex in bondage. When the race becomes free her battle will have been won, and she can begin to build up a new and glorious race."

Wallace's eyes glowed as the enthusiasm wherewith he had spoken sent the blood bounding through his veins. Imelda saw that Margaret's eyes rested with something more than mere admiration on his darkly handsome face. All in an instant she understood—"Margaret's love." It shone in the depths of her deep blue eyes, it trembled upon the sweet, dewy lips, it burned in the glow of her cheek.

Imelda's eyes reverted again to the face of the young man with renewed interest; but her searching glance could detect nothing to his discredit. It was a frank, open, manly countenance wherein she gazed, a face women would involuntarily trust and little children love.

"At the same time," now spoke Miss Wood, "you will permit us to begin to exercise just a little of that freedom now. We will begin at home with our individual selves and proclaim that no man shall ever say to us, 'Thou shalt,' or 'Thou shalt not.' How is it Miss Ellwood and Miss Leland?"

The question was put rather laughingly and banteringly, as she turned first to one, then the other of the two girls. Imelda had no answer but a heightened color, but Margaret held out her hand which Miss Wood readily clasped.

"I am with you," she said. "I intend to win my lover's love and hold it too, but I will never buy it at the price of my freedom."

"Bravo!" came simultaneously from the lips of the gentlemen, while the hand of the elder gently patted her shoulder.

"That is what I call making remarkably free with my daughter. She belongs to me and I object," and the pleasant face of Mrs. Leland became visible in close proximity to her daughter and Mr. Roland. Margaret's laugh rang out in sweetest music.

"Now! now! Mamma, you know better than that. If I am your daughter, I am not your property. Don't you know if I find pleasure in feeling Mr. Roland's hand on my shoulder—why—you have nothing to say." This last was said in so saucy a manner that it caused a general laugh, which having subsided, she with sudden recollection added:

"Pardon me. I almost forgot, mamma,—this is the very dear friend I have so often told you about,—Imelda Ellwood." Mrs. Leland's eyes rested for a moment searchingly upon the face of the young girl; then, satisfied with what she saw there, clasped both hands in hers and in a few words caused her to feel quite at her ease. Then seating herself, she said:

"Proceed now. I know that I have broken into the midst of something very interesting."

"Only a continuation of our discussion," replied Mr. Roland. "We have been considering the rights of women in particular, and those of humanity in general. The reason in this case is, to convince a beautiful woman and win her as a convert," bowing to Imelda, "which I hope is justification in this case for becoming eloquent. I can assure you that you have missed something, Mrs. Leland."

"Well, if such is the case, I am sorry, but who is the convert that is to be? You, Miss Ellwood?" looking inquiringly into Imelda's face.

"Just so," she answered, "and if I can gain a clearer insight into things, the efforts of my friends may prove successful. But I must remark that I seem to have gotten into a very pronounced set of radicals."

"Are you frightened?" asked Wilbur Wallace with a laugh, in which the rest joined.

"Not in the least," she retorted, "although the term 'radical' always left the impression on my mind of something of a rather wild character. But really, if what I have seen of them this afternoon are fair specimens, they are a very well behaved species."

A general laugh followed. Mr. Roland pronounced it almost six o'clock and time to disperse. As a parting admonition Miss Wood turned to Imelda.

"You seem to be a young woman of more than ordinary intelligence. It is such as you whom we wish to win, to take an interest in the fate of womankind,—in the fate of humanity. Permit your friend, Miss Leland, to induce you again to join this circle, and I hope when next I see you that I will find you one of us, heart and soul. Good bye, now, friends, may your every effort be blessed with success." With these words they parted, she clinging to the arm of Mr. Roland, leaving our little group of four alone. Arriving at the outside they found that it had already grown quite dusk. For a moment there seemed to be an indecision on the part of Margaret and Wilbur as to which direction they should take, when Mrs. Leland decided the matter for them.

"Come with me to the nearest car, Margaret. It will take me almost to our door, so I can very well go alone, while you and Wilbur can accompany Miss Ellwood to her home." Imelda protested, saying she was as well able to go alone as Mrs. Leland, but the elder lady insisted, supported by her young friends, and as a matter of course carried the day.

"By the time you return," she said, "I will have luncheon ready. Good night, now, Miss Ellwood, I will not say good bye, as I hope to see you often." Waving her hand in adieu, she mounted the car and was gone.

Five minutes walk in another direction brought them to the car that it was needful to take to reach Imelda's home, and soon they were being whirled along to their destination. The car was almost deserted, which gave them an opportunity to continue their conversation. Margaret did not say much, but seemed rather to enjoy listening to her friend and lover as they traversed the same ground that she had passed over not so very long since, for although the daughter of a radical mother, that mother had not always been radical. The time was not very far gone by when the old prejudices still held her in bondage, and the fear of what the world might say, restrained her in all she would say and do.

Margaret long felt the influence of those earlier teachings. It had been harder for her to break away from the old beliefs and superstitions than for her mother; but—"Love works wonders" was true in this case. Wilbur Wallace was of that type of men who are sure to win conviction where once they gain a foothold. Gifted with a bright intellect and a manner of speech both positive and fluent, he carried conviction to the minds of his hearers. It had been at an entertainment, to which she had accompanied her mother, that Margaret had first met Wilbur. The young couple had from the first been attracted, which attraction soon ripened into more than mere friendship.

But young Wallace was not without bitter experience; as he had observed home and family life he had found it anything but perfect. He had seen a sweet and gentle mother suffer from the arbitrary monogamy of her married life to such extent that it had laid her in an early grave. The lesson of the ending of that life had entered like a corroding iron into the soul of her first born, a boy then but eighteen years of age. From the hour his idolized mother was laid beneath the green sod he had never entered his father's home. Life was a problem he had set himself to study, and the more he studied the greater the problem became. But he was not easily daunted. He kept his eyes open, thus soon discovering that the world was full of wrongs that needed righting.

Soon Wilbur Wallace's name was classed among those who were laboring in the cause of the poor and lowly. But woman's cause seemed ever to lie nearest his heart. The memory of one sweet woman lay enshrined within the depths of his heart; for her sake he sought for truths that should be the means of saving other women from a like heart-break. The faces of two weeping girls, as he had seen them last, would arise before his mind's eye, and more firmly than ever did the resolve become rooted to save them from a like fate. The years had rolled by; he was twenty-seven and his sisters young women of twenty and twenty-three. He had never seen them again, for many miles separated him from the place that had known his childhood days.

CHAPTER XII

Then had come the hour of temptation to him. Sweet Margaret had come into his life, and he found himself shaken to the very depths of his being, but he came forth conqueror. He loved the girl with all the power of an intense nature, but he would never seek to bind her. His love should bless her but never prove a scourge. The girl's heart had grown faint when it had caught his meaning. Love, sweet, pure soul-redeeming love, had come to her, but not such as the world knew it. She was not to know the meaning of the word wife. O, how her love had been tested! But love had conquered, and together they had studied the problem that had at first appeared as though it would prove the shoal upon which their bark of life was to be wrecked. But the skillful hands of reason had warded off the dreaded disaster and had safely guided them through the rocks out into the smooth waters of the mid ocean, but for the present they were adrift; as yet they could not see the shore, the haven where they might safely be anchored. Now and then this caused the trusting maiden an anxious pang, the honorable man a deeper pain than he wished to betray, but the sky was clear, bright sunshine and smooth waters made the way very pleasant. So they were content to drift on.

Margaret had learned to understand the meaning of the glorious freedom that her lover sought to secure to her. She had looked deep into the mysteries of married life with the aid of that mother whose experiences had been so terrible. She had learned also to walk with open eyes and to read the signs as she walked. And oh, how her pure soul revolted at the hideous sights that were covered with a filmy veil, sights that the gauze like covering made only the more horrible by the vain attempt at concealment.

She lifted the smiling blue eyes to the clouded face of her friend who seemed almost to have forgotten her presence.

"Well, Imelda, what do you think? Do you now understand how I could express myself as I did some days ago?"

"I understand now, as I did then, that you had just cause to mistrust the present institution of marriage. I do not blame you, but there is still much that is not clear to me. What else can we do, if we would not sacrifice nature's truest, purest instincts?"

Margaret slowly shook her head, and scarcely above a whisper came the words:

"I do not know."

Wilbur had been observing the girls and had heard the low-spoken words. A sad smile played about his lips.

"Wait," he gently said. "The problem is too great to be solved in one short afternoon. It has caused me considerable thought for quite a number of years. As yet I have found no satisfactory solution, but do not despair of eventually doing so. When woman becomes conscious of her true worth she will soon find means to have that worth recognized. I think, however, for a first lesson, Miss Ellwood has done extremely well. Suppose we discuss some commonplace subject for a change. The weather for instance. Have we not been having some very fine weather for October?"

Both girls looked up, first at Wilbur, then at each other. There was nothing remarkable about discussing the weather, but just at this moment it sounded ridiculous, and but for the fact that Wilbur's face was like an impenetrable mask they would have burst out laughing. As it was they controlled the desire and soon found themselves discussing plays, literature, art, etc., which they found very interesting.

The minutes passed by and soon they arrived at their destination. The parting words were said, Wilbur giving expression to the sincere wish that she would again join their circle.

And Imelda did join them, again and again. She seemed drawn to the circle in the lecture room by some magic force. Question after question on that radical platform was brought up for discussion. The fields of science also were explored. She soon found that she was able to learn at that place more in a few short months than in all probability she would have learned in the outside world in years.

Many were the battles she was called upon to fight with the deep rooted superstitions of other days. Idol after idol crumbled to dust beneath the merciless fingers, but bravely she held out while scale after scale fell from the weak eyes until at last they grew stronger and she could see as with a new light. Bright and clear was now what had seemed dark and murky before. The new truths burst upon her in all their splendor and at last Imelda was ready to take her place in the world as an inspired priestess of the new realm of thought; of the new truths by means of which the world should be renovated and womankind uplifted.

Thus time had slipped by and brought its changes to Imelda. Her mother had been laid to rest at her father's side, and in spite of the desire of her friends to share their home, she had made one for herself. Humble though her little attic room might be she was queen in its realm.

They were indeed dark days that now fell to the lot of Imelda. It was hard to hide the aching heart beneath a smiling exterior, but it was part of her daily task, and bravely did she accomplish it. But when she returned at night to spend the evening alone in her little room, it was then that she was often overcome; it was then that the over tired spirit gave way to grief. As she looked around at the many little mementoes of earlier and happier days, they brought vividly to her memory the times when her father, with his favorite child at his side, had permitted her to look into the depths of his artist soul. If home had not always been the most pleasant of places, yet at those times she had not known the meaning of the word sorrow as she now knew it. Father and mother were now sleeping in the silent grave. The brother and sister who ought, by nature's ties, to be more closely drawn to her now than ever before, were, she knew not where. And in the new light in which she now looked upon the world, she felt more sorrow than anger toward the wayward absent ones. O, if she could but have the assurance that the future would develop the better part of their natures she felt she could willingly forget the past. Could she but find them! She thought that perhaps there might yet be a way of reaching their hearts; but never a word did she hear from either. If it had not been for the friendship of Margaret, who was more and more a true sister to her, her life would indeed have been lonely and dark.

Nor was Margaret her only friend. Among the circle of radicals where Imelda was a constant attendant she found many that were sympathetic in more ways than one, but none attracted her more powerfully than did Mr. Roland. He was more like a father than a mere friend, and fatherly had often been the advice that the kind and sympathetic old gentleman had given her. One other, also, had an influence over her life and strongly did she feel herself attracted in this direction. That other was Wilbur Wallace. In spite of the love he bore the winsome Margaret, the sad dark-eyed Imelda had the power to stir his heart to its very depths. Fain would he have folded both sweet girls to his great loving heart and cherished them there as priceless treasures. Margaret saw and understood what was going on in the heart of the man she loved, but she understood also that that which was "her own" would remain her own, and she "feared not."

Margaret was right. Even though Imelda's head was sometimes pillowed on the breast of her lover and even though he should kiss the tears from the sad eyes and hush the fear of the trembling lips, what of it? The love that was to throw Imelda's whole being into a tumult was yet to be called forth by another. This love that she felt for Wilbur Wallace was a sweet, tranquil affection, undisturbed by the passions that clamor for possession. Knowing and understanding this, the two girls were more firm friends than ever. If now and then Wilbur felt a stronger emotion; an emotion that would cost him an effort to subdue, no one but himself was aware of it. He knew that the time had not as yet come that it would be practicable to give vent to his feelings in the manner that he felt was right and natural, and that the well being and happiness of both these girls was far too dear to his noble heart for him to cause them one needless pang.

Thus matters stood when one day Margaret startled them by stating her determination to prepare to go upon the stage. She knew that she possessed dramatic talent of no mean order, and had often expressed a desire to choose the stage as a means of earning a livelihood. Nor did she meet with opposition now from her friends, although they were at first somewhat taken aback. Within a week she was in the hands of a competent teacher. This, of course, necessitated study, and instead of spending so many of her evenings as she had hitherto done in the society of Wilbur and Imelda, she was forced to devote her spare time to books. This fact caused Imelda and Wilbur to be more often thrown together than ever before. Now it was music they practiced together; then it was a new book they read and discussed, while now and then they would go and hear some good opera. As a general thing when such was the case Margaret would go also, as she passionately loved the queens of song; and her sweet lips only curved in a happy smile as she observed the good understanding between the two whom she so dearly loved. That such a thing could be possible as Imelda winning her lover from her never once entered Margaret's mind. And she was right. Wilbur Wallace did not hold lightly the gift of his Margaret's love.

CHAPTER XIII

Thus matters went on. The cruel, piercing winter months had waned; balmy spring with her flattering promises had again visited the land, and in turn was now giving place to the sultry days of summer. The tired shop girls, behind their counters, looked as though they could barely drag their weary limbs along. Imelda had for some time felt as though she could not possibly hold out much longer when, near the close of an unusually hot and close June day, a lady, small of figure and dressed in the airiest of summer costumes, came tripping down the aisle and stopping just in front of Imelda's counter said:

"Some real laces, please."

With a start and smothered cry of "Alice!" Imelda went forward and the little lady caught the stately head and drew it down, imprinting the warmest of kisses upon the pale lips.

"Still in the old place? I thought I would find you here, providing you had not done as I did—got married and settled down as the queen of some fair home."

A silvery laugh dropped from the cherry lips, but the laugh sounded just the least bit forced, and the bright glow on the rounded cheek,—was it really the flush of perfect happiness? Imelda looked long and carefully into the blue eyes, but though they were clear she could not read within their depths, the dimpling smile hid everything, if there was anything to hide.

"Why, where did you get your cranky ideas? O, I forget,—you still live in Chicago, which city, as I believe, has known many changes, and, I suppose, the people who inhabit the dear old place must of course change with it. But Harrisburg is a rather conservative town, you know, and radical or progressive ideas are not much indulged in by its people. How is it? am I right? have you been imbibing some of these new foolish notions?"

Imelda smiled. This little chatterbox was rattling on at a great rate, on a subject she evidently knew little about, and had already exhausted her store of knowledge. What would she think if she knew exactly what Imelda's views at present were? The girl behind the counter had an idea that her visitor would be somewhat shocked. So she only answered:

"Maybe I have, it is in the air, you know, like a contagious disease." Alice laughed.

"Is it dangerous?" she asked, but not waiting for a reply she continued:

"Have you time? I would like to have you with me this evening so that we could enjoy a quiet dinner together. May I call for you?"

A flush stole over the pale face. When had such a pleasure ever been offered her? For a moment she hesitated, then threw scruples to the winds.

"Yes; you may come. I will be ready. This is indeed kind of you to make me such an offer, and I assure you I shall appreciate it."

The dainty gloved hand was raised in a mock threatening manner.

"If you speak again in that strain I shall punish you by failing to put in an appearance. But I must not forget—your address, please." Imelda wrote name of street and number on a slip of paper and Alice Westcot tripped down the aisle and out to where her carriage was in waiting. Imelda's lips quivered as she watched the friend of former days pass out.

There were but few of the girls in the store now who had known Alice. The few who had seen the meeting between the two wondered who the richly attired lady could be who was on intimate terms with the sad faced but well liked companion and co-worker who had a smile and kind word for all but who made friends with none—none except the jolly, mirth-loving but proud Margaret Leland.

Imelda sighed as the form of Alice disappeared. Who would have thought, looking at the dainty figure, that in former years she had stood at the self-same counter where Imelda now presided. That she had wealth at her command was easy to be seen. But was she happy? If she was not she knew well how to hide it. No casual observer would have noticed anything wrong and when her carriage in the evening drove up to the number that Imelda had given her the pretty figure was robed in daintiest white. When Imelda appeared in the doorway in her plain black lawn and simple sailor hat she hesitated a moment. She knew she would look out of place at the side of this richly attired lady, and she would rather not go. But already Alice was calling to her to come. "For," she said, "we want a good long evening together and we cannot afford to waste time."

Imelda hesitated no longer. Why should she? Did the possession of wealth alone make Alice Westcot her superior? She told herself, No! They had been friends in the days of long ago, Imelda had found Alice a dear girl, sweet and pure and true, but for all that she knew that mentally this little woman was not her equal.

So she took her place at Alice's side without further hesitation and they were soon whirling along toward one of the beautiful parks. Imelda gave herself up to the luxury of such delicious comfort, such sense of pleasure as seldom came to her. Alice chattered on at her side, telling her all about her life; telling her of the many bright spots it contained; of the beautiful home with its richly furnished rooms, its charming grounds and surroundings; of the husband who showered wealth upon her; of the two pretty blossoms— her little daughters, one dark eyed with glossy curls like the father and who was named Meta, while the youngest was fair and flaxen-haired like herself, and had been given the name of Norma.

Imelda listened like one in a dream. Was Alice's life all sunshine? She made bold to ask her. For a moment the bright sunny face clouded, then a silvery laugh rippled from the ripe red lips.

"Why not? Certainly it is sunshine, all sunshine. Have I not everything my heart desires? No more hard work, no more eking out and economizing, no more planning how to make both ends meet. My husband's purse is open to me always. I have nothing else to do but be happy."

And then, not giving Imelda time to ask any more questions, she in turn began to question her. She poured such an avalanche of questions upon her that Imelda did not know which to answer first. So bewildering was the torrent that Alice was obliged to repeat them more slowly. Imelda answered them all to the satisfaction of the persistent questioner who gradually came in possession of all the dark facts that had brought so much pain into the young girl's life and only at the close of the story did she understand that Imelda was all alone and her tender little heart swelled and two pearly drops fell upon the hands of the girl as she lifted them and pressed them to her cheeks.

"My poor, proud girl," she said, "how you must have suffered! Listen, Imelda. How would you like to live with me? O, no!" she said as she looked into the surprised eyes of the girl, and read therein a refusal.

"I understand you too well to offer you a home without a way of earning it. I understand your proud nature better. But I would like someone trustworthy to take care of my little daughters. For really I am too much of a butterfly to have so grave a charge on my hands without some one more competent to aid me. I do not understand how to train my babies. But you, who have had so much experience, would know always what to do and they really are such dear little darlings. I am sure you would soon learn to love them and then you should be treated as just the lady that you are, not as a servant but as my own dear friend, and you should have so much time all your own when you might read or paint or study, and you shall cultivate that precious talent of yours, music. Say yes, dear, you shall never be sorry for it, I promise you," and the little cajoler wound her arm about the neck of the dumb-founded girl and laid her face against hers and coaxed and kissed and plead until Imelda gave the so much desired promise. Then Alice was happy as a child and said that Imelda must leave the store instantly so she could prepare to go with her when she should return to her home.

"I expect to remain only a little over a week, and until then you shall come and live with me at the hotel where I am staying." But to this Imelda would not listen. It was all so sudden she could hardly realize what it involved. A sharp pang entered her heart as she thought of Margaret and Wilbur. Ah, yes, it meant to give up these tried and trusted friends. No! oh no, she could not leave without devoting some of the last hours of her stay in the dear old city that had always been her home, to the friends whose lives were so closely woven in with hers. She finally succeeded in making Alice understand as much. In the morning when she told Margaret, it seemed at first as though she could not comprehend it. The large soft eyes filled with tears and the sensitive lips quivered when the comprehension came home to her, but she bravely choked a sob as she said:

"You are right. Why should you wear out your life, standing day after day behind the counter in that store, when opportunities are offered you that do not fall to the lot of every working girl. Yes, it is certainly my advice to accept this offer, and make the most of it. But I insist that you spend the evening with me at my mother's home. We must make the most of your short stay with us."

Imelda did not refuse. She felt it was not so easy to sunder ties. She also felt a sadness steal over her as she thought of how soon she was to turn her back upon all the scenes of the old life, and some very sharp pangs made themselves manifest.

CHAPTER XIV

The evening found her with her friends. After supper Wilbur came and was told of the projected change. He bent a quick searching glance upon Imelda and in the eyes that met his he thought he read a subdued pain. All through that evening Imelda was unusually quiet. Wilbur and Margaret played and sang but Imelda only listened. Mrs. Leland once in passing behind her chair, laid her hand upon the glossy dark hair, slightly bending the head so she could look into the dark eyes, saying in a low tone:

"Are the dreams of the future not bright, dear Imelda? Don't let the shadows of the past follow you into the future. Keep a brave heart and it will be strange if the future does not contain for you something for which it is worth your while to work and wait."

The dark eyes of the girl filled with a pearly mist.

"Thank you, Mrs. Leland. When you, who have certainly seen some of the very darkest sides of life can still give such encouragement there must indeed be a bright side to all things, only I am parting with so much that is pleasant in the present, while the future is yet a sealed book. Not knowing what it may contain, it is not very wonderful that I should feel the least bit sad."

"But you are to be an inmate of a beautiful home and the companion of the friend of former days." Imelda smiled.

"Yes, of former days, indeed. In the present she is no longer all-sufficient. I have been walking in the pathways of progress. She has been lingering in those of blind faith, of contentment and of duty. I fear there will be many lonely hours for me."

"There may be," said Mrs. Leland, "but also, maybe, you can take this little girl by the hand and lead her by your side. Who knows what your work in this new life you are about to enter really may be? So be of good cheer. At all events it is not to another world, or even to another continent you are going. You can send us your thought and your love and receive a return in a few days. I know Margaret and Wilbur will both expect a great many of the white-winged messengers, and they will keep your fingers busy in their spare moments."

She bent and kissed the warm lips of the girl and passed out of the room, soon returning with a basket of luscious fruit. For a time the music was hushed while the fruit was discussed. But as all things, the best as well as the worst, must come to an end, so with Imelda's visit to her dearly cherished friends. As the evening was far advanced when Imelda rose to go home, Margaret coaxed her to remain with her.

"For I am," she said, "so soon to lose you altogether, that I want to make the most of the short remaining time." But Imelda was longing to be alone.

"Not tonight, dear. Tonight you must excuse me. I cannot help it, but I have so much to think about, so much to do yet. But tomorrow night, if you wish I will come and remain with you," and with that Margaret had to be content. "Instead," Imelda went on, "I would have you come with me. It is not so very late yet, and a walk will do you good. Wilbur will make it doubly pleasant coming back. What say you?" But now it was Margaret's turn to shake her head and say:

"Not tonight. But that does not mean that you will be permitted to go home alone. Wilbur will take care of you. Will you not?" Wilbur smiled.

"It seems I have nothing to say in the matter but am quietly disposed of," he said with a spice of mischief, "the arrangement suits me, however, so I will not object. Or, have you objections, little girlie?" He looked at Imelda in such a quizzing manner that the tell-tale blood dyed the pale cheeks to a dark crimson.

"If you desire objections, Mr. Impudence, it will not be a difficult matter to satisfy you." Whereupon the young man, in mock humility, begged her not to deal with him too severely, plead for pardon, and solemnly promised that he would not offend again. Thus laughing and jesting they prepared to part for the night. Ready to start Imelda stood some moments at the door gazing up into the starlit heavens. Wilbur in the meantime wound his arm tenderly about his beloved Margaret. For a moment she was enfolded in a close embrace; pressed to his manly breast, his lips closed over hers in a tender clinging kiss. "My own precious one," he murmured,—"you love me?"

"As my life."

Again their lips met, then he stepped forward to Imelda's side and together they walked toward the humble home of the girl. For awhile neither spoke, and when at last their voices did find utterance it was only to speak of commonplace matters. Their hearts were too full to converse much; least of all of that which was uppermost in their minds. Imelda's leaving would make a great change for them all, and Wilbur felt that it would make a decided change in his life. He almost feared to give expression to his feelings,—certainly not under the starlit heavens. So, when after a quiet walk through the nearly silent streets, they reached the home which soon would know Imelda no longer, he stopped, loth to leave her, and she, as if divining his thought, simply said, "Come," and just as simply he followed her up the three flights of stairs into the little room where he threw himself into an arm chair at the open window. Imelda was about to strike a light when he said:

"Don't, please; come and sit here with me. It is easier to talk with only the light of the moon." And Imelda did as he requested, moving her chair so that she sat just opposite him, but for awhile it seemed that the moon, which was full and flooded the city with its pale silvery glory, was not going to prove an inspiration to conversation, for the moments slipped by until half an hour had passed, and as yet neither had spoken. But now Wilbur turned and laid his hand gently upon that of the dreaming girl.

"Imelda!" Low, soft, tremulous, the name dropped from his lips. She started. Why was it that the mere sound of her name should thrill her so?

"Imelda!" Again the low-spoken name came to her ear like sweet, thrilling music, and suddenly, ere she knew how it had happened, she found herself encircled by two strong arms, her head pillowed upon the heaving breast, and the bearded lips pressed close to hers in a burning kiss. Tender words and endearing names greeted her ear.

"O, my darling, it is hard to see you go, not knowing when, if ever, I may see you again, and just as you were becoming so dear to me."

"But Margaret?" came in a trembling whisper from Imelda's quivering lips. He held her closer still as he made answer.

"She is the dearest, sweetest woman that ever loved a man."

"But she trusts you," came from the trembling lips.

"And why should she not? Am I not trustworthy? Darling, she knows the love I bear her is all her own, and surely, you do not think her so small that she should deem it necessary in order to hold her own, my heart must be held in such narrow confines that none other, though she be equally pure, equally good, may find room therein? You do not think that, do you? No, my love; Margaret is too true, too noble a woman to fail to understand that no matter how boundless the love may be Imelda has won, it cannot detract one iota from that which is hers in her own right. I could not love her less if I would, notwithstanding the new love which you, my darling, have won, and I cannot believe that Imelda has been one of our number all this time without having learned to understand that there is nothing so pure as the love that is free, free to bring blessings upon the object that inspires that love. Love is limitless. Each new object that finds its way to the innermost recesses of a true lover's heart brings new stimulus that each in term may reap the benefits, the added blessings that are bound to come with the calling into life of each new love."

Wilbur Wallace was laying his whole soul bare before the pure eyes of the young girl, and O, what a storm of emotions swept over her soul! What a new import, and how different, these words conveyed from the standards that had been taught her from her earliest infancy. A little over a year ago she would have believed it to be rank treason to passively listen, with such a sweet sense of enjoyment stealing through her veins, to such passionate words of love from Wilbur's lips,—and now? Well! try as she would, she could not detect a feeling of guilt. On the contrary she was conscious of being very happy at that precise moment, and the conviction that had for some time been making itself manifest,—that it is right to love, and to enjoy that love, whenever and wherever Cupid may make his appearance, was forcing itself more clearly upon her mind. She now began to believe and understand that nature is right. That love must always be right, and so her answer to Wilbur was only to nestle closer to his side.

It was not the first time that he had encircled her waist with his arms, and kissed the ripe dewy lips. She had always permitted it, smiling like a happy child, as she looked into the pure dark eyes above her. Often he had drawn both fair girls to him, an arm about each slender waist, a fair and a dark head resting upon either shoulder. Margaret never thought that Imelda was robbing her, and into Imelda's head the idea never entered that such proceedings were not right, although he had never folded her quite so closely, nor pressed her lips so firmly as he had done tonight, and now she felt he was giving expression to more than the friendship he had hitherto tendered her. With a mighty bound her heart told her that Wilbur loved her! And Imelda?

O well, she was a woman! and as far as we have known her we have every reason to pronounce her a true woman, true to all of nature's holiest instincts. So, who would or who could blame her when she gave herself up to the subtle warmth that had crept into her heart and pervaded her whole being? She felt her pulses throb and thrill, and knew she was under the influence of the sweetest of all human emotions, but feeling them to be pure she gave herself up to the influence of the hour, and to the love that had unawares crept into her life.

Yes! Imelda now knew that she loved, even as she was loved, and the minutes passed until they grew to hours—hours of pure holy joy, and when Wilbur left her the dawn had crept into the east, and with his kisses resting upon her lips she still sat at the open window, dreaming of the raptures that life—sweetened by magic love—had brought her. And soon the waking dreams merged into the sleep of youth and innocence as the brown eyes closed; and still the smile hovered about the dewy red lips as they in tender cadence whispered—"Wilbur!"

CHAPTER XV

The morning hours passed. The sun rose high in the heavens and still Imelda slept; slept until the noonday rays fell across the fair flushed face. The heat soon made the room uncomfortably warm, waking the sleeping maiden who, confused at first, did not understand how she came to be sleeping at the open window. But all in a moment memory returning with a swift rush, brought back the sweet hours of the departed night. The red life blood stained the fair cheek and obeying the first impulse Imelda's face was buried in her hands, hiding the blushes that stained it. Such holy memories she would keep hidden even from the sun's bright rays. Then brushing the tangled tresses from her brow she cooled the burning face with fresh cold water, darkened her room and disrobing lay down upon her bed to rest the aching limbs that had become cramped by reclining so long in an uncomfortable position.

But the desire to sleep had fled. Thoughts in the brown head revolved in chaotic confusion. The sweet love dream wove rosy fancies until chased by the more realistic thoughts of the near future, causing a feeling of sadness until rose-hued love again conquered.

Thus for an hour or more, in sweet reveries indulging, and when the excited nerves were becoming soothed, and soft slumber gently closing the drowsy eyes, a low rap sounded upon the door. The next minute Margaret was sitting upon the edge of the bed, chaffing and teasing Imelda for being so lazy.

"It is easy to be seen," she was saying, "that you were born for something better than standing behind a counter, measuring laces. What a perfect lady you would make, to be sure. Your very first holiday you must use in practicing the airs, the manners of a fine lady." Her clear sweet laugh rang out while she bent and kissed the red lips of her friend.

Imelda's soft rounded arms wound themselves about the fair form bending above her and drew her close to her fast beating heart. Laying her lips to Margaret's pink shell-like ears, she rapidly whispered; then drawing back, eagerly did she look into the now quiet and pretty sobered face of Margaret, who seemed to have sunk into deep thought.

"Margaret," whispered Imelda. "Margaret what have you to say?" The large blue eyes rested lovingly on the dark face before her, darker hued still because of the burning blushes that were mantling it. Margaret's answer was to bend low and lay her face close to hers. Her eyes shone brightly as she clasped Imelda to her breast.

"What have I to say? Why, as you followed the dictates of your heart you have done perfectly right. Wilbur is so grand so noble a man, how can a woman help loving him? You did not think I would find fault with you for doing precisely as I have done? Maybe, if I thought it were possible that you could win him away from me it might be that I would not treat the matter so coolly," [a new light dawned in Margaret's eyes] "for I am only human, and I love him, O, how I love him! I find in him my nearest realization of heaven—as I can think it. He is to me life itself. If the star of my love were suddenly to set I think my life would go out with it. My love has power to sway me like a storm-tossed bark, like a mighty oak in the wind. And you, Imelda? Tell me what is your love like." The waves of rich blood were flooding the face of the questioned girl.

"Not like that," she said. "Mine is a quiet joy; it is peace; it is balm. Like oil on troubled waters; a calm after a storm; a haven of rest. To lose him would bring me pain, deep and lasting, but not a complete wreck. But O, Margaret, I don't want to think of anything like that. The mere thought hurts."

How long the girls would have gone on in this strain can never be known, for at this moment a rap again resounded on the door of the room. Imelda, frightened, quickly drew the covers closely about her form, the next moment she was merrily joining in the silvery laugh of Alice who had entered without waiting to be bidden. The dainty figure was attired in rich black lace that became the lily fairness of the sweet face exceedingly well. It was the first meeting between Margaret and Alice.

"A pretty, merry child," was Margaret's inward comment.

"Proud and haughty," was Alice's first thought. That was always the first impression Margaret made on others, and only in the measure that new acquaintances won their way into her heart did she unbend; only to the nearest and dearest did she show the child of nature that she really was. It was not long, however, until winsome, pretty Alice had found that way, and for a while Margaret dropped the proud air that became her so well and descended to the mimic and burlesque. She recited selections of emotions and passion, until tears filled the eyes of her auditors, then suddenly, in the twinkling of an eye, the broad brogue of Irish Bridget caused them, with blinded eyes, to hold their sides, convulsed with laughter. Then followed a negro song, ending with an Indian war-whoop; whereupon she sat down upon the floor at their feet and asked them if they did not think it rather foolish to so exert themselves with laughing, such a warm day. "It is so exhausting, you know, and so vulgar!" and waving her fan back and forward in the most approved languid, lady-like style, she elevated her slightly retrousse nose, while her companions went into new convulsions of laughter.

Leaving them to recover their composure she rose and stepping to the window drew aside the curtains. In a moment she was lost to her surroundings; her thoughts following her eyes into the distance, into the future. Incomprehensible dreamer she was, as she gazed up into the azure sky. The pearly teeth sank deep into the crimson lips. Tightly the white slender hands were interlaced, while the large eyes became soft and lustrous, a mist rising therein, and presently tears were falling upon the folded hands, recalling her from dreamland to the realistic present. Just then Imelda's arm was wound about the snowy neck and her quick eye caught sight of the tear drops. Her heart gave a quick apprehensive bound.

"What is it?" grasped the paling lips as she caught the tear-bedewed hands in hers. "Am I the cause?"

But already Margaret's mood had changed; a bright smile played about the sensitive mouth.

"No, dearest," she said, "how could you."

But Imelda was not so easily satisfied. The cruel fear entered her heart that Wilbur might be the cause. The painful thought was reflected in her eyes. All in an instant Margaret understood. Folding her arms about her friend's neck she said:

"Not that, Imelda, never that! I am not so foolish, but I do not understand myself today. It is a day of my many moods. I am as changeful as an April day. I was thinking of the future, what it may bring me. Do not think, silly child, that your pure love for Wilbur has caused my tears. Not of that was I thinking. Oh, the curse of poverty! I love beautiful things. I love fame. I love wealth. I love a home, and I love little children. [This last came almost in a whisper.] What will, oh what will the future bring? Any of these? and which of these? will any of my dreams be realized? Sometimes a sort of despair comes over me when I think of the hours of trial, of pain, of suffering my dear mother has been compelled to endure, with her nature so well fitted to enjoy and to bless. A kind of wild anger sometimes takes possession of me. It has been nothing but plod and work. Then I think if her fate is to be mine, over again, I could curse the day I was born.

"But those feelings do not often last long. The determination to conquer buoys me up. I mean to sway the world, and—I will! I will fight for freedom until I obtain it. I will not permit myself to be shackled and fettered. Society has placed fetters enough upon me at my birth; and I will not add to their number. Free as the wild winds I mean to be. I will conquer fate. The day shall dawn that victory shall be mine; and then those I love shall be happy as the laughing sunshine of a summer's day.

"And to curb some one else!—to curb you, my sweet Imelda, could I do that and be consistent with my ideas of justice? Never again, my dear girl, never again insult me with that suspicion. Now good bye, my precious one, this evening I expect you to be with me."

Bending she kissed her, and without bestowing a single glance upon the surprised Alice, Margaret was gone ere Imelda had fully comprehended her meaning.

CHAPTER XVI

Imelda had seen Margaret in similar moods before, and she knew of the intensity that sometimes lurked beneath the smiling exterior. She knew Margaret's most dearly cherished desire was some day to be a mother. To press the rosy dimpled infant, the child of the man her heart owned king— to her jubilant heart was her dream of dreams. But with this gift that she so craved she demanded no common conditions and environments. To call into being a perfect child she must be a perfect mother, and she understood, only too well, that she could not be that, surrounded with imperfect conditions.

Something had vividly portrayed this dream before her eyes today. Imelda understood the fierce storm of emotions that sometimes shook the nature of the proud girl to its very foundations. But Alice did not understand. She was rather frightened than otherwise at the storm that had so suddenly burst from the lips that had but a short time previously been overflowing with gayest merriment. The depths of feelings thus exhibited was a revelation to her. She had never heard such wild, such passionate words from any one, much less from the lips of a woman. In a helpless manner she turned to Imelda for explanation. But Imelda appeared to have forgotten the presence of Alice, as she sat blankly staring after the receding form and at the door through which she had passed, and only after Alice had twice spoken her name was she recalled to herself. With a deep heart-felt sigh she arose and began arranging her simple toilet, but never a word did she say of the queer manner of her friend, until again the voice of Alice aroused her.

"What was it you said? O, the meaning of this strange outburst. I don't know if I would be able to explain the moods of Margaret. I doubt if anyone could explain them, but she is the dearest, sweetest, noblest woman that ever lived. Her life, like mine, has been overshadowed by those of her parents. She understands the meaning of the finger of scorn, and her proud spirit rebels against it."

"The finger of scorn? What do you mean? Explain yourself."

"Margaret's mother is a divorced woman."

"A divorced woman!" broke, in a surprised cry, from the lips of the young woman. Another question seemed to hover on them, but checking herself she waited an answer. Imelda smiled. She understood what was going on in the other's mind. When, in all the past, had a woman gone through the dread ordeal of the divorce court that the world in general and women in particular did not believe that she was not in some way to blame for all the shame that had been heaped upon her? She who had the strength to dare to go through the calumny of the divorce court was, in the minds of many, composed of some grosser material than that was used in the composition of women in general, and little Alice Westcot was by no means above the common.

How could she be? Had she ever been taught otherwise? She had yet to learn that the divorced woman, instead of being a coarse-grained creature of the slums is more often possessed of a nature most refined, and far superior to her surroundings. She had yet to learn that it was for that very reason, often, that the divorced woman bears the shame, the disgrace and the calumny heaped upon her by the cruel process of the law, in order to escape a state so distasteful to her sensitive soul that death itself is preferable to the continued endurance of bondage. Imelda knowing this could only smile, but she hastened to say:

"Yes! her mother was married to a man that Margaret is anything but proud to acknowledge as a father. He was coarse and brutal; often descending to so low a level as to strike the woman who was the mother of his children. Margaret's mother was a woman very sensitive and refined. The only wonder to me is that she ever could have made the selection that she did, unless the fact that she was little more than a child could be considered an explanation. He drank, he cursed her, he struck her. He did not provide. The more she worked the less did he do, and the more he depended upon her efforts to gain a livelihood, until finally one day she took her babes (she had two of them) in her arms and left the man who had made of her life such a miserable ruin.

"As time passed he sought to induce her, by every effort in his power, to return to him; but his efforts were unavailing. She would rather, she says, have thrown herself with a babe clasped in either arm into the cold waves of the darkly flowing river than again return to the bondage from which she had escaped. For, added to all the other indignities she had been forced to bear, were the constant outrages perpetrated upon her womanhood, and which she could no longer endure."

"The brute!" broke, in a passionate exclamation, from the lips of Alice.

Not heeding the interruption, save by a quick sharp glance at the young woman by which glance she noticed that her lips were compressed and the delicate hand clinched, she proceeded with her story.

"Finding her mother could not be induced to return he finally entered a suit for divorce, and here the demon nature of the man showed itself in its most depraved form. It would have been the easiest thing in the world to have obtained a divorce upon the grounds of desertion, as nothing could ever have induced her to return to him, but that did not suit his vile purpose. He circulated all the unclean, defaming reports about her that his low mind could concoct, which brought Mrs. Leland to the verge of insanity.

"At last it was all over. Once more she was a free woman, but defamed and disgraced before the world. It was then she registered a vow that the world should yet pay her the respect that was her due, and nobly has she kept her word. Her daughter Margaret can go with head erect into the best society, while she herself is everywhere treated with the most marked respect. But for all that, Margaret has oft times felt the stigma her father has placed upon her mother, and through her upon her own name, and many of these fierce outbursts, — one of which you have just witnessed, are due to that fact. But Margaret, like her mother, is pure gold, and no taint remains upon her, or upon her equally true and pure mother."

As Imelda finished speaking she finished also her toilet, and sinking into a low rocker, in a tired manner, laid her head against its back. Presently Alice slipped forward and knelt at her side. She laid her face against Imelda's knees but said nothing. For a few moments the young girl permitted her to retain this position, then laying her hand upon the fair head and gently brushing the blond hair from the white temples, said:

"What is it, Alice?" A change had come over the merry features. A hitherto unthought-of sadness dwelt in the light eyes where also a suspicious moisture was visible, and with a noticeable effort she conquered something that was gathering in her throat.

"Nothing," she replied. "What should I have to say? Only Mrs. Leland's history has placed a new light upon divorce in my eyes. I have never heard a case thus discussed, or seen it placed in such light before. She was at all events a brave woman, and I would like to meet her. As for Margaret I know I shall always love her."

"If you really wish to meet Mrs. Leland nothing will be easier," Imelda said. "I am to spend the evening with them. You can accompany me and judge for yourself."

"Thank you. But you must remember, Margaret has not invited me. So you see I cannot go."

"Nonsense! I see nothing of the kind. Margaret is not responsible for the oversight she has committed and I will take it upon myself to introduce you into their pretty but simple home. But really, I feel hungry. I have not taken food today, and my stomach demands its rights."

"Not taken food today? Why, Imelda! what do you mean? Do you know what time it is?"

"I must confess that I have not been troubling myself to ascertain, so cannot answer your question."

"Well, you seem to attach little importance to the craving of the inner man—or woman, which is it in this case?" laughed Alice. "But for all that, will answer my question myself for the enlightenment of your pitiful ignorance. It is now half past two. I am usually not any too early a riser myself but long ere this I generally have eaten my second meal."

"Little gourmand!" smiled Imelda. "I wonder you do not say it is time for a third one." Alice laughed lightly.

"That is a libel," she said. "I protest; but in order that you may be no longer exposed to the danger of starving yourself I insist that you now go with me. I will take care of you in the most approved style."

Imelda protested. "A glass of milk, some fruit and a piece of cake, will be all-sufficient and I have a supply of that on hand." But Alice insisted so strenuously that Imelda succumbed and in a short time both were comfortably seated at a table in a restaurant awaiting the dainty viands that Alice had ordered notwithstanding the protesting looks of Imelda. But Alice only laughingly shook her head and proceeded to call for some little extras. It seemed to afford her a peculiar pleasure to press these little attentions. She was happy to be able to contribute towards furnishing some little pleasure for the friend for whom she knew life had hitherto not turned the sunniest side, and Imelda soon came to understand that it was useless to protest against her friend's generosity.

Having finished their meal they seated themselves in the carriage that stood in waiting, and were soon bowling along the shady drives. For awhile thought was busy with each of the fair occupants. Imelda was thinking of the changes that had come into her life, past and present. How many sighs, how many tears lay in the bitter past. She shuddered as with cold, on this blazing hot day. No, no! She was done with it. She did not desire to resurrect its skeleton memories, even though some dearly loved ones belonged to that past. But the present? Were not the changes the present was bringing also fraught with bitterness? Yes, but not without hope. The green banner of hope was held high, indicating the coming of better times. There would be sweet memories mixed with the pain of parting. And the future? She would win it, she would conquer it. She would not be less brave than Margaret who so earnestly vowed to conquer all obstructions.

CHAPTER XVII

While such thoughts surged through the brain of Imelda, what was it that clouded the brow of fair Alice, causing now and then the ruby lips to part with a tremulous sigh? What caused the eyes to grow dim, the child-like mouth to quiver? Was there a skeleton in her closet also? Ah, could we always but lift the veil and look underneath! What aching, breaking hearts the smiling lips sometimes mask. Imelda looked up just in time to see a bright drop splashing upon the dainty gloved hand, but which was hastily brushed away. Another moment and the young woman was laughing and chatting in a way that showed a light and merry (?) heart underneath, and Imelda forbore to question. The two had a very nice drive, enjoying the parks and open air sports. The hours of rest were doing Imelda a world of good, reviving her spirits and calling a rosy hue to the pale face.

The evening found them at the home of the Lelands, where they were both heartily welcomed. Alice watched the faces about her, wondering whose lover the handsome Wilbur Wallace was. She read in his face an almost worshipful love when his eyes rested on the proudly regal Margaret, while they followed with a passionate intensity every movement of the queenly Imelda, which glance would soften to a holy glow when he bent his head above her and when his hand touched hers. Alice felt the warmth of Mrs. Leland's motherly manner, and soon found that her heart was in every word she uttered. Although here and there a silver thread could be seen among the brown, her manner was as bright and youthful as that of the young girl's. Later the generous hostess brought in fruits, cake and cream, and merry sallies were passed round, while the refreshments were being discussed. Music and singing came in also for their share, and Alice felt that she had passed a very pleasant evening indeed.

The absence of all formality was not the least pleasing feature. The naturalness of every movement and action was refreshing in the extreme to Alice, whom the wealth of her husband had led, during the years of her married life, into those circles of society where empty phrases and society small talk are paramount, but which must be delivered in a stiff, formal, cut and dried manner. To talk, to act, to laugh, to eat, to drink, to sleep, to rule—that is society life; anything but to be natural. O, how homelike the little circle was! The evening passed by and the time came for parting. Margaret reminded Imelda of her promise of yesternight, and tendered the same invitation to Alice, but the latter did not accept.

"No! no! I would only be intruding. It is enough that I am about to separate these precious friends without intruding upon the last days and hours they can have together. With many thanks for the pleasant evening I have spent I will bid you good night. Tomorrow is another day when I shall see you again." Leaning back in the cushions of her carriage she was rapidly driven to her hotel. Wilbur kissed both fair girls and for a moment his arms wound about Imelda's form. She could feel the beating of his heart and heard his rapid breathing. She smiled into his face, wound her arms about his neck, laid her cheek against his, for an instant touched her lips to his whispered "Good night," and the next instant had slipped from his embrace, and from the room.

Margaret was standing at the window gazing at the starry heavens when she heard the door close after Imelda's retreating form. Turning she saw that they two were alone. Again she turned to the window giving him time to recover himself, and when a few minutes later she crossed the room to his side Wilbur had regained his composure. She laid both hands upon his shoulder and looked into the dark eyes.

"Wilbur," she whispered. Only that one word, the mention of his name, but O, it spoke volumes. The next moment he had caught her to his breast and covered the fair face with kisses.

"My darling! my darling!" he said. "You love me, you trust me?" There was a suspicious moisture in the dark blue eyes as she crept closer into his arms.

"You know I do." The girl's heart was passing through a fiery ordeal. Would she prove pure gold? Long were they locked in each other's embrace, not a word was spoken, but the lips were sealed each with the vibrating glowing lips of the other. Holding her thus close he drew her to his knee as he sank into the swelling cushions of an arm chair, and Imelda's dark head had for several hours pressed the snowy pillow ere Margaret sought her side. She leaned over and kissed her on the forehead when the white lids opened and the soft arms closed about the neck of her friend. Thus the two clasped in each other's arms a dark head and a fair one pressing the same pillow, their breath mingling, they fell asleep, and not until Mrs. Leland gently shook them and laughingly called them the seven sleepers, did they awake.

"I am afraid you would be 'my ladies' of the first water could you live according to your inclination. I believe girls are naturally lazy." Thus teasing and laughing she moved about opening the shutters and letting in the bright sunshine.

"Only see how you have let the golden hours of the morning fly away lazily hugging your bed." But the smiling faces on the pillow did not look as though this moralizing had anything to do with them. Margaret saucily told her mother that she (her mother) was only sorry that she could not lie there at that hour and enjoy a lazy nap, but if she would be kind enough to cease moving about and give them a little chance they would think the matter over, and in a little while come downstairs and have some breakfast.

"Which means, you saucebox, that I am to leave the room and go to prepare your breakfast. Very well, Miss Indolence, but I hope you will condescend to make your appearance when it is prepared." Thus bright and cheerful the new day began, and in a little while fresh and rosy, attired in white muslin dresses they made their appearance. Margaret had insisted that Imelda should wear one of her own snowy robes for the morning.

"I am tired of seeing you in this everlasting black." So the somber gown had been laid aside and when later in the day Alice came to carry Imelda off she clapped her little hands in delight at the sight of the spotless robes. She wanted her to retain the pretty dress for the day, but to this Imelda would not consent, so she had her way. Then Alice asked Margaret to join them for the day. "I shall need your advice and help." Both girls looked up with a questioning glance, but Alice shook her head and said:

"No! I will answer no questions, only come." They were not long in doubt, however, as to what it was that Alice wanted Margaret's advice for. They drove up to a large dress goods emporium where they selected a variety of beautiful fabrics. Soft gray woolens and dainty white muslins; also a handsome black silk. At first Imelda did not understand that they were meant for her; and when she realized it; it was too late to protest. She was scarcely more than half pleased, as Alice counted out the price for the pretty material, and made up her mind to accept it only as a loan, and so she told Alice. Alice did not object, only said:

"There are many things you will need and it will not be a question of how soon you will return the amount; that can be settled some day when you leave me. I would far rather, however, have made you a present of these few necessary articles." Imelda flushed.

"If you do not wish to offend me, you will cease to speak in such a strain. I can understand that I look very much out of place with my plain black muslins, but as your companion, nursery governess to your children I will hardly need much costly apparel."

"As my friend," corrected Alice. "Whatever else you may be; whatever position you may insist upon filling, I wish it distinctly understood that you are my friend. An orphan, in reduced circumstances, if you will, but always, most assuredly my friend." Thus the matter was settled for the present. Imelda bit her lip. Alice did not understand that the act of kindness, as she meant it to be, was, and must be most galling to the proud spirited girl; but no further comments were made at that time. The fair trio with their purchases next drove to a dressmaking establishment. Under protest Imelda was measured, and the order given to have the dresses made on short notice.

"You have nothing to say in this, only to obey," Alice had said with merry laughter. Thus the days slipped by one after another, until Imelda's trunks were packed, awaiting the expressman to take them to the depot. She herself was arrayed in her traveling dress, a plain soft gray serge, seated at the window awaiting her friends who had promised to escort her to the depot, Alice having said that she would meet her there. Tears stood in her eyes as she let them wander over the familiar objects that she was to take leave of now forever. Many a little trifle was stored away in the bottom of her trunks, but other and larger articles she was now forced to part with. Many a token had been given to Margaret, but there were still others that had to be disposed of, which Wilbur had promised to do, and as she now heard a familiar step coming up the stairs she quickly, with a convulsive start, laid her hand upon her heart and turned her face to the window. Another moment an arm had drawn her into a close embrace and she lay sobbing upon a manly breast.

CHAPTER XVIII

Quite a while she lay thus, for the first time giving full vent to her feelings. She had not intended to do so, but of what avail are good resolutions when the heart is full to overflowing; when every fiber clings to some loved object from which it is about to be separated, and she had not known how close her heart had clung and was clinging to this handsome, noble man, this lover of her best, her almost only friend. In spite of all the teachings and theorizing of later days the thought would steal into her mind—was it right? Is it right? Was she, O, was she wronging that noble girl? But Margaret's clear eyes still wore the same sweet, shining light that they had always been wont to wear. Always cheerful, always loving. If she considered herself wronged she certainly understood how to most successfully hide it.

But in giving shape and being to such a thought, was she not wronging Margaret? Her ideas of right and wrong were far too lofty to permit her for one instant to entertain such a sentiment. Would not the idea that those precious friends by their love were wronging her, be equivalent to placing a curb upon the natural outpourings of their hearts? Would not this thought be an infringement on personal liberty? To prove that she had been wronged Margaret must analyze the how! Could it in this case be otherwise than that some one person had taken or appropriated something that was her own, her personal property? Now how could any one rob her of her own? She knew and felt that that which was her own no one else could take from her, for just as soon as that which she had thought her own was appropriated by another, the unquestionable, the insurmountable truth confronted her that the said object had not been her own. Or, again, if such could once have been the case it proved now her inability to hold it and consequently at the same time proved her unworthiness. Are we, is anyone, justified in an attempt to forcibly retain that which in nature is attracted elsewhere?

Margaret in her reasoning would have answered "No!" Therefore it was the height of folly to speak of robbing her. And when the object in question, as in this case, was the heart of a man, was it not a question so easily answered as not to leave a shadow of doubt that he who bore the heart in question in his bosom was the natural owner thereof, and as such, was possessed of the indisputable right to dispose of it?

But Imelda, through his love for her, might sway that heart? O, yes! that was her right, as he had granted it to her. That another, equally pure and good girl had the power to win and sway him also proved only to her that his nature was more grand, his character more noble, his mind more pure, and his heart vastly larger than that of other men. No! Margaret did not feel herself wronged, although she knew that Imelda held an equally warm place in his great heart.

But as yet Imelda did not fully realize and understand the full grandeur of Margaret's nature; how wholly uncalled for her fears were; and when she gave expression to this fear that was making havoc with her peace, Wilbur who knew and understood the noble sentiments of his brave Margaret answered the agitated girl:

"Where is the usually clear-headed woman, the woman who has discussed so often these questions of right and wrong? of individual liberty, of universal liberty? the question of the emancipation of women from sex slavery? the woman who has been claiming and agitating for herself, and for her much wronged sex, the right to the indisputable ownership of herself? In accordance with all this, would you now place all your holiest and purest feelings and desires in a bondage most unnatural? Would you not by such action admit the right of one person to dictate a 'thou shalt' and 'thou shalt not' to another? Look up, my sweet. You do not think me, and believe me, still so far in the old ruts and so deep in the old superstitions and prejudices that in order to love one girl I must prove false and disloyal in my allegiance to another.

"See! as yet we have not arrived at the point of action. We have not yet the strength to stand and walk alone. As yet we are only theorizing. The few advocates of Love in Liberty with whom we have been associating in an intimate circle are not egotistic enough to expect our women, our girls, to shake off the restraining hands of society and act in accord with their beliefs and views. That would mean ostracism. We dare not place so heavy a load upon weak shoulders without giving them the assurance that at all events their future is provided for. Stern, demoralizing poverty binds our hands, and until ways and means are found which will show us in a clear light the road we are to travel we must conquer nature's desires and wait, patiently wait. But shall this circumstance prevent us also from folding the sweet loved ones to our hearts and from laying the kiss of pure and holy love upon their lips? Never! Imelda, you would not ask it. What is it to us if the whole world declares the human heart is capable of only one small dwarfed love. We know better; we who have been developing under Nature's teachings.

We will follow nature's promptings and permit our hearts to expand in the sunshine of their beauty, wherever and whenever this beauty bursts in its glory upon us."

Placing his hand gently under and raising the tear-wet face until he could look into the shining moist eyes, and bending low his lips pressed hers in a long and lingering kiss, and by and by under the influence of his caresses and soothing words a quiet peace stole over Imelda, only that subtle pain that held her heart, as with an icy grip would torment her and—well she knew what caused it.

"But,—'Harrisburg'"—Wilbur was speaking—"is not the end of the world by any means. We will meet again, my love. I feel it. Probably when the clouds have passed away, when we can see clearer and know what we can do and ought to do. And then, who knows, in that unknown future into which you are about to step, may be a work for you to perform. Your destiny may be lying awaiting your coming. There you may find him who will prove your best loved one. Nay, sweet one; shake not your head. I am not vain enough, not conceited enough to think that I alone should possess the power to sway your gentle heart. No! I hope you may prove yourself stronger and greater than the common everyday woman, whose ideal of pure love is centered in one poor, weak mortal with his one, two, perhaps more, sterling good qualities yet who will prove himself lacking in others equally good, nay, perhaps better qualities, which will be represented in another man but which by her must be passed by unnoticed because not centered in the person of her one love. No! my darling. I hope the time will come when a grander passion will come to you than I have inspired."

Wilbur smiled as he again folded her close and kissed the trembling lips. "I appreciate the sweet tender love that fills and swells your gentle breast, but I know, if you do not, that it will be another than myself who will be able to shake this woman's heart of yours to the very foundation of your being. Under the influence of a mightier love than you have yet felt you will awake to your full strength. Then will come the time when you will arise to the height and glory of your work in the cause of humanity, in the cause of womankind."

He spoke the words soothingly, smoothing the glossy dark braids, as if thereby to cause the pain of the present hour to gently pass over. Did he feel that his words would prove prophetic? With a swift motion peculiar to herself she threw her head slightly back looking upward into the earnest eyes, taking his face between both her hands, she said, softly, gently:

"Wilbur, you are a man among men! A friend whom any woman might well count a priceless treasure. Whether or not it is true that my heart will find another whom, in time, it will own king, this much I do know, that I know of no place where I would rather rest than in your strong sheltering arms, but the time has come that I must stand alone. I am about to weigh the last anchor that holds me to the old life. In a few hours I shall be speeding away, cut loose from all the old ties. I will be brave now, and calmly look the coming time squarely in the face." Saying which she disengaged herself from the encircling arms.

"Where is Margaret?" Scarcely had the question dropped from her lips when the answer came just outside the door.

"Here! I am late, I know, and that too when I wanted to be here early in order to have one more hour with my darling girl, ere we are parted. But mamma was quite sick this morning; something unusual for her, as she generally has such good health. I left her sleeping, however, and feeling much better." This last in answer to the anxious inquiry that fell from two pairs of lips at the same time.

"O, my precious, precious darling, must I really lose you? I cannot realize that it can be true that I am to lose my friend, my Imelda;" and the two girls sank into each other's arms, clasping each other in a tender loving embrace, mingling their pain and tears. Wilbur stepped to the window and studied the tops of the buildings upon which he gazed in order to give these two tried and true friends an opportunity for a last exchange of a multitude of thoughts and emotions that were thronging their breasts and seeking utterance in incoherent speech. But time is merciless in its flight. Wilbur turned to remind the girls that the final moments were drawing very near.

CHAPTER XIX

"Mrs. Westcot will be getting uneasy if we tarry longer and indeed we certainly will have no time to lose if we wish to meet our little friend at the appointed hour."

Thus admonished the girls made haste to prepare to leave. A few minutes later the three were seated in a car hurrying toward their destination. Imelda had bade Mrs. Leland farewell the evening before—at whose home had been spent the last evening the three friends were together. She had also found present there quite a number of her radical friends whom Mrs. Leland had notified of the coming departure of Imelda Ellwood; and had invited them to meet her at her home. All who had received an invitation had come, for Imelda was a favorite and had found her way into many hearts. All were sorry to lose the society of the intelligent young lady friend and co-worker in the cause of humanity. None had expressed more deep regret at the loss they were all about to sustain than our white haired friend, Mr. Roland. He had taken Imelda by the hand, long and earnestly had he spoken, giving her much fatherly advice, privately and otherwise, as to the life she was about to enter upon. Among total strangers the fact that Alice Westcot had been a girl friend in former days did not weigh much with the old man. She was only one weak woman. In the midst of these new surroundings Imelda would often find it difficult to walk erect and self-reliant in the new path.

"It will hardly be an atmosphere of truth," said he, "with which you will be surrounded, but rather one of deceit and falsehood. Your powers of discerning the pure from the debased will be severely tried. There will be work to be done, for the true worker is ever on the alert. You must be an opportunist, ever awaiting the chance to strike while the iron is hot. Ever keep your eyes open. Point out the defects of a rotten system; the unholiness of an unmated marriage; the uncleanness of lives united without love; the loathsomeness of keeping up the semblance of love when it has long since become a putrid corpse. Keep your mind clear. Never let lust—passion—in the guise of love, draw near your side, tainting your fresh young life with sickening noisomeness. It is difficult to see clear in the dark labyrinth of society customs, and you may stumble and fall. And oh, the difficulty of rising after such fall! If it requires almost unlimited strength to obtain a firm foothold at any time in the whirlpool of fashion and custom, it will require strength superhuman to rise in a struggle in which you have once sunk, and it will take all your strength of will power, all your keen sense of honor and justice, all your sweet natural purity and self conscious pride to always hold that queenly head erect and walk firmly among the slippery pitfalls that unseen may lie along your every path."

It was not a very pleasant contemplation that her aged friend had called up before Imelda's mental view, but probably a much needed and wholesome lesson. "Forewarned is forearmed," and if Imelda's future was to escape the temptation that so often besets the lives of beautiful women, so much the better for her, as it would save her many little struggles of the soul. But on the other hand it would never tend to harm her that she knew something of the dark precipices of life. So she thanked Mr. Roland for the well meant kindness that had prompted his words, and in bidding him good bye she had permitted him to kiss her young fresh lips, well knowing that only the most disinterested concern for her future prompted the action.

One and all of the many kind friends had a parting admonition, a well meant advice, a loving word of farewell, all expressing the hope at some future time to meet her again. Mrs. Leland had folded her in her arms and held her there as a mother does her tired babe, and indeed Imelda had been tired. The events of the evening had been full of conflicting emotions. The taking leave of friend after friend was not a light task, and it had been a drain upon her strength. She would have much preferred to spend this last evening quietly in the close circle of her most intimate friends, and yet she also knew that she owed it to these others who had always shown themselves so appreciative of her friendship, of her small endeavors to aid them in their grand work of humanity. She felt the desire to see them all once more before forever stepping from the enchanted circle, and above all she would have been sorry had she failed to receive the parting clasp of Mr. Roland's hand.

When it was all over, the lips quivered and the eyes filled with tears, as she laid her face to Mrs. Leland's. The young matron gently passed her hand over the dark head brushing the heavy waves of hair from the white brow and in doing so discovered that Imelda was feverish. There had been too much excitement and she feared it might prove detrimental to the health of the young girl, so she had a nice fresh cup of tea brought for her, then folding her close in a farewell embrace she kissed her again and yet again, giving her much good counsel and many cheering words. She had then sent her home, as she insisted upon going. More like a sister than otherwise did Mrs. Leland seem to the parting girl as indeed she always felt thus toward the young matron. The girls never thought of keeping secrets from her; she was one of them, as she always made it a point of being in the confidence of Margaret, which was given voluntarily, as indeed it would have been difficult to be in the society of this woman and not have full confidence and trust in her. She won it from them and the girls knew only too well they could find no better place for the safe keeping of that which they wished to entrust to her.

But we have been devious and must hasten to rejoin the three friends as they now meet the little lady so anxiously awaiting their arrival at the depot. Her face lit up with an unmistakable expression of relief, the words she spoke the next moment giving proof of the anxiety to which she had been subjected.

"O, at last! at last! I thought you would never come. I had all kinds of visions—of runaway horses, of some great fire, of some accident wherein you figured as the heroine. Then too I thought you might have changed your mind at the eleventh hour. Indeed I felt quite miserable."

The whole company laughed. Imelda kissed the little excited woman.

"You seem to have but a poor opinion of me. Don't you know that fickle-mindedness is not counted among my faults? We still have fifteen minutes left I believe," looking up at the timepiece in the central waiting room, "so just please calm yourself. I am a fixture. You need not fear that you can easily rid yourself of me now." Imelda continued in this light tone. The others imitating her example. The object to be gained thereby was easily discerned, for neither wanted to display the aching heart that lay hidden within the bosom, but for all that none was deceived. The eye so eloquently speaks the language of the heart and their telegraphy was sending swift messages back and forth. All too quickly the passing moments flew. The train was ready and would not wait. Both fair young travelers were safely seated in their Pullman car. The last farewell had been spoken, and as the puffing engine steamed out from the depot the fluttering of white handkerchiefs was the last view the friends had of each other. With tear-wet eyes Margaret watched the outgoing train, Wilbur's face bearing almost as sad a look as her own. When would they meet again?

CHAPTER XX

Thus had come the beginning of the new life and the past lay enshrouded in shadows. Almost at the threshold of that new life Imelda was met by him whose coming Wilbur had, in last moments preceding the sundering from the old life, prophesied. With Wilbur's kisses yet warm on her lips, every beat of her heart responding to the love he bore her, there had been room in that heart to receive the impress of another's image. While still the memory of Wilbur's caresses thrilled her the kisses of the new-found lover sent the blood bounding in ecstacy through her veins. Those precious friends of the past, would understand? But Norman,—would she ever succeed in leading him to such heights of progress as to enable him to see by the light of understanding the glorious beauties of a boundless freedom?

As yet she had not reached the topmost heights herself, was not yet standing in the full glare of light that should show her the path that lay in the direction of perfect freedom. But she had seen the brilliant star in the distance and she knew of dark depths that were concealed, the dungeons where prejudice and superstition held in bondage all of nature's pure desires. She vowed never, never to wear the galling yoke of marriage.

She was deliriously happy in this new love. She found their thoughts blending in all things pertaining to nature. Only as yet Norman had paid little attention to progressive thought on this particular subject. Possessing an innate veneration for all women, he expected to find heaven in the arms of one. That such a thing is not possible we would by no means assert, for, contrary to the general rule that arbitrary laws prove the ruin of loving hearts and sensitive lives, there are cases where the one love has proved to be the happiness of a lifetime; but it is time that we rid ourselves of the illusion that a compulsory marriage law can command such fidelity and steadfastness that such cases instead of the rare exception—as they really are—will be the rule. The knowledge of perfect freedom—the freedom that means none may have the right to say, "Thou shalt" and "Thou shalt not,"—with the power this knowledge can give we rise to glorious heights, and in such knowledge is created a love which in its abandonment to love, its power to achieve, its strength to endure, a life opens before us that can never be attained when fettered within prescribed limits.

It was thus that Imelda felt, and to point out to Norman the way wherein he would be enabled to obtain the same views was what she felt to be now her task. But oh, the difficulty, the magnitude of her task! At least such it seemed to her.

Then, too, there arose another specter from the dark past. Norman Carlton was the descendant of a proud family. In time past they had ranked with the proudest and wealthiest of the country, and were still reckoned among the first. His mother was a dainty aristocrat, his sisters cultured and refined ladies. No doubt the pride of blood had been instilled into his mind from early infancy. Would his love stand the test of Imelda's past? Her father? Yes, her father had been a man as cultured and refined as ever a Carlton had been,—she felt that. But on the side of her mother she knew it was different. Then like dark apparitions appeared before her mind's eye the forms of Cora and Frank. These two were certainly living proofs (if they were yet living) of bad blood in her veins. How would it be when this record of her gloomy past was laid before him? Would he stand the test?

True, Imelda understood, with the high ideals she possessed, that if he did not stand those tests he was unworthy her love. But again, love in its unborn glory fails to grasp such philosophy, and longs only for the completion of the union of loving hearts. With all these difficulties in mind Imelda was not looking to the distant future. It was rather the near future with which she had to contend, the winning of her best loved lover.

After parting from Norman under the waving maple trees and after being refreshed by a healthful sleep her mind wandered to those other friends in their distant western home, and, grasping her pen, she spent two hours in writing; at the end of which time two closely written sheets lay before her. Having sealed and mailed the same she joined Alice and the two little ones at the breakfast table. Lawrence Westcot had breakfasted at a much earlier hour and had gone to his business. Usually Imelda joined him, as she was an early riser, but this morning the early hours had been given to her letter which had been directed to Margaret.

"Rather an unexpected pleasure," was Alice's comment as Imelda made her appearance and seated herself at the table. She generally came to assist the little ones, as they were sometimes unruly and clamorous until the hungry little stomachs had been satisfied. But that she should wait so long ere satisfying her own physical wants was a new departure and Alice looked as though she would like an explanation. Imelda smiled.

"I have been writing letters," she said.

Alice did not seem wholly satisfied. The new sweet light that shone in the young girl's eyes could hardly have been produced by the doubtful pleasure of writing letters in the early morning hours. (Alice always found writing letters a task.) But she asked no questions at present, though a troubled look shadowed the blue eyes as she turned her attention to discussing the dainty meal before her. Imelda attended to the wants of the little ones first and then sent them scampering off for a morning romp. Scarcely had their childish forms disappeared from view when an anxious "Well?" dropped from the lips of Alice. Imelda smiled. Feigning not to understand, she repeated the "Well," with an additional "What is it?"

"O, pshaw, Imelda," she said, "You cannot deceive me; something has happened, and you may as well tell me first as last."

Imelda's laugh rang out merrily at this assumption of the little lady.

"Your sense of perception is very acute this morning, but I will no longer keep you in suspense. Norman Carlton made me an offer of marriage last evening."

"You have accepted!" exclaimed Alice. For the moment it was hard to read the pale, immovable features.

"No I have not accepted." Alice sighed, while a puzzled expression settled upon her face. She found the young girl rather difficult to understand. Why was she so slow in telling what there was to tell?

"Finish your breakfast, Alice, and then I will tell you all." Thus assured a little more attention was paid to the tempting viands, but Alice for some time was toying impatiently with her knife, waiting until the imperturbable Imelda should be done with her breakfast. Presently she folded her napkin, thus indicating that she was through. Then she arose and said:

"Come, Alice, we will go either to your room or mine where we can talk undisturbed." The proposition met the favor of the young woman and soon they were seated in the cosy room of the fair mistress.

Alice listened while Imelda took her into her confidence and told her the story of her love. She knew of Imelda's aversion to marriage. She had come to understand some of her views and though she did not indorse them yet she could not but recognize much in them that would prove an everlasting blessing to humanity could they be put into practice. She felt if it were opportune she would not hesitate to hold out her longing hands for the tempting boon of freedom. Had she not told Imelda of moments when she felt like cursing the fetters that bound her even though they were golden? But Lawrence Westcot was known as an honorable man; one who heaped upon his wife golden favors; who daily sought to strew her pathway with flowers. All of this was true, yet time and again the blue eyes would fill with tears. The merry sprite was not always such when within her own chamber, and Imelda's confidence called forth no answering smile, and yet Imelda knew she always wore her brightest smile when the handsome young man was a visitor at their home. With an effort Alice banished the gloomy look and wished her friend happiness when she would become the wife of Norman Carlton.

"But," said Imelda, "have I not told you? I will never be his wife."

CHAPTER XXI

"You will never—be—his wife? And yet you are happy—in his love? Imelda, what do you mean?"

"I mean," Imelda replied, "to be wiser than you were, little one. I mean to always keep my lover."

This was too much, and Alice burst into tears. That Imelda was surprised was a mild way of expressing her emotion. A dim suspicion was born in her mind, which, however, she tried to repress. No, no; she did not believe it,—and yet it might be. She would watch, she would see. Taking the excited little woman in her arms, Imelda kissed and tried to soothe her, and after a time was apparently successful. Then she went to look after her little charges. No sooner had the door closed upon her retreating figure than Alice with trembling fingers locked it and casting herself upon the bed burst into a storm of sobs, for which there was no apparent cause, and which were so passionate that the merry mistress of the beautiful home could scarcely be recognized.

Surely a strange creature is woman. Of unfathomable depths her caprices; whose moods are so various that it would prove an almost impossible task to solve the pretty riddle. In some such way as this the conventional novelist would doubtless comment upon the action of Alice, but we know better than to judge her thus. It was neither a caprice nor mood that caused the bitter sobs to shake her to her inmost being. She was no riddle. It was all plain enough to those who would see. Nature's voice was clamoring for nature's own. But man-made laws, with iron hand, stood between.

Alice had not known why,—why, spite of the disgust she sometimes felt at the life surrounding her, she yet was light and happy. She had not yet understood what it was that brought the sunshine to banish the clouds of her life. But what had she to complain of? If you had asked her I doubt if she would have been able to clearly answer the question, yet it was all so clear, so apparent.

Her husband was all that has been stated, but no special credit could attach to him for that. Wealth was his to command. He never thought of refusing any wish of hers that money could satisfy. If any one had accused

Lawrence Westcot of unkindness to his wife he would have opened wide his eyes in surprise. Did she not have everything that heart could desire? That she would turn from him when he approached her; that little ripples of disgust shook her frame as he bent to kiss her; that her eyes would flash in angry scorn when he attempted to secure to himself the rights the law gave him—certainly was not his fault. That he was not fine-grained enough to desist on such occasions could be no reason for laying blame on his shoulders. Was she not *his*?—his by the wholly rites of matrimony? And why should she not comply with his desires and demands?

And yet, handsome Lawrence Westcot was a favorite wherever he went, especially with the fair sex. Strong, healthy, full of spirits, there were few who stopped to look for traces of greater refinement, but rather enjoyed the fiery look that would sometimes cause a rush of blood to the fair face that came under its power.

But we will leave Lawrence Westcot for the present and return to Imelda. As nothing happened during the hours of the day that would be of interest to us we pass them over until the shades of evening brought her handsome lover to her side. She had donned a soft white cashmere. No ornament of any kind, only a snowy rosebud nestling amidst the dusky coils of hair. The flushed cheek and the happy light in the dark eyes made a picture to gladden the heart of any lover. She was sitting in a reclining position in a large arm chair, shading her eyes from the bright light of the chandelier, with a fan artistically finished with black lace, sparkling with diamond dust, a present of the fair Alice, who was sitting at the piano, softly playing an accompaniment to a sad little air that she was singing. A mass of pink gauze enveloped Alice's slender form like a cloud, from which the shoulders rose and gleamed like marble. A beautiful picture, thought Norman, as he stood in the open doorway.

But another had also been feasting his eyes upon the fair form. From the low French window which led to the balcony without, another pair of eyes were gazing upon Imelda's fresh young beauty. Lawrence Westcot was standing there in the shadow of the night. Not a glance did he have just then for the little woman who was his wife and who was softly singing to herself. His whole being was thrilled by that other who now glanced toward the door. The look which beamed from her face at that moment was a revelation to him and the look on Norman's face corroborated it. Muttering a curse his teeth sank deep into his lip. Quickly he stepped further into the darkness and was lost in the winding walks of the beautiful garden.

Intuitively Norman knew, when his eyes rested on Imelda's figure, that she had dressed for him. Never had she appeared anything but beautiful to him, but tonight she seemed to surpass herself. He had never seen her in anything but somber black, or at best in a soft, unassuming gray gown; so that the effect of the pure white of her attire this evening was a revelation. After greeting the hostess he seated himself at the side of his loved one. Alice meanwhile, continuing her singing, evidently trying in vain to hide the tears in her voice. But her fear was needless. The world for these two did not extend to where she was sitting. They were wholly absorbed in each other.

Finding herself so utterly overlooked, Alice rose from her seat and gliding to the open window soon found herself gazing up into the starlit heavens. What was it that so rebelliously stirred her inmost soul? Had the two in the parlor wronged her in any way? Were not both dearly loved friends, and was it not her desire that both should be happy? Slipping down from the balcony into the walk below which was flanked on either side with blooming plants, Alice fled down, down until the splashing of a fountain greeted her ear, beside which she now sank. Dipping her hand into the cool water she let it play over the white fingers. Her bosom heaved and in a little while the crystal drops from her eyes mingled with the sparkling waters of the fountain. She was fighting out a battle, here under the starlit heavens. How dare she own even to herself what it was that moved her so? Was it the poisoned arrows of Imelda's views that had sunk deep into her soul?

"No, no!" was the answer she made to this question; "Be truthful. When you acknowledge so much, go farther and acknowledge still more. Remember this man was your friend long ere Imelda came to be a pleasant companion in your house; long ere you ever heard one word of the girl's beautiful doctrine. His voice was music, his smile heaven to you.

"But oh, I did not, could not know," continued the unhappy woman to herself. "Only when she came and told me of what she had won, did my heart awake and realize what its cravings are; what all this sunshine in my life means. Now all will be darkness, utter darkness!" and as if the climax had now been reached the white hand covered the quivering face, and the pearly drops trickled from between her fingers.

After awhile the storm in the heaving bosom was somewhat allayed; her breathing became more regular, the sobs ceased and removing her hands she was about to lave the tear-stained face in the cool water when she became aware of the near presence of a man, whom she now saw was leaning against a large fir tree and watching her every movement.

The suddenness of her discovery almost caused Alice to scream. Although the man had risen she could not for the moment decide who he might be, as he was standing in the shadows, but seeing that he was discovered he stepped out into the full light and—with a gasp Alice recognized her husband. How long had he been standing there, how long had he been watching her? A somewhat defiant air settled upon her countenance as without a word she proceeded to lave her face, as she had intended doing.

"Rather a queer place for making your toilet, is it not?" he queried. "I believe there could have been more suitable places found in your home."

Alice would rather not have answered, but felt it was not good policy to pass his words over unnoticed.

"I have a splitting headache, and came out into the open air and it was very tempting to feel the cool water on my burning temple."

His lip curled. "I have not the least doubt," he made answer, "that your head aches. It seems to be the natural result when a woman indulges in such a 'good cry' as I have witnessed during the last half hour. Was the cry a result of the headache or the headache the result of the cry?"

Alice detected the sneer underlying the words, but chose to appear unconscious.

"Whichever you please; my pain is great enough to cause the tears, and tears again are liable to produce headache."

"Prevaricating!" he sneered. "But, my lady, I see deeper, and have been seeing rather deep for some time past. But to change the subject, I have had a revelation tonight. Our friends, your friend and mine, have concluded to become more than friends; that is, if appearances do not deceive."

His eyes were resting searchingly upon the face of the woman before him, and his cunning was in vain. Not a line of the pale face moved. She continued laving the aching brow and swollen eyelids and vouchsafed him no answer.

"You heard what I said?"

"I heard what you said."

"Well, what do you think of it?"—this time impatiently.

"Think of it? What could I think of it but that Imelda could not do better. I must compliment you on having a friend whom I consider a gentleman in every respect."

"O, indeed! It is quite a compliment I must acknowledge, but if you think you have washed yourself enough permit me to remind you it would now be in good taste to return to the house and pay just a little attention to our guest."

For some reason he was pleased to be most sarcastic tonight. Such moods she feared. His tongue was then sharper than a two-edge sword. So then she drew the filmy lace handkerchief from her bosom and proceeded to wipe the water from her face. Suddenly, and taking her quite unawares, he bent and kissed the white shoulder. As if stung by an asp she pushed him from her with such force that he nearly fell backward into the water.

"How dare you?" she exclaimed. His face was white to the lips.

"I will show you how I dare if you dare to repeat such an action. A pretty pass it has come to, if I may not kiss my own wife when I choose. Return to the house with me at once. This moonlit show has been kept up long enough."

CHAPTER XXII

Without a single word Alice turned and walked back to the house with her husband at her side, but when they returned to the brightly lighted rooms they found them empty. Norman and Imelda had disappeared.

Alice, to avoid further persecution, fled to her own room where she hastily disrobed and sought her couch, but her temples were throbbing in a manner that did not promise sleep. She lay for some time pressing her hands to the aching head, when she heard steps outside her door and immediately after a quick rap. She recognized both step and rap. She lay with bated breath, giving no indication that she heard, when the rap was repeated more loud and forcible than before. Again no answer. A third time the rap was repeated, accompanied by a loud demand to open immediately.

"Not tonight, Lawrence," came in pleading, quavering accents. "I am sick tonight."

"Open!" he demanded.

"Please, Lawrence," pleaded the voice within.

"Will you open?" came threateningly from the outside. Trembling in every nerve Alice rose and unlocked the door to admit the man she called husband.

"What do you mean?" he asked, grasping her arm in a manner anything but gentle, "what do you mean by locking your door?"

By this time Alice was wrought up to a hysterical pitch. With a quick movement she threw off the hand that held her.

"I locked the door to be safe from intrusion. I am sick tonight, and wish to be alone."

"I dare say," was the unfeeling response. "If it had been some one else who wished admittance, our honored guest, for instance, the door would not have been so firmly locked. Your husband, however, is not so welcome."

"Lawrence!" almost shrieked the sorely tried woman. "How dare you!"

"O, I dare anything, as you will soon find. Just now, I order you back to your bed, and to keep quiet until I join you, in a few moments."

"Lawrence! You—do—not—mean to stay?" gasped the poor suffering woman.

"Well, I—just—mean—to—stay;" mimicking her frenzied appeal.

"But I am sick tonight, oh, so sick!"

"The sickness then must be rather sudden. But madam, it is rather a flimsy trick to rid yourself of your husband's presence. I advise you, however, to take matters more coolly. By this time you ought to understand and to know who will come out victor."

And Alice did know who came out victor in this instance. But the morning dawned upon a fever-flushed face, and ere the sun was many hours in the heavens a doctor stood at the bedside of the little wife, who gravely shook his head as he listened to the ravings of his patient, which—if such utterances can be relied upon—revealed a tale of woe to the attendants that ought to fill the heart of every true woman and man with horror.

The hours passed into days and the days into weeks, and yet the fever raged unabated. Imelda, who passed the days and nights in sleepless anxiety at the sick woman's bedside was well nigh worn out, even though an experienced nurse was there to share the responsibilities and care. The little ones were banished to another portion of the house, so that their childish prattle and laughter might not disturb the sick mother. Lawrence Westcot came and went to and from the sick chamber, wearing a gloomy countenance, but his presence there was not at all helpful, as it invariable caused the patient to be very uneasy and restless, even though he did not come within the range of her vision. She seemed to feel his presence and the physician fearing the effect upon her nervous system advised the husband to make his visits short. Sometimes he bent above her, laying his hand upon her fevered brow. Unconscious though she was she would with a quick nervous movement throw his hand aside, muttering incoherent words.

Both Imelda and the nurse observed that invariably the sick woman would be worse after those visits of the husband; although of short duration they were glad when they were over.

Almost three weeks passed ere the much-feared crisis came. By this time the patient was very weak and it was apparent that life hung by a thread. Anxiously bending over the couch the two friends watched while the clock ticked the hours away. Slowly they crept on; slowly, softly, almost imperceptibly the life of the sufferer seemed to ebb away.

Twelve, one, two o'clock, and still no change. Half past two, the door of the room softly opened and Lawrence Westcot entered. Imelda's heart gave a bound. Why must he come at such a time? Stepping softly he drew near.

Imelda placed her finger upon her lips in token of caution. Coming close to the side of the dying woman he stood gazing down upon her. What his thoughts might be could not be known from the calm, unmoved appearance of his countenance, but certainly they were not pleasant thoughts. How could they be, when he so well knew what had brought his wife so close to death's door? If she should die, would not her death lie at his door? Would he not be compelled to own himself her murderer?

Five, ten minutes passed, then Alice moved. Imelda laid her hand upon his arm and bent a pleading look upon him. Immediately he stepped back into the shadows of the room and there waited the issue. Restlessly the head moved upon the pillow. The eyelids quivered and fluttered open, the lips moved, Imelda bent to catch the low whisper that was merely a breath.

"Water!" came faint, scarcely audible, from the fever-parched lips. With a teaspoon a few drops at a time were administered, the patient apparently gaining strength from the cooling liquid. The blue eyes opened wide, but they were clear with the light of reason. Presently they closed again, and soon a slow, even breathing told that sleep, natural restful sleep, had once more come to the sufferer's relief. The nurse bent above her and listened, laying her fingers upon the fluttering pulse. Presently, standing erect, she whispered:

"She is safe for tonight. I will continue the watch. Miss Ellwood, you had better retire and rest."

Imelda's breast was heaving. The strain had been a severe one, and feeling that it would be impossible long to control herself she hastily left the room, followed by Westcot. Just outside the door he laid his hand upon her arm.

"She will be saved, you think?" He seemed to be anxious and serious. Had not this man with his cruelty almost murdered the woman who was as yet lying at death's door? It cost Imelda an effort to be civil.

"I believe so," she answered. "According to the doctor's statement if she should safely pass this night there is every hope of her recovery."

For several moments he did not answer, then—"Thank you," and ere Imelda was aware of his intention he had taken her hand and lifting it he quickly touched it with his lips. With a hasty movement she withdrew her hand, but before she could speak he had said "Goodnight," and swiftly walking away left her standing there alone.

Imelda stood looking at the hand he had kissed, and then with an unconscious movement drew her handkerchief across the spot his lips had touched. She shuddered. What did it mean? Without waiting to answer her own question she turned and hastily sought her room. She was tired, O, so tired. Never since Alice had been tossing in the fever had she known what it was to sleep a whole night through. Snatching an hour, or two at most, always ready at a moment's notice to return to her post at the side of the sick one, she had scarce found time to eat or catch a breath of fresh air, — and now it was three o'clock in the morning. O, how tempting looked the snowy draped bed. She felt as if she could sink into its soft embrace, never to rise again. The night was already well advanced; two or three hours at most was all she expected to sleep. The faithful nurse was just as much in need of rest as herself. A moment she hesitated. Should she risk it? The nurse was positive that for the rest of the night Alice would sleep. She no longer hesitated, but hastily disrobing and donning a snowy nightdress, scarce had her head touched the pillow when she was already unconscious and in the land of dreams.

CHAPTER XXIII

For the first time Imelda's mind was free. She had left Alice sleeping. Not in a dull, feverish stupor, constantly interrupted with delirious mutterings but sleeping, actually and really sleeping. And although her breathing was only a gentle fluttering, it was so weak, it was a quiet sleep, and she knew that for a few hours, at least, she could safely trust her to the faithful nurse. So Imelda slept the sleep of the just.

When the morning sunlight streamed through the open window, flooding the room with its bright glory, a servant had softly entered and with deft fingers closed the shutters, darkening the room so that the slumbers of the completely exhausted girl might not be disturbed; the nurse meanwhile remaining faithful and true to her trust. Now and then a maid softly opened the door to listen, but Imelda slept on, and when the doctor came he gave the order to let her sleep by all means, until she should awake of herself. So the hours of the day passed and the evening shades were falling ere that death-like sleep was lifted and Imelda opened her eyes. The deep hush and darkness that prevailed left her for a long time in semi-unconsciousness, a delicious drowsiness folding her in its power, but by and by it passed away, leaving her brain more clear, and presently, all in an instant, she knew and remembered.

But how long had she slept? It was three o'clock when she sought her bed and only two hours before the morning light would appear. It was still dark, yet she did not feel as if she had slept only a short time, but rather had the sensation of having slept a long while, she was so wide awake, and— yes! she was hungry, very hungry. She reached out her hand for her watch, which she remembered having placed upon the stand near the bedside. It was there, but when she placed it to her ear she made the discovery that it had stopped. Then she struck a light, having a lucifer always within reach. By the flickering flame she saw that her watch had stopped at twenty minutes of two. A puzzled look overspread her face. What did it mean? Just then she thought she heard a footstep outside her door; the next instant the door was softly opened.

"Who is there?" she hastily inquired, her heart giving a bound, as she was not in the habit of leaving her door unlocked. Could she have forgotten it? A soft laugh answered her.

"Is it you, Mary?" she asked, recognizing the voice.

"Yes, Miss Imelda, it is I. Have you decided to return to life? I was beginning to fear you were going to sleep right over into the next world."

"Why, what time is it?" was Imelda's next question, still surprised and puzzled.

"Almost eight o'clock."

"Eight o'clock! Why, Mary, you ought to have called me ere this. Mrs. Boswell ought to have been relieved some time ago. But why is it so dark? I thought I had the windows open."

"So you had. I made free to close them but will open them now," saying which the girl unfastened and opened the shutters. Instead of the bright sunshine, as Imelda had expected, only a hazy twilight filled it with dim shadows.

"What does this mean?" she stammered. "Why, it is quite dark. Did you not say that it is almost eight o'clock?" She was growing impatient. Mary's laugh again rang through the room.

"Yes," she said "it is eight o'clock, not in the morning but in the evening."

Imelda was sitting bolt upright in bed now.

"What! Do you mean to say that I have slept all day through?"

"Just that, and nothing else."

"O, that was wrong! I ought to have been called long ago. How is——" she stopped, a sudden fear holding her tongue a prisoner.

"Mrs. Westcot is getting better,"—supplementing the unfinished question and answering it at the same time. "She, like yourself, has been sleeping all day."

"And Mrs. Boswell——?"

"Has also had a nap while I sat with Mrs. Westcot, and if you will rise and dress I will prepare you some—breakfast," and laughing again she disappeared leaving Imelda to her own reflections, but first having lit the gas overhead. No hesitation now. Hastily she arose and quickly made her toilet. Donning a wrapper she twisted the dark hair into a shining coil, and in a few minutes descended to the dining room where Mary had spread for her a tempting meal.

Imelda was a favorite with the servants, who were always willing to do a favor for this fair girl from the west, who was so considerate. It was well known that Mrs. Westcot was also from the western metropolis, and they often wondered if people in the west generally were so kind and considerate. It would have been impossible for the gentle-hearted Alice to assume aristocratic airs, therefore she could always depend upon her servants, and all hearts were filled with fear while the gentle mistress was raving of real or fancied woes, and when at last, after weary weeks, the crisis was over, it was as if a heavy cloud had passed away, and the gloomy faces were bright.

Having done ample justice to the generous repast, and feeling much refreshed, Imelda sped to the chamber above. Softly she opened the door and moved to the bedside. Mrs. Boswell was sitting with her elbow resting upon the bed, her head upon her hand. She never moved as Imelda stepped to her side. Bending down she found that the nurse was fast asleep. A pang smote her that while she, in the strength of youth, had slept the day away the much older woman had continued at her post. True, Mary had said that she had relieved her for awhile, but Imelda knew that she, like herself, needed a good long rest, and she decided that she should have it. Seeing that Alice too was sleeping, she gently touched Mrs. Boswell on the shoulder and slightly shaking her the nurse awoke with a start. Imelda held up a warning finger to prevent her from making an outcry. But the woman was frightened. She felt guilty at having been found asleep at her post of duty. Hastily reaching for her watch she breathed a sigh of relief.

"Only ten minutes," she whispered. "She has been sleeping so long," indicating Alice, "that I suppose the quiet has overpowered me."

"And no wonder," said Imelda, — "you are certainly in need of rest. I will now take your place while you sleep all night and all day tomorrow, too, if you wish. So just give me the directions for tonight, and then away to your couch." The woman smiled.

"Thank you. I am only too glad to accept." After giving the proper directions she added: "And now if you will excuse me I will accept your kind offer and sleep. Mary took my place for several hours or I fear I could not have held out. In the morning I will be ready to take my place again."

So the nurse withdrew and left Imelda alone with her sick friend, and as she largely imitated the example of the young girl and slept until the afternoon of the next day, Imelda had a long watch before her.

But we are forestalling. While the nurse has gone to recruit her strength in sleep we will remain with Imelda and follow the outline of her thoughts as she watched her sick friend. Over three weeks have now passed since the promenade of the lovers in the moonlight under the silver maples, — the evening after that on which for the first time she had discarded her mourning garments, when they had spent two happy hours together, Imelda adroitly preventing a repetition of the pleadings of the night before. She was happy, and was willing that Norman should know it. He in turn had been content to drink the kisses from the dewy lips and leave the morrow to take care of itself.

Since that evening Imelda had seen but little of her lover. If he came in the evening she scarcely ever had longer than a half hour to give him. The cloud that hung above this house was too dark to admit of much happiness or joy for them. On the other hand it did not give them the leisure to discuss the question nearest their hearts, and Imelda did not wish it just now.

Long ere this, had the answer come to the long letter that she had written to Margaret. But not alone in Margaret's delicate tracing had the answer come. A long letter had also come in the bolder handwriting of Wilbur Wallace. Her heart gave a bound as she recognized the hand, while the rich blood rushed in a hot wave to her face dyeing her temples, ears and neck. What would he have to say? With a beating heart she had opened it. Something impelled her to lay Margaret's aside until she first perused Wilbur's letter.

CHAPTER XXIV

With Imelda we will read Wilbur's letter:

"My Darling: The fact that I am writing this to you must of necessity be proof that Margaret has laid before me your letter containing the news that already the event has come into your life which I, in our parting hour, prophesied would come. Though I still claim you as my darling, and though my heart still goes to meet you with the same tender emotions, I cannot do otherwise than say I am pleased. I am glad that that other has so soon stepped into your life, and, building upon the past, I take the responsibility on myself of giving the advice you ask of Margaret.

"The fact alone that you love this man, that your heart has so fully gone into his keeping, is to me the best evidence of his trustworthiness. Not but that you, as well as many another, are liable to make mistakes as to the character of any individual you may come in contact with, but in a case of spontaneous love I feel and know that the purity of mind itself, of which you are possessed, would intuitively recognize that which is not equally pure.

"That Norman should still be bound by old superstitions and creeds may prove an obstacle to the speedy consummation of your love. It is here your work begins; here your strength will be tested. If you would be a priestess in our holy work you will be expected to remain true to the sentiments you have so often expressed. Your soul must remain free and unfettered, even though the man may be purity personified. Not a semblance even of the power the law gives to a husband must you put into his hands. If your love is great enough to trust him he will be generous enough to trust you, or he is not the man he has represented himself to be. If he is not generous enough to trust you, then your intuition will have been at fault—the blindness of a common love has been laid upon your vision.

"Where lies the beginning of your work?—you ask. I will tell you. Your first duty is one that you owe to him and to yourself. You say that in your past life lie hidden many dark spots. It is your duty in this case to lay bare these dark spots in the full light of day. It is thus you will test his strength of character. As he comes of a long line of Puritan ancestors this will be necessary. The old prejudices may be so deeply rooted that, rather than take to his arms one who, although not responsible for the actions of others, may by the ties of blood be allied to those that are, he may be willing to crush out a love that would leave his own heart mangled and bleeding. If such should be the case, my little girl, I understand full well that bitter pain must then for a while gnaw at the cords of your heart. But it will pass, and in passing leave you purer and stronger than ever.

"If, on the other hand, he stands the test I feel sure it will be only a short time until his whole soul will come to understand the grand sublimity of full and untrammeled liberty. Love cannot be fettered. Love will always remain free; the greater his freedom the more certainty is ours of retaining him to make bright our lives. Try to fetter him, he unfolds his wings and mockingly takes his departure. Then, what are we to do with our empty lives?

"In justice to woman we must admit that she is at the greater disadvantage, no matter in what light the case may be placed. In marriage, it matters not how just may be the man whom she calls 'lord,' she is, she remains, his property, according to the mandates of the law. No matter how willing he may be that she shall enjoy perfect freedom, society takes it upon itself to place a watch upon her. If her husband has no sense of honor, or of what is due to himself, the stern finger of the law points it out to him. Society prepares a code for her that she is bound to respect and accept as her guide. The path which he is asked to walk is not nearly so straight. There are many recesses and angles in it, if he chooses to explore them. If he does so quietly nothing will be said.

"On the other hand, we know only too well if woman refuses marriage, it is equivalent to throwing away all hope of ever enjoying life as nature has designed. If she dares to thus enjoy she is ostracized from society.

"At the present time we are still in the dark. But may we not hope, sometime, to grow strong enough to defy the mandates of society? May not love find a way that shall yet defy all the lynx-eyed agents of a corrupt moral code? May we not hope that man and woman both may yet be natural as the new-born babe, when it is first placed in the mother's arms—at nature's fount?

"Will you be strong, my Imelda? Think you, you can take your Norman by the hand and lead him on until he stands upon your own sublime heights? Until he stands at your side? Then side by side to explore the unknown heights that still lie beyond your field of vision?

"Be brave, my precious one; be strong, and when the time comes when we shall meet again (and I feel that it will come), and I fold you to my heart, pressing warm kisses on your lips, some prophetic spirit tells me that your Norman will stand by and understand.

"There must and will come a time when the full glory of a free love will be understood and enjoyed. So look up to the goal in view; bravely work on, and remember there is strength in the knowledge of unity of thought and purpose of those who work in a like cause, even though your friends with their supporting love are distant. Remaining as ever, loving you with a love that is absolutely pure, I am yours for truth of purpose, and for the best humanity.

Wilbur."

A long drawn sigh escaped the lips of Imelda as she laid the closely written sheets upon her knees. Well she knew that he was right. In the still hours of the night watches, by the side of the sick friend the thought had come to her again that open truth was the only course for her to pursue. But oh, how gigantic the task appeared. In all the three weeks the subject had never been touched upon again by them. Few indeed had been the moments she had been able to accord him, her strength being tested to its utmost in her capacity as nurse. Being well aware of the state of things Norman Carlton was far too noble to press for the reason of the loved girl's views at such a time. For the present he accepted the boon of her love as a priceless jewel of whose possession he was assured.

But Imelda knew that the hour was coming when he would expect an answer to his question, and, as Wilbur had stated, it was then her work would begin. If she dreaded that coming hour, was she to blame? Folding the letter she placed it back in the envelope and with the action there came to her with overwhelming force, the realization of the grandeur of this man's character. What purity, what nobility! Even as the new love more fully filled out her life so did she understand better the true worth of the man who had first called her love into being.

"O, Margaret darling," was her mental comment, "when your heart chose Wilbur as its best beloved, it made a grand selection; no one will ever find his way into your life who will be able to look to you from a loftier height than that upon which he stands."

Recalling her wandering thoughts she next opened the epistle from Margaret, for such it proved to be. Such a long, warm, glowing letter; overflowing with the love her pure young heart contained. She had filled page after page, concluding with the words:

"And now my dearest girl, I think I have made my meaning clear. I have given you the best advice that I know of. I know, however, that it is the same as Wilbur's, only perhaps in other words, and I feel that now we shall not be disappointed in our brave girl. Let me add one thing. I understand fully how difficult the making of such a revelation will prove; and yet it *must* be made. I can see nothing else you can do and remain true to yourself and lover. Not the shadow of a suspicion, of a deception, must lie between you. I will not say disgrace; that will exist, if it exist at all, only in Norman's *mind*. But now for my advice:

"Write the history of your life. That will be easier. You can tell him all, everything, without the disadvantage of seeing in his face the emotions that such a history might call into play. He will have time to think and understand the full import of it all. You will not then receive an immediate answer prompted by an impulse that might prove a barrier to your love. Cool, calm reflection is necessary in such a case, and as my own Imelda possesses her full share of common sense she can but see the wisdom of such a course.

"Be brave, my dearest friend, my own loved one. If this man is worthy of your love he will stand the test. If he does not stand it, then I can but say he was not worthy. And now remember—three hearts beat in love for you, and the united strength of that love is bent on the success of your heart's dearest hope (for of course my mother knows), and hoping to be reunited in a not too distant future, thus writes and advises your most sincere and loving friend,

Margaret."

This letter had been folded and placed side by side with that other one. Long had Imelda sat with bowed head and folded hands. Yes! both kind and loving friends were right. An inner voice told her this was the only course to pursue. But the condition of the sick friend had not permitted her to think of it. Every minute of her time had been devoted to her. Her lover must wait until the dark, uncertain hours would be past; but now as Imelda sat and watched the peaceful sleeper, she realized that she could not spend the long hours of the night watch to better advantage than in the performance of this duty. The dreaded hour had passed; hope and sunshine were again seeking admittance at the portals of this home, and Norman was waiting, patiently waiting, for his answer. So when the morning broke, with its pale light, she folded the closely written sheets. With trembling hands and beating heart she wrote the address and sent them to their destination. Would he stand the test? When tried by this crucial ordeal, would he prove faithful and true?

CHAPTER XXV

The sultry summer day was at its close, and Norman Carlton had just finished reading the letter that Imelda had written the night before. A troubled look was upon the frank and honest face, as he stood at the open window looking out at the falling shadows, but seeing nothing. In one hand he still held the fateful sheets; the other hand he held to his aching temples. He stood and gazed until dusky twilight faded into starlit night. Ever and anon a deep sigh escaped the drawn lips as he thought, and thought, and thought.

But what was it he thought? Did that miserable tale of woe show him only the impracticability of an alliance with a child of the people? A woman whose mother had no right, according to the views of society, to the title of "lady;" whose sister had made an outcast of herself; whose brother might, even now, be occupying the cell of a criminal; whose past life had been one long privation and struggle with fate. His own lady mother and sister! Was it not his duty to first consult their views, their feeling upon the matter?

Or was it that he was made of more noble material? Were his views so broad that it was of no consequence what the world might say? It could hardly be expected, when we consider the training of his past life, that he would now have no battle to fight. It was not pleasant to know that the woman who had won his love should be so unpleasantly connected, but while this knowledge was to him most depressing, it also had the effect of raising, many fold, the respect he held for her. What could have been easier for her than to keep these matters secret? It gave him a better insight into the nobility of her character. She at least was truth itself. She would prove trustworthy. She was above reproach. He was doing battle with the old prejudices based on society codes, as they rose, one by one, to assail his love.

But to do him justice his love wavered not for one instant. If the setting be tarnished, will that fact diminish the lustre of the diamond? He knew that his jewel was of the purest; why should the setting trouble him? But all was not yet plain to him. He remembered that night under the maples; when she had refused him marriage—not love. Love she had given then as freely as now. He saw it then, he knew it now. But now again she makes the same refusal. "You understand now," she wrote, "why it is that I cannot marry you."

His noble manhood was all alert now. Does she think so meanly, so basely of him as to suppose that he would add to the burden that had so many years been resting upon those slender shoulders, by withdrawing his proposal? If that is what she thinks, her opinion of him is not so exalted as he could wish and—he must seek her—must see her tonight. With him to think was to act, and a few minutes later finds him on the way to the woman of his choice. It was with a dazed feeling that he stood upon the marble steps awaiting an answer to his ring. What would be the outcome of this night's quest?

His card again found her at the bedside of the patient preparing for another long night watch by herself. Her heart beat high when the little bit of pasteboard was placed in her hand. Mrs. Boswell had not yet retired. She saw the flush steal over the fair brow and an understanding came intuitively to her as to what it meant. It was not so many years ago that she too had received a lover's visit, and she knew so well that since the illness of Mrs. Westcot the young girl had no time to spend on friends or lovers. So she kindly said:

"Go and see your friend. I am not tired tonight and can well remain several hours longer." With an appreciative "Thank you" Imelda accepted the kind offer and descended to the drawing room, where but one jet of gas was burning which but dimly lit the room.

Scarcely had she entered when she felt herself folded with strong arms to a wildly beating heart. Lips that whispered, "My own love," were pressed firmly to hers. Her heart was full, her bosom heaving. That he held her thus was ample proof that to him she was just as lovable now as before he knew her wretched story. Brushing the soft dusky waves of hair from the flushed temples, he asked:

"Will my girl have a little while to spare for me tonight? I would have you walk with me under the maples. Will you come?" Without a word she turned to the hallway and taking a soft white scarf from a rack, threw it over her shoulders and said:

"Now, I am ready." Together they wended their way to the silver leaved trees where once more they paced back and forth, his arm about the graceful form, his head bent until it rested against hers. Every attitude betokened the love they bore each other. O, how he talked, how he plead. But the slender girl at his side was strong and firm. She understood the ground she was treading upon. She met him at every turn.

He loved her, and as he listened to her arguments, as he watched the sparkle of her eye, as he got a better insight into her life, he felt that here was indeed a woman of superior qualities, a woman possessed of rare intellect.

And as she met him, point after point, he began to see things in a different light. Dim and hazy at first yet still he saw a difference. Not that he showed an inclination to acknowledge the truth of any of the pictures she painted. O, no! not quite so easy are deep-rooted superstitions and prejudices uprooted. Yet she gave him food for thought.

She pointed out to him conditions as they exist throughout the country, She showed him how one vexed question is entangled with another. She drew his attention to the masses of workers who with their dollar a day,— sometimes a little more, sometimes even less,—have no time for self-improvement, no time for healthful recreation. That recreation which is of an elevating character, is quite unattainable and that which is within their reach is of the most demoralizing kind. The swilling of vile drinks, with vile companions in dens still more vile.

She spoke of the overburdened wife and mother, wearing away her life in drudgery and loneliness. At the close of his day's toil the husband brings no love to the cheerless home. That which he had named and believed love on their wedding day has long since fled; yet of this union springs unwishedfor children; children gestated in an atmosphere of hate; idiots and criminals ushered into being to fill our prisons and insane asylums. The employer class, on the other hand, feast upon the wealth these unfortunates produce, and by their excesses sow the seeds of crime in their offspring.

"On all sides," said Imelda, "through the force of circumstances young lives are lost in the sloughs of vice and shame. Woman sells her virtue to the highest bidder; the one for a passing hour, the other for a life time. Which of the two is the worse? The merciless and unnatural codes of society demand the unsexing of woman by strangling nature's desires, then these codes permit one man to drive her to the grave or to the mad house through the power given to him by the law. The woman that would be true to her normal instincts, the woman that would practicalize her natural right of being a mother, must first sell herself for all time to some man, who, in return, forces upon her what at first was a pleasure and a blessing but now a hundred-fold curse. To surrender herself in love with holiest emotions is a sin, is a demoralization. To endure the hated embrace of the man who long since murdered every trace of that holy love, is a duty and virtue.

"To escape such thralldom is to her an utter impossibility, as the only way out lies through that most damnable of abominations, the divorce court, where every pure instinct of a sensitive woman's nature is outraged to such extent that generally she prefers, of the two evils, the marital outrage to that of the divorce court.

"And yet the world goes on. Ignorant mothers bear and rear ignorant children. From their birth nature is strangled. They are fed and clothed in an unhealthful, unnatural manner, so that the wonder is, not that there are so many small graves but rather that so many survive. The little girl with propensities to romp is told she is a hoyden, a tomboy. The boy with refined sentiments, that he is a 'sissy,' and so on throughout the long category. We are bound, fettered, on all sides from the cradle to the grave. No matter what misery, what woe, springs therefrom, never go your own way but travel only that which is mapped out for you by custom which has been foisted upon society. O, it is so unnatural, so miserable, this binding, this fettering, this laying down laws that are made only to be broken."

She had spoken rapidly, and had warmed in her enthusiasm. Her head thrown slightly backward with a motion most graceful, her eyes shining with a glory that was beautiful, and Norman did not fail to be struck by it.

"How can it all affect us, my sweet?" he asked. "Are we not far above all the horrible pictures you have drawn?"

"I hope so," she answered. "I do, indeed, hope we are above it, but don't you see every picture has its ground work in the 'Thou shalt not,' of some law? Every picture has its clanking chains and the heaviest is always the marriage chain. Don't you see, don't you understand?" He folded her close in his arms, an action which she by no means resented.

"And must our sweet love be sacrificed because of those horrible conditions? Have you not more faith in the voice of your heart?" Tears sprang to her eyes. O, how hard it was to steel that heart to the pleadings of the precious voice. How could she make him understand that he possessed the unbounded trust, the most unconditional love of her whole being?

"I have all the faith in the world in you," she said, as with trembling fingers she caressed the fair locks that fell in clustering masses over the open noble brow.

"Can you not see, can you not understand that I love you with all the strength of my being? Let us be happy now, in the present, in that love, and trust to the future to lift the veil, to dispel the clouds,"—and he could not dissuade her. He kissed the tears from the shining dark eyes. His love for her grew with every hour. He realized that bitter suffering in the past had sown the seed of the present strength of character and growth of views to which until now he had given but a passing thought.

CHAPTER XXVI

But now? One thing Imelda had achieved. She had led Norman into the realms of thought. She had made him think as he had never thought before. He now began to see the real cause of human misery. Asking a few well directed questions he soon had the missing links needed to supplement Imelda's life history. She told him of the fair-haired girl whom she loved better than a sister; the girl whose mother's life had been blighted through that self-same marriage curse. She told him of that cherished friend who through the same curse had seen a worshiped mother laid beneath the sod — which tale she ended by requesting him to write those friends; to become acquainted with them; to test their friendship. Norman agreed to do this, and not many days later a letter of his was speeding across the prairies bearing his worded desire to know better those who had in earlier days befriended his Imelda, and who wielded such influence over her.

But to those enthralled in love's golden fetters time speeds on rapid wings. When Norman looked at his watch he found it pointing to half past ten. A pang smote Imelda's heart as she thought of the lonely watcher up in the sick chamber, and hastily sought to disengage herself from the encircling arms of her lover. A half dozen more love-laden kisses and the young girl was bounding across the open grounds followed by the fond eyes of her lover who watched her until she disappeared within the portals of the house ere he wended his way homeward.

No sooner had Imelda stepped into the hall, softly closing the door behind her, than, from the open door to the right, leading into the drawing room, stepped Lawrence Westcot. Imelda drew back. She did not care to encounter anyone just now, least of all Lawrence Westcot. Planting himself directly across her path, but speaking with faultless courtesy he said:

"Miss Ellwood will you grant me the favor of a few moments conversation?" at the same time holding open the door for her to pass through. Imelda paused, hesitating. What could Lawrence Westcot desire to say to her? Besides it was already late. Her conscience smote her for having absented herself so long from the sick room, and she certainly felt no desire to be alone with this man at this hour of the evening. But he was waiting, holding the door for her to pass through, quite as a matter of course. Much as she was disinclined to do so she yet felt that she could not refuse without appearing rude, and so, reluctantly passing him she entered the room, while he closed the door after them.

The room was dimly lit, as before when she had entered it earlier in the evening. Imelda paused under the single burning jet. He came forward and turned it to a brighter blaze, then wheeled forward a chair for her to be seated, but which she declined, shaking her head in a positive manner.

"I beg your pardon, but I would rather not, Mr. Westcot. It is time I return to Alice. Mrs. Boswell kindly relieved me this evening of several hours of responsibility. I have already overstayed my time. I do not wish to give it the appearance of an imposition, so if you have anything to say to me I must beg of you to hasten."

She had taken a step or two backward and stood with her hand resting upon the back of the chair Westcot had placed for her, the soft folds of the white shawl that had been loosely thrown over her head and shoulders, the glow of health and happiness upon her cheek and in the dark brown eyes—Lawrence Westcot felt the magic beauty of the picture before him. It was doubtful if he heard a word of what she had spoken; certain it was that he paid no attention to it. Suddenly Imelda became conscious of his burning gaze, and in a moment her face was dyed from brow to chin with a hot wave of color, and again she spoke:

"If you have something to tell me, Mr. Westcot, will you please do so without loss of time? I do not wish that Alice should be waiting."

"Let her wait," he said hastily, huskily. "She is not wanting for anything. I have just come from there. Mrs. Boswell is with her and can manage very well. Besides, why should you make such a prisoner of yourself? The nurse is paid for her work; let her do it. A little while longer will not hurt her."

Utterly surprised, Imelda for the moment was unable to speak, but almost instantly recovering her self-possession:

"Was it to tell me this you have asked me to come in here?" He heeded not the withering scorn in her voice, but stepping nearer he possessed himself of one of her hands.

"Why should I not tell you that, and a great deal more if I choose? True, you never gave me a chance, but can you not see that I madly love you?"

"Sir! You forget yourself!" Imelda snatched her hand from him and stepped several paces backward. Nothing daunted the next moment he again was at her side.

"Why should I not tell you, and why should you not listen? Do I not know your views on love and marriage? According to them you cannot deem my love for you a crime because I am a married man." With these words he attempted again to take her hand, but she, by mustering all her strength pushed him from her with such force as to almost unbalance him.

"How dare you?" she articulated. The face that only a few moments ago was dyed scarlet was now ashen in its pallor.

"I dare it because I love you," came in low, almost hissing tones from lips that were now pale as hers, while his black eyes glowed like living coals.

"Do you think I will meekly surrender you to that—no! I will not call names—to that so-called friend of mine? I tell you no! a thousand times no! I acknowledge no barriers, as I know you do not, and I swear to you that you must and shall be mine!"—and ere Imelda was aware of his intention he had gained her side, his arms like bands of iron were laid about her shoulders, and the next instant she felt his hated kisses upon her lips. For a moment she was powerless, and only for a moment, when with strength of desperation she tore herself from his embrace.

"You are the most despicable creature upon this earth! I will tell you what barriers stand between us. First and foremost your utter lack of manhood. By whatever despicable means you may have obtained an inkling of my views, let me tell you that you have failed, utterly failed to get the least gleaming of the truth. Know that a creature so wholly devoid of principle and honor may never hope to win the favor of a free woman. Know you that love can neither be forced nor bought. When you come to realize and understand this you may speak to me again—not until then."

With an imperious movement she swept by him, leaving him bewildered and, for a moment, totally subdued. Had he failed to understand her? What a glorious creature! and what superb scorn. Did she know what stood between Alice and him? At the thought of Alice a dark frown swept over his face. What was the meaning of that?

Upon winged feet Imelda flew up the broad stairway and into the sick room. Her strength was at an end. Staggering she would have fallen, had not the nurse seen her condition in time and caught her in her arms. Carefully she laid her upon the lounge. Alice was sleeping, as indeed the last few days and nights she had slept almost constantly, which fact enabled the nurse to pay all her attention for the next half hour to this new patient. Finally Imelda returned to consciousness, but only to break into an uncontrollable fit of weeping. For a little while the nurse permitted this fit to have full sway, but when the storm had spent itself and Imelda became more composed she stepped to the stand where there was quite an array of medicines. Mixing a soothing draught she handing it to Imelda, saying:

"Take this," and, quite as a matter of course Imelda drank the cooling drink.

"Now," continued Mrs. Boswell, "go to your room and lie down." But this time she was not so readily obeyed. Imelda's frame shook as with a chill.

"I would rather not. Please let me remain where I am. I shall soon recover and be all right again."

"No! no! the sick room is no place to sleep. I insist that you go to your own room and bed, if you would avoid being sick yourself."

But Imelda on no account would have traversed the lonely hallway again tonight, for fear of meeting in some shadowy nook the man she had just left below in such a storm of passion. Mrs. Boswell soon realized that for some unaccountable reason Imelda seemed afraid, though this was a weakness she had not hitherto noticed in the girl, but she understood too well that she was in need of perfect composure and rest, and the sick room was no place for these. Stepping to the bedside of the sleeping patient she bent over her and listened for a moment to the quiet breathing; then she said:

"Come, I will go with you. It will be perfectly safe to leave our patient for a few moments." Then taking the agitated girl by the hand, she led her through the hallway to her own room. Lighting the gas jet she next turned down the bed clothes and quietly but quickly assisted her to disrobe and helped her into the snowy night robe. She would then have tucked her into her bed but Imelda refused, as she wished to fasten the door after the retreating form of the nurse, who thereupon returned to the bedside of the sleeping Alice to watch the night away when she herself had expected to spend it in needed rest and sleep.

CHAPTER XXVII

Since recording the events of the last chapter, weeks of summer sunshine have passed away. Alice, dressed in a soft fleecy white cashmere wrapper, is reclining in her own cozy room, upon a comfortable lounge which has been drawn closely to the open window from where she can watch the golden rays of the setting sun as it disappears beyond the distant hills. Pale and wan she looks, but the sparkle of returning health is in her eyes as they rest now and then upon the forms of her two little girls who are seated in childish fashion upon the floor, and with their baby fingers trying to wind wreaths of ferns and flowers that are heaped in a low basket that has been placed with its contents at their disposal.

Imelda in one of her soft gray gowns was seated in a low rocker. The book from which she had been reading was lying unnoticed in her lap; her eyes, too, were wandering through the open window to enjoy the golden glory of the setting sun. For a while nothing was heard but childish voices in childish glee. Both fair women were busy with their own thoughts. Imelda had lost some of her wild-rose bloom. The clear-cut features were almost colorless as marble. There was a constrained look upon them; yet now and then they would brighten as with an inward light, and reflect the happiness that she, in those moments, felt; but they soon gave way again to that other look, a deep sigh betokening the change of thought.

As the last rays of the sun died out in a golden halo, Alice slowly turned her head and for a while lay watching her friend. "A penny for your thoughts, my dear," she said with a smile, thus recalling her to present things.

"They are not worth it," Imelda made answer. "They are but vague and unreal dreams." Alice's pale face quivered.

"Vague and unreal," she repeated. "Ah, my precious, as long as they are vague and unreal, you may count yourself happy. It is the real and tangible that makes life a burden. Why have I returned to it? I am sure I would have been many times better off had they laid me beneath the green sods." A pitiful quiver was in the sad young voice, and Imelda felt a sudden pain at her heart as she heard and understood. The next moment she knelt at the side of the invalid.

"Why should you talk like that? See, that is why you should be here," pointing to the little ones. Little Norma was laughing and clapping her chubby hands. She had just succeeded in crowning, with the work of their childish hands, the elder and more stately Meta who was attempting a dignified mien under the high honors. The dark-eyed elf looked so comic that Alice could not repress a smile even though a tear trickled over the pale face. Just then a step in the hallway was heard, and the next moment a figure stood in the open doorway.

"Papa! papa!" Norma's baby voice rang out, and the next instant the little one flew to meet him. He stooped and lifted the flaxen-haired child to his arms. The baby arms were twined about his neck. But little Norma's welcome seemed the only one that was accorded him; even Meta hung back, shy and quiet. She walked backwards to where the fair young mother lay, who clasped the child to her fast beating heart. Imelda rose quickly from her kneeling position and stepping to the open window turned her back to the other inmates of the room. Lawrence Westcot saw and understood. For just one moment his black eyes emitted a flash like a smouldering flame and his white teeth sank deep into his nether lip. But not one word passed those lips that would have betrayed what was taking place underneath the quiet exterior. He had not seen Imelda since that night three weeks ago, when his words had been like cruel blows to the pure, proud girl. She had managed to keep out of his sight, and he did not possess the courage or daring to force himself into her presence. This lack of courage kept him also from the sick room of his wife, which was probably most fortunate for her chances of recovery. Never once, since her return to consciousness, had her eyes rested upon his face. If she missed him it certainly did not cause regret. It is more likely, however, that she did not think of him at all, in those days.

Certain it was that when he suddenly stood, unannounced, in her presence her heart gave a great bound and then seemed to stand still. Could she have thought that he would never come near her again? But the silence was now becoming oppressive. Not a word from anyone only little Norma's cooing, caressing—"Papa, papa," as the little hands patted the dark inscrutable face. With the little one still in his arms he took several steps forward toward the frightened little woman seated upon the lounge. With a start and a gasp she drew Meta with one arm still closer to her, while the other hand was uplifted in a manner intended to wave him off. Seeing the gesture he instantly stopped. An indescribable look passed over his face. Could it be pain? He hesitated a moment, then kissed the baby face and set little Norma down.

"Papa is not wanted here," he said in a tone that sent a strange thrill to the heart of either woman. Was it the same voice they were wont to hear? No sneer, no sarcasm. How husky it had become! Did it not sound like regret? Ere they could recover from their surprise he was gone and they were once more alone. The excitement that those few minutes had brought had been too much for Alice. The next moment she was sobbing hysterically, and for the next half hour Imelda had her hands full in trying to restore quiet and peace. For seeing the mother weep caused both little girls to fling their playthings aside in true childish fashion and join with their tears. Alice was still very weak, or this episode could scarcely have affected her as it did; and to do Lawrence Westcot justice, he had no intention of inflicting pain when he went to his wife's room that evening.

Nevertheless Imelda felt bitter as she reflected what life must mean to this timid, nervous little woman when the mere sight of the man to whom she was bound could throw her into such a hysterical state. O, how wrong it all was, how wrong! After a while, however, she became more quiet and at Imelda's suggestion she soon retired. Imelda mixed for her a soothing drink and soon had the satisfaction of hearing the even, regular breathing of the sleeper. Long ere this she had sent both little girls away with their nurse, so she had the hours of the summer evening to herself. It was quite warm, the evening shadows were deepening, and following an inward prompting she soon found herself in the garden walks, wending her way to the fountain. This was a favorite place with her. Its cooling spray was so pleasant after the oppressive heat of the day. She dipped her hand into the cooling liquid while her thought strayed away to distant friends.

The evening before she had spent in the society of Norman, who had that day received a second letter from Wilbur Wallace. He had expressed himself well pleased with the tenor of those letters as they showed to him the writer as in a mirror of light, and of whose character he was forming a high opinion, even though he could not yet second all the ideas placed before him for inspection. Yet, although he found these ideas impracticable in the extreme, as he expressed it, he could not but pronounce them exalted and pure, beyond those of men in general. Imelda longed to see these two men friends, and the prospects were that her wish would be gratified.

Another thing that had proved of interest to Norman was that Harrisburg had been the early home of Wilbur Wallace, the discovery of which fact was as much a surprise to Imelda as to Norman, as he had never made mention thereof. He gave as a reason for not having done so that the place held little of that which was pleasant to his recollection. It was beneath the waves of the Susquehanna that his mother had found her watery grave, and if it were not that his sisters still lived there he would have been glad to forget that there was such a place. But, he had gone on to say, in his last letter to Imelda:

"Since you, my precious friend, have made your home in Harrisburg, I have often desired to tell you that my idolized Edith, who is the eldest, and the equally precious younger sister, my sweet Hilda, are living somewhere at no great distance from your present home. So many years have passed since I have seen them that they have grown almost strangers to me. Do you think you could take interest in them sufficient to visit them in my name? Both dear girls often send me long and affectionate letters, wherein they tell their 'stranger' brother all about their girlish affairs, and if there is any saving virtue in thoughts transferred to paper I may hope to keep those blessed souls pure and unstained through the strength of the love that they bear me."

"Could she be sufficiently interested in them?" Imelda smiled as her heart warmed to those unknown girls. She would love them as sisters of her own. Had she known she would long since have hastened to meet them; now she must wait a little while longer until Alice would be stronger, so that she could either leave her or persuade her to come with her. She thought of them this evening as she playfully let the water run through her fingers. In her mind she pictured the meeting with them and then she thought of the report she should send Wilbur, and then her thoughts strayed away to her own wayward sister, of whom she had never again heard so much as one single word, or received one sign of life. She did not know if she was still among the living.

Imelda's heart grew warm and yet sad. What had become of Cora? To what depths had she sunk? or had there been enough latent good hidden somewhere in her character to once more extricate herself and rise to higher ground? "Cora, O Cora! where are you to night? Don't you know your sister loves you?" and as if in answer to the prayerfully spoken words a voice at her side low and intense spoke her name. "Imelda!" As though the voice had struck her speechless, she stood with stiffening white lips unable to move or speak until her name was repeated.

"Imelda!" Then — —

"Frank!" broke from them in a husky whisper.

CHAPTER XXVIII

"Frank! You? Where did you come from?" turning to the form that from the darkness had stepped to her side. The old reckless laugh rang upon the still night air:

"Not afraid of me, sister mine, are you? I have come from somewhere out of the darkness surrounding us, but I am not dangerous. I have never done anything worse than steal when I was hungry; but as that happens on an average about twice, sometimes thrice a day I have that unpleasant duty rather often to perform. But what is a fellow to do? The world owes me a living, you know, and exerting myself to the extent of taking something wherever I can place my hand upon it is about as much work as I care to do.

"Say sis," he went on in his reckless manner, to the horror-struck girl, "you couldn't give a fellow a little spending money, now could you? You are in a pretty feathered nest here, you must admit. I always knew and said such saintly goodness and beauty must have their reward. I knew too you were not quite so innocent as you would have us believe. Say, now, honor bright, how much is this most honored brother-in-law of mine worth? To judge from the appearance of yonder noble mansion and these surrounding grounds, he must command more than a few thousands, and as I would like to put in an appearance at your next grand entertainment a few hundred would not come amiss. You would not like to be ashamed of me, eh?"

Almost paralyzed with horror Imelda listened. Was this man, who was scarcely more than a boy, her brother? Oh, shame, shame! Her brother, born of the same mother! She understood. He thought she was married and he asked her for some of that supposed husband's money. Was it possible that the man sleeping in his far western grave was the father of them both?

"Well, 'Melda, can't you give a fellow an answer? I am waiting patiently. Gad, but you have managed nicely. It seems I struck it handsome when the brakeman found me snuggled away in a freight car, the other night, and insisted that my room at that particular place was more welcome than my presence. Think I shall remain here, instead of playing tramp any longer. It will certainly be a change. Only I suppose I can't present myself in my present plight at the front door of my illustrious brother-in-law's mansion. So, sis, you will have to fork over some of the shiners so's I can make the desired change."

"Frank!" now broke in Imelda's horror-struck voice. "Frank! Will you stop? How dare you think any of all the terrible things you have been saying? You seem to take it for granted because you find me here in the grounds of a handsome home that it is my own. I am not married, as you seem to think, but am only a servant in the house you see yonder. So you see all your talk about a rich brother-in-law is the veriest nonsense, and the sooner you leave here and find yourself some honest work to do the better it will be for you."

"Look here, 'Melda," he cried, catching her roughly by the arm, "you can't come any such chaff over me! I want money! I know you have it, and I swear you are going to give it to me." Imelda felt the blood in her veins turning to ice, not from fear, but from the horror that her brother had come to a level such as this.

"Let go of my arm," she said in a calm, even voice. "Have you ever known me to speak a falsehood? I have no money, and what is more, if I had I should not give you a cent. You know me well enough of old to know that I never say what I do not mean; so I repeat, let go of my arm and leave these premises as quickly as possible. Until the time that you can prove yourself a man I forbid you ever to speak to me again. Go to the home of our childhood and at the graves of those to whom you owe your being, make the resolution that you will be a son worthy of your father, and if you can keep that resolution a time may come in the future that you may again call me sister. Now for the last time, go," —saying which she brushed his hand from her arm and turning walked quickly away.

She had not proceeded a dozen steps when she ran into the arms of someone standing there in the darkness. A cry broke from her lips. She was almost overcome with terror. Were the grounds infested tonight? Her heart throbbed with such force it seemed she would suffocate. She could not utter a sound. Who was it? She only heard a heavy breathing and on trying to extricate her hands they were held tighter.

"Don't fear," spoke a voice which sent a new thrill of fear to her heart, for it was the voice of Lawrence Westcot!

"Don't fear, you are quite safe. I have heard the greater part of what transpired a few steps from here, and I will walk with you to the house."

Imelda was too weak to protest much against this offer. She shivered as he drew her arm through his and led her silently to the house, but in spite of her terror and repugnance at his touch she could not but notice that he treated her with profound respect. He led her to the entrance, opened the door and held it for her to pass through.

Without a single word she left him. Scarcely able to keep on her feet she dragged herself up the broad stairway to her room; then without removing any of her clothing, she sank upon the bed whereon she lay long hours without moving so much as a finger. As the morning dawn stole through the windows she rose and disrobed, a storm of sobs shaking the slender figure while tears bedewed her pillow.

On the following day, and on many following days it was difficult to say which of the two, Alice or Imelda, was the paler, the more listless; whether in the depths of the blue or brown eyes lay hidden the keenest pain.

Norman came and went. He saw the change in the girl he loved but could not fathom the cause. He asked if she were sick; a shake of the head was the only answer. It was all she could do to restrain the tears in his presence. It would have been a luxury to sob her unhappy story out upon his breast, but shame sealed her lips. So she bore her sorrow as best she could, and in time its keen edge wore off. Frank seemed to have disappeared as suddenly and completely as he did once before. Now and then, as the memory of that evening more vividly rose before her mind's eye, she would whisper to herself.

"O father! my ever dear father! how thankful I am you did not live to realize all this. How thankful that your proud head has not been bowed with shame such knowledge would have brought you," —and as these thoughts seemed to give new strength her own head would be uplifted, while a look of pride could be read in that high-bred face.

CHAPTER XXIX

The events recorded in the last chapter had for a while caused to be forced into the background the desire in Imelda's heart to become acquainted with the sisters of Wilbur. The affair with Frank was of a nature so unpleasant that the remembrance of it seemed to crush out all youth and life in the proud sensitive heart, but as time is wont to heal all wounds so also did the effect of that dark night's occurrence gradually vanish. As the days and weeks went by on the ceaseless wings of time Imelda again became interested in what was going on around her.

Toward evening of a sunny day in August when Alice had been feeling better, brighter and stronger than usual she expressed the desire for a drive. Accordingly the carriage was ordered. Both little girls, sweet as snowy blossoms, in fresh white dresses, looking dainty and charming as two little fairies, were lifted upon one of the seats, their lively spirits keeping busy the hands and mind of their young governess. Alice leaned languidly back among the cushions and let her eyes rest alternately upon the glowing landscape and upon the two restless little elves. As it had been quite a while since they had the pleasure of driving with their pretty mamma it was really a treat for the little ones—this driving past pretty gardens filled with gorgeous flowers and trees laden with ripening fruit. Soon they were passing through the more thronged streets when suddenly,—no one knew just how it happened but some boys were playing in the streets. Either in their play or because they had been quarreling among themselves a stone was thrown. Then followed a plunge and a rear of one of the horses, a piercing scream from the inmates of the carriage, and then horses and carriage went plunging down one of the busiest streets—the flying figure of a woman as she hastened to get out of the way—a horrified cry at her having been run down—the figure of a man standing in the path of the runaways, a firm hand grasping the reins of the beasts as with an effort almost superhuman they were brought to a standstill. Snorting, trembling, restive, it was no easy matter to hold them, but the young man with the almost boyish face was equal to the task. A crowd soon gathered around. The carriage door was opened and the frightened ladies and children lifted therefrom. Alice could scarcely keep upon her feet. Just then it was remarked that someone had been run over and injured,—a young girl, someone else added. At hearing this Alice would have fallen had not Imelda caught the swaying figure in her arms.

"Oh," she cried, "I hope she is not killed or seriously injured. We must find out who she is and how badly she has been hurt, and—oh, wait! Where is the young man who so bravely rescued us, periling his own life to save ours. Where is he? Who is he?"

Upon looking round they found that he was still holding the horses, patting and coaxing them, speaking to them as if they were intelligent beings, while the driver was also busy trying to pacify them. Upon request someone spoke to the young stranger, telling him that the ladies whom he had just rescued wished to speak to him. A comic grimace for a moment distorted the handsome face, then a merry smile played about the ripe red lips, then quickly stepping to the sidewalk, he dropped his hat and bowing asked if he could be of any further service. As he stood with uncovered head awaiting the pleasure of the ladies a sensation flashed through Imelda's mind that somewhere she had seen this face before. The poise of the head, a trick of the hand, even the very smile playing about the lips seemed familiar, but she found it impossible to place the resemblance. Alice in the old impulsive manner held out both small white hands to him.

"You will permit me to thank you, will you not, for the service you have done us today? But for your bravery we might all have been killed." The boyish face dimpled all over with sunny smiles, as he tossed the fair hair from the heated and damp brow.

"I beg your pardon lady, but I think almost anyone would have done as much. It was not so wonderful a thing for me to do. I am used to the handling of horses, it was only a spicy adventure, that is all, and if I thereby was of any important service, why, I am only too glad, I can assure you."

"But will you not give us your name? I want to know to whom I am indebted."

During all this time Imelda was studying the youthful face of this stalwart young stranger. Where had she seen that face, or one like it? Meta was clinging to her skirts, her great dark eyes staring at the handsome boy, for he really was little more than that. Little Norma was clinging to her mother and was still sobbing in childish fright. Ignoring the question of the young mother the young man laid his hand upon the head of the sobbing little one, which action hushed the sobs, while she lifted her blue eyes in wonderment to the smiling face.

"Never mind, little pet," said he, "when you are a young lady you will have forgotten all about the naughty fright you have had today. Don't you think so, little Dark Eyes?"

This last to Meta who never for a moment had let her shining dark orbs wander from the fair face of the young rescuer.

"I don't know," was the naive answer the sweet childish voice made, which provoked a merry peal of laughter from the boyish lips. Alice too was smiling now, but if he thought to divert her thoughts from the question she had asked he was mistaken, for as soon as she could again recall his attention she repeated the request.

"Well now," the young man replied in a hesitating manner, "I really have not done anything worth mentioning, and— —"

"Please," interrupted Alice. "I want so much to know. As an additional favor I ask it."

"Very well, then," he answered with a sort of desperation, at the same time hunting in the depths of his pockets and fishing therefrom a bit of pasteboard.

"I believe my name is scrawled on this. If that is of any value to you, you are certainly welcome to it," and with that he handed her the little white card.

"Osmond Leland," Alice read. Like an electric shock did the words thrill Imelda. Her hand caught the arm of her friend.

"What is the name? Read it again. I fear I have not heard aright."

"Osmond Leland," repeated Alice. "I am sure that is the name written very plainly," and she handed the card to Imelda. The young man began to look with surprise at the beautiful agitated face of the lady who seemed to find something queer about his name. She turned to him with a quick imperious movement. All in an instant she knew why his face seemed familiar.

"I beg your pardon, Mr. Leland, but have you not a sister?" A flush slowly mounted his brow, even to the roots of his hair. The surprised look in his face deepened. Who was this lady that she should ask him such a question?

"I believe I have a sister. Yes, but how could you know of this?"

"Her name is Margaret?" entirely ignoring the latter part of the young man's answer.

"I believe that is her name," he again answered becoming still more mystified.

"And her home is in Chicago, where she lives with your mother?" Again the flush mounted to his brow. There was a little stiffening of the lines about the mouth as he answered somewhat coldly.

"She lives in Chicago with her mother," placing a marked emphasis upon the "her." Imelda noticed it and a pained look crept about her lips. She hesitated, scarcely knowing how to proceed. Alice was watching her. Quickly she understood that the young man who had rendered them such signal service must be the brother of the precious friend of Imelda, whom she herself had learned to love in the short time she had known her, for her own sake. Imelda had told her all the sad story. The boy had been many years under the influence of that worthless father. Had he instilled the poison into his heart? It would almost seem so. How would Imelda proceed? She seemed to hesitate for a few moments, then suddenly, —

"I left Chicago only a few months ago. Margaret Leland was my most precious friend in that great city. A woman pure as pure gold; reared, instructed and cared for by her mother whose life is consecrated to truth and purity. Margaret Leland and her mother are women whom any man in the land might well be proud to own as sister and mother."

Imelda had spoken quickly, her words savoring just a little of excitement. They sounded like a defense, with just an undercurrent of pleading for justice for those loved ones, to one whom fate had placed in a position where he was ignorant of that which ought to concern him most in life. He seemed to understand her desire. After a slight hesitation, his embarrassment growing greater every moment.

"If the ladies will kindly permit I would be thankful to avail myself of the permission to call upon them."

Imelda reached out her hand.

"I would be so pleased. I will have much to tell you." Alice, in her turn, hastened to express her pleasure, giving him her card, and while she clasped his hand in both of hers she gave him, as a parting salutation:

"Do not forget or hesitate to come. I, too, know both sweet ladies referred to. Let me assure you they are ladies, pure and good." Then giving her driver orders to wait she again spoke to young Leland, telling him that they were anxious to ascertain the truth of what they had heard, that a young girl had been injured; whereupon he offered to accompany them. They retraced their steps the distance of a square, where they found quite a number of people gathered who were discussing the accident. Upon inquiring they found that the girl had been picked up bleeding and in an insensible condition, but that before she could be taken to a hospital a young lady, opposite whose home the accident had occurred and who had just returned from shopping, had opened her hospitable door and had cared for the wounded girl. Some bystanders remarked that in all probability her kind action would not meet the approval of her father, or that of her stepmother. But Miss Wallace, it was replied, had a mind of her own, and usually she followed its dictates. The house was pointed out to Alice and Imelda, and to judge from the outward appearance it was by no means the abode of poverty. Mounting the steps they rang the bell. Upon stating their errand, they were asked to enter.

Young Leland here bade them farewell for the present, promising them soon to call at the home of the Westcots. The anxious ladies were then shown into the parlor and left to themselves. They could hear that there was a commotion of some kind. There were hasty steps to and fro; voices in the distance; orders given, etc. After a while the door opened and a beautiful dark eyed young lady entered. In a voice full and rich she said:

"If I have been rightly informed, you ladies were in the carriage that dashed over the unfortunate girl who has been hurt?"

Both ladies had risen.

"Yes! to our great sorrow, such is the case," said Alice. "Some boys were throwing stones and hitting one of our horses caused the sad accident."

"And were none of you hurt?" looking from one to the other and from them to the little ones.

"No, thank you; not hurt at all. We escaped with only a terrible fright, but the unfortunate young girl,—who is she? Is she seriously injured?"

"Who she is we have as yet no means of ascertaining as she is still unconscious. From appearance she is a working girl; she is very plainly dressed, but there are evident marks of refinement, as though she might have seen better days. How seriously she is hurt we also do not know. As I have said before, she has not yet regained consciousness. We know, however, that she has been hurt about the head. An arm also is broken, but the doctor hopes she is not inwardly injured. She seems to be in a weak condition of body as from recent illness. I have left my sister in charge while I came to you, ladies, so as not to leave you too long in suspense."

It was evident the fair speaker was desirous that her callers would take their leave, as her attention was doubtless required somewhere else. Imelda had not spoken. She experienced again the same sensations that she had when she first saw young Leland. Again the face before her seemed strangely familiar, but she was unable to place it. Was it to be a repetition of her former experience of an hour ago? But how? Alice was in the act of leave-taking, giving minute instructions as to her place of residence in case of an unlooked-for development of the case, for she said:

"I feel as though we are in a measure responsible for the sad accident, and I shall want to know if there are any serious results." Ere the young lady could give an answer Imelda could no longer resist the impulse to speak what was in her mind. Laying her hand upon that of the beautiful stranger.

"I beg your pardon," she said, "but will you kindly tell me with whom I have the honor of speaking? I do so much want to know your name." The great dark eyes sparkled as she answered:

"The favor you ask is but a small one indeed, and easily granted. My name is Edith Wallace."

"Edith Wallace!" echoed Imelda. "Are you a sister of Wilbur Wallace?"

For a moment a look of surprise rested on the face of Miss Wallace; then,

"Is it possible! can it be Imelda Ellwood?"

"I am Imelda Ellwood." In a moment the hands of both fair girls were joined in a firm clasp and, as if drawn together by a strange magnetism, their lips also met.

"Wilbur has told me all about you, but as he did not send me your address, my sister and I had to wait patiently for you to come to us. And this, I suppose," turning again to Alice, "is the lady with whom you make your home?" An introduction followed and instead of dismissing the two, Miss Wallace now insisted that they should remain awhile longer. "That is," she added, "if you can pardon my seeming neglect, as my attention will have to be a divided one. My sister Hilda is with the patient and the doctor at present and to them I must soon return."

"Take me with you," pleaded Imelda. "I have had a great deal of experience with the sick and maybe shall be able to be of some help to you. Besides, I feel curious to see this girl. I feel somewhat guilty as to the cause of her suffering, although we were the unconscious and unwilling cause. Yet I feel we owe her more than the wornout phrase, 'I am sorry!'"

Protesting yet consenting, Edith after having again excused herself to Alice, who was by this time reclining in a large easy chair, and having supplied the little ones with a charming picture book, she led the way. Leading her guest up a softly carpeted flight of stairs she noiselessly opened the door into a large airy chamber furnished in light refreshing tints. Snow-white curtains draped the windows while the bright light was toned to a mellow glow by wine-colored blinds.

A sweet-faced young girl was sitting at the side of the snowy draped bed, watching the pale face on the pillows. So intent was she that she never turned her head at the entrance of the new comers, thinking it was her sister alone that was returning. The light brown hair was a struggling mass of curls that, although brushed and combed, constantly escaped from their confinement. The face was almost colorless, the brow rather low, and the eyes a deep, dark gray. Tender, loving, with a full share of animal spirits, Hilda Wallace was loved wherever she went. Not quite so beautiful as the elder sister, Edith, she was just as attractive in her way.

In the one quick glance Imelda gave her she understood her fully. Before the watcher and obstructing the view, stood the doctor with the forefinger of his right hand resting upon the wrist of the girl's left and uninjured hand. With his left hand holding his watch he was counting the pulse beats. At the foot of the bed stood a woman of about forty years, apparently the housekeeper. Her eyes were bent as intently upon the quiet form as those of the others in the room. Edith stepped up to her and for a few moments whispered in her ear. Nodding assent and softly tiptoeing the housekeeper slipped from the room. Edith gently moved around to the other side of the bed and bending over the sufferer listened to the almost imperceptible breathing.

"How is she, doctor? Do you apprehend any danger?"

The man of science shook his head. "Not immediately," he said, "but she will require careful nursing. She has an ugly cut upon the head and we will have to prevent inflammation or brain fever may set in. It is important to keep her head cool. Do not forget to change the ice bandage every few minutes. The broken arm is nothing serious in itself and will soon be all right, but it may add to the fever the first two or three days. She ought to have been taken to a hospital instantly. I am afraid it may be some time now before she can be removed."

"That is not to be considered," said Edith. "We have room enough and also willing hands that it will do good to get some practice in the art of relieving pain, and if it should prove necessary we can call in the help of a professional nurse. But I wish I knew who she is. I am sure her friends must be very anxious about her."

The doctor merely nodded his head in a grave manner, giving vent to some very expressive grunts. "Very well," he said, "very well; if you are so willing I am sure I am more than satisfied. I know I can trust the patient in your hands, Miss Wallace. You and your sister are a host in yourselves; so in your care I leave her. My part of the work being done for the present I will now go. Should there be an undesirable change, let me know;" and with a few more general instructions he bowed himself out. Edith would have followed but he prevented her from doing so.

"No; I can find the way myself while your place is here—and—good evening, ladies,"—and he was gone.

Until now Hilda had not spoken a word. Her whole attention was directed to the care of the sick girl, every few moments lifting the cloths from her head and replacing them with others taken from a vessel of ice standing by the bedside. All this time the sufferer never spoke, never moved. Imelda could not see her face as it was turned partly away, and partly concealed in a deep shadow. Edith now spoke.

"Hilda, do you see this lady?" whereupon the girl's head quickly turned.

"O, I did not know that there was anyone here," she said in tones of liquid music. Hastily turning to Imelda, "I beg your pardon"—then to Edith. "Whom did you say? I don't understand."

"Which is quite natural," answered Edith smiling, "as I have not said who; and as I know you will never guess I may as well tell you. It is Imelda Ellwood; the young lady Brother Wilbur has so often told us about."

"O! Imelda Ellwood!" exclaimed Hilda, with a glad little cry, her face brightening with a sudden joy. "I am so glad," and impulsively extending both hands she kissed her in greeting.

Just then a smothered sound was heard from the bed. With her well hand the wounded girl grasped the cloth from her head and dashed it across the room.

"Who said Imelda? Where is she? I know of but one Imelda, and she is far-away. Ha! ha!" laughing wildly.

"I wonder what Imelda would say? my beautiful and good sister Imelda, if she could see me tonight. Would she soil her pure hands to wash mine? I thought I heard someone speak her name. Say, do you know her?"—and her glance travels unsteadily from face to face. As her eyes rested upon the white face of Imelda they settled there in a stony, set manner. Her lips twitched convulsively as she slowly raised herself upon her well arm. With a quick movement Imelda now cast aside the hat that she still wore. The next instant she had caught the weakened but fever-flushed form in her arms.

"Cora!" She spoke the name calmly, and in a tone of voice tender and gentle, as if the meeting and finding of the wayward sister here was a matter of course. Laying her cool hand upon the heated brow and gently brushing the tangled hair therefrom.

"Cora, be calm and quiet or you will harm yourself. Come, lie down and go to sleep." From the manner in which these words were spoken one would scarce have thought that anything unusual had happened. The influence of both words and manner was instantly felt by the suffering girl. Obediently she permitted herself to be laid back upon the pillows. Her eyes closed. Her hand went up to her head; then to her injured arm, thus indicating where the pain was that tortured her. Hilda had by this time replaced the cold cloths. Low moans escaped the lips of the patient and soon two large tear drops stole from beneath the closed eyelids. Imelda gently brushed them away, now and then murmuring a caressing word so low that only the prostrate girl could hear. Her hand passed back and forth across the fevered brow. The magnetic touch seemed to do her good. Gradually the sufferer became more quiet, and when the parched lips asked for water it was Imelda's hand that passed the cooling drink. In a little while the breathing became more regular, and presently Cora was asleep.

In all this time there had not been spoken one word of explanation. Whatever of curiosity the sisters may have felt none was expressed. Quietly they waited until their guest should of her own accord explain what seemed so strange. When Imelda felt certain that her sister was fast asleep she gently withdrew her hands and raising her eyes to those of Edith she indicated that she wished to speak to her. Not wishing to make the least sound in the sick room the two went out together, leaving Hilda once more to watch with loving care at the bedside.

As soon as the door was closed upon their retreating figures Imelda turned and looked Edith Wallace full in the face. It was an ordeal she felt called upon to pass through, and though a severe one she resolved to meet it bravely.

"Do you understand what that girl is to me?" pointing to the door of the room wherein the sick girl lay.

"I have an inkling," replied Edith, "but do not quite understand."

"She is my sister!" Like a wail the words came from Imelda's lips. She had managed to hide her real feelings while in the atmosphere of the sick room, but now she was in danger of losing control of herself.

CHAPTER XXX

"Come with me," said Edith, and she led the way to a room at the other end of the hall.

"Here we will be undisturbed, and you can tell me all you wish to impart. But I wish you to understand that I expect you to say nothing that may cause you pain to recall. The fact that this girl is your sister makes her much less a stranger to me than she would otherwise have been. Come, sit here in this chair, here where you will be shaded from the rays of the setting sun. Now, if you are comfortable you may proceed."

What a cozy, homelike room it was. A bright glowing red was the predominating color, softened by the lace curtains and snowy draped bed. Here and there was a dash of gold. The warm hues seemed just suited to the glowing beauty of the girl who sank into a seat opposite the chair wherein she had placed Imelda, and here, in the cool half-dark room, was told the sad story of how this wayward sister had left the home of her childhood to go with her lover.

Of her own suspicion, however, that Cora had never been a wife Imelda could not bring herself to speak. How could she know how these sisters would judge? She only told that from the hour that Cora had left her home until now they had never seen her; never heard from her, "and now I am afraid," added Imelda, "she will be a burden upon your hands, an imposition upon your kindness for an indefinite length of time."

"Hush! Not so, my friend," interrupted Edith. "I may call you friend, may I not? Would I not have done as much for an utter stranger. Why then not do it for one whom my brother holds most dear, meaning yourself, of course; and I can not help accepting your sister in the same light. But," she added smiling, "do you not think we have treated your friend Mrs. Westcot, rather badly considering it is over an hour since we left her alone to pass the time away as best she could,—and now the shades of night are beginning to fall."

Imelda uttered a little frightened cry. "O, I had forgotten! Poor Alice. I must go to her at once. But first, if you will permit, I must see Cora is still resting." So, stopping for a moment to inquire of Hilda as to the condition of the patient, and being assured that she was still asleep and perfectly quiet, the two found their way down the wide stairway to where the little woman had been left to entertain herself. Here they found that that tired little morsel of humanity had fallen fast asleep in the depths of the large arm chair wherein she had settled herself, while the little girls seeing "Mamma" asleep and having been taught at such a time to be very quiet had climbed into a chair, which Meta had pushed up to a window, and were watching the stream of travel and traffic on the street.

As the door opened little Meta turned her head and seeing Imelda uttered a glad cry. It had been a tiresome task to entertain the baby mind of Norma, and the little heart beat joyfully at the prospect that the charge was over. The cry woke Alice who started up a little confused, but immediately she remembered where she was. Edith apologized for her seeming neglect, but added:

"I am sure you will excuse me when you fully understand. I will go now and see to arranging our simple evening meal, for of course you will take tea with us. In the meantime your friend will make the necessary explanation." With these words, having first lit several gas jets, and ere Alice could formulate a protest she withdrew and left the two friends alone.

But Imelda spoke not a word. Exhausted and broken-hearted she sank into the nearest chair and bowing her head upon her hands her overcharged feelings gave way. Breaking into an uncontrollable fit of weeping, sobs shook the slender figure while tears trickled fast through her fingers.

Alice was speechless. Surprise at this seemingly uncalled for outburst of feeling, seemed for the moment to rob her of the power of utterance. The little ones stood with eyes wide open, wondering why "Aunty Meldy should try!" as little Norma expressed it. By and by Alice collected her wits sufficiently to take the hands of the weeping girl and drawing them from her face asked her what it all meant. When Imelda had somewhat conquered her emotions she said:

"Alice, you have been a true friend to me always. You have made me your confidant in many things. You know much of my earlier life, but not all. You knew I had a sister and brother; you think they are dead, as I simply told you that I had lost them, but the inference is not true. Both have stepped out of my life and have been as dead to me, for several years. I have sometimes almost wished they were indeed dead. Wild and wayward they had cast aside the restraining influence of home and had gone—we knew not whither. Never a sign of life did they give, and my mother went to her grave calling vainly for her absent ones.

"Within the last few weeks, however, the knowledge has come to me that both are alive. Several weeks ago I encountered Frank in the grounds of Maplelawn. Laboring under the misapprehension of believing me to be mistress of the handsome mansion he asked me for money. Finding I occupied only a servant's position he had no further use for me, and disappeared as suddenly as he had appeared. I know not what has again become of him; and"—with a choking feeling in her throat—"upstairs with a broken arm and a bleeding head lies my sister Cora! Do you now understand?"

Imelda turned and going to the window gazed blankly into the darkening night. She had spoken hastily and in broken accents, as if ridding herself of a very disagreeable duty. It was not pleasant to speak of these family affairs. For her they meant shame and disgrace, even though her whole being recoiled from word or act impure. Her burning brow was pressed against the cool glass and her hand upon her aching heart. Many indeed had been the trials she had been called upon to bear. Had it not been that such rare and true friends had been hers to smooth her rough pathway, and had it not been for the love of a true man's noble heart, she would often have found life not worth the living. As she stood there waiting she knew not for what, a hand stole softly into hers and a gentle voice said:

"Imelda! I am sorry, so sorry for you, but—I wish I had a sister! I have no one in all this wide world that has a claim upon me except my children. There was a time when Lawrence was my heaven, but now—you know and understand—that time belongs to the past. You have a sister. Let us hope that the finding of her will prove a blessing to you. The same blood flows in your veins. It were strange indeed if some of the same noble emotions did not also move her heart." Imelda was moved. She had never heard Alice speak with so much depth of feeling. She had not thought her friend possessed so much real character.

"Thank you," she said. "I hope so, indeed; but do you understand? I will now be compelled to remain here for some time to come. The doctor says it will not be advisable to have her removed; so I am in a manner bound to remain, which means that you will for a time have to do without me."

By the sudden pallor of Alice's cheek it was very plain that she had not thought of that, but bravely she put down all feelings of self.

"Very well, we will get along without you until such time as your sister can with safety be removed; then we will have her brought to Maplelawn where you can nurse her until she shall have perfectly recovered." Imelda started.

"Oh, no! That would be kindness too great to accept. It would be too much; besides how would Mr. Westcot accept the situation? It would be an imposition; there is no gainsaying that. No! no! Alice. I cannot accept your kind offer. As soon as it is safe she will have to be removed to a hospital where I shall make arrangements, if at all possible, to have the care of her. If that cannot be done, why then—I shall have to do the best I can for her."

"Nonsense, Imelda, do not speak like that. Lawrence has never yet refused me an expressed wish and I certainly do wish to have you near me as much as possible. But there will be time enough to discuss these matters later, for the present it is undoubtedly understood that you remain here. The rest we will trust to future developments. Just now," she said, in order to change the subject, "I wish you to help me lay this sleeping child upon the tete-a-tete, as she is becoming quite heavy;" and while Imelda was arranging an easy position Edith returned.

Alice was more anxious to return home now, as she would have to do so without her trusted and faithful companion, but Edith insisted on refreshments first, and while they were being partaken of she sent out a servant to have Alice's carriage brought up to the house. But the carriage was already waiting for them, and had been for some time. Osmond Leland had been possessed of forethought enough to attend to that matter. Edith explained to her guests that when she and her sister were alone they dispensed with the culinary art to a great extent, as they were both fond of fruits, and in the summer it was no difficult thing to have a variety of fruits on hand.

"Maybe I am a little indolent," she explained smiling, "but I do not like to roast my brains above a great fire, and by the same token I do not like to see someone else do it either; so this is the result."

There was no occasion, however, for Edith to make excuses. The ladies found the simple meal very refreshing. After it was over Imelda told Alice what few articles she deemed it necessary that she should send her; for as a matter of course she would remain for the present, and take upon herself the chief care of the wayward but now suffering sister. With the two sleepy little girls Alice was then snugly tucked away in the carriage and the driver being cautioned to be very careful, replied there was positively no cause to fear. It was not likely that a similar accident would again occur; had it not been for the throwing of that unlucky stone the trustworthy beasts would never have played such pranks. With a wave of the hand Imelda saw the carriage disappear, and with a heavy heart she again ascended the stairs to relieve the patient Hilda, and to take upon herself this new duty of nursing back to life wayward, erring Cora. To life? and what else? The sequel will show.

CHAPTER XXXI

In the days and nights that followed Imelda had every opportunity for studying this sister pair, with whom her manner of becoming acquainted was so different from that she had pictured. The first week was a trying time. Fever flushed the cheeks of the injured girl, tossed her head upon her pillow, and in her delirium she spoke of many things that caused Imelda's face alternately to pale and glow.

If any reliance could be placed upon those wild utterances, "storm tossed" would rightly apply to the life she had been leading. In her troubled dreams she was living in an atmosphere that was strange to the much tried sister. At intervals she would recognize Imelda for a few moments; then there was a subdued light in the feverish eyes, a nervous twitching about the lips. Her hand would come creeping in a hesitating way, groping for that of her sister. Imelda thought she understood. Gently pressing the groping hand she would lay her cheek to that of the suffering girl and whisper,

"It is all right, Cora, never mind." Sometimes in lucid intervals, tears would force their way from under the closed eyelids and roll down the faded cheek. Imelda would gently wipe them away and kiss the parched lips. But invariably the next moment wild fancies would hold sway and she would talk of things the patient sister could not understand.

Edith and Hilda were of the greatest help to Imelda. They would insist upon relieving her that she might refresh her tired frame with hours of balmy sleep, and also insisted that she should occasionally take a walk in the evening or morning air. Hilda more particularly proved herself a valuable assistant. The soft magnetic touch of her hand seemed to give ease to Cora in her most restless moments.

For more than a week her life hung in the balance. But her strong youth conquered, and after the ninth day reason returned to its throne. The gash upon the white forehead would be a disfigurement for life. Happily the prevailing fashion of hair dressing would almost completely hide the disfiguring mark. The cruel wound was yet far from being healed, but the danger was past. It now only required time for her to gather strength. Already she could sit daily for a few hours in a comfortable arm chair and enjoy the sweet pure air at the open window.

The Wallace sisters had positively refused to listen to any arrangement for removal of the patient. "She will remain," they had said, "until quite well." And here she still was, after two weeks had passed. A marked change had come over her. Imelda saw she was no longer the reckless, daring Cora of old. A spirit of refinement rested on the white brow, and shone in the no longer defiant eyes. There was a story in the pained lines of the decidedly pretty face. The loss of blood, the ravages of fever, and the pain of the broken arm had robbed her of every vestige of color. The ugly gash upon the white forehead had now healed enough to remove the bandage, and only a narrow strip of court plaster was needed to cover the still festering edges.

As she was somewhat of the same build and size as Hilda, that maiden had robed her in a pretty pink tea gown with a white silk front, trimmed at the neck and wrists with a soft fall of rich lace, a white silk cord encircled the waist. The heavy light brown hair had been combed school girl fashion, and hung in two plain braids over either shoulder. With the front hair Hilda had gone to some extra trouble to have it look nice. It was a mass of fluffy, curling ringlets, only at one end peeped the court plaster, merely indicating what was hidden. With that look of sadness, that was so new to the elder sister, and which softened every line of her face, Cora was far more than merely pretty.

As yet the time that intervened since the sisters had seen each other last had not been touched upon. Both seemed to avoid it as if by mutual consent. Today Cora lay back in her chair, her gaze fixed intently upon the outside of the window, but it was doubtful if she saw what was transpiring there. Imelda had been reading, now she also was resting. The book lay in her lap while she too permitted her gaze to wander. After a time, however, she recalled her wandering looks and directed them upon the face opposite her, and in doing so she saw that two pearly drops had stolen from beneath the half-closed eyelids and were slowly trickling down the white cheeks. Imelda noiselessly sank on her knees at her side, and taking the well hand of the girl in both of hers, she laid it against her cheek.

"What is it, Cora?" she asked gently. "Can you not trust your sister and tell her all?" But as if the words had loosened the flood gates of her soul the tears gushed forth in torrents from the hazel eyes; the white teeth sank deep into the quivering lips, as if to quell the sobs that broke from them. Drawing her hand away from Imelda she covered her face while she sobbed as if her heart would break. For a while Imelda did not speak, but permitted the storm to spend its strength, knowing full well she would feel all the better for it. When she had become more calm Imelda passed her arm about her waist and leaned her head against Cora's arm.

"Won't you tell me?" she again pleaded. Again the lips quivered and the tears flowed.

"Oh, Melda, Melda, how can I? You in your purity cannot understand. If I tell you all you will withdraw your clean immaculate hands from me and—Well, what matters it? I have chosen my path and no doubt can continue to walk in it. When a girl once steps aside from the straight way it is not supposed that she should ever wish to return. That circumstances rather than desire could send a woman on the downward course to ruin is not considered at all probable. I may have been wayward and wilful in the past. I know I was not good and gentle and dutiful as you were. But I was not possessed of the same strong nature, and if I have done wrong, believe me, Imelda, I have also suffered."

There was bitter pain in the words that seemed to dry the hot tears. Her mood was changing. She was at this instant more like the Cora of old than she had been since the accident. Imelda did not like it; she feared it might lead her back to the old defiance, but she hoped not. It should not, if womanly ingenuity could prevent it. So she determined not to notice the underlying bitterness. She pressed the unhappy girl's hand and said:

"Don't be too sure of so easily ridding yourself of your sister. I do not intend to lose you again. Do you think it was for the mere pleasure of the thing that I have been watching with you night and day for the past two weeks? Oh, no! Since I have found you I intend to keep you with me. An only sister is not lightly lost sight of."

This last caused Cora quickly to turn her head.

"An only sister? What about—little Nellie?"

A sharp pang pierced Imelda's heart. The question showed her that Cora did not know of the changes that had taken place. But as she hesitated Cora seemed to understand.

"Is little Nellie dead?" she asked.

"Yes!" softly answered Imelda's voice, as her arms tightened about Cora's waist. "Little Nellie is sleeping in our mother's arms."

Imelda felt the tremor in the weakened frame, but no answer came from the pallid lips. But when she looked up she observed the tears again stealing from beneath the closed lids.

"Dead! dead!" she whispered, "and I was not there. Maybe it was better so. If she had known all that had taken place in my life it would only have added another bitter drop to her already overflowing cup. But you, Imelda! What are you doing here so many miles from our western home? How came you here?"

"Do you remember Alice Day, who used to work at the store where we were both employed?"

"Yes."

"Well, you also remember that it is long since she is no longer Alice Day but Mrs. Lawrence Westcot. Lawrence Westcot's home is in Harrisburg and I have the care of her children, two sweet little girls."

"Here in Harrisburg?"

"Yes, here. And just here, I may as well tell you of another circumstance. On the day which came so near being your last our old time friend with her two little girls and myself were out driving in her carriage when through the throwing of a stone our horses took fright, and like mad they dashed through the streets and—Well, do you understand the rest? I was in the vehicle that caused you a broken arm and an almost broken head." Cora smiled sadly.

"A pity it was not wholly broken,"—for which she was reproved by Imelda.

"Don't let me hear such words again. I will not listen; but first tell me why you should use them and then let me judge."

"Let you judge,"—fell in bitterest accents from Cora's lips. "Chaste, honest, truthful, will you be able to judge me?"

"I hope so, and as I hope that I am all that you say, you must not forget to add 'just.' That is another attribute to which I aspire. Now trust me, little sister, and ease that aching heart. You will feel better when it is all over; I am very sure." So at last Cora gathered up courage and began the confession that in the last few days so often had hovered upon her lips.

Cora told how short the dream of happiness had been that had enticed her to leave home and listen to the tempter's words. How the promised marriage had been put off from day to day, and from week to week, until the truth burst upon her that he never had had any intention of making her a wife. A scene similar to that recorded somewhere near the beginning of this narrative was again enacted. Cora was no less emphatic in her demands than her mother had been before her. But there was a difference: Herbert Ellwood was a gentleman; one of nature's noblemen. But Tom Dixon did not know the meaning of the word "honor," and when he was tired of his plaything he simply cast it aside. Neither threats, tears or prayers could avail anything. Alone, a stranger in a strange city she was helpless. He had taken her as far as New York, and for a while the disgraced girl was tempted to end her life in the quickest way possible. Desperate indeed was her position;

without money; awaiting an event which, if nature had justice done her, should be the crowning joy and glory of a woman's life, but which, instead, made her a wretched outcast, a homeless, friendless wanderer.

Her voice was husky and her cheek fever-flushed as she proceeded with her story, not daring to meet the eye of her sister.

"I had been considered pretty, I know, both of face and form, and these drew the attention of a man who had protected me from the brutal insults of some roughs, and who, noticing my condition and circumstances, and, attracted by something that even now I cannot account for, took me under his immediate care and protection. I soon discovered that he possessed a tender heart, as well as a well filled purse. Placing me in the hands of a skillful physician he procured a nurse, and, when my baby was born, saw that I had every attention.

"At first I hated the little innocent because of its father, but after it had lain in my arms and at my breast the unnatural feeling gave way to one that might have brought me some happiness if I had been permitted to keep it. But just two weeks from the day I first felt the touch of the baby lips the little unwelcome life went out, and I was left more wretched than ever.

"I did not love my new lover, (for such he was). I don't think I was then capable of love. My heart was so full of bitterness. But Owen Hunter had been kind to me when he who according to nature ought to have protected me had cast me off. This stranger had cared for the despairing outcast and tided her over the stormiest waters. But there came a day when he seemed to expect a return, a compensation.

"He came to call upon me one evening about two months after my baby was born. As he often came this fact was nothing new, and his coming always brought with it a certain degree of pleasure, but on this particular evening he drew me upon his knee, fondled me, paid me pretty compliments and ended by making me the blank proposal to become his mistress.

"I had been passive under his caresses, never thinking what it all meant, but now it burst upon me like a thunderbolt, and I saw only a repetition of past experiences. I cast off his encircling arms and tottering to my bed threw myself down and gave way to an outburst of tears and sobs. For a while he let me have my way; then came and sat beside me upon the edge of the bed and talked to me for some hours. He was enamored of my pretty face; called me beautiful, and wanted me all to himself. He promised me a life of ease; lots of money and pretty clothes. He said he could not understand how a man could be so heartless as to cast aside a girl so pretty. He loved me well enough, he said, to have cared for my little babe had it lived. He thought he had proven to me that he was trustworthy, and if I was but willing to try him he was sure I would never rue it.

"As I said before, I did not love him, but I felt a kindly feeling for the really handsome man, which feeling I tried to persuade myself was love. I was cast adrift without a friend or a dollar. What more natural than that I should give heed to the sympathetic voice? Then the thought came to me: If he so loved me he might be willing to make me his wife. So permitting him to take me in his arms and kiss me I took his face between my hands and asked him, would he not marry me? He laughed, as if it were some good joke, but held me all the closer, and still laughing shook his head.

"'Make you my wife, little girl? No! no! It is not a wife that I want, but someone to love me; someone to whom my coming will be sunshine; whose laugh will be music to me; who will be sure to make the evenings I am with her happy ones, and wives don't generally do that!'

"I did not understand then what he meant though I did so later. What I did understand was that he refused to marry me. Whatever else the offer contained it was not fair promises that he did not mean to keep. Well, why should I continue? I felt that here was a haven of rest, what else was open to such as I? My past would always be a barrier to my moving among so-called respectable women, and I was desperate.

"To make a long story short I accepted his offer. But this man was truly kind to me. Through it all he never once attempted to take a liberty I had not first granted to him. He never forced his attentions upon me. He soon seemed, however, to understand better how matters stood. A change came over him. Although many were the evenings that he spent with me he was not the same. I missed the joyous happy laugh, and his impulsive caresses were toned down to a light kiss, given at his coming and going. He no longer remained very late. He brought me books and flowers; he prevailed on me to take an interest in many studies, offering to be my teacher. A handsome piano found its way into my rooms on which he taught me to play. Having made the discovery that I possessed considerable talent in music and also that my voice was above the common, he did not rest until a competent vocal teacher was procured for me. Evening after evening he was at my side aiding me in my studies; leading me on and on until I was surprised at the capabilities that had lain dormant in my nature. I awoke to a hunger and thirst for knowledge, and day by day I applied myself more diligently to my studies. I was beginning to be ambitious, the wellspring of which I did not as yet understand, but I would see the smile of pleasure and approval light up his face and I felt rewarded. One evening when about a year had passed he paid me this compliment:

"'My little girl is quite an accomplished lady now.'

"I can yet feel the flush of pleasure, the blood mounting to my brow, as he laid his hand with caressing touch upon my head, lightly brushing back my hair. The action was new. Long ago he had laid aside the lover and was merely the friend and teacher, and it puzzled me to understand the meaning of it at first. I had not heeded it much, but gradually my feelings had undergone a change. He always treated me with such perfect respect just as if I were some high-bred lady. I learned to admire him first and then a warmer feeling crept into my heart. When evening came I counted the moments until he would arrive. Sometimes it would be late, then a spirit of unrest would make me miserable with the fear that he might disappoint me, and when such would be the case, as it sometimes happened, the spirit of unrest and disappointment would not let me sleep. I awoke to the knowledge that I loved him now if I had not done so during those first weeks of our acquaintance, and with this knowledge another feeling made itself apparent. I felt that I was under obligation to him. He was keeping me as a lady when I had no right whatever to accept anything from him. One evening I electrified him by telling him that I was going to look for work. For a moment he looked at me as if he thought I was not in my right mind, then he peremptorily asked:

"'What is the meaning of this foolish notion?'

"'I have been a burden on your hands long enough.'

"He laughed,

"'A burden? Well! well! What put that idea into this little dark head?'

"'Is it then so strange that I should desire to turn to practical advantage all the knowledge I have gained through your kindness? I am sure it is time I sought, in some measure, to repay you, and how better can I do that than by doing something practical?'

"A troubled look rested on his face as his eyes searched mine.

"'Will you believe me, little one, that the evenings spent here are the one pleasure in which I indulge? the pleasure to watch your mind expand and grow; the one pleasure which nothing else can replace? And what of your studies? They are as yet by no means complete. What is to become of them while you work to earn a living?'

"The sound of his voice changed. 'I do not want to hear such foolish words again. Until your studies are mastered you are to think of nothing else.' That vibrating voice robbed me of all power of resistance; and so no more was said on this subject, but I felt my heart go out to him more and more.

"But why did he never caress me now? Did he no longer love me? Considering our relations in the early part of our acquaintance it was strange; but I felt a restraint that would never permit me to show what I felt. The day he paid me the compliment of being an accomplished lady I felt my heart leap with joy. O how I longed to throw myself into his arms and repay him in a warmer manner than I had ever dared show him. But this indefinable something stood between us and held me to my place. The next evening, and every evening after that, I took extra pains with my dress. I wanted to look nice when he came, and with greater impatience than I had ever known I awaited his coming. Often I succeeded in drawing a word of praise from him which would send the blood bounding through my veins.

"One evening about a week after he had so effectually overruled my intention to seek work I arrayed myself in a soft gown of purest white, a color which Owen most particularly admired. But on that evening I waited in vain. The hours came and went but they did not bring Owen. The next evening the same experience was repeated and every evening for a week, but the man who had become so dear to me did not come; and the thought was slowly forcing itself into my mind that he would never come. If in the past there had been hours of despair the prospect of the coming time seemed so much darker that truly life would not be worth the living if I was again to be forsaken.

"With weak and trembling hands I once more arrayed myself for his coming. I wore a loose robe of creamy silk fastened only with a white silken cord at the waist. My last week's experience had robbed me of the roses that the few previous weeks had called to my cheeks. It was Sunday evening and I hardly dared hope that he would come that night. It was the sweet Maytime and a great bunch of lilacs filled their room with their fragrance. The evening was warm. Doors and windows were open, and I think I must have fallen asleep in my rocker for I heard no sound, yet was aroused suddenly by the feeling of a face close to mine. For a moment I was frightened and involuntarily uttered a cry, but the next moment seeing who it was, and forgetting everything but that he, my friend, my lover, had returned, I sprang to my feet and with the cry, 'Owen! Owen!' I cast myself upon his breast and twined my arms about his neck. In that moment I knew that he had not ceased to love, as I had feared, for holding me close in his arms he pressed me to him and almost smothered me with his kisses, whispering again and again,

"'My little girl, my own little woman, you love me now, my sweet? I have not waited in vain?' I answered him only with a happy laugh. My heart was too full for anything else, but he understood, for he again rained kisses upon my face calling me by every endearing name that love had ever invented. He never rightly explained why he had remained so long away, but I understood then that circumstances over which he had no control had caused it, and little did I care in my new-found happiness, for I was happy,—happy as I had never thought I could be. I sat upon his knee with my arms clasped about his neck until away into the night. We had not struck a light; he would not let me be free long enough to do so. There was no need, he said, and I know that not one softly whispered word of love was lost, and with the most perfect ease his lips found mine. The hour had come and gone that he was wont to leave me, but as midnight approached he laid his lips to my ear and whispered words that for a moment caused my heart to stand still; and then to bound as if to break its confines. The past year had made a different woman of me and I now, as never before, wanted the respect of the man whom I loved. He felt my heart beating so madly and I know he guessed the cause. He laid his face to mine and pleadingly, tremblingly spoke:

"'Darling, can you not trust me? my timid fluttering birdie? I would not harm one shining hair upon this precious head.' And I did trust him, for O Imelda, I loved him, I loved him. You, looking down from your pure and lofty heights can not understand it, but it was all so different from that first experience that I had. I tried to realize the enormity of my wrong-doing but I could not feel impure when I was in his arms. My love for Owen was something different from what I had hitherto deemed love to be. I felt myself lifted above everything sordid, everything unclean. Every feeling, every thought connected with him was as something holy, and now, as then, the thought will force itself upon my mind: How is it possible that true, pure love can ever be deemed impure! when its fires are so purifying only holy emotions find room in the heart.

"But our love was without sanction of either church or state and therefore the world would place its seal, its stamp of 'outcast' upon the brow of such as I. But is it not somewhere written that much shall be forgiven to those who love much? And the short time that followed I was madly, intensely happy, while Owen seemed to be no less so. He would catch me in his arms and lift me up as if I were a baby while his blue eyes shone with a light as of heaven.

"'My own darling! my precious one!' O, how often did he say these words while I pressed his fair head to my heart and thought heaven was in his arms." Cora broke off with a choking sob, while the tears once more rolled down the pale cheek. Imelda was still upon her knees at her side, was still fondling the white hand when Cora again turned to her:

"Why don't you turn from me? I who have been a mother, who have granted to man the greatest boon of love a woman can bestow,—without first being a wife! Why are you not angry with me? I am sure I deserve it!"

"Why, my poor, dear Cora! Why should I be angry with you? For loving a noble man? I hope I am not so narrow, and that I am able to judge you more fairly."

Cora's hazel eyes expanded to their utmost extent.

"Melda, what do you mean? I do not understand. Do you not curse him and despise me?"

Imelda shook her head.

"Neither," she answered. "Although I do not quite understand, yet according to your description of the man I get the impression that he was noble and good. Nothing at all to warrant a judgment so cruel from me. But now you must keep calm or I shall not permit you to speak farther. I insist that you lie down and rest, as this excitement may prove injurious to you."

"And if it should make an end of my miserable life it might be the best thing that could happen to me. I have been of but little good in the world,— only to bring pain and sorrow into the lives of others."

"Now, now, Cora! Is it right you should talk like this when you have but just finished telling of the love of your Owen and the happiness you have brought to him?" Cora put her hand to her head.

"You confuse me," she said. "To hear you speak like this causes me to doubt my senses. I do not understand." Imelda smiled.

"But you will understand, by and by, when you know all. Now I am waiting to hear the rest of your story."

"The rest of my story? Would that it ended there; then, maybe, I might still have some faith that my life is not all in vain. But to return and finish. My dream was too bright and beautiful to last. Such intense bliss is not for this world. I ought to have told you before how I lived. Owen had furnished a small house for me in princely style. It was far up town and stood in a grove of trees and isolated from the neighborhood. A most beautiful garden was attached to it with richly scented flowerbeds and vines and ivy-covered arbors. Certainly a lovely spot and a perfect lovers' home. From the windows I could see the blue waters of the Hudson and often I watched the stately steamers proudly sail up and down its silver-hued bosom. As I stated once before, Owen had procured a nurse to attend me in my hour of trial, a faithful colored woman, and she had lived with me from that time on, keeping my nest a bower of beauty. She always thought I was Owen's wife and he said nothing to dispel that belief. She probably often thought it queer that during all that year he had spent only a few hours in the evening of each day with me, but she never said anything.

"One day when I was more happy, if that were possible, than usual, a carriage drove up to my little heaven. A footman opened the door and a richly attired lady stepped therefrom and slowly came up the shaded path. Old Betty met her at the door; I heard them speak but could not understand what was said. The old woman led the lady into our cosy little parlor and then came to me in my own pretty bed chamber upstairs. She brought me a card upon which I read, 'Mrs. O. Hunter.' She was a woman of perhaps twenty-eight or thirty years of age, very tall, a decided brunette with flashing black eyes. Her features were sharp, and a look indicating that her tongue could be as sharp. I looked helplessly at her and then at the card in my hand."

"'Mrs. Hunter?' I said, bowing—but her stiff head never inclined. In a haughty, heartless manner she spoke,

"'If you are able to read you ought to find that correct. Mrs. Owen Hunter,'—with a decided stress upon the 'Owen.' I was beginning to feel dazed. 'Mrs. Owen Hunter'! My Owen's name. Who could she be?

"'Well?' I asked.

"'Well!' she repeated. 'Does not that speak for itself? If not I will endeavour to be still more plain. I am tired of having my husband spend his nights away from home. I warn you, girl! Owen Hunter is my husband, and the father of my children. If I still find, after this, that he continues coming here, I shall find means to put an end to it, and to make it go hard with you!'

"I was as if stunned! My head swam, as I listened to this threat. My Owen the husband of this woman! Impossible! Surely, surely, there is some terrible mistake here. Not for one instant did I permit myself to believe the cruel accusation that had been hurled at me, but without deigning me another look she turned in haughty scorn to leave the room when her eye caught sight of a crayon picture—Owen's picture, my most especial pride, which had been placed upon an easel. A look like a thunder cloud passed over her face, and before I could think what her intention might be she had swooped upon it, knocked it down, and setting her foot upon it crushed the glass into a thousand pieces, cutting and hopelessly ruining the precious picture. With a cry of dismay I stepped forward, but it was too late, and with a mocking laugh she swept from the room, leaving me in a heart-broken condition.

"I had not known that Owen had a wife, and as yet I could scarcely believe it true. If such was the case I knew full well it was to her he belonged and not to me. How I managed to live through that day I do not know. My heart felt like stone in my breast; no tears came to ease or quench the aching, burning pain.

"In the evening Owen came whistling up the garden path, his handsome face all aglow with the sunshine of happiness. He came bounding into the room where I was sitting and the next instant he had caught me in his arms and was madly straining me to his breast, smothering me with kisses. But suddenly he seemed to discover something amiss in my manner. Holding me away from him the better to look at me he said,

"'What is it, birdie? not sick are you?'

"'Yes,' I said, struggling with the tears, —'heart-sick.'

"All the sunshine, all the laughter was gone from his face in an instant.

"'Explain, sweetheart, what is it?' For answer I pointed to the ruined picture.

"'Why' — —he stammered. 'What has happened?'

"To speak would have been impossible. I felt as if a cold, unseen hand was clutching at my throat. So I merely handed him the card with the name of 'Mrs. Owen Hunter' upon it. I shall never forget the look of dismay that passed over his face.

"'Do you mean to say she has been here?' he articulated. I merely inclined my head. His arms fell slowly away from me and stepping to the open window, he stood looking out into nothing for a long time, —so long, indeed, that I thought he had forgotten that I was there. When he turned back to me his face looked in the gray twilight as if it had aged ten years.

"'And will my sweet love send me away because of this woman?' He asked the question holding my hand in both of his, closely pressed to his cheek. His voice did not sound the same. All the laughter, all the life had left it. I saw he was suffering, and the knowledge did not tend to lessen the pain that was tugging at my own heart. I answered his question with another.

"'She is your wife?'

"'She is. But what of that?' —doggedly.

"'Only that you belong to her, and not to me.' Then he caught me in his arms and held me so fast he almost crushed me.

"'No! no!' he huskily said, 'it is false. I do not belong to her. It is you that holds me, body and soul. That woman never married me, —only my money!'

"'But your children?'

"'What children?'

"'Why, yours—and hers.'

"'There are none!'

"My head swam; she had said, 'The father of my children,' and he said. 'There are none.' I looked into the clear blue eyes and believed him. But in spite of that I knew my dream of bliss was ended. In his madness he made the proposition that we should leave together,—go to some distant city, to Europe, anywhere where we could remain together. The world was wide and in some small corner we would find room where we might be happy.

"But to this proposition I would not listen. My mind was already made up. I would leave—leave without saying a word about it. I could not bear the thought of being the cause, perhaps, of his ruin. If I told him I knew he would never consent; but this one last night he was mine, and with that shadow threatening to engulf us we loved with the intensity of despair. But before the night had waned, clasped closely in his arms he told me the story which had wrecked his life."

With a weary movement Cora leaned her head against the bolstered back of her chair. Imelda saw that her sister was exhausted. Reproaching herself for having permitted her patient to do so much talking she gave the order, "Not one more word!" and helping her to disrobe she gently assisted her back to her couch. With a new tenderness she arranged the pillows and then insisted upon perfect quiet.

"Tomorrow will be another day, and time enough to proceed."

Cora did not protest, and soon the weary eyes were closed in slumber. Long did Imelda watch the sleeping girl while she was conscious of a new feeling toward this erstwhile wayward sister. Her heart went out to her as it had never done before, and henceforward she knew she would not be quite alone in the world as she had been. She felt that she had now found her sister, in more senses than one.

Just here it might not be out of place to make mention of that other pair of sisters to whom these two were at the present time under such heavy obligations. It had seemed rather queer to Imelda that the two should be all alone in this large house, as she had understood from what Wilbur had told her that the sisters lived in the home of their father who with the second wife had quite a family of children, but of whom there was not a trace to be seen. Only a day or two ago, however, Edith had explained to Imelda how matters stood.

CHAPTER XXXII

From this explanation it was evident that neither of the two elder daughters had any too much love for the stepmother, who was domineering in character. Of late years the freedom-loving Edith had refused to submit to her many dictations. She absolutely refused in any manner to be a subordinate. When Hilda found her sister making such a brave effort to free herself from the domination of the stepmother she was not long in following her example. The stepmother appealed to the father, who in turn ordered his daughters to explain.

Edith did explain. She said that Hilda and herself were now old enough to judge for themselves in all personal matters. They demanded freedom in all their actions. If it were refused them at home they would seek a home elsewhere. With youth and health they were confident they would not starve.

But Edmund Wallace was a proud man. After the disastrous ending of his first marriage, with the second wife, brilliant and fashionable, at his side,—a woman who seemed better to understand how to manage her husband than did the timid Erna before her, Mr. Wallace had been more successful financially. Dabbling in politics he had secured to himself political and social position and hence the idea that his daughters should leave his house to find a home elsewhere was not at all to his liking. Such a thing would draw attention, and cause unpleasant notoriety. So, for once, he sided with his daughters and gave his wife to understand that they were at liberty in all personal matters to do as they pleased.

The haughty woman was almost strangled in her anger, but found herself forced to submit. But if she could no longer domineer there were a thousand other ways in which she could make the lives of the girls a daily torture. The result was that Edith again turned to her father, telling him that under existing circumstances they could not and would not longer remain. So another and more decided change was made. A room was assigned to Edith and Hilda as their "sanctum." Through the political influence of the father positions were secured for both girls, which furnished them with pocket money to spend as they saw fit. The salary of each was sixty dollars per month, twenty of which each contributed toward keeping up the establishment. This arrangement made them independent, and from the day it was made both refused to take part in the household duties. Mrs. Wallace had to procure hired help. Then it was she came to realize the full value of these despised stepdaughters. But as she considered it beneath her dignity to unbend towards the girls there was a constant frigidity between them.

There were four children from this second marriage, two girls and two boys; the girls being the eldest. All four were away at school. Mr. and Mrs. Wallace were away spending the hot summer months at some mountain resort. The girls having vacation, nothing averse, took charge of the house, expecting later in the season to spend a week or two on some quiet country farm. To the circumstance of the absence of the rest of the family was it due that Cora had found such a haven of rest under this roof prepared by the kind and loving hearts and hands of this sister pair. That she herself was the sister of one who had such a warm friend in that absent brother who to them personated the whole of manly graces and perfections, made it to seem more like a privilege than otherwise that they should have been permitted to lavish their tenderest care upon her; besides the sufferer had won for herself a place in these sisterly hearts that was all her own, a place that no one would be able ever to deprive her of.

Alice had often called during the past two weeks but as yet had not seen the injured girl. Somehow Cora had always been asleep and it was deemed unwise to awaken her. Norman also had found his way several times to the Wallace abode, as indeed it would have been strange if he had not. When making his first visit he said:

"It seems we are destined to love under difficulties—always someone claiming the love and attention of the woman that I would fain monopolize." When he heard that in this case the claim came from the lost and erring sister a cloud had for a moment rested upon his manly face. Then gravely and tenderly he had said, kissing the pure forehead of the girl he loved,

"Do what you think is your duty, and what you think is best, my sweetheart. I would not have you do otherwise,"—and then Imelda had gone back to her sister's bedside with a much lighter heart and with a new sense of happiness. Today, as she stood watching the face of the sleeping sister, thoughts and feelings came crowding upon her that she herself might have found difficult to analyze. Poor Cora, thought Imelda, how manifold and how oft painful had been her experiences. If she had dealt many a cruel blow to others, in the thoughtlessness of youth, it was very evident that she had suffered much and keenly, and yet—looking at her experiences without prejudice, was she not, in some respects, more to be envied than to be pitied or condemned? This very reckless daring that was Cora's chief characteristic, had secured to her a term of such intense, such exquisite happiness that Imelda, with her high strung morals, could never hope to attain, and as she bent to kiss the sleeping girl she whispered:

"You possess more courage than the sister you think so pure. You are more true to nature and to yourself than I."

When Cora awoke, refreshed from a long sleep, she would have resumed the recital of her story but Imelda positively refused to listen. Instead the invalid was again arrayed in the pretty wrapper and, with the assistance of Hilda, was led down the broad stairway to the handsome parlor. Here the trio of girls read, played and sang for her amusement, and several times during the evening Cora's clear, sweet laugh rang out, making music in Imelda's heart. An unbroken night's rest followed, and the next morning found the sisters once more seated by the window and Cora ready to take up the thread of her narrative where she had left off the day before.

"Owen Hunter was the only child of very wealthy parents. They were the possessors of millions. All the advantages that wealth can procure had been his. At college he had graduated with the first honors. He was gifted with talents of high order—a poet born; a musical genius, and his gift of song alone would have made him famous, had he so desired. But, as is so often the case with natures of this kind, he was very impulsive. The blood in his veins was extra hot, and at the early age of eighteen he had got himself entangled with a dark-eyed southern beauty, whom he deemed the perfection of all womankind. His mother had died when he was sixteen, else she might perhaps have been able to guide him with loving gentleness where reason and parental commands failed. The girl with whom he had fallen so madly in love was also wealthy, and had had the benefit of a thorough education—that is, a fashionable one. She knew how to dance, how to bow gracefully. She possessed an exhaustless supply of small talk, quick of repartee, brilliant and witty. She knew how to haughtily snub a social inferior—and so on through the long list of fashionable accomplishments.

"Owen saw only the fascinating smile and the wild, witching beauty that had set fire to his brain. For some reason his father was opposed to an alliance with Leonie Street. Perhaps he better read beneath the attractive surface. But Owen was determined, and when he was scarcely twenty he married the girl who had so completely bewildered his senses. Young as he was he was at the head of a large business firm. His father of late had been in poor health, and upon the young man's shoulders was laid the burden that had become too heavy for those of the older man. And when his father died, stepping into his inheritance he found himself worth some twenty millions of dollars.

"Long ere this, however, Owen Hunter discovered that he had made a grand matrimonial mistake. The woman he had married was only a fashion plate, with this difference. A fashion plate is called inanimate, whereas Mrs. Hunter was possessed of a temper so fiery that she became quite dangerous when something occurred to arouse her ire. In her passionate moods she was so vulgar as to be disgusting. One babe had come, but as if her passion was a poison that killed, the little thing lived only a few days, and none other ever came.

"Of short duration had been their honeymoon. She managed soon to thoroughly disenchant her boy husband—to cure him of the infatuation that had led him to brave even his father's displeasure; displeasure which might have meant a great deal to him, as his father was noted for a certain bull-dog tenacity or stubbornness. When once he took a stand, either for or against, he would hold to it, to the bitter end, no matter if later he found that only he was in the wrong and all others in the right.

"Since there was no sweet baby smile to woo and win the hearts of these two, Owen and Leonie Hunter daily drifted farther and farther apart, neither caring, or little caring, what the other was doing. His millions were at her command wherewith to satisfy her every whim, and this wealth enabled her to worship at the shrine of fashion, to her heart's content. Their 'home' was a mansion; one of the most beautiful of homes but Owen Hunter only went to it to sleep, and not always then. Sometimes home did not see him for weeks at a time. The clubs suited him better than the princely mansion which contained his dark-browed wife. His wedded experience had made him reckless, and he made the most of what his wealth would buy him. He was not by nature bad; not by any means. He was only what circumstances had made him. Deep down hidden in the innermost recesses of his being were the germs of a noble manhood, but those germs were fast going to decay for want of the magic touch which would waken them to life and growth. Sometimes he felt heart-sick and soul-weary when he realized that with all the wealth at his command there was none so poor as he; that his bosom bore a starving heart. In all the vast multitudes of the great city there was not one face to brighten at his coming, to smile a welcome at his return to the place he called home.

"In a mood like this, one evening as he was passing a deserted thoroughfare he was attracted by a woman's cry. A woman was struggling in the grasp of a man. A well directed blow felled the ruffian to the earth while the rescuer caught an almost fainting girl in his arms.

"That was the way in which I became acquainted with Owen Hunter. He offered to see me to my home. I told him I had none. He seemed to understand it all in a moment, and afterwards he told me that he did so understand. A young woman whose condition was so apparent, and no home, could have only one story to tell,—a very common story, and at that moment he felt, as he afterwards explained, just as forlorn and alone, just as hopeless and homeless. It was as if I had touched a hidden wellspring. He drew my arm through his and said:

"'Come.'

"I was trembling in every nerve. The terror I had undergone almost paralyzed me. He saw I was almost unable to stand."

"'Will you trust me?'

"One look into the clear eyes told me that it would be safe, and I only nodded my head. I could not trust myself to speak. I hardly knew how it happened, but in a few moments more I found myself seated in a closed carriage, and that night I slept safely housed, with a little confidence in mankind restored.

"You know the rest. I told you the story yesterday; of how he came to love me and I him, until our love glorified our lives. Never until the darkly passionate woman stood before me did I know that another had a stronger claim upon him than I. He did not know through what chance she had become possessed of his secret. He felt sure she cared little, only it gave her a chance to empty the poison vials of her temper and spleen in a manner that she was conscious would strike me in a vital spot.

"'She thinks to part us, loved one,' he said, 'but she shall not succeed. I will not sacrifice the only bright spot that makes my life worth living. You, my darling, have redeemed me. You have taught me the bliss of the love of a true woman. You have made a new being of me, and to you I belong; while you are mine by the might and power of that holy love that you bear me.'

"O, Imelda, forbear to judge me from the high pinnacle of morality and purity upon which I know you stand. Although I had made up my mind to disappear out of his life—that he should not know what had become of me,—but this one last night I wanted to be happy, happy in the present hour and in the feeling that he was mine and I his. I would not think of the morrow and what it would bring. I only gave myself up to the hour and to my love, and when the bright sun of another day had risen he still held me so closely in his arms that it seemed he meant never to release me.

"'Have patience, my own one,' he said, 'if you should not see me for some time. I will have much to arrange, but when all shall have been attended to I will fly to you, never again to leave you; for I cannot, I will not give you up.'

"I thought my heart would break, as he held me in his arms, whispering to me his plans of hope and happiness. But I forced back the scalding tears and with smiling lips kissed him goodby. I stood at the doorway and watched him out of sight.

"'Out of sight!' Could it have been out of mind as well, it would then not have been so hard to bear. I re-entered my room, threw myself upon my bed and wept myself to sleep.

"Long hours I lay thus. When at last I awoke the sun was high in the heavens; my limbs were weary and my heart heavy, but I knew I had work to do, the hardest part of which was to write Owen a letter wherein I should bid him farewell, as I thought it better to part than that I should be the cause of his ruin. I had some money, money he had given me, and many valuable jewels and trinkets. To me they were possessed of a double value as they were the gifts of his love. I packed a trunk with such things as it seemed necessary that I should take with me; selecting the plainest of my dresses. Then having sent old Aunt Betty on an errand, I managed to procure a wagon to take my few belongings to the ferry and thence to the depot and—I have never seen him since.

"It is only two short months ago, but to me it seems ages. Not caring whither I was going, as all the world was alike to me, I procured a ticket with scarce an idea where it would take me. My trunk checked, I patiently waited for my train. For two hours I never stirred, gazing fixedly at my tightly clasped hands. Had not the strangeness of my demeanor attracted the attention of an old gentleman who kindly asked me where I was going, I might have missed my train. He doubtless saw something in my face that was not quite satisfactory for he asked to see my ticket and found that my train would be due in a few minutes. Taking me under his immediate care he saw that I was made comfortable, as, fortunately, he was to take the same train, and was bound for the same destination.

"How I reached Harrisburg I suppose I shall never know, for one day I awoke to find myself in a hospital bed, my face wan and thin and too weak to lift my head. I was told that I had been brought there four weeks before, delirious with fever, and that I constantly required the care of several nurses. But youth was in my favor and I soon regained health and strength, and in two weeks more I was discharged. It was the old gentleman who had befriended me on the train who had also caused me to be taken where I would be cared for during my illness, and through his kindness it was that I found my belongings when able again to care for myself.

"It had been just two weeks since my release from the hospital when the accident occurred that brought me here. If my thoughts had been with me I don't think it could have happened. But Owen's image still lives in my heart. It is not so easy to obliterate it therefrom, right or wrong. I still love him."

Here Cora's overwrought feelings again gave way, and she sobbed as if her heart would break. Imelda gently placed her arm about the weeping girl's neck and pressed her against her own bosom. Tenderly she brushed her hair and kissed the tear-wet eyelashes. With a quick unexpected motion Cora caught the hand that was caressing her cheek and pressed it to her heaving breast.

"Can you still find room for me in your pure and stainless heart? Can you still love me? But oh, you can't understand how hard it was to give him up. Indeed! indeed! I have tried so hard to overcome this love, but it is stronger than I. It overcomes me."

Imelda bent and kissed the quivering lips. "Poor little sister! Have I been so cold and merciless in the past as to cause you to believe that I am so small and narrow as to heap censure upon this bowed head? to still farther lacerate your bleeding, aching heart? No, no! you poor child. If in the past you have been childishly wayward I may not always have rightly understood you. If you have dared to fly in the face of society, of man-made laws, it is you who have been the sufferer, and when the sweetest boon that comes to woman's life was held out to you and you were brave enough to grasp it and to bask in its glorious sunshine, I certainly cannot condemn you. I had not dreamed that the material of so grand a woman lay hidden beneath the surface of that saucy, independent child. A grand and glorious woman indeed is my sister Cora, and I am proud of her!"

Cora's great hazel eyes were opened wide with astonishment. As if by magic the tears ceased to flow; her face grew deathly white; huskily she whispered,

"What is it you mean, Imelda? I do not understand. I have heard your words but have not caught their import. The Imelda that I know regarded a life such as I have been leading a deadly, hideous sin, and your words almost imply that— —I— —have done right."

"They do imply it, darling! I think you have been brave and true and strong. It might be, though, that it was because you were not so strongly bound, as I, by the fetters of prejudice, but I also am getting rid of these fetters and hope soon to be a free woman, and in the measure that I am gaining liberty I understand better what it means to others to be deprived of that precious boon. Sister mine, my eyes have been opened to many evils existing in this world, and the starvation of woman's sex-nature until marriage, when the starvation generally changes to surfeit and sex slavery is one of the greatest evils that this world knows. A few men are intelligent and noble enough to understand this; men who suffer almost as much from this accursed system as do most women, and, little girl, your Owen was one of these noble men. After all you have told me about yourself and him I am rather surprised you did not dare the world and claim your own."

"Imelda! This from—you! I wanted to save him from himself. I know he would never have given me cause to rue it had I entrusted myself, my life, to his care. He was too noble, too true for that. But you know the law gives him to that other woman, and how it would have hurt him in the society wherein he moves and in which he ranks so high."

"I understand. Love blinded you to your own interests while you sought to guard only his, forgetful of the fact that every pang that was torturing your own heart would find an echo in his. Oh, what a horrible structure is society; built as it is upon the quivering hearts of poor bleeding humanity!"

Cora listened in open-eyed wonder to the words that fell from the lips of her sister. To her unsophisticated ears they sounded like rank treason, only that she knew that Imelda's mind and heart were not capable of treason. Long and earnestly therefore did the elder sister talk to the younger one, trying to make clear her views and theories, and as Cora caught their import a new hope, like sweet balm, crept into the weary heart. Was she then not the loathsome and vile thing the world would have her believe herself to be? Could it really be that true love, soul-elevating, ennobling and purifying love, does not need the sanction of state and church to give it those redeeming qualities? O, how like another being she would feel if the sweet consciousness could be hers that she was not unclean and defiled; but that her love was just as pure and holy as in its highest, noblest sense it ever could be.

CHAPTER XXXIII

Long ere this the assurance had been Imelda's that Edith and Hilda were both true sisters of their brother Wilbur, and that they espoused sex reform in its highest sense, and when an hour later these two bright girls joined the Ellwood sisters Cora was again surprised to hear the same sentiments voiced in equally strong language. Hilda knelt beside the dumb-founded Cora, and while playfully fondling her hand told her of plans that had been maturing in that youthful head.

"Sometimes," she said, "when we shall have more money at our command than now, we will build ourselves a home. O, such a glorious, beautiful home, in some retired or isolated spot, and our lovers shall come and share it. But only just so long as they are our lovers, for we want no masters. We shall be strong enough, and capable of standing at the head of our home ourselves, and directing its management. Don't you think so? Our home shall be our kingdom, and we shall reign queens therein, and our lovers will be our dear friends and comrades, instead of husbands. Will not that be glorious?"

With an experience such as hers had been it was not much to be wondered at that Cora became an apt pupil of this, to her, new doctrine, and of which this trio of girls were such enthusiastic advocates. Edith and Imelda smiled as they listened to the glowing description of Hilda's home while a new and wonderful light began to glow in the hazel eyes of the bewildered Cora, and then she began to question, and all the time one utterance of Hilda's kept ringing in her ears: "When we shall have more money." When? But first she wanted to know and understand, and for a while she kept the trio busy answering her questions. She had become deeply interested and now wanted fully to understand.

"How many are there in this scheme? How many such daring members are there?"

"Well," answered Hilda, "there are four of us here; for of course you are in it. Then that wonderful brother of ours is the lover of a sweet girl in that western home of yours. Margaret Leland is her name."

"Margaret Leland!" interrupted Cora, and looked inquiringly at Imelda. "Was there not—"

"The same," said Imelda. "She was employed at the same store where we used to work, and for years has been my best friend. It is to her largely that I am indebted for my present views. But now please let Hilda proceed."

"Well," continued Hilda, "Margaret's mother comes next. From all accounts we could not well get along without her and—well, I don't know. Is there anyone else?"—looking inquiringly at the girls.

"I think," answered Imelda, "It will be perfectly safe to count Mrs. Westcot in—'Alice Day,' Cora, I was speaking of her before. That makes seven, I believe, and who knows, by the time 'our home' is built there may be as many more."

"And how many lovers are there?" asked Cora. This caused a little laugh.

"One I know, and two I believe," was Imelda's answer to Cora's question. "Wilbur Wallace, the brother of these dear girls, we can be sure of, and Norman Carlton I hope may soon be able to see clear enough to be willing that woman should in all things decide for herself."

"Who is Norman Carlton?"

A beautiful rosy color swept over Imelda's sweet face, and Cora was answered. "O," she said with a slight gasping sound, "now I know how you understood so well." Then Hilda spoke:

"I have been waiting for Edith to make some kind of announcement, but she sings 'mum.'"

"Hilda!"

"Edith! I am not afraid, sister mine. You know you met a very interesting gentleman last year in our rambles on the mountains."

"Yes! but child, you also know that we have not seen him since, and as we had just received a call to come home immediately we left without a word of farewell;—then again we did not get a deep enough insight into the views of Paul Arthur to enable us to ascertain whether or not he is a free lover."

"O, but I heard him express himself very clearly at one time on the subject of marriage. 'It is the grave of love,' he said, 'the altar upon which the holiest emotions are sacrificed.'"

"It may all be true," Edith replied, "but as I remarked before, we may never see or hear from him again."

"But," Hilda said, kissing Cora's pale cheek, "have you no contribution to make in the shape of a lover?" slowly the rich color swept over the pale face; involuntarily her eye sought Imelda's. Was there a meaning in the glance? She smiled.

"Can you see the rising sun?" Imelda asked, but for answer the pearly drops filled the sad eyes. "O, if I dared hope." To the inquiring looks of the sisters Imelda replied:

"When Cora is stronger I am sure she will tell you her story in all its details, as you have proved yourself so trustworthy. A cloud at present overcasts the heaven of her love; but don't clouds always in the course of nature move on, and are not the heavens always so much clearer and more beautiful after their removal? So hope, little sister. I expect ere long to look into the sunny laughing eyes of your Owen. The world is large but not so large but that the divine magnet of love will attract and direct each one to his or her affinity."

Thus bringing hope and cheer to the weary aching heart of the girl, the days, one by one passed by.

Several weeks more had now passed away. Cora had gained rapidly in strength, and as Mr. and Mrs. Wallace were now daily expected to return home and the girls wishing to avoid an explanation it was thought best to remove the patient to the abode of the Westcots. Alice was also anxious to have Imelda return as she was fast losing all control of her little daughters. Tender, loving mother that she was she was totally unfit to train her little ones. Besides she was not yet really strong.

With an unwilling heart Cora had bade good bye to the sisters who had shown her so much kindness and love. Imelda's eyes, too, had filled with tears as she kissed both gentle girls, but she carried with her the promise that she should soon see both at "Maple Lawn." Cora's cheeks were tinged with a faint peach-bloom color denoting the return of health, and her eyes sparkled as she and Imelda were swiftly driven along towards the outskirts of the city where the Westcot mansion was situated amid its beautiful gardens. Just as the setting sun was casting the last golden rays across their path the carriage drove up the beautiful maple-drive to where little Alice, in daintiest of white gowns, was awaiting them, her eyes sparkling with joy at the prospect of having Imelda once more with her. The little girls also, arrayed in their pretty white dresses, were watching for their "Miss Meldy." They clapped their little hands and fairly danced with delight when the figure of their young teacher alighted. They grew somewhat quieter when a second lady, so pale and languid, stepped from the carriage and slowly followed the more quickly moving Imelda. She caught the little ones in her arms and they clung to her as if they would never again let go of their beloved friend. Alice, finding herself overlooked in this meeting, turned to Cora. Holding out both hands in welcome she made the sad-eyed girl feel that her words were no formal phrase, but that they came from a warm impulsive heart.

"I hope not to be a burden long," said Cora. "I am beginning to feel quite strong now, and in a short time hope to be able to look about for some work to do."

Alice laid her hand upon her lips.

"Not one word more. A burden indeed! On the contrary I feel as though I had a great deal to make good. This, (touching with her dainty finger the red mark which was just peeping from beneath the mass of ringlets that covered the young girl's forehead) this will be a constant reminder of what might have proved a fatal accident, and as yet I have had no opportunity to right the wrong that has been done." Cora protested but Alice had her way, as that little woman invariably did have. She herself conducted her up the wide staircase to the room which had been set apart for her and which adjoined Imelda's.

"I thought you two might want to be near each other," she explained. "Better now let me help you dress for dinner. I will be your dressing maid. How long do you expect still to nurse your arm? It must be tiresome to have it so tightly bandaged."

Cora smiled.

"O yes," she said. "It will be quite pleasant when I shall be able to move about with more freedom again. I will not then feel so much as if I were a constant task on some one's hands, so almost perfectly useless."

"Please don't!" in a pleading manner the little woman spoke the words. "Can I not make you understand that you are not a task and burden? Had it not been for that almost fatal drive those long weary weeks of pain would have been spared you—"

"And in all probability I should have missed meeting the best of friends,—would have failed to find my one, my only sister. No! no! the little pain that I have endured does not so much matter, and if you can all have patience with me until my strength returns and I am once more myself I am sure I have every reason not to complain, for the good the last few weeks have brought me far outweighs everything they may have contained of unpleasantness."

Thus chattering in a friendly way Alice was endeavoring to array Cora in a pretty gown of soft, clinging, warm-hued material, but the fussy little woman was far too excited to be of any real use, and not until Imelda appeared, already dressed, was her toilet completed. With deft and ready fingers Imelda lent the needed assistance, then selecting some of the bright-hued flowers from a vase filled with the various blooms of mid-summer, and which was standing upon a small table near one of the open windows, she twined them in the dark chestnut coils, then fastening a bunch at the snowy throat and standing at a distance she measured her sister with a critical and admiring look.

"Now look at yourself. Do you think you would please a fastidious eye?" The vision that met her gaze as she turned to the mirror was a mixture of girlish sweetness and of serious womanly dignity. Returning health and strength were filling the fair form with a roundness and tingeing the serious, half-sad face with exquisite color. Cora gave more than a passing glance at the reflected full-length image, and while she looked the eyes of both fair women in attendance were watching her face, and presently they saw the lips quiver, the eyelids droop and the crystal drops force their way from under them and cling like liquid pearls to the dark lashes. Imelda's face bent over her sister's till it rested on the dark-crowned head. Instinctively she felt what the thoughts were that caused the tears to gather, but she had not one word to say. Cora's well hand went up to Imelda's face and her lips whispered,

"He whom my appearance would please is not here; so what does it matter?"

Imelda shook her head and forced a smile to her lips.

"Ah, but, little sister, it does matter. Don't you know that you are to meet someone else tonight that I wish so much to be pleased!" Playfully smiling she lifted the drooping face and looked into the tear-wet eyes. The questioning look in them suddenly gave way to one of understanding.

"I had forgotten that I was of some importance tonight. Yes, you are right. It does matter, and I do want to please."

Dinner was now announced and the trio descended to the dining room. Here Lawrence Westcot was awaiting them. Imelda had not seen him since the unpleasant meeting with Frank in the garden, and unexpectedly finding herself opposite the dark-eyed passionate man threatened momentarily to disconcert her. A flush mounted to her brow, then receded, leaving it marble white. But quickly regaining her self-possession she saw that no one had noticed anything amiss. Mr. Westcot came forward and in a few well chosen words expressed his pleasure at her return: next he acknowledged the introduction to Cora, for a moment closely studying her face. The dinner came off rather quietly to say nothing of the feeling of restraint felt by all. Alice seemed to have lost the fear that for so long had been a drawback to her full recovery, at least it was not now so apparent, but there was no confidence as yet established between herself and Mr. Westcot. They were more like strangers who found the task of getting acquainted a tedious and irksome one. Imelda, with the consciousness that the memories of the past brought her, felt great constraint, and it is not to be wondered at that Cora felt the influence thus brought to bear upon her, and felt quite uncomfortable. The ladies spoke in monosyllables, and although the efforts of Lawrence Westcot to produce something like a flow of conversation, to bring a feeling of harmony to the little company, were almost incessant they fell decidedly flat. So when the meal was brought to a close the feelings that were retained were anything but pleasant. Lawrence made his excuses almost instantly and withdrew, thus clearing the field and leaving the ladies to themselves. They were not slow in taking advantage of the fact that they were alone, and as the husband paced the veranda the voices of the chatting and laughing women came very clearly to his hearing. A bitter smile curved his lips. He felt that he was no longer welcome in his own home. Yet was any one to blame but himself? But what had he done, he asked himself, other than men were wont to do? Nothing! he felt sure. But an inward voice whispered,

"These women are not like other women. You have not understood them, but have taken it for granted that they were the same. When too late you recognized the fact, and all your efforts to set yourself right in your own home have been vain. Yet have these efforts been all they should have been? Have you in reality done all that could be done?"

He leaned against a pillar and gazed into the darkening shadows of the coming night while thought chased thought. Yes! he would make one more effort, for was not the life he was leading in his palatial home fast becoming unbearable? While he was dreaming with open eyes a queenly head appeared before him, crowned with a glorious wealth of dark hair. Passionately dark eyes emitted flashes of fire, scornful in their scintillations.

Passing his hand over his eyes with an impatient movement he heaved a weary sigh and in a tone that was almost a moan the words broke from his lips, "Why, O why is this all!"

Just then a step aroused him, and glancing up the friend of other days stood before him. Very seldom indeed had Norman Carlton favored Maplelawn with his presence in these later days. The harmony that had once existed there was broken, though he did not understand why, and in consequence remained away. Westcot had long ago recognized the injustice of the unmanly words he had in a fit of passion hurled at his wife, and if he had needed proof that he was wrong, Carlton's remaining away during the enforced absence of Imelda Ellwood and his sudden reappearance at the very moment of her return, ought to give him that proof. But to do him justice, he no longer needed it, and if he believed he had read correctly a secret page in her life he knew only too well who it was that had digressed farthest from the prescribed line. Norman would have passed him but he laid a detaining hand upon his arm.

"I understand the attraction," said Westcot, "but no harm will be done if you will give me a half hour first. We have been drifting apart, and I would not have it so. Something has gone out of my life, leaving it empty; and sometimes life itself seems a burden. Will you assist me to make a reparation?"

A look of surprise overspread the face of the young man. Then he hastened to say:

"Certainly I will. Have we not always been fast friends in the past? I have no desire to let a friendship of almost life-long standing die a death so sudden."

"Then come," said Westcot, and together they wended their way through the grounds, and were soon lost in the shadows. When they returned an hour had passed. Both faces were perhaps a shade paler, a shade more serious, but the old confidence has been restored. What overtures had been made, what words spoken will never perhaps be revealed, but firmly clasping hands Norman spoke:

"You have my advice!"

"And I will follow it!"

"Thank you! You have spoken like a man. Under the circumstances I think it is the only way that is open, and I am a poor judge of human nature in general, and of women in particular, if such proceeding as you now contemplate will not restore peace and confidence to the little circle under your roof."

With a last glance into the eyes of the other he dropped his hand and entered the room where the trio of women were trying to while away the hours that were to bring at least one fair girl's friend and lover. Just as he stepped across the low French window Imelda was running her fingers across the key board of the piano. Cora was standing by her side. Ere he had advanced more than a step a voice of singular sweetness arose and filled the room. In an instant more a second manly face appeared in the frame of the open window. All unconscious of her audience the girl gave full vent in song to the feelings that swelled her breast. The notes rose and fell and vibrated, until the very air seemed to be full of life and feeling. With bated breath the men stood and listened, forgetful of aught else but the rare sweet music of the young pathetic voice; a voice that possessed the power of carrying them away beyond themselves. The song was a translation from the German by Heine—the famous "Lorelei," a selection well calculated to try the strength and compass of the voice that attempts it. Its weird and melancholy pathos moved the inmost hearts of the listeners. As the last vibrant notes died away the sound of applauding hands fell upon the ear, and hastily turning the trio espied the two men standing just where they had entered. A blush overspread the face of the fair singer. It was the first time that other ears than those of Owen Hunter had listened to the magic sound of that voice when raised in song.

With a quick movement Imelda stepped forward and with outstretched hand greeted the new comer. By the heightened color of her face and the happy light that shone in the lustrous dark eyes Cora quickly judged who it was that so suddenly had stepped into their midst, and in a moment more was bowing in acknowledgement of the introduction which had followed. As she felt the searching glance the clear eyes bent upon her Cora again felt the tell-tale blood mount to her face, but with an effort overcoming the embarrassed feeling she openly returned the look. That which Norman Carlton saw within the depth of the hazel eyes must have been satisfactory for, extending his hand with a firm quick motion he said;

"I am"— —pleased, he was going to say but changed it to—"glad to meet Imelda's sister"—emphasizing the "sister." "I hope we may be friends."

"Thank you." Scarcely above a whisper, and with a fluttering breath, the words dropped from the slightly trembling lips, and one felt, rather than heard, the depths of feeling contained in the two little words. In that moment Cora knew that she had found another friend. His words were no idle phrase. Imelda also understood, and her heart gave a great bound. Did it not mean much? She took a step backward,—she wanted the two to become better acquainted. Would they have anything to say to each other? A little while she would leave them together. Turning to the side of Alice who was carelessly standing just a little beyond, plucking the scarlet blossoms of a geranium to pieces, while her glance traveled a little nervously to the man who was still standing by the open window. What did it all mean?

For weeks now Mr. Westcot had studiously avoided meeting his wife. His meals were either taken late or away from home, and the drawing room had not once known his presence in all that time. Was the old life about to be taken up again? The white teeth sank into the red lips and a tremor seized and shook her form. She raised her hand in search of a support. Imelda saw her reel, and with a quick movement caught her in her arms. But another had watched this little by-play, and a few strides brought Lawrence Westcot to the side of the woman he called his wife. Pouring a little ice water from the pitcher that was standing near by he held it to her lips.

"Drink," he said. Quietly obeying she drank a few swallows. Pushing a large easy chair forward in such position as would shield her face from the glaring light of the chandelier, he would have led her to it, but she evaded his hand and managed to reach it unaided. Bending over her he inquired the cause of her sudden indisposition. Nervously she answered:

"Nothing. It is nothing. I will be better in a moment. The coming home of the girls must have excited me. I thought I was stronger than I am." Was it an anxious look he bent upon her? He did not speak, however, and quietly withdrew.

CHAPTER XXXIV

Cora and Norman had not seen any of this by-play. He had taken her by the hand and led her to a tete-a-tete, and seating himself by her side soon had drawn her into conversation. A group of exotic plants was, by this movement, placed between themselves and the others, and as scarce a word had been spoken they were in ignorance of what had transpired. Lawrence Westcot now raised his eyes to Imelda who had stood during the scene without speaking. She read in that glance a request which he presently put into words.

"Will you favor me with a few moments of your presence?"

Once before he had asked of her that question, the memory of which sent the rich blood in hot waves over her neck and brow. What did it mean? The words she had uttered when in righteous indignation she had swept from his presence now came back to her:

"And until such time, do not dare to speak to me!"

Only once before had he "dared" to speak; that was when she so unexpectedly ran into his arms. Then it had not been of his seeking; but now? An anxious look gathered in the sweet brown eyes.

"Will you, please?" he asked.

The tone as well as the words were full of entreaty, so, silently she moved forward a step and bent her head in token of acquiescence. A glad light for a moment lit up his eyes, then stepping to Alice he said:

"You will excuse us? I will try and not keep her long."

A look of wonderment filled her eyes. When had Lawrence ever paid open attention to Imelda? Again the question arose in her mind, "What does, what can it all mean?" But she readily answered, "Certainly, I will excuse you. I shall do very well. I feel so much better now." With a low "Thank you," he turned from her to Imelda whose hand he took and placing it on his arm led her to the open window leading to the veranda, followed by the eyes of the surprised Alice.

Imelda understood, but only the quick indrawing of her breath gave token that the idea of going out into the open air under the starlit heavens had anything unpleasant in it for her. Slight as had been the sound and involuntary the action, Lawrence Westcot had taken note of it. His teeth sank into his lips but otherwise he gave no sign. Down the garden pathway to the fountain's edge whose silvery sparkling waters had witnessed so many and so very different scenes he led her, and then quietly dropped her hand. Stepping back a pace or two he folded his arms and confronted her. For a minute or more he did not speak, although his lips twitched nervously. Was he waiting for her to utter the first words? If so, he was doomed to disappointment for the proud lips did not open.

"Miss Ellwood!"

A slight uplifting of the head, that was all. Whatever he had to say, she would not help him one iota.

"Miss Ellwood, a man does not often find himself placed in a position quite so awkward as that in which I find myself this evening, in having asked you for this interview." He paused a moment ere he went on. "Some two months ago I spoke words to you that tonight I feel ashamed of. I approached you in a manner that was ungentlemanly—unmanly. For the feelings that had crept into my heart I make no excuse. I simply had no control over them. A hot, fierce desire and longing for something that was denied me; a confused comprehension of what that something was, made me unjust—and—cruel to the woman who is so unfortunate as to be my wife. Having through the merest chance overheard a conversation of yours and hers, thereby gathering something of your strange ideas and opinions, but utterly failing to comprehend them, I permitted the passion that had taken possession of me to have full sway. A woman who does not believe in marriage, what would you?

"In my insufferable conceit I supposed I had but to stretch out my covetous hand in order to satisfy the fire of my passion. I was rudely brought to my senses by the reproof of a pure mind and by the righteous scorn of insulted purity. In an instant, almost, I came to understand my mistake and would have given much to have been able to recall my words. But you had dealt my pride an ugly blow. It was not an easy matter to humble myself to the woman who had treated me to well merited scorn. I had hoped time would close the breach and that this painful scene would be spared me. Men of world are not wont to retract insulting words, especially when defeated in their object. But something besides wounded pride would not let me rest. There is something here," — touching his breast, "a painful aching void that makes life a mockery, a misery. The unmanly act of that evening is a burden which at times is almost unsupportable. Will you help me remove it? Will you say that you forgive?"

He had spoken in hasty, jerky, broken sentences. In a pleading manner he held out his hand to her. But the girl stood with downcast eyes and did not see it, and the hand fell nerveless to his side.

Slowly she raised the white lids. In the uncertain light of the starlit night he could not see into the depths of the dark eyes, but as he bent closer he thought they were dimmed, and that her voice was vibrating as she now in turn extended to him her hand and simply said:

"I forgive you."

Hastily the hand was grasped and bending over it with the same pleading accents in his voice he said:

"May I?"

"Yes," came in soft accents from the trembling lips. An indescribable sensation stole over her as she felt the pressure of the warm bearded lips upon her hand. A feeling of gladness filled her heart. She felt that the emotion displayed by this man was genuine, and that she knew she might safely trust him. She laid her other hand gently over his that was holding hers and softly spoke:

"It is enough, please. I feel that you have spoken the truth, in recognition of which I feel bound to pay you honor. Let me hereafter see on your face the light of self-contained manhood. I am more glad to be able to respect you, the father of my two precious charges. Now let us return. Alice was not feeling well and Cora may wonder." His only answer was to again kiss the hand that was still resting in his; then again placing it upon his arm together they retraced their steps to join their friends in the parlor.

As Imelda and Westcot re-entered the drawing room they found Cora and Norman so deeply interested in conversation that their entrance was not heeded. Cora's cheeks were glowing and her eyes shone like twin stars as the words flowed in a stream from her lips. Alice was sitting quiet and unobserved in the shadow of the aforementioned group of exotic plants, listening to every word that fell from the ruby lips. Cora spoke well. Norman had said but little, but that little to advantage. Adroitly asking a question here and making a remark there he had succeeded in drawing her out and was surprised to find how well informed she was on many subjects of which most young women have absolutely no understanding. Cora had studied to advantage; for with love to teach, it had not been so much a task as a pleasure. It was also a pleasure for her to converse with this refined and handsome gentleman. Until now Owen Hunter had been the only man of that type she had ever come in contact with. It had seemed to her that there was none other. But to her surprise and great pleasure she found that her sister's lover was in every respect the equal of the man who until now had stood out in her life alone.

Just as Imelda and Westcot were entering, the poets, both American and foreign, were being discussed, and Norman felt a little surprise when Cora said that Shelley and Byron were her favorites. In speaking of these he found her most familiar with Byron,—"Queen Mab" being the only production of Shelley's she had as yet read, while he could mention scarce any of Byron's works that she was not familiar with. When asked, which she liked best, she unhesitatingly replied, "Manfred."

"What! that gloomy pessimist, who continually takes you to the very depths of despair, and finally closed so tragically?"

"Yes. I like it because it portrays so truthfully and vividly the heartaches that so often lie hidden beneath the smiling exterior. It lifts the veil and shows the hidden woe. Oh, why must all nature be thus perverted? Why must all the grandest passions thus recoil upon themselves? The story makes me shudder as if I stood upon the brink of a chasm. It chills my very blood, but it has a weird, strange fascination for me. I always return to it and it has done much to stimulate my dormant brain to action. It has taught me a lesson in thought."

The re-entrance of Imelda and Lawrence at this juncture brought the conversation to an end. A hasty glance from Norman showed him that an understanding had been effected. A quick look passed between the two men and a feeling of gladness entered the heart of Norman, for the sake of all concerned. For a short time the conversation became general, then Cora was asked to once more sing for them. After a little hesitation she did so, and the strains of sweet "Annie Laurie" filled the room. No noisy applause greeted her when she had finished, but every head was bowed and some of the eyes were moist. The last lines had been sung with even more pathos than the first, but the fluttering, quavering sound indicated something more than pathos. Cora was fatiguing herself. In an instant Imelda recognized the fact and hastily arising said:

"Not another line. We have been forgetting that you have been ill, and are taxing you beyond your strength. Come, you must retire at once and I will attend you." But Cora shook the brown curly head.

"No! no! I shall not accept your service this evening. You will remain right here, while our friend here, I know, will assist me for this once. Am I right, Alice?"

"Most certainly. Right you are, and as we are two to one, Queen Imelda is overruled. So just consider yourself sent about your business while I shall tuck the covers about this little girl's form." Thus jesting and laughing Alice in triumph bore the tired Cora off to her own domain. At the same time Lawrence also discreetly withdrew. "To indulge in the solace of man," was what he said, to seek the companionship of a cigar; thus leaving the lovers alone. So many weeks had passed since an evening of undisturbed quiet had been theirs that now they had so much to say that the hours sped far into the night ere they finally separated. After Cora and Alice had bidden them good night and Lawrence had withdrawn, Imelda said:

"Look," struggling from his embrace, "what I have got! a long sweet letter from my Margaret, with one enclosed from Wilbur. She says she is getting along much better and faster with her studies than she had at first expected, and she now hopes that in the fall she may begin with her chosen work. Listen to what she says:"

"My Own Imelda!—To use the expression of gushing school girls, I am just dying to see you. Save my mother and Wilbur, I have no one to whom I can talk just what is in my mind. I have many radical friends here, in dear old Chicago, but none quite far enough advanced to admit them into the innermost recesses of my heart. It is so hard, so very hard, to replace a tried, a trusted friend. In all probability this very circumstance is not without its advantage as thereby I am better able to apply myself to my studies. During the evening hours I have an assistant and it would be natural to suppose that during those hours my studies would progress the most. But, strange to say, we continue to rehearse the same first act—somehow we cannot get beyond it—with some variation, it is true, but in reality the same. I expect after a while we shall surely be perfect. But of what the second contains I am at present not able to give you an idea. It is still a sealed book. To confess the truth however, I care but little, so long as the first act gives such exquisite pleasure, I am perfectly willing to let the second take care of itself. All the same my arms are in the best of trim to give you a good hugging—a regular bear-hug. Maybe I can impress you. If so, let me know.

"Do you know I almost envy you your present surroundings? You have so many to love now. No, I don't, either. That is not just the right thing to say. Rather, I am glad, O so glad, that you have found that wayward sisters of yours, that was. See, darling, how our doctrines have been verified in this case: that we are just what circumstances have made us. Who would have thought that the wilful Cora could be transformed into so noble a woman! But then you know love works wonders, and undoubtedly Owen Hunter must be one of nature's noblemen, else the love upon which he fed the starved heart which gave itself into his keeping could never have produced such wonderful results.

"Now, my Imelda, it will be yours to develop the germ which this man has implanted, and when they again meet—which I feel assured they will do—he will not find occasion to regret the enforced separation. And now, kiss for me that precious sister pair who so truly belong to us. When your letter came, telling us all about them, describing their persons and characters so minutely that we imagined that they were bodily transplanted into our very midst, Wilbur could not restrain himself. His eyes filled with tears— tears that with overflowing heart I kissed away.

"O my precious friend, will the time ever come when we shall realize some of our dreams, or will fear, like a dark pall, always keep our heaven, our paradise, enshrouded in darkness and gloom? When these thoughts come to me I am sad. But you know I do not approve of that. I shake it off; and indeed I have not much chance or time to indulge in gloomy thoughts, as hard work stands by and keeps my mind busy.

"Jesting aside, my rehearsing is not all play, and my teachers are more than satisfied with me. They have given me the best of hopes that I shall, in the coming fall, be able to fill an engagement of some note. They tell me my talent is remarkable and that I must succeed. Professor Morris has written to the managers of several first class companies and daily expects an answer. Now, my girl, please do not accuse me of what is vulgarly termed 'self-conceit,' but you cannot know what it means to me to be successful. I love the profession that my talents fit me for, only second to that other object that thrills my whole being. I love, O Imelda, how I love Wilbur, the king of my heart. I love humanity, the down-trodden, and I love the liberty to do and to dare whatever my heart desires. And among those desires by no means the least is my love of the stage, despite the stigma that clings to it. But where so great the stigma as that which has fastened itself to the term 'free love?' or, for that matter, to any other reform?

"Two days later: The answer has come. An engagement has been secured me and—Hurrah! Imelda. In a few more weeks I shall be off on the road to see how easy or how hard it is to win bread and fame. If everything continues as favorable as the beginning appears to be my success is already assured. The vacancy that I am to fill is that of a leading lady, and I know I must strain every effort to please. My mother scarce knows whether she is pleased or sorry. I am sure she is the best mother any girl ever had, and while she is ambitious for me—while she desires to see me successful, her heart cannot conquer all its foolish fears. She fears the men of the world, and the very fact that radical ideas have been nurtured in my mind may bring me danger. But she forgets it also has brought me a knowledge that I could not well have acquired otherwise. I have been taught by object lessons, and I have learned to read character. It will not be an easy matter to try to pass off on me the spurious for the real, the genuine. Wilbur I know trusts me more fully, and why should he not? Does he not know that he is, and always must be, the best love of my heart? Always? Well, until I find some one who has scaled the ladder of life to a grander manhood, to nobler heights, he certainly will stand first, and I know so well such men are rare. He is glad for my sake that I have found an opening, but sad when he remembers that it necessitates a separation. He does not want to show the latter feeling, as he fears to cast a shadow on my glad prospects, but then you know, love is quick to note when every cord is not tuned to harmony.

"As yet I do not know at all where our company will be booked, but I do hope that sometime during the coming season we may stop for a week in Harrisburg. Do you think such a possibility would contain anything pleasurable?

"And now—but no! I was going to tell you another piece of news, but that will be Wilbur's privilege, as he, too, wants to write a few lines. But I really must bring this to a close, or it might prove a task instead of a pleasure to read it. Kiss all those precious friends for me and say something nice to that one particular friend who is not a friend but something so much warmer, and soon, soon send an answer to your homesick, loving—"

Margaret.

Folding the closely written sheets Imelda looked up into Norman's eyes and said:

"Well, sweetheart, what have you to say to my Margaret?"

"That she is a precious, sweet girl, and a true woman. I hope that she may indeed be successful in her chosen profession. But what has our friend Wilbur to say?" Without further comment Imelda unfolded another document and began to read:

"My Precious Friend:—I wonder if, after all that our Margaret girl has written, I shall be able to find something more to say. I am sure she has told you all the news there was to tell and maybe if I should write too lover-like, someone would object. How is it? Do you think Norman Carlton would grudge me the kiss which I am craving and longing for? Methinks I read between the lines of the truly grand letters he has been writing us lately, a broadening, a widening out, that was not there at first. I believe him indeed to be a grand, noble nature, possessed of a high type of manhood. I am positive the germ is there, even if yet somewhat hidden and undeveloped, and it behooves you, my little girl, with womanly tact to develop it that he may yet stand in our foremost ranks, working for the universal good of humanity and for the special good of sister woman. I expect when we meet to take by the hand a brother worthy of the name.

"With his natural reverence for womanhood it seems to me it ought not to be a difficult task for him to understand the injustice, the unfairness, aye, the cruelty that is being dealt out to woman; to always doom her brain to slumber, to inactivity; to expect her to stand with idly folded hands, denying her the right to be her own judge pertaining to matters of womanhood; deeming her incapable of understanding her own affairs; dooming her always to submit quietly to what man may wish to impose upon her; using her as a pretty plaything with which to amuse himself in any manner man may see fit. O it is horrible to place woman, the creator, the builder of the race, on a plane so low, and I cannot think that Norman Carlton fails to see these things in their true light.

"It is wrong to seek to bind love in any way, and, try as we may, it cannot be done! Love, the spirit, will ever be free. 'Tis only the body, the house, the casket, that we can fetter and defile, and by that means it, the body, becomes but an empty casket, which will soon fall into decay when it has nothing to sustain it, while the little love-god goes wandering on and on mocking and laughing at our futile attempts to hold him fast.

"Then why should such attempts be made? Cherish him with tenderness, strive to stand high in his regard, strive to attain to a noble manhood and womanhood and he will forget his gypsy habits, his proneness to wander. Feed and nourish him with that of which he is most in need; develop for his especial benefit that in your own character and nature which commands respect and admiration, and you will find him willing to be held in his allegiance. You can do much to win him but you cannot hold him by force, because there is absolutely no holding him. It cannot be done, and it is wrong,—it is a sin and a shame, a crying shame, to attempt it.

"Ha! ha! On the old track again! Always the same; always preaching; but I cannot help it, my dear. It seems to have become my second nature. But now I have a piece of news for you. Margaret did not tell you all.

"When this fair lady-love of mine will have taken to walking her own way I know there will come many weary lonesome hours, for the coming winter, so we have been laying some plans how to make them less irks me. Maybe it is premature to say what these plans are, as much may happen to prevent the realization; but here they are:

"About the time you expect sleighing in your eastern city, I intend, in company with our fair Margaret's mother, to set out on a trip. Do you understand? My heart yearns for those precious sisters of mine, mere babes almost they were when I saw them last. I want to clasp them in my arms and kiss their lips, red with the wine of life; while Mrs. Leland, I know, will win a place in the heart of every one with whom she comes in contact. Yet I believe there is a particular reason that actuates her in making this trip. There is a secret yearning and longing that will not be quieted.

"By writing of the accident which reunited you with your sister you aroused her mother heart by bringing before her mind's eye her son Osmond. The hope to again call her boy her own is the mainspring of the desire to make this visit. How is it, little girl? Shall we be assured a welcome? But there! I ought not to have asked this last question. It was out of place, for of course we shall be welcome. But methinks it is time to close or I will have covered as much paper as Margaret has done, and it is not my desire to weary you. With the same cherishing love as of old, I am as ever

Wilbur Wallace."

Imelda folded these sheets also and laid them to the others, but Norman did not speak. With his head leaning on his hand he sat staring into vacancy, Imelda gently, tenderly took his head between her hands and bent it back so she could look into the clear blue orbs.

"And what does my Norman think of Wilbur now?"

"That he is right in every instance."

CHAPTER XXXV

The brown curly head was resting on the snowy pillow. The maimed arm had been tenderly cared for, and already the tired eyes were drooping. It had been such an exciting day. So many changes had taken place. Cora's heart had been stirred to its very depths and it was a relief to be at last alone. Alice was bending above her, and to bestow her a good night kiss upon the faintly smiling lips.

"Good night, dear one. I hope you may spend this first night within the walls of this home in restful sleep. I, too, am tired and wish to rest. If you should require anything, ring this bell, and I know Mary will instantly attend to your wants. The fact that you are Imelda's sister will alone insure you the entrance to her heart."

"O thank you! thank you ever so much. Everybody is so kind to me. I do not deserve it, I am sure."

"O yes, you do. How can you speak like that? And now once more, good night." Two pairs of warm clinging lips met in a loving kiss, then the form of Alice vanished, and Cora was alone. In but a few minutes sleep had closed the tired eyelids and happy dreams brought sweet smiles to the rosy lips.

Alice glided quickly through the silent hall until she reached her own cozy, comfortable room. It was in utter darkness, which fact, however, did not intimidate her in the least. At times she rather liked the darkness. It was then so pleasant to sit at the window star-gazing, and let her thoughts wander whithersoever they would. So she crossed the room to where a comfortable rocker was standing, and sinking into its depths with a weary sigh, she prepared herself for her favorite indulgence. Hastily undoing the fastenings of her dress she then clasped her hands above her head, gazing up into the starlit heavens, gently rocking back and forth in the darkness.

Suddenly she stopped and listened. It seemed to her there was someone else in the room. She could have sworn that the sound of heavy breathing had been borne to her ear, though now that she listened, everything was quiet. But the feeling of another's presence seemed conveyed to her in the air itself—she felt it. With a quick nervous movement she rose and walked across the room. She could feel her very lips grow cold, but with a strength and courage of which one would scarce have believed the little woman capable, she controlled every outward manifestation of fear, and securing a match she deliberately struck it and, mounting a chair, lit two jets ere she ventured a single look about her; then with a smothered, frightened cry she would have fallen had not the man, whom she had seen and recognized, caught her in his arms and prevented a mishap. Gently he lifted her down and reseated her in the rocker at the window. He, too, was pale, white to the very lips, as he saw the impression his presence made upon the pale little woman. He stepped back a few paces and waited for her to speak, and when no sound came he hesitatingly, in trembling accents, articulated her name.

"Alice!"

But her only answer was a frightened look. Holding both his hands to her in a supplicating manner, venturing a step nearer,

"Alice, am I never to be forgiven? Listen to me! If ever a man has been thinking—if ever it has come to a human heart, or understanding, that a great wrong has been committed, it has come to me. I know I have wronged you. I know I have acted like a brute! But I would, in some way or measure, make good the wrong I have done."

The hands of Alice were closely pressed upon her wildly beating heart. Her lips were twitching in a manner that caused Lawrence's heart to give a bound. In a moment he had forgotten that he was the supplicant. He knelt at her side and caught both her hands in his, pressing and chafing them.

"Alice! Alice! little girl. Don't look at me like that. You need not be afraid of me now, or ever again. I mean every word that I say. Come, trust me! It is the one boon I ask"—and he gently drew the excited little woman nearer to him, winding his arm about her as tenderly as of yore. Laying his face to hers, his lips touched the pretty pink ears.

"Little sister," he whispered, "can you, will you once more trust me?"

"Little sister?" Had she heard aright? What was the meaning the words conveyed? A hysterical sob broke from her lips, and as she permitted him to enfold her in his embrace, with an impulsive movement she placed her hands on either side of his face,

"Lawrence! Lawrence! do you mean it? You have not come to mock me?"

"I mean it, little girl, every word of it. Henceforth, you shall be my dearly cherished sister, with just the same liberty and privileges I would grant to her, were you really a sister and dearly loved as such."

A few moments she leaned back that she might the better look him in the eyes. Then she wound her arms about his neck and nestled her head close upon his breast and the words,

"I love you, Lawrence," thrilled him to his innermost being. He understood well the meaning of those words. He had called her sister, and he knew the love she gave him now was the same as every pure woman gives a dearly loved and cherished brother.

Once again a week had passed, and again merry laughter resounded through the rooms. Happy voices were heard blending in song while skillful fingers evoked sweet strains of music. But faces which were new within these rooms—though not new to us, were revealed in the bright light. Edith and Hilda Wallace had found their way into this enchanted circle tonight. Alice was seated at the piano. Her fingers lightly running over the keys, playing the accompaniment to Cora's rich sweet voice as it rose and fell in the cadence of sweet strains of song. The two were like a world unto themselves tonight, paying little attention to the others, each of whom was absorbed in giving attention to someone else. While Hilda actually seemed to fascinate Lawrence Westcot,—so absolutely was his attention riveted upon the sweet serious girl who possessed such a fund of knowledge that he thought he never had been so rarely entertained, Edith had taken Norman Carlton in tow, and by her serene and placid manner had so captivated him that for the past hour he had actually forgotten his queenly Imelda, who in her turn was talking just as seriously to a smooth-faced boy whose bright, intelligent countenance was a perfect mirror of the emotions that were being stirred within that young breast. Sometimes the blue eyes flashed, and with a quick peculiar motion of the hand he would toss back the fair hair from the white open brow; then he would ask question after question that, with never failing readiness, Imelda would answer.

"Wait right here," she said, "I will return in an instant,"—and in a very short time Imelda reappeared, carrying a small package in her hand. Before undoing it she laid her hand on his.

"I may call you Osmond, may I not?" The clear eye met hers in a responsive glance; in turn he laid his hand over hers and in a tone which had a hearty ring he replied:

"Certainly! It will afford me the greatest pleasure to have you do so."

Reseating herself in the chair she had a few moments ago vacated, with deft fingers that were slightly trembling, Imelda undid the cord that bound the package. The next moment Margaret's sweet face was brought to view. The boy's hand trembled as he reached for it, and in his face was reflected the emotions that were stirring his young soul. Imelda watched him closely, as for a long time his eyes were riveted on that fair reflection, and when with a fluttering long drawn sigh he laid it aside without comment, she also said nothing, but handed him a second portrait; this time the face reflected being that of Mrs. Leland.

It seemed almost Margaret over again, the resemblance was so great; only where time had touched it; the years having left their trace—but only lightly. The brow was just as smooth as that of the young girl, the eye as clear and sparkling; the hair dark and full. But there was a line about the expressive mouth,—an expression on the face that was not on the younger one, and which only experience could have stamped thereon. It seemed to the boy standing there, holding in his hand the picture of his mother, as if in the eyes gazing at him there was a pleading, yearning look that went straight to his young heart. His sensitive lip quivered and with another sigh he laid this picture also down. He kept his eyes downcast as if he dared not look into those searching dark orbs that were so eagerly fastened upon him. In a little while a woman's soft hand was laid upon his and— —

"Osmond,"—a pleading voice spoke,—"do either of those faces portray aught but purity? Do you think your mother" (laying her hand on the picture), "with a face like that, could be capable of anything but what is good and pure and noble?" His eyes were raised to hers, and they were dim with unshed tears.

"I don't know. But my brain seems reeling. When I look at the face of the girl you say is my sister a feeling comes to me as though I should be proud to proclaim her as such to the world; while she who is my mother seems to draw my very soul from me. Looking at them both a feeling overcomes me as if I had lost something to which I had a right, but which has been withheld from me. But when I recall all that which my father has told me of bygone years it seems as if they were handsome, glittering, fascinating serpents looking up at me, luring me from my allegiance." Imelda took both the boy's hands in hers.

"Look at me," she said. "In the first place, tell me—do you think I could be guilty of all the cruel, unholy things that have been reported of your mother?"

"Why, no! no! A thousand times no! It would be impossible. One look into your face, into your eyes, would convince me of that."

"Thank you! but do you think, my young friend, that I could hold one near and dear who is so vile as you have been taught to believe your mother to have been? Now listen: I do not want you to take my word for all that I have told you of these my best friends. Only wait, come here often. Here you can become acquainted with the sentiments that fill your mother's whole heart and soul, and which find a reflection in every word uttered by your fair young sister. You seem, despite all the prejudices with which your young life has been poisoned, to yet have remained pure in heart. You are brave and truthful. Now from this time forth in justice to your mother, study your father; his modes of life; his sentiments; his every action, and compare it to that which he has told you of the woman who, being the mother of his children, ought to be shielded and protected by him from every breath of scandal; instead of which protection he has blazoned such awful tales about her that it takes almost superhuman courage and bravery on her part to live them down. So I ask you again, in justice to the woman who is your mother, will you henceforth keep your eyes open?"

A dark wave of color swept over Osmond's face, then with outstretched hand, he said:

"I promise you that I will!"

This conversation closed, the pictures carefully laid away, their attention was called to the other occupants of the room. The first words that greeted their ears fell from the lips of Hilda. They listened.

"You speak of the prevailing spirit, of too little charity of man to fellowman," said Hilda, "and again of single instances where charitable deeds rise to the heights of grandeur, only regretting that they are too few, too rare to be of any real value to humanity. Aye! they are indeed too rare; but I do not believe in charity. I do not like her. I have no room for her. Does she ever draw near to the side of justice? Is her garb not rather a cloak wherewith to hide all the abounding and heartless cruelty which seizes and retains the lion's share of the product of all the weary hours of toil that produce the wealth wherewith these deeds of charity are done?

"But that is only one kind of charity. That charity which is supposed to overlook, to condone, and even to justify what society treats as faults and sins—O, how I hate it! For while charity pretends to do all this, in reality it condemns every idea, every thought, every action that is not in strict conformity with the prevailing standards and customs of artificial society. Charity enchains liberty; it blindfolds and fetters justice. No! a thousand times no! I scorn charity, no matter in what garb she may seek to approach."

Hilda's dark gray eyes shone with a lustrous light as she finished her animated speech. Imelda thought she had never seen her so attractive.

"Bravo, little girl," she exclaimed, "your words ought to inspire brave hearts to noble deeds."

Hilda blushed as she replied,

"O no, I do not aspire to so great honor; but at times I feel I must give way to my feelings. They oppress me so."

"Will you permit me to ask a question?" It was Lawrence who spoke.

"A dozen if you wish."

"Then tell me what would you put in place of charity which you so discard? You cannot but acknowledge that there is great need of a helping hand."

"Thank you, Mr. Westcot. Had you tried for a week you could not have asked a question that would afford me greater pleasure to answer. 'What would I substitute for charity?' Why, Justice! Justice every time. Where Justice reigns there can be no place for charity. She will not be needed. She will have lost her vocation. Let justice be done to the great masses, to the struggling individual, and where would there be occasion to call for the assistance, the services, of the haughty dame with her mock humility? None whatever! Where plenty and peace have found a home there will be no occasion to air her gaudy plumage. And in a short time her very name will have assumed a strange sound. Aye, it would be forgotten from little usage; would become extinct, obsolete. Once pushed into the background she would quietly step down and out and be heard of no more."

"And," added Edith, "with the advent of justice and the exit of charity another thing would become extinct, and that is power—the power of money. When justice is done, the toiler, the producer, receiving the full value or equivalent of his labor, it would be impossible that a few favored idlers should grow fat—in wealth and ease, while the masses starve. No more strikes, no more robbery, no more bloodshed. Peace, happiness, prosperity—would not that be an ideal world?"

Here the refrain was taken up by Imelda.

"No strikes, no robbery, no bloodshed! Do we properly consider the full import of these words? We hurl the curse of baseness, of low and brutal instincts, we charge the birth of vice, crime, hatred and what not, all upon those who toil and produce. If in a measure it is true that the very air surrounding this class of humanity is often pregnant with all the elements that breed a state of things so depraved, is it to be wondered at? Let us take into consideration what the women of the despised classes are called upon to pass through. Let us ask the why and wherefore. When hunger and starvation stares her in the face; when the demon drink has entered her home; when the husband and father is thrown out of work through no fault of his; when the monster monopoly has shed precious blood, and made her home desolate—what then, think you, breeds in the heart of woman?

Her every thought, her every breath, must of necessity be freighted with—murder! Then the little helpless unborn, the human embryon, that is being gestated and fed with such nourishment—must not a race of murderers, of criminals of every description, be the product of such creative conditions?

"When mothers are free to choose the fathers of their babes; when they can have just the conditions their hearts long for; when they can be free from care and anxiety; when every woman has learned the science of becoming a perfect mother; when every mother understands the fearful responsibility of becoming such; when every father is filled with a sense of the high honor that has been conferred upon him in being chosen to be such; when, in consequence, he recognizes the duties he owes to woman and her offspring, and when, in every act of his life he seeks to aid her in perfecting the coming being; then, and not till then, may we expect peace and joy and happiness. And to bring about such a state of things justice must be done."

Strange words these, that fell for the first time, upon the ear of young Osmond Leland. He heard thoughts expressed that struck him as grand, lofty, sublime, but—but—did they not savor of—well, the insane? Was there any sense in dreaming of such impossibilities? As each of these young ladies in turn had spoken they had appeared to him as though surrounded with a halo, such a sublime light had shone in their eyes. But again, it seemed, to him, as if their reasoning was devoid of reason, and his mind reverted to the discarded figure of charity. He could conceive of no other way to reach the suffering masses. Until now he had scarcely thought of it. But now? What sort of women were these that could express themselves thus? What was it Imelda had said?

"Wait, and come often. Here you can become acquainted with the sentiments that fill your mother's heart and soul, and that find reflection in every word uttered by your sister."

He could not comprehend the reasoning of these young women, but the air surrounding them seemed so truly holy and pure; such as had never been his fate to come in contact with. And his mother and sister?—Were they as these? Had he much to forgive his father for? He felt dazed. Was this also a case where gross injustice had been done?

"But how, young ladies, would you make all your grand ideas practicable?" asked Lawrence.

"By proclaiming liberty," answered Hilda. "Liberty will insure justice, and justice liberty. The two combined will make truth possible. To be truthful is to be natural, and nature is pure, nature is chaste. Only think what it all would mean to be free! We hear the cant of freedom, of liberty, of a 'free country,' all around us, when in reality it is all a miserable sham!

Every word must be guarded, every action fettered. We must eat, drink, sleep, walk and talk all according to a prescribed fashion; must bow to fashion, to custom. We may not even welcome a child to our arms when we desire it, unless we have first allowed shackles to be placed upon our freedom; unless we have first bartered our womanhood for motherhood—often turning what should be a priceless boon to a most bitter curse."

Hilda's eyes were sparkling with brilliant flashes, but the eyes of Cora, who with Alice had drawn near, were downcast, and on the dark lashes clung two pearly drops. Music and song had ceased; the two performers, Alice and Cora, had for some time been listening to the soulful words that were being spoken. The sweet lips of the agitated girl were quivering as with pain, her hands tightly clasped as she repeated, "turning the precious boon so often into a bitter curse." Turning to Hilda and kneeling at her feet Cora laid her face upon her knee.

"Is the curse never to be lifted?"

"Yes! When woman is ready to be blessed; when she has learned to keep herself pure; when the sacred temple of her body no longer is invaded by the curse of lust; when man no longer dares to intrude, to force his unwelcome attentions upon her, but patiently bides his time at a respectful distance."

"You speak of the 'millennium,' of the perfection of the race. Must our lives be one long sacrifice to secure that end?" Hilda shook her head as with both hands she lifted the tear-wet face.

"I hope not! Whilst we all have a work to perform in the meantime, I believe we may yet be able, in our own lives, to so far lift ourselves out of and above all the pains that make life such a weary round of toil, as to be able to enjoy just a little in advance, of what the coming future will bring the now enslaved race. When we are brave enough, when we are strong enough to live as our inmost convictions tell us is right and true and pure, we may then hope for a little happiness, or perhaps a great happiness, just as we make ourselves ready to receive and appreciate it. And I feel so sure, so sure that here, just right here around us, a band is forming, true and staunch, that by its unity will enable us yet to realize what now seem but dreams!"

"You are speaking of that ideal home of yours?"

"Yes! If only—if only—I could once see the way clear as to where the means are to come from. Money! 'Filthy lucre,' as it is called, I fear is the rock that will upset our plans." But now Cora's eyes were shining.

"Money, money," she murmured. "I think I know who would furnish it—only, will he not spurn me now after I have disappointed him so, and brought the bitter pain to his heart? O, will he believe that it was all for love of him and not for myself that I seemingly flung aside the priceless treasure of his love?"

"If it is really that; if his love is a priceless treasure, he but awaits the call and you will find him at your side."

"And she," murmured Cora "whom the law gives to him and him to her,—she will never willingly give him freedom."

"Wait and you will see!" came the assuring answer. "Somehow I feel that all will be as we desire."

CHAPTER XXXVI

Neither of the men could quite understand the last words that passed between the girls, but Norman understood enough to know that whatever might be their meaning no ignoble subject would be thus discussed. Lawrence Westcot shook his head, but trusted. He was beginning to find these girls very trustworthy. Only Osmond felt as if standing upon some unseen brink. Hilda's enthusiastic words and manner had not been clear to him. He had caught the words but not their full import, and yet—what was it she had been saying about womanhood being sacrificed, of being "bartered"? Had she meant that marriage necessitated such sacrifice? But surely, surely she had not meant that a child could be welcome without the marriage blessing—a child outside the sacred fold of wedlock? In a dazed manner his hand went up to his head. "Here you can become acquainted with the sentiments that fill your mother's heart and soul, and find a reflection in every word uttered by your sister." As with a red hot iron the words seemed burned into his very soul. These his mother's sentiments? This his sister's religion? His eyes rested upon the faces of the girls; a sweet purity was reflected upon each while Hilda appeared surrounded with a halo. Some strong impulse drew him closer to them; he felt uplifted, borne upward, floating in cloudy mists—a feeling of widening, expanding, filled his being until the words of Hilda again came surging in his ears, "we may not even welcome a child to our arms when we desire it unless we have first permitted our freedom to be shackled, made a barter of our womanhood for motherhood, thereby turning the precious boon into a bitter curse." Blank horror made his blood run cold; he felt as if an icy hand was clutching at his throat.

"What is it—are you not feeling well?" Imelda asked the question and Edith's soft warm hands gently pushed him into the nearest chair, handing him a drink of ice water. She understood perfectly well what it was that ailed him, and feared they might have repelled him so much that he would not again seek their presence. So with her ready woman's tact she led the conversation to other subjects. Music and art, the beautiful in general, were discussed, and finally a request was made that Cora should sing again ere they parted for the night. She surprised them by singing a hymn. But all understood there was a meaning underlying the usual import of the words, "We shall know each other better when the mists have rolled away."

It was with very mixed feelings that the good nights were spoken, and as Hilda's hand for a moment lay in Westcot's a look from his dark eyes flashed into hers, a look that sent the warm blood in a glow to her face, flooding it to the very roots of her hair. Accompanied by the two young men, Norman and Osmond, the sisters were rapidly driven home, the pressing invitation "to come again," still ringing in the boy's ears; and when at the door of the home of this sister pair Hilda also held out her hand to Osmond asking him to call there. After a moment's hesitation he placed his hand in hers and promised.

Days and weeks had again sped on, each day bringing its own events and lessons. The summer's sunshine had changed to the glow of autumn, and just as marked had been the changes with many of our friends. More firm had become the bond of friendship and love that bound them together, more clearly defined—because more clear the ideas, the ideals that formed the central attraction around which love and friendship clustered; day by day they understood each other better, and also themselves better, and their lives became purer, higher, nobler.

But still they were waiting, waiting. They recognized that their work was not yet done, but pulses beat higher, eyes shone brighter, smiles more radiant, as they were learning the old, old story over again. At least several of our charming circle were being blessed with that experience. Lawrence Westcot's heart was once more drinking in the lessons of love, and his nature was broadening and expanding under its influence, while Hilda seemed almost glorified, as she moved about, soft snatches of song dropping from her lips. Edith was almost as happy, sunning herself in the reflection of her sister's new-found love. Alice also saw and was happy. The old child-like merriment had returned and the rooms resounded with merry jests and silvery, tinkling laughter.

One evening when Alice had surprised Norman in the gloaming she had not been able to resist the longing, yearning spirit. Creeping up behind him her little snowflake hands had closed his eyes. Ere he had caught the meaning of it a pair of warm dewy lips had been pressed to his. Then she would have fled, but quick as lightning her hands were made prisoners and, despite the desperate struggles of the furiously blushing little woman, she was drawn into the circle of light where Norman in a most wicked manner enjoyed her dire confusion. But presently drawing her to him and enfolding her in his arms he whispered:

"Now for revenge!" The drooping moustache brushed her face and for a little while Alice felt herself smothered; so sweet, so clinging, so really in earnest were the kisses which were pressed upon her lips, and when a few minutes later she came flying into the presence of Imelda, who had both the little girls standing at her knees trying to teach them some object lesson, the young instructress looked up in some surprise at the disheveled figure. The fair hair was tossed and its owner was pressing both hands to her flaming cheeks. Ere Imelda could frame the question that was trembling upon her lips Alice had sank beside her on her knees and hid her face in her lap.

"Don't say a word," she whispered, "until you have heard what I have to say," and drawing the dark head down so that she could place the rosy lips to her ear, she hurriedly whispered a few sentences and then drew back to watch the effect. Imelda's face betrayed nothing; she only placed her arm about her friend's neck and for a few moments laid her face upon the fluffy hair, then after kissing her repeatedly she said, with a sweet smile:

"I believe it is about time that these little folks receive their evening meal and then to bed. So, for a little while I must be excused."

An hour later as Imelda was standing in the embrasure of a window, a manly head bent above her; an arm tenderly drew her head to be pillowed on his breast while the whispered words, "My own, my best beloved," caused her own heart to beat in answering throbs and a sigh of sweet content parted her lips.

Only Edith, in those days of pure happiness, wore a look in the dark eyes that portrayed a something hidden in their fathomless depths, a far-away dreamy look that spoke of hopes not yet realized. Sometimes when no eye was looking a suspicious moisture would gather in the dark wells and for a while would dim their glorious luster, but not for long. Where there was so much warmth of heart and joyousness of spirit it was not possible that one whose life had been so practical would cast a shadow upon the bright faces around her.

There was yet one other whose happiness consisted in dreaming of the future and waiting hopefully and patiently what it might possibly bring, and that other was Cora. But not in idleness was she waiting. He should not have reason to think that she had wasted precious time; so she had studied on. Not only studied but already she was using her talents to advantage. As soon as she was strong enough she had insisted on doing something to be self-supporting, and through the aid of her friends she had been successful in obtaining quite a class of music pupils, foremost among whom was Meta who gave promise of future wonders. One hour in the early morning, however, found her with another pupil, and that pupil was Imelda. Much as she desired it Imelda had not hitherto found the time and opportunity to apply herself to this study, for which she possessed a talent that surpassed even that of Cora, whose music had settled in her throat rather than at the ends of her fingers. More than once Cora had said:

"Not long till you must have a more competent teacher." Thus the sisters daily grew more close together with an appreciation of sisterly love in their hearts such as is rarely known by those who have been cuddled in the lap of fortune since their infancy.

But there was still another—another growing daily in light, in breadth and in intelligence. Osmond Leland had returned again, and yet again, to the charmed circle and was, as it were, born into a new life. And as, day by day, he better understood the sweet purity of these girls, so also did the events in connection with his old life stand out in glaring contrast. To his sorrow and dismay he found, upon close investigation, that his father's life was neither pure nor truthful. Contrasted with the pure nature-love and poetic beauty displayed in every word spoken by these new friends the coarse and lewd jests indulged in by his father and his companions could not fail of effect. It was but a short time until he felt his soul revolt at their ribaldry. More and more he felt himself attracted and, still more often he found himself seeking the society of the coterie of fair girls who each in turn imparted their ideals and dreams to the susceptible young heart, so eloquently that it went out to each and all in answering throes, and at the same time there was born in that heart a secret yearning and longing for the mother and sister who were as strangers to him. Often when he sought the Westcot home at an earlier hour in the day he had the, to him, rare pleasure of a romp with Alice's baby daughters. Norma would clap her chubby hands and scream with delight, while Meta's dark eyes would glow and sparkle. But while Norma, with all a baby's delight of pulling her victim's hair would soon tire, and was content to cuddle up in his lap where she would often fall asleep, Meta would softly steal up behind and take possession of him in a more gentle manner. Her soft little fingers had a peculiarly tender touch as she patted his cheek and toyed with his hair, arranging the blond curls into a mass of ringlets. She would thus keep her fingers busy for an hour or more, and never seemed to tire. The dark eyes would have the same glad sparkle at the end as at the beginning, and Osmond seemed to enjoy the performance as well as the little ones. On several occasions he had stretched himself out upon the carpet when the serious bright-eyed sprite would lift the fair head and pillow it in her lap and while toying with his hair would put him to sleep. This would afford her extreme pleasure. She would not permit anyone so much as to whisper while she guarded his slumber.

The young mother and her girl friends watched the play with amusement and pleasure. Was there already a spark of the future woman in the little child's heart?

Thus the autumn with its gorgeous colors had come and gone. Chilly days and raw wet nights were now in order, but the glowing fires in the grates added to the cheerfulness of the rooms and the closely drawn curtains closed out all that was unpleasant and dismal. Then came the icy frosts and the first snow and with it a letter from Wilbur announcing the long promised visit to himself and Mrs. Leland. Edith and Hilda were almost wild with joy and anticipation. At last! at last! this so long, so sorely missed brother coming home to his own, to clasp them in his arms, and they counted the days and hours until he should be in their midst. But theirs were not the only hearts that beat high at the contemplation of the coming event. Imelda was scarcely less excited than were the sisters. With a tender cadence the name "Wilbur" lingered upon her lips, but not for him alone did her heart beat with joy. Mrs. Leland received no small share—her bonny Margaret's mother. And yet another heart beat with a strange flutter in anticipation. Osmond, when told of his mother's expected visit, had turned white to the very lips. Faint and trembling he had sunk into a chair, and for the remainder of the evening had been unusually quiet and absent-minded.

"What is it? Not pleased, Osmond?" The boy looked up into Imelda's eyes and she saw that his own eyes were filled with tears.

"Do you know, do you realize what this meeting may mean to me? My heart is going out in advance to the woman who is my mother. I know I shall love her. I know that I shall find her all that my mind has pictured. I know that I shall find in her eyes a new life; in her eyes and arms, such as I have never known. But what else will it mean for me? Great as has been the fall of respect for the man who is my father, when I contrast his life and teachings with what I have here been taught,—yet for all that he is my father! That fact remains. The forming of new and purer ties means the sundering of some old ones, and although I can only win thereby an untold amount of good, the fact still remains that it hurts."

Imelda's hand gently passed over the clusters of fair curls as she said,

"I can but honor you for an emotion that is the surest proof of a heart good and undefiled. I feel certain that if you will follow its dictates you will soon be able to judge whether it was affection for you which caused your father to pierce your mother's inmost soul by depriving her of the child she had nourished with her heart's blood. Can you think of more refined cruelty than to rob a mother of the babe that has lain for months beneath her heart, and that, with the most excruciating pain and with great peril to her own life, has been born into the world? Do you think a father's affection can excel, or even equal, the love of a mother? Then think of the years of hungry yearning that have filled that gentle soul." —

The boy had not answered, but throughout the evening had remained quiet, lost in thought. But after that, day by day a restlessness had come over him scarcely permitting him to remain any length of time in one place. More glaring became the father's coarseness as with a critical eye the boy followed his movements—his actions and his words. Often he found himself remonstrating with him. At first these remonstrances had elicited blank surprise, then he had been rudely laughed at and taunted that he must have fallen in love with some Sunday school Miss.

"That's all right," Mr. Leland had said. "Couldn't help being sweet on the little creatures myself. In fact am so occasionally yet, but not to the extent that it is going to interfere with any enjoyment in life. Don't be foolish, boy. Kiss the pretty soft lips and tell her pretty nothings to satisfy her; that need not prevent you from doing just as you please; and by no means, let me tell you, will it affect me. Girls are pretty playthings that help to while away the time, but the man is a fool who permits one of them to affect him more seriously. I have had a dose of it which I have no desire to have repeated."

Fearing a tirade against a certain woman who all unconsciously had grown into his affection he swallowed his disgust and left his father to himself. Judging his mother by those other women whose "sentiments" were the same as hers he came to wonder how it had come about that she could have linked her fate with that of his father. He reproached himself for entertaining such thoughts, but yet was unable to banish them. And so it came that often and still more often Osmond found his way to the Westcot home. Sometimes he would also wend his way to the home of the Wallaces, but as the sisters had no control there outside their own sanctum it was not quite so homelike and harmonious, not quite so natural and free. More often he would stop at their door only a few minutes to leave it a little later with both sisters under his care. Thus it was that time went by and the change, the most important event in young Leland's life, came nearer.— —

All day long the soft, fluffy masses had been falling, noiseless, incessant, covering hill and plain, and enveloping the world, as it were in one vast winding sheet. The merry sleigh bells were tinkling, but it was more work than pleasure to be out in the soft yielding masses of fresh fallen snow. The hearts of the young beat with glad anticipation of coming pleasures, but older and wiser heads took it not so lightly. They looked more seriously at the mass of whirling fluffy flakes as they came piling down faster and even faster until you could see scarce a half dozen feet before you, while anxiety crept into many a heart. And not without cause. Already every train was late, and there was much fear of trains being snow-bound. In the evening, when in spite of unpleasant weather our friends gathered at the Westcots' they wore very serious faces indeed. According to the dispatch they had received, informing them on what train the dear expected ones would leave Chicago, they would be due in Harrisburg the following morning at ten o'clock. If they had started at the time intended they would in all likelihood be detained many hours. If they were fortunate enough to lie over in some city there would be no harm done, but on the trackless prairies it would be far from pleasant at the best. There was no music and singing that night. Too much anxiety for merry-making, and at a much earlier hour than usual they again dispersed. Edith and Hilda's hearts were heavy as they kissed their girl friends good night. So long, O so long they had hoped and longed and waited for this brother to come, and now—Surely, surely their fondest hopes would not be thus rudely shattered. With a mighty effort the tears were forced back and bravely they clung to cheering hope. Just as they were about to descend the stone steps leading from the front of the building, two strong arms wound themselves about Hilda's form and lifting her bodily carried her safely to the waiting cutter. Warmly and snugly she was tucked in by loving hands and just for one moment a pair of mustached lips touched hers, then the words were whispered in her ear: "Courage little girl! be brave and strong. Tomorrow evening someone else will be claiming kisses from these sweet lips. Our precious ones will surely come."

It was the first time Lawrence had put his love into words and action, and the trembling lips of the blushing maiden thanked him for the sweet cheering words.

Norman had performed the same office for Edith. To save her feet from damp and cold he also had carried her down to the waiting cutter and tucked her in beside Hilda. Then taking his seat beside Osmond, another hasty good night, and soon the tinkling of the bells were lost in the distance.

Osmond was quiet; he had been quiet all the evening. Scarce a word had dropped from his lips. It is very doubtful indeed if the girls felt more keenly than he the danger threatening the travelers. The tension on his nerves drove him almost mad. He dare not give expression to his fear. It meant so much, so much—this coming of his mother. If she should perish! With a sudden clicking sound he clinched his teeth while the horror of the thought caused him to close his eyes. Would he then be able to say, "It was all for the best"?

The dismal drive came to an end. The girls were safely seen inside their home. Osmond was next deposited at the door of his father's dwelling and shortly after Norman also was housed within the four walls of his room. When the morning broke the snow was still falling with a likelihood that there would be no change very soon. The trees were bending and breaking under their load and only with the greatest difficulty could either man or beast move about. Trains which had been due the day before could not be heard from, owing to the fact that in many places the telegraphic wires had been broken. Evening again came, but as yet no news from the expected train whereon our travelers were supposed to be.

About noon the fall of snow had ceased: a change of temperature had set in; gradually it had been growing colder until at midnight of the following night the cold had reached an intensity which was almost unbearable. This added greatly to the horror of the possible situation of the travelers, and our friends were in a fever of anxiety. With blanched faces they moved about in their respective homes scarcely able to endure the dreary hours of waiting.

Again the night passed and another intensely cold day was ushered in, and not until noon did any news reach them. A message was wired from Pittsburg that the train had been snow-bound in Ohio. Rescue trains had been sent and in all probability if nothing farther occurred to cause another delay, the train would reach Harrisburg by Thursday evening where it had been due Monday morning.

Impatience must be curbed. Another night and day must pass ere they could hope to fold their loved ones to their bosoms. But tedious as the hours had moved, the day was at last nearing its close, only a few more hours and then?—Just as the clocks were striking the hour of nine the puffing monster came steaming into the city with its load of human freight.

CHAPTER XXXVII

Heaving bosoms, concealing madly beating hearts, were hidden under the heavy fur-lined wrappings. In the excitement and bustle of the jostling throng our waiting friends greatly feared missing the travelers in the murky light, but just as the train was again pulling out, Imelda espied a lady and two gentlemen who seemed hopelessly seeking someone judging from their hurried glances. Quickly walking up, that she might the better look at their closely muffled figures, she was recognized by the lady traveler, and,

"Imelda!" broke from her lips as she stepped forward and folded the girlish form in her arms, kissing her again and again.

"Dearest Mamma Leland!"—and the kisses were returned with interest. When released it was to be again enfolded in a pair of stronger arms—this time a perfect bear's hug. Then followed hasty introductions. Several more embraces, wordless, but nevertheless speaking volumes, and then Norman spoke:

"Save the caresses for an hour later; they will keep, I am sure. This weather is not at all inviting, so pile into the waiting sleighs; that we may go where a welcome is prepared for you."

"One moment,"—It was Wilbur's strong pleasant voice. "I make bold to bring you a fellow traveler who has been of great value to us. Mr. Paul Arthurs, I think deserves a better fate than to be left to the tender mercies of a cheerless hotel on a night like this." These words were followed by a hearty invitation and welcome. At first Mr. Arthurs protested against intruding so summarily on perfect strangers, but was shortly overruled, and a few minutes later the sleighs were flying over the smooth surface of the already beaten track, and in a very short time the piercing night air was exchanged for that of the warm rooms at the Westcot mansion. Willing, friendly hands were assisting each of the travelers to warmth and comfort. Mrs. Leland was supplied a soft warm robe, a loose wrapper from Imelda's wardrobe. As there was no possibility of procuring their trunks before morning, dry hose and fur-lined slippers were provided for the weary nether limbs. After a refreshing bath Imelda's deft fingers neatly and tastefully arranged the tired woman's hair. Then telling her that she looked ever so much better than a half hour previous, she escorted her to the parlor to find that the men had just preceded them. Both the gentlemen guests had been supplied from Mr. Westcot's wardrobe, and they looked fresh and bright enough to give the impression that they were there for an ordinary social call. Wilbur's eyes lit up with a bright gleam as Imelda entered. Without a moment's hesitation he held out both hands and drawing her close, held her face where the full light of the chandelier overhead fell upon it—for a minute drinking in the full glow of her beauty, watching the rich color come and go in the fair cheeks. Then taking the sweet proud face in both his hands he kissed the ruddy lips, once, twice, thrice.

"Now," he said, "I want to look at someone in the——daylight I almost said; 'tis the gaslight, I mean, which is almost as bright."

Norman was standing near, leaning with his elbow on the piano, watching the scene before him with a warm light in his eyes. Understanding well who Wilbur's "someone" was, he stepped forward and extended his hand with a pleasant, happy smile lighting up the handsome manly countenance. For a few moments the black and blue eyes met, each reading in the depths of the other's soul; each satisfied with what he saw and read there. It was a moment, "When kindred spirits met," when "soul touched soul." As they stood there, man to man, hand clasped in hand, each knew and felt that he had found a friend worthy of the name, and when a woman's soft hand was laid on theirs, as if in blessing, it was Norman's lips that touched the woman's hand, but Wilbur's dark face was laid close to hers, and as their lips met the whispered words fell upon her ear:

"Imelda, gem of women, in this precious brother you have found a jewel worthy of the finest setting. You have been a sweet and successful teacher."

With the pure love-light in two pairs of eyes reflected in her heart she turned to leave them together. Little gushing Alice was just getting through making Mrs. Leland welcome when the eyes of the latter fell upon a sweet face, lit up by a pair of dreamy hazel eyes. Something in the face struck her as familiar, but she was unable to place it. The girl saw and understood and was in the act of moving forward when Imelda caught the look on Mrs. Leland's face. In a moment more she stood at Cora's side, laying her face to hers she said:

"Do you understand?"

"I do," Mrs. Leland replied. "It is your sister." Here again after a few moment's conversation Imelda had the satisfaction of knowing that two hearts, both dear to her, would meet and love.

In glancing about she espied Edith deep in conversation with the stranger, the traveling companion of Mrs. Leland and Wilbur. He was holding her hand in a close clasp and looking into the dark eyes in a way wholly surprising in a stranger on such short acquaintance. The color was coming and going in the sweet face and her eyes had in them most plainly an answering warmth. He certainly was a very handsome man; one that any woman would be apt to turn and look at again when meeting him in a ballroom or on the street. Fair, with a light curling beard and a free open countenance; tall and well proportioned he was a picture of manly beauty. Edith looking up and, seeing her friend's perplexed and wondering gaze, smiled and beckoned,

"You are surprised, I see, at our seeming unwarranted familiarity, but do you remember the day when Cora made her first appearance downstairs after the accident, and we were weaving such golden plans for our future? Well you also remember that Hilda spoke of a gentleman we had met in one of our summer vacations in the mountains? I see you do remember. I had thought the friendship of Mr. Arthurs was to be only a pleasant memory when lo and behold I recognize him in this traveling companion of our loved ones, and to make the surprise more complete, Harrisburg was his destination, as he was coming here on matters of business and intended remaining in the city for sometime."

Imelda expressed her delight in finding in him a friend of her friends, and was about to move on when Mr. Arthurs asked for Hilda. That maiden was discovered serenely smiling and rosily blushing while listening to some, from all appearance, highly interesting tale of Lawrence Westcot's. Edith forthwith drew her new-found friend in the direction of the two.

With a happy smile upon her face, reflecting the sunshine of her heart in her eyes, Imelda was flying from group to group when they suddenly rested upon the sad face of a boy whose form was half hidden in the heavy curtain of a deep bay window to which he had withdrawn himself. In a moment she saw it all. The boy had requested not to be introduced to his mother at the depot. He would wait a more favorable opportunity.

"It would only excite her," he said, "and be very unsatisfactory."

His request had been granted, but in the excitement that followed he had momentarily been forgotten. Not dreaming that her son might be among this group of bright intelligent people Mrs. Leland was giving her every thought to winsome Cora whose heart was being drawn out to meet hers in glad response.

Imelda crossed the room to where Osmond stood. His eyes filled with tears as she approached,

"Why so sad, my boy? Cheer up! Do you think you are now ready to look into your mother's eyes?"

"My mother! how strange the words sound; but I am afraid!"

"'Afraid!' Afraid of what?"

"Of the disappointment that may possibly fill them when they rest on me. It would hurt if there should be but a momentary reflection therein."

Imelda's gentle hand lifted the chin of the boy that was drooping in a dejected manner,

"Those words that speak of the fear of a disappointment show that you have not known a mother's heart. Come now and have this fear cast out," — and taking the trembling boy by the hand she drew him from his hiding place and approached with him the woman to whom he owed his being. Laying one arm about his neck Imelda drew his face to hers, with her other hand she touched Mrs. Leland's arm to draw her attention.

"See! Mamma Leland. Who is this I bring you?"

It was a moment of intense expectation. Mrs. Leland quickly turned, and for a moment stared—then gave a quick gasp. That face! Just for a moment she had thought it was Margaret, so great was the resemblance, but only a moment. His look was strange and yet not strange. From his face she glanced to that of Imelda, and back again to the boy. She rose from her chair pressing both hands to her madly beating heart. Her face became deathly white. Slowly the boy's hands were extended towards her—an agonized pleading look lay in the large blue eyes.

"Mother!" broke from the pallid lips.

"Osmond!" echoed the mother, and then she folded her long lost child, her darling boy! in close embrace near to her wildly beating heart.

For a moment Mrs. Leland felt faint and dizzy, then her pent-up feeling found vent in a flood of tears, with which were mingled those of Osmond. The tension on his nerves had been too great, but both strove hard to conquer their emotions, and for some time they sat in a wordless embrace, reading what they felt in each others eyes. Tenderly her trembling hand smoothed the sunny locks and the pearly drops again gathered in her eyes as she thought how her baby had been permitted to grow and develop, until he stood upon the brink of manhood without the guidance of her hand. His boyhood's years—they had come and gone without bringing her mother's heart the privilege of watching over the tender soul's moulding. O, to have been with him! to share his joys and to soften and smooth his childish troubles.

But now? Why dwell upon the past with its many bitternesses and trials? Did not the present moment outweigh all the sufferings? all the dark hours of woe? Her boy was still her own, with a soul pure and true. Should she not rather be thankful? With an overflowing heart she drew the boy's face down to hers, giving vent to all the pent-up feelings that were causing her heart to heave and her lips to seek a loving, clinging mother's kiss. Imelda's eyes filled with tears; without another word she gently touched Cora's arm and together they withdrew, leaving the two to enjoy their new-found happiness.

Imelda drew her sister in the direction of the piano, where Norman and Wilbur were still standing, welding the friendship that was to last throughout all the years of their after-life. With a little dextrous movement the girls managed to reach the instrument without attracting the notice of the men and only when Cora's rich, sweet voice filled the room with joyous song did they become aware of their close proximity.

Every voice was hushed, every word suspended while she sang. Who was this girl, possessed of such a glorious voice? When the music ceased and the song ended Cora turned and faced her audience. Wilbur was struck with the rare beauty of the face, coupled with a strange sense of familiarity. Imelda smiled, as she caught the puzzled look upon his face,

"It is Cora, Wilbur." That was their introduction—just as a matter of course—feeling they would need no other. But Wilbur was not satisfied, and begged that Cora would sing again; and she, nothing loath, did sing again. It was the first time this week she had sung—with the anxiety for the possible fate of the absent ones she had had no heart to sing. But tonight she felt happy; so why should she not? Turning over the pile of music her eye fell upon "The Wandering Refugee." The music was sweet, if the words were sad; and as the sad, sweet strains filled the room their influence was felt by everyone present, toning down the exciting joy that filled every heart. Just as the last notes died away a rasping noise was heard at the window. Glancing up they became aware of a white face being pressed against the large pane. Only a momentary appearance, and almost in an instant it was gone. But in that instant both girls had seen it and—had they recognized it? Both pairs of lips breathed the prayer—"I hope not!"

Such a wretched looking, such a deathly white face! Imelda quickly moved over to the window, but no sign was to be seen of a human being. Had they been mistaken? Was it only a chimera of the brain, conjured up by the sad, weird words of the song? Heaving a deep sigh she turned away, shaking her head to the enquiring sister. No one else had seen the face at the window.

At this juncture Alice claimed her right as hostess, and insisted that all should direct their steps to the dining room, there to partake of a warm repast which had been prepared for the hungry travelers. Around the table another hour passed by in pleasant conversation in which many a treasure of mind was unfolded, and where bright eyes sent electric sparks back and forth—sparks that were ever ready to kindle love's fire wherever they might happen to alight, until at length, breaking in upon the running conversation Westcot said,

"Will not someone be kind enough to relate the experiences and dangers of the late journey?"

Wilbur laughed.

"I suspect they are greatly magnified—in your imagination greater far than in reality. Snow-bound we were; that is true enough; not a pleasant experience, I grant you. By the storm-king we were forced to remain in one spot, consumed more or less with anxiety and by impatience to move onward. The change to bitter cold caused us some suffering, but being well supplied with wraps and blankets its keenest edge was blunted. Perhaps the greatest danger that menaced us was the lack of provisions, but that also was warded off.

It was night when our train was brought to a standstill, and when the morning dawned we saw only a vast unbroken field of snow, spread out before our eyes. The outlook was far from cheerful. Not having thought of such an emergency we had supplied ourselves with no provisions whatever, and the probability was that we would become acquainted with empty stomachs before reaching our journey's end.

"Just opposite us across the aisle our friend here, Mr. Arthurs, had taken his seat and, as misery loves company, it was not long ere he made our acquaintance. Pardon me, Arthurs," laughed Wilbur, "I did not mean that you were so very miserable but that we were all so miserably situated that your kind heart prompted you to lighten our misery by coming closer to us. Well, as the day wore on we all became uncomfortably conscious that there were appetites waiting to be appeased. The supply carried by the train was not a large one and the steward was asking shameful prices. Mr. Arthurs made the proposition that we make an attempt at exploration, to see if there were no human habitations near. At first Mrs. Leland would not listen to such a thing, fearing we might get lost, but her fears were overruled and we made preparation for a tramp through the deep and softly yielding snow.

Following the base of a hill, near which our train had stopped, we walked about a mile when in the distance we discovered quite a village. It seemed an endless tramp but at length we managed to get there and make our needs known. The villagers proved to be a rough but kindly disposed people and, combining business and humanitarianism, some hours later they brought to the cold and hungry travelers a supply of hot coffee and sandwiches at reasonable prices. This removed the deadly fear of starvation, and although the temperature was very, very cold our situation was endurable. Towards evening of the second day rescue trains arrived. The snow had been cleared from the tracks by the persistent labor of many men who had worked night and day with their shovels, and soon we were once more speeding on our way rejoicing.

"By this time our new friend had proved himself a friend indeed, and having made the discovery that his destination was the same as ours we invited him to make one of our party. And to judge from present appearances he is not at all sorry for having accepted the invitation."

Every eye turned in the direction of Mr. Arthurs, at whose side Edith had found a seat. So deeply was he interested, just then, in something Edith was saying that neither had heard the closing remarks of Wilbur, but at the sudden hush both looked up to find all eyes resting upon them in smiles. A flush mantled their faces, but, joining in the laugh at their expense the matter was quickly disposed of, and now, having satisfied their hunger Norman said he thought it time they were seeking their respective homes, the night being far advanced, and rest being much needed. Both Wilbur and Mr. Arthurs spoke of going to a hotel, which proposition was most strenuously objected to by the Westcots who insisted that they make their home with them during their stay in the city.

But to this neither of the young men would listen; for this one night, however, they did not refuse to accept the kindly proffered hospitality. Tomorrow they would make other arrangements. Hasty preparations were then made for the departure of the others, and Mrs. Leland's heart contracted painfully at the thought of letting her boy go from her, even for one night. But chiding her selfishness she gave him a good night kiss. As Norman opened the door, the outer vestibule door and was passing down the stone steps he suddenly stopped. Across the lower step a dark object was lying which proved to be the cold and stiffened form of a man.

CHAPTER XXXVIII

Norman's cry of alarm soon brought the others to his side. To the question, "What shall be done with him?" Alice replied,

"Bring him in immediately."

So the inanimate form was lifted and carried inside, not to the heated rooms but to one where the fire had gone out, leaving it cold and chill. Imelda and Cora stood with clasped hands, a frightened look in their eyes; looking at each other, expecting what they dared not think or breathe aloud.

The body of the unfortunate man had been carried past them without either having caught a glimpse even of the white face, leaving them in cruel uncertainty as to the identity of its owner. Norman spoke of procuring a doctor when Paul Arthurs spoke:

"With the kind permission of all present I offer my service, as I am a physician." This was news, and under the circumstances a very agreeable surprise. The offer was most gladly accepted. Requesting Wilbur and Norman to lend their assistance Doctor Arthurs began the work of trying to resuscitate the seeming dead body, and for two long hours the three worked hard and faithfully. When they had about given up all hope of recalling the fleeting spark the discovery was made that the blood was beginning to circulate while faintly perceptible respiration gave hope of returning consciousness. After a thorough cleansing the body was wrapped in a soft, warm blanket and put to bed. The chances now were that a life had been saved, but—to what end?

The young physician had made a sad discovery, one which indicated that the patient was at best the victim of an incurable disease. He who lay before them unconscious of his condition, was but a boy in years but already a physical wreck, through the indulgence of a most pernicious sexual habit. Hollow eyes and sunken cheeks told the sad tale. The drawn white face was encircled by clusters of dark, curling hair; in health he evidently had been a handsome lad. Now his appearance was anything but prepossessing.

"There we see the result of ignorance on the part of some one," spoke up the young physician. "The ignorance of parents in regard to the meaning of childhood, or the ignorance of a boy who did not know, or understand, the meaning of life, and the right uses of life-giving organs and forces."

Neither of the young men had a word to say, but stood with eyes riveted on the ghastly face. Why did that face seem so strangely familiar? and while they looked this strange feeling grew. Like a flash a revelation came to both and their eyes met in a sympathetic glance. Norman became white to the very lips. In Wilbur's eyes was a troubled look, as he met the glance of the other, but across that motionless form he extended his hand to the other who without a moment's hesitation placed his own therein. It was like a compact, this involuntary action, and in that silent clasp there was something conveyed that told to each that they had drawn a step nearer to each other; that in the future they would stand still closer as friends. Wilbur turned to the young physician, pointing to the prostrate form,

"We have made a discovery!"

"And which is— —"

"That this unfortunate young man is Frank Ellwood!"

"Frank Ellwood? Who is he?"

"The brother of the sisters, Imelda and Cora Ellwood."

"Ah!" The word was long drawn and hesitating. Paul Arthurs did not as yet understand; so, briefly as possible, Wilbur related just enough to enable him to grasp the situation.

The young doctor's face became sad and overcast. O, why is this young life blighted? Why should this burden be laid upon those young shoulders? But he felt it would not be for long. Disease, with its fatal clutch, had fastened upon the vitals of the young man, and it was only a question of a very short time until the fell destroyer would claim the victim for his own.

When an hour later, with returning consciousness Frank opened his eyes it was to find two fair faces bending over him, faces wherein only love and compassion were to be seen. While Imelda gently brushed the dark hair from the pale face Cora took his hand and laid her face upon it. In his weakness he saw but did not understand. As if their presence brought him peace and comfort he again closed his eyes and soon the regular breathing told that he was in the land of dreams. Gently, lovingly, the sisters nursed the erring brother back to life, with never a word of reproach for the wasted past. They understood only too well their task would be of but short duration, and when the paroxysms of coughing shook the weakened frame it was all they could do to stay the tears that would well up in their eyes.

But soon the time came when he asked to have their joint presence explained, and it was Cora who told him all—all the bitter struggles and experiences of both their lives; of the heavy overhanging clouds, but which clouds were now beginning to show their silver lining.

Frank made no comment. He seemed broken in spirit as well as in body. The once strong and healthy young athlete seemed now only to desire rest and quiet, and when the glad spring time came with its new life and budding joys, its sunshine and song, they folded the waxen hands upon the pulseless breast, decked his coffin with the first sweet flowers of spring and laid the emaciated body away from sight.

Poor boy! Wayward and reckless from his childhood up he had plunged headlong into all the vices that lure passionate youth from virtue's path, and yet—had he sinned more than he had been sinned against? If he had erred, if he had gone wrong, surely he had paid the forfeit. It was a heavy price, that of his young life, and it ill becomes us to sit in judgment upon him. Lawrence and Alice had insisted that he remain an inmate of their home, and a bright sunny room had been placed at his disposal, where he remained until the end.

In the meantime much of interest had transpired, ere the dawn of that sad spring morning. On that memorable night that had brought so much of joy, and also so much of pain—the finding of the long lost brother—our friends had separated as they had at first intended doing, with the difference that those departing had remained a few hours longer at the Westcots than they had expected. With the feeling of uncertainty as to the fate of the frozen man none experienced a desire to leave until the news came that he would recover temporarily at least; and when the suspicions of the sisters had proved to be correct—that the unfortunate stranger was indeed their brother, so long dead to them—then, as the hour was very late, whispering words of hope the good nights were at last spoken. The Wallace sisters with Osmond and Norman as escorts were rapidly driven to their home; Edith's hand had been held just a little longer and closer by the young physician than would seem to have been necessary, and Mrs. Leland had held her boy very close as though the separation about to take place was for an unknown period of time, instead of only one short night,—but finally they were whirled away over the freezing snow, and in due time deposited each at their respective doors.

Mr. Wallace did not often inquire into the doings of his daughters. Long since he gave over the attempt to control their actions, feeling that they could well be trusted. On this occasion, however, the hour had been so unusually late when they had come home that he could not refrain from asking where they had spent the evening, or rather night, as was in the "wee sma' hours" that they had sought their room. A moment Edith hesitated, then,

"At the Westcot's—they are entertaining visitors from Chicago, the belated trains causing us also to be late."

Edith again hesitated before answering. Should she tell the truth? It was extremely distasteful to this pure-minded girl to speak a falsehood. She felt she could not possibly keep the fact a secret that her brother was in the city. The sisters exchanged a quick apprehensive glance, then endeavoring to appear calm as possible Edith said:

"The interest might possibly be greater than you think, and you will perhaps agree with me when I tell you that one of them bears the name of Wilbur Wallace."

Mr. Wallace, who was just partaking of his morning meal, arrested midway the cup which he was about placing to his lips and stared at his daughter as if he had not heard aright.

"Who? What is that you say?"

"Wilbur Wallace," repeated Edith with slightly trembling voice. Slowly the cup that was poised in mid air was again replaced upon the table.

"Do you mean to say that it is your brother to whom you refer?"

A slight inclining motion of the head was Edith's only answer. She almost feared to look at her father, and when she did so she found the strong man had turned deathly pale; his lips twitching nervously, and presently with a gasping sound came from his lips:

"Wilbur! Wilbur!" and his head sank upon his hand, in which attitude he remained a long while, then slowly, without again speaking, he rose, donned overcoat and muffler and went out into the crisp, wintry, morning air. His manner was a mystery. The girls looked at each other and shook their heads.

In the evening when they again met at the family table he looked more like himself but was strangely quiet, not at all like the Elmer Wallace who was wont to carry himself with an air of such importance and assurance. Even his wife took note of the matter and inquired as to the reason, but received no answer for her pains.

Several days thus passed by. Regularly each evening after supper a span of horses with a dashing cutter drove up to the door; a youthful driver would spring therefrom and would carefully tuck the waiting girls therein and drive away, returning always a little before midnight. Then there was a change. Beside the boyish figure a more manly one had taken its place.

Tall and well built, every movement of that form betokened health and strength. At such times the face of another and older man could be seen at the window, watching the figure of the younger man as he sprang to meet the girls. Eagerly he listened to catch the sound of the voice speaking words of greeting to the sisters, watched him tuck the robes closely about them, heard his deep-toned laughter mingle with their silvery ripples, and in a few seconds more they would disappear. Long hours would intervene, but when the tinkling bells announced their return, as though it had been watching for their advent, the face at the window was always there, until the good nights were spoken and the merry music of the bells was lost in the distance.

But Mr. Wallace never asked for his son; though deep down in his heart a longing was making itself manifest. Now that he knew that his first born was once more near him in the same city, to look into his eyes, to clasp him to his bosom, to have a share in his life, was a desire that was daily growing upon him. Yet he could not bring himself to sue for it. Day by day the longing grew stronger until it became almost unbearable. This longing was the more strongly felt when he glanced at his younger children, the result of his second marriage. All of them, the whole four, had not been sent, this season, to boarding school, as they were not at all well, and they had made life anything but pleasant for the rest of the household. The eldest boy, Homer, the father had hoped would soon have been ready to graduate, but the lad showed an unaccountable aversion towards his books. He was surly, sullen and irritable, with a languor of manner that caused the parents to fear that he might be breeding some fever. The others were no better. Elmer was hollow-eyed and nervous. The girls, Hattie and Aleda, were fretful and hysterical to a degree that made life a misery to those about them.

The parents were anxious and fearful, pampering them in mistaken kindness, thereby making perfect tyrants of them all. Only Edith and Hilda would not submit to the whimsical demands of the younger children, and when Mrs. Wallace complained and lamented about the ill health of her darlings Edith would reply:

"Insist on it that they all take exercises every day—exercise of a nature that will tax their strength, and ere long you will see a change."

"Yes, I am sure there would be a change. You certainly are the most heartless girl I have ever met. Compel my sick children to work? I believe it would please you if they should die, for that is what such a course would result in, I am sure."

Mr. Wallace would look at them, then at the bright and cheerful faces of his eldest daughters. Then he would remember the face and figure of the stalwart young man whose movements he had of late been watching from the window and would wonder how it was that the children of the delicate Erna should be healthy and robust while these younger children, whose mother was apparently so strong and healthy, should be so delicate, apparently candidates for early graves. More than ever he longed to be reconciled to his first born. But his stubborn will would not bend. Had Wilbur come to him he would have welcomed him with open arms, but that he should go to Wilbur his iron will and stubborn pride would not permit. So he stifled the voice of his heart, only he could not cast out the longing therein, and day by day he grew more restless, dissatisfied and irritable while the state of affairs at home grew daily more unpleasant.

One day, it was clear and frosty, Mr. Wallace was on his way home to dinner, walking along at a brisk pace. Part of his way lay along the railway track, when at a short distance ahead of him he saw a boyish figure in which he recognized his son Homer. The boy was walking at a very slow pace with downcast eyes seemingly forgetful of his surroundings when the rumbling of the wheels of an approaching train was heard. The boy however, paid no heed. Mr. Wallace gave a cry of warning but the boy was so lost in thought that he never heard. The train was approaching at an alarming rate of speed.

"Homer! Homer!" the distracted father cried, but unconcerned the boy walked on. Mr. Wallace started on a run but despaired of reaching him. He repeated his warning cry when suddenly the boy tripped and stumbled, almost fell—recalling him to himself, but the nearness of the approaching train, the certainty of impending fate seemed to stun him and he stood stock still, with white set face, awaiting the coming shock. Mr. Wallace calling again, "Homer! Homer! quick, aside," covered his eyes with his hand so as not to witness the dread disaster.

The next moment the train went speeding by, sending the icy chills through his veins. Dreading to look up, expecting to see only the mangled remains of his child Mr. Wallace with white lips and blanched face, opened his eyes to see a stalwart, manly figure, a face encircled by clustering dark locks, lit up by piercing black eyes, and in his arms holding the half-fainting form of Homer.

The revulsion of feeling was so great that the strong man reeled, and when he saw and recognized who it was that had been the savior of his boy a film gathered over his eyes. He staggered as he made his way to where the stranger stood, still clasping the careless boy in his arms. Both hands were outstretched to clasp those of the rescuer but the stiff lips refused to articulate the words he would have spoken.

Hilda's Home | 213

By this time Homer had recovered himself sufficiently to free himself from the firm clasp, and to say,

"All right, old man! No need of being so scared. I have not gone to 'kingdom come'—not just yet."

But not on the boy were the eyes of Mr. Wallace riveted. As if fascinated they hung upon that other young face while his own was working strangely.

"I presume you are the father of this young man?" spoke a clear, full-toned, manly voice.

"Wilbur!" came in husky, broken accents from the pallid lips of Mr. Wallace. "Wilbur, do you not know me?"—in a hesitating, supplicating manner, extending both hands to the young man.

Wilbur started and changed color, retreating a step and bending a searching glance upon the elder man. "You are——my——"

"Father!" interrupted Mr. Wallace. "Yes, I am your father, and the boy whose life you have just saved is your brother."

The boy gave vent to a long drawn whistle,—

"Say, Gov'nor! this is news. Where did you manage to have him stowed away all this time?"

The face of Mr. Wallace flushed darkly red.

"Homer, I am ashamed of you. You would please me much by being a little less ill-bred." Then turning again to Wilbur and again extending his hand,

"Will you permit the past to be forgotten? Must I ask in vain that my boy, my first born, will lay his hand in mine?"

The husky pleading of the voice touched Wilbur. After a few moment's hesitation in which the past seemed to confront him,—in which he seemed to hear the splashing of the icy waters of the Susquehanna river as they closed over the head of the hazel-eyed little mother, so many years ago—a shudder passed through his frame; then his eyes fell upon the boy, almost a young man, but with a sullen look on the otherwise fair face, thereby marring its beauty—the disrespectful manner towards his father, showing an equally marred character. Then his eyes turned to the face of the father who had so long been a stranger to him, and what they saw there again touched his better nature. No! it certainly was not the face of a happy man. There were lines in it that the flight of years alone had not traced. It looked careworn and worried. Slowly, involuntarily his hand was raised and laid in the outstretched palm whose fingers closed about it almost like a vice.

Several moments passed ere Mr. Wallace had controlled himself sufficiently to speak, then hurriedly, anxiously, —

"You will go with me? I want you at home."

Wilbur shook his head, but his father only held his hand the faster.

"I will take no refusal. For once I am going to give Edith and Hilda a pleasant surprise. Come, Homer, we will not keep them waiting at home for us any longer." Without answering the boy turned his steps homeward, while Mr. Wallace drew Wilbur's arm through his.

"You will come I know, and the girls will be happy."

Half reluctantly and wholly longingly he permitted himself to be led away and almost ere he knew he found himself standing at the door of the well known house before which of late he had so often stood.

CHAPTER XXXIX

Edith gave a gasp when she saw the noble form of her brother enter the door at her father's side; but she welcomed him by laying her white round arm about his neck and kissing him. Hilda stood for a moment looking from one to another in a bewildered manner, then a bright light almost transfigured her face. Gliding to her father's side she surprised that individual by winding her arms about his neck and pressing her fresh dewy lips to his. Then laying her cheek to his whispered:

"I thank you from the bottom of my heart."

What was it that arose in his throat and dimmed his eye? When had a sweet woman's kiss been pressed upon his lips before. He laid a trembling hand upon the back of a chair to steady himself while his eyes followed the hazel-eyed girl—so like the Erna of long ago. For just one moment it had seemed to him that it had been she who whispered that "Thank you." That it had been her cheek resting against his. A sigh escaped his lips as he thought of how short duration had been their happiness. Why had it been so short? Even now he could not understand; but he felt a glow of satisfaction, such as he had not known in many a long year, as he watched the group of three. For the first time a feeling of conscious pride swelled in his heart at the thought that they were his children. Mrs. Wallace, when she entered the room in her sweeping robes was not exactly delighted when the guest of the evening was introduced to her, but had enough of good grace to tender him a kindly welcome when she heard of the service he had rendered her own son. Besides this splendid young giant commanded her respect whether she would or not. She always did admire handsome men, and Wilbur was decidedly handsome. So once more—what he believed would never again be possible—Wilbur found himself sitting at his father's table, partaking of his bread, of his hospitality, and felt conscious that he was doing right; knew that his idolized sisters sanctioned it. Both were extremely happy and, conscious of that happiness, Wilbur felt as if inspired, and talked as he had never before talked. His sisters were proud of him and his father was surprised and astounded at the store of knowledge he possessed, at the ideas that had possession of his active brain, and a new light dawned upon his mind.

It was, he now began to see, this brother who had been the teacher of the sisters, developing them into the splendid independent women that they were. Even Mrs. Wallace became interested, although most of that which he said was as so much Greek to her. It was of so foreign a nature to her. She found more to disagree with than agree to, yet she found herself listening to every word. Stranger than all, Homer was aroused; his senses were alert. Where had he ever heard such doctrines propounded before? Certainly not in such a strain. Yet he had heard them, and with his mates of the boarding school had jeered and laughed and scoffed at what they termed "would-be-reformers." Now he began to see how much superior were these thoughts when compared with the useless studies with which his head had been crammed, and with the teachings of the dime novels which he and his mates had devoured—inflaming their passions and leading to the formation of vile habits.

While Wilbur was speaking he had been watching the flushing and paling face of the boy. A suspicion of what made him languid and nervous and sullen forced itself upon his mind and he forthwith made up his mind to take the lad in hand. He also observed that none of the other children possessed a healthy color, but with this one he was, for the moment, most interested. He remained all the afternoon, partaking again of the evening meal, thereby causing him to draw still nearer to the slumbering heart and senses of Homer; at the same time winning his way into the hearts of all the others. So when after supper as usual a double-seated cutter drawn by a span of fiery horses came dashing to the door, Wilbur surprised that young gentleman by inviting him to join them.

"It will do him good," he said, glancing at his father.

Thus Homer made the acquaintance of this circle which was to influence all his after-life. As soon as an opportunity offered Wilbur drew young Arthurs aside and had a prolonged conversation with him, their eyes frequently resting on the pale face of the boy. Presently Mrs. Leland was also drawn into the conversation and when it ended all understood what was expected of them.

Mrs. Leland drew near the boy who was a stranger in their midst, and in a pleasant motherly fashion began to talk to him, gradually drawing him out, finding much intelligence stored away in the youthful mind but which had all been going to waste for the want of a guiding hand and skillful touch to turn it into proper channels. Edith and Hilda watched while a feeling of joy filled their hearts. Was there really something more than self-will, indolence and haughty overbearing in the nature of the boy, hidden beneath that repellant exterior? Presently it was Imelda's turn to exert her gentle influence on him in her bright, animated manner, and when Cora's voice filled the large room with a burst of song he felt as if lost in a new world. The two sisters knew he was taken care of, and in their turn devoted themselves to the invalid. Poor Frank! They had the satisfaction of seeing his face light up and the color come and go in the wan cheeks. He had learned to love the circle which nightly met here, where naught but love seemed to reign, while Mrs. Leland was almost worshipped by him. Was ever mother so kind to erring boy before? If his own mother—but here he stopped. She too had been erring, suffering. She belonged to his wasted past. She had been an over-indulgent mother to him, in spite of her fretfulness and peevishness, and at this late day he felt that it would be wrong for him to throw a stone upon her grave. While Hilda toyed with his white hand Edith was standing at the back of his chair, smoothing back the clustering locks from his brow. A sense of peace and quiet came over him, such as he had not known in the olden days. Now and then a much meaning look passed between the young physician and the elder sister, calling forth a warmer hue to the fair cheek. Hilda enjoyed the same kind of by-play with Lawrence, to whom it seemed impossible to gain more than a few moments at a time at her side, while Mrs. Leland was more successful with her boy lover. When the good nights had been spoken and our party was whirling homeward, Homer was very quiet, He was deeply impressed with all he had seen and heard, and his thoughts were busy.

Next morning, earlier far than had been Homer's habit to rise, two strong, young figures appeared at the door asking admittance, and sending the merry tinkle of the bell through the rooms. Wilbur and Osmond, ready for a hunting trip, had come to take Homer with them. The boy was tired from being out so late the evening before, and at first was not at all inclined to join them. It seemed he could not muster enough of will force to face the crisp morning air, while Mrs. Wallace objected with all her strength, being positively sure that her darling would take cold because he was not at all strong. But Wilbur carried his point. A half hour later, warmly clad and well equipped for their day of sport they set out, being soon joined by Dr. Arthurs, Norman and Westcot, they formed quite a party of hunters. As they started away from the Westcot home a pair of dark eyes, watching them from the window of the invalid, grew dim and a pair of lips quivered in helpless longing. But fair woman's hands took him in tow and made it so pleasant and entertaining that he forgot the manly sports the others were following.

The hunters were out long hours. Up hills and down valleys, through woods and meadows, across rocks and frozen brooks they went. Warming to the excitement of the sport, which sent the blood bounding through his veins Homer forgot he was weak and tired. The reaction set in, however, and when they returned he slept long hours, but when the evening came he was ready and anxious to go to the home of the Westcots.

Next morning another excursion had been planned and again they carried Homer with them. This time they managed to take Elmer also, in spite of the protests of the anxious mother who saw certain death in store for her pampered darlings—tramping about these rough mornings through the snow; and when she saw them return so tired they almost fell asleep on their feet she felt more anxious than ever. Soon, however, a change made itself manifest. They were less fretful and discontented. Their eyes were brighter, a more healthy color tinged their cheeks, while they ate with an apparent appetite.

Paul Arthurs now frequently called at the house. He also prescribed a new course for the younger children. He forbade sweetmeats, spices and condiments. A simple diet of bread, milk and grain foods, fruits and nuts, he told the mother, was far more wholesome than the meats and highly seasoned food they had hitherto been accustomed to.

"Give them a daily bath, then rub them until a warm glow shows itself; then plenty of outdoor exercise. The cold will not hurt them, but rather benefit them. Let them go coasting, skating and snowballing until they are tired out, so tired that they scarce can keep on their feet, and my word for it, Madame, if you follow this course, you will soon have the satisfaction of seeing the glow of health in the faces of your children. They need no medicine. They are suffering from a nervous debility that only exercise in the open air and wholesome simple food will correct. I look to you," turning to Edith, "to see that these directions are carried out. You understand, I am sure?"

Edith as well as Hilda did understand. The young doctor as well as the girls did not dare to tell Mrs. Wallace the true reason of the delicate state of health of all her children—that the seeds thereof had been sown in the abominable boarding schools she would have considered highly improbable. At however slight intimation of the real cause she would have been liable, in her passion, to turn them all from the house and thus her children would have been robbed of the only chance of regaining their health. So they wisely kept the secret they had penetrated and insisted on a course of treatment that these pampered darlings thought extremely cruel. But soon the effect was apparent, and there was hope that the morbid cravings might be destroyed, and a strong and pure manhood and womanhood be secured to them in the future.

So it was that a new life entered this house, and in a manner scarcely noticeable. A better footing was established between the stepmother and the daughters. There was more peace and quiet. Once in a while the order was reversed and the circle would gather in the Wallace home, but not often. There were many reasons why it should not be the same. The visitors were made welcome, it is true, but the entertainers must at all times be guarded in their speech. They could not be quite themselves; and then Frank never gathered enough strength to bear the fatigue of the drive back and forth in the cold night air. One or the other would remain at home with him, as in spite of his protests his sisters and friends would not consent to leave him alone.

Mr. Wallace had tried hard to induce Wilbur to take up his abode in his house during his stay in the city, but in this the son was obdurate. He had buried and consigned to oblivion much of the past, for the sake of his sisters and also for the sake of those other children who were also his brothers and sisters, and whom he would, as it were, snatch from an early grave, but he could not bring himself to lay his head on the pillow beneath the roof that should have been a loving shelter to his own precious mother; in the home of the man who should have loved and cherished instead of driving her with his criminal neglect to a watery grave. When such thoughts came to him it was all he could do to curb the ill-will that would fill his heart, and only by the force of his strong will did he succeed in banishing a feeling of hatred.

Meanwhile Wilbur became more dear day by day, to the father, whose heart went out to the children of his first marriage as it had never done to the younger ones.

Thus the weeks passed away and Christmas was drawing near when the mail brought a letter from Margaret to her mother. A cry of joy broke from her lips as she read its contents.

"What is it?" cried the girls in chorus.

"O, listen! It is almost too good to be true!"

"And now, dearest mamma, let me wind up this epistle by a little bit of news. By some strange and opportune circumstance we have no engagement for two weeks, beginning with Christmas morning, and now I mean for a short time to join that precious circle of which I have heard so much. O, you don't know how impatient I am as the time draws near. I am longing, am homesick for you all. It is sweet, this thing called fame and homage, to be greeted and rewarded with applause, but the heart-felt affection of your loved ones is something different, and O, so much more satisfying."

This indeed was news and joy. Imelda knelt at Mrs. Leland's side, laying her head upon her motherly knee,

"O, I am so glad, so glad! for once our circle will be complete." Glancing up, her eyes met those of Cora. The look of pain and silent reproach therein pierced to her very heart. Hastily rising, with a quick step she was at Cora's side, winding her arms about her she laid her face to hers.

"Forgive me, little sister. For a moment I forgot that we cannot be complete until one more noble man, your own Owen, shall have joined us."

Cora smiled through her tears.

"There is nothing to forgive, only sometimes I grow so hungry, so heart hungry, so love hungry. I know everyone here loves me, yet— —"

"Yet the supreme love, the love of him who makes life's sunshine for you, is wanting; is not that so? But why, little one, do you not send him the word which will bring him to you?"

"I do not know; but I have the feeling that for some reason it would be useless. I will wait a little while longer."

So a few more days went by and at last Christmas morning dawned. A solitary watcher paced up and down the platform in front of the depot awaiting the arrival of the incoming train, his impatience not permitting him to seek the warmth indoors as many others were doing. Up and down, up and down, he paced, the dark eyes glowing in their suppressed eagerness when at last the whistle sounded on the clear, crisp air and a few minutes later the thundering train discharged its load of human freight, and was again putting away on its eastern course. A tall, fair-haired woman was seen casting searching glances about when a pair of arms were laid upon her shoulders. She was gently turned about, almost at the same moment a pair of moustached lips pressing hers,

"Margaret, my rare, sweet Margaret!"

"Wilbur!" Another kiss followed, then quickly she was assisted to a seat in the waiting cutter, snugly tucked in with warm robes and furs and in a few minutes more they were speeding along over the frozen snow.

"My mother, is she well? and Imelda, and Alice, and her babies, and all the rest whom I have not seen, are they all well and happy?"

Wilbur laughed. "One question at a time if you please, my girlie. But as to each and all I can give the same answer, so will I answer them all at once with the one little word 'Yes,' and they have sent me along to greet you, not but one and all are just as eager and impatient to greet and welcome my darling. Only they have kindly conceded the privilege to me to be the first to embrace my girlie, for which I certainly am thankful. For when that bevy of women once have you in their clutches—there now! I retract that word, but it is certain when they have secured you I may not hope to again speak to you in a hurry. For some time at least they will own you."

By this time they were leaving the turmoil and noise of the city in their rear and as the roads were quiet and deserted, the arm of the young driver gently stole about the slender waist of the woman at his side. Nothing loath the fair head rested against his shoulder while the blue eyes looked up into the black ones with love unutterable. Again their lips met in a clinging kiss.

"O sweetheart and lover, it seems so good once more to be able to nestle in your arms."

To press her still more closely was his only answer. Thus laughing and talking, loving and kissing, they enjoyed to the utmost that drive in the crisp, cold air, and soon they arrived at their destination, where many open arms were extended to receive the fair Margaret.

"My darling!" and

"My own mamma!" were the caressing words exchanged as Mrs. Leland folded her daughter to her heart. But not for long was she permitted to hold her there. Imelda's brown eyes were beaming with love and pleasure. Alice was eager for a kiss, her two pretty babies wanted to be noticed by this new auntie. Then Imelda drew her aside where the hazel-eyed Cora was standing with one arm laid lovingly about the shoulders of a pale-faced young man. Margaret needed no introduction. By letter she had long since known of the finding of both of Imelda's wayward ones, and a single glance told her all. She took the girl's face between her hands and gently kissed the cherry lips.

"I am so glad for your own as well as for Imelda's sake."

This was her greeting and Cora understood, for her eyes filled with tears. Frank's hand she took between both of hers and knelt at his side.

"And you are the brother I have so often heard her speak about. For Imelda's sake you must be my brother also, as my own brother has been absent for so long a time I can scarce remember him."

Frank's face became sad and his eyes misty.

"O, but your own brother is so much more deserving than I. Would that my record were as clean."

Margaret shook her head.

"Not so downcast and self-reproachful, my boy. We are so much the creatures of circumstances we cannot well help doing just the things we do. The past you have done with, only the future is yours, to make that what it should be will be your task, your duty, your pleasure."

In his turn Frank shook his head.

"No! no! even that boon will be denied me. My bad deeds can't be undone; to atone for them will not be permitted me. My days, my hours, even, are numbered. No, no, please don't. I understand what you would say. Why should such a truth-loving woman as you seek to deceive me. I know it all, and I suppose it is best so. Look, there at your mother's side another awaits to welcome you, one who is nearer and dearer to you than such a poor wreck of humanity as I could ever dare hope to be."

Following the direction indicated by Frank Margaret saw, standing at her mother's side, an arm thrown caressingly about her shoulders, a young man as yet almost a boy, fair sunny locks thrown carelessly back from a broad and open brow, a look of longing in the frank blue eyes, and suppressed emotion quivering about the sensitive mouth.

Slowly Margaret drew herself up to her full height, with her eyes fastened on that boyish and yet manly form. Was it—O was it— —? Her mother's hand went up to his face and drew it close to her own, holding it there, the other hand she extended to her daughter. With bated breath Margaret crossed the room.

"Is it— —"

"Your brother."

Then both of Margaret's hands were extended and both were clasped firmly and tenderly, and,

"Osmond!"

"Margaret!"—spoken in a breath, and Margaret knew that at last her mother had her heart's one desire; her boy, her baby is once more her own, and the sister is clasped in her brother's embrace.

"O, this is indeed a merry Christmas, and you are the nicest Christmas gift I could have wished for. But how is it, mamma, that you have not written this to me?"

"Because I so sincerely hoped and believed that you would make it possible to spend a week with us, and I wanted to surprise you. Have I succeeded?"

"Indeed you have, my darling mamma. But is this boy always so tongue-tied, having just nothing at all to say?"

Osmond laughed,

"I believe you are a saucebox! But that isn't a bit nice of me, is it? to call you names in the first moments of our acquaintance—with the first words I address to you. I promise you to try and do better and say something nice. I don't believe you are easily spoiled and feel that I may tell you, that already I am proud of my sister. I think they have named you well—Margaret. A daughter of the Gods, divinely tall and most divinely fair——"

"For shame, Osmond; to try to pay your sister compliments in such wornout phrases."

A laugh followed and the ice was broken. Margaret felt and knew that she should love this brother. As the days of the following week glided by she gradually came to know all there was to tell and to learn. Osmond told her all about the father who opposed his coming here, when by accident he discovered that it was the boy's mother he daily went to see; of the battle he had fought and how he had come off conqueror; of how there had been much in common between them; but that of late he was daily drifting more and more away from his father; then of how he had come into this circle, and how he had gradually come to hear and then understand their ideas; how he had come to know and understand what true womanhood and manhood were, what they meant, and that he now knew that his mother and sister were sweet and pure and true, notwithstanding the teachings of his father.

Then Margaret had come to know the sisters of Wilbur, and knew not which was the most love-worthy, the stately Edith or the sweet, gentle Hilda. She saw the heightened color in the cheeks of the former when the young physician was holding her attention; she saw the sparkling light in the eyes of the latter and the answering light in those of Lawrence Westcot; the adoration in Imelda's glance as it rested on the splendid figure of Norman Carlton, whom indeed she found to be all her friend had said of him. "One of nature's noblemen" was the best she knew how to describe him. But to which, indeed, of the manly faces and forms should she not have applied the same appellation? And O, how she enjoyed the society of this bright circle! how swiftly the hours and days flew by. How soon she knew her short vacation would be over and that again she must away to her work.

She loved her work but she could not help feeling sad that her visit would be of such short duration. She would nestle closer to Wilbur's side, and just a little more passion would creep into her kisses, when she was folded against his heart, at the thought of the coming separation.

So the first week of her vacation neared its close, and all felt more than ever before the rapid flight of time, when one evening Norman joined the circle holding a telegram aloft.

"Look," he said, "this announces the visit of a friend of olden days, a college mate, a most precious friend whom I will turn over to the tender mercies of our ladies; a splendid fellow, wholesouled and true. Maybe you girls can make another addition to our circle. He is well worth the winning, though he be a married man."

CHAPTER XL

We must now retrace our steps for some months back to the golden summer time.

In the great eastern metropolis, on the sunny banks of the beautiful Hudson, almost hidden within a grove of wild plum and cherry trees, stands a cosy cottage. Snowy lace curtains drape the windows. Creeping vines almost cover it like a heavy green coverlet. On the shady porches are arranged a profusion and variety of richly blooming plants. The grass plots surrounding the house are dotted with beds of rare flowers which fill the air with fragrance.

But in spite of all the tempting beauty of the place there was an air of desertion about it that one felt rather than saw. The sultry summer day was drawing to its close. Evening was casting its lengthening shadows across the paths. Many of the beautiful blossoms drooped their heads as if weary and sad, while every window and door was closely fastened.

There was not a single sign of life about the place, when suddenly the click of the garden gate was heard, and a man with hasty steps came walking up the path. His face was pale and handsome, his eyes blue, and his drooping, silky mustache a decided red. The hair of the head, however, was of a darker hue, a handsome brown. He was admitted to the house by an old negress, whose face wore an extremely doleful expression.

"Hello! Aunt Betty, what's wrong? Your young mistress is well, I hope?" But not waiting for answer he pushed by her, and was half way up the stairway when the old woman's voice arrested his footsteps.

"No use, Massa Hunter. The young Missis is not upstairs."

"Not upstairs! Then where is she, pray? Tell me at once."

For answer the old woman covered her face with her snowy apron and burst into tears.

"What is the meaning of this?" the young man demanded. "Has anything happened? Where is Cora? Don't you see how you are torturing me?"

"I don't know. Indeed I don't! She just put on her plainest dress and says to me: 'I is going away, aunty, you can keep dis as a present from me,' and she gi' me a purse all filled with gold. 'You is to remain here,' she says, 'until the massa comes and den you gi' him dis.' Then she gi' me lettah, and dat is all I knows."

His face was ashy white and his hand shook as with palsy as the negress handed him the missive which he instinctively knew was a farewell from the one woman who was dearer to him than life. A deadly fear crept into his heart as he went into the little parlor and closed the door as if to shut out the glad sunlight while he read the words that had been penned with a broken heart. Here and there a stain, a tell-tale mark had been left by a falling tear.

"You will forget," she wrote, "that such a one as I have ever crossed your path. It is better thus. It seems my destiny only to bring pain and suffering to those who love me.

"Do not fear I may sink again to the level on which you found me and from which you rescued me. You have taught me a woman's real worth and no degrading action or word shall ever again soil my life. I was reckless and daring to accept the priceless boon of your love without first inquiring if you were free to love. I did not know, O, I did not know, that law and custom had already bound you to another. I cannot permit you to make a criminal of yourself, and when you return I will be gone. Don't seek to find me. What would be the use? The world is wide and somewhere I shall be able to live out this life which consists of so much more pain than joy. I am young and strong, and shall find work somewhere. Good bye! Farewell, my Owen, my lover. Reserve in your memory one little spot of green for your own unhappy.

Cora."

The closely written sheets fluttered from his hand and fell unheeded to the floor. His head sank upon his arm where it fell upon the table. Thus he sat long hours. The day had gone out in the gloaming. The twilight hours passed and ushered in the dark night and still he sat there. Then he arose and dragged his weary footsteps to the pretty bed chamber which was to know her no more. There, where he had spent so many sweet and indescribably happy hours, he threw himself upon the bed and buried his face in the snowy pillows which her head had so often pressed.

At sunrise he left the sacred abode. He told the old negress to remain and take care of the little home just the same as if her mistress were there. Giving her a well filled purse he turned his back upon the place where love had been wont to welcome him and went straight to the mansion where dwelt the haughty Leonie, his wife.

"I will never give in! Never! never! I would scratch the eyes out of her white face first!"

The shrill voice almost shrieked the words and the black eyes of the angry woman flashed fire as the white face twitched with fury which transformed it until it became almost hideous.

"I would murder the brazen hussy ere I would — —"

"Not another word! I will not hear your vile tongue defame her whose shoes you are not worthy to wipe. Yon have driven my poor girl away. If sin there be, it is mine. She never knew I had a wife. She was content to give me her love until you drove her forever out of my life. So on that score you can rest easy, but I repeat that I will not continue this farce any longer. I have crossed the threshold of the dwelling that you call home for the last time. I shall sever now and for all time every tie that binds me to you. You can retain this house if you wish it. I do not want it. I shall deposit a million dollars at my banker's to your credit. Then you can apply for a divorce just as soon as you may desire."

To be mistress of this lordly mansion was by no means a small thing. When he made the declaration that she was to retain it together with a princely fortune, an iron band seemed to loosen from about Leonie's throat but she gave no sign of her intense gratification.

Just then the tinkling of a bell was heard in the distance; a few moments later a servant appeared with a card. Before Leonie could step forward, Owen had already secured the card and as the man again noiselessly withdrew he cast a quick glance at the name inscribed thereon,

"'Wilson Porter!' Your name, fair lady, has lately often enough been coupled with this one, and as Wilson Porter is neither a fool nor a knave, to the best of my knowledge, I am sorry for him. He deserves a better fate than to be drawn in by a woman of the Leonie Hunter stamp. The immaculate woman who could hurl such withering scorn on an unfortunate sister really ought not to throw stones as she herself is the inmate of a glass house."

He turned and left her standing there, and as he opened the door to pass out he lifted his hat to Wilson Porter who had come to conduct Leonie to Mrs. Van Gorden's reception.

For days and weeks Owen kept up an incessant search for the missing girl but no trace could be found of her whereabouts. His face became haggard, his manner nervous and restless. Sleep fled his eyes, and as summer gave way to autumn, followed by dreary winter, the conviction slowly forced itself upon the mind of the lonely and embittered man that his dream of bliss had ended.

Never in all this time had he seen Leonie. His life with her had been a miserable failure and he never wished to see the dark passionate face again. And in reality Leonie cared very little for the doings of her truant husband. Now as before she queened it in society. As a matter of course it was accepted that Wilson Porter on all occasions should be her escort. The society world had become accustomed to that fact; there was no longer anything new and strange about it.

But if Leonie cared little, Owen cared still less, and as on the clear frosty night of Christmas eve the clanging of the merry bells were calling the orthodox masses both rich and poor to commemorate the birthnight of a world's redeemer, he stood watching the surging masses with a scornful smile curling the finely chiseled lips, he murmured:

"I wonder how much Christian love and charity has done to make the world better. Bah! nothing but cupidity, sordid lust for gain, fill the hearts of one class, whilst superstition, prejudice and ignorance rule the other. The one class rivets the chains; the other hugs them. O how beautiful the world might be if poor groveling humanity would but be natural. Of all things under the sun possessed of life and motion the human family alone is taught it is wrong to be natural, that it is right to outrage nature's laws, even though death be the penalty.

"I wonder if, in all New York to night, there is one who is more wretchedly poor and desolate than I am, with my millions? Of what use are they to me? They cannot buy me happiness."

The heart-sick man paced the streets until they were wholly deserted. A restless spirit kept him on the move until the bells of the Christmas morn proclaimed "Peace upon earth, good will to men." Again the scornful smile curved his lips as he whispered: "Where is it? O, where is this chanted peace?

As he was beginning to feel tired and was about to return to his hotel his attention was attracted by the movements of a man a short distance in advance of him who was staggering along the street as if intoxicated. Impelled by some strange fascination Owen followed, never for a moment taking his eyes off the figure in advance. The reeling man soon came to Riverside drive, and thence to the Park which he entered and passed through the winding paths down to the river's edge. His movements became more and more suspicious. Owen quickened his steps almost to a run and just as he was on the verge of taking the fatal leap he reached the side of the stranger, and hastily grasping him by the arm he quickly drew him back. The man reeled and almost fell from the force of the impelling motion. When he regained his equilibrium he turned his white and stern face upon Owen who dared to interfere with his actions.

"Let go my arm," came in a husky gasp from his lips. "By what right do you compel me to remain where there is nothing but pain and sorrow, where all is cruel deceit, blackness and lies, while down there in the clear depths peace and rest await me?"

Owen retained his grasp while he looked the other full in the face. He saw it clearly now. The man was not intoxicated; he was sick. The eyes glowed feverishly from their hollow sockets, his cheeks were sunken, what were to be seen of them, for the lower part of his face was covered with a handsome flowing beard.

"You are sick," said Owen, "and are raving."

"Sick? Yes! Raving? Ha! ha! ha!" The wild weird laughter made Owen think he was confronting a madman. "So would you rave were the bloodhounds of the law hunting, dogging your every step." Another chill crept over Owen. Was it a desperate criminal he had encountered? Had he made a mistake in attempting to interfere with the action of this stranger? Then again, when he looked closer, he did not believe it. By the bright light of the full moon the face before him showed not a single trace of what he would expect to find in the face of a criminal. Sick and delirious he might be, but nothing else. Speaking in an authoritative manner he said:

"Come with me. This is no place for you. I will see that you are taken home and cared for."

"Home! Ha! ha! What a mockery the word is. I wonder if any one ever has known by experience what the word implies?"

Owen was beginning to feel the effects of the cold. Here by the water's edge it was doubly keen and the standing still added still more to it. Once more he spoke. "Come, you can not stand here all night, and surely you have thought better of the rash action you contemplated. At any rate I shall not move from your side until you come with me."

A bitter smile for a moment rested upon the bearded face of the stranger, then he said:

"Very well, some other time will do as well. Lead. I will follow, and then explain why on this night of all others, when the world is rejoicing over the birth of a redeemer I came so near seeking and finding a watery grave."

Owen accompanied the staggering stranger to Seventh avenue where they had the good fortune to find a cab. Both men got in and were driven rapidly to the hotel where Owen was staying, arriving there just as the gray dawn was breaking. Having reached Owen's rooms the stranger sank exhausted into a cushioned chair. Owen assisted him to disrobe and placed him on the couch where he was soon sleeping soundly, then stretched his tired limbs upon a lounge and in a little while he also was in the land of dreams.

It was almost noon when Owen awoke. He arose and walked over to the bed whereon the stranger was still sleeping. While debating the advisability of awakening the man before him the stranger opened his eyes. A bewildered look for a moment filled them, then returning memory brought with it recognition of the face before him and the circumstances which brought him into the present surroundings. A bitter smile moved the bearded lips as he half rose. Leaning his head upon his hand he let his gaze wander about the luxurious apartment; biting scorn was in his words as he spoke:

"It is not likely that you, who can afford surroundings like these, would ever attempt so desperate a deed as you prevented me from doing a few hours ago."

"Why did you do it?"

"Why did I do it? You cannot realize to what utter despair and darkness you have called me back. I will have all these battles to fight over again, and the struggle is not an easy one, I can assure you."

The bitterness that rang through every word betokened a despair that was deep seated, and Owen's heart was touched deeply.

"Tell me, and let me judge. But first, however, I think it would be advisable to take care of the inner man. So while you arrange your toilet, I will order some breakfast. It is somewhat late in the day for that meal and all the more necessary that it should be partaken of."

Accordingly a generous repast was ordered which was served in an adjoining apartment. After they had finished their meal they drew their chairs before the fire. The stranger leaned his head with its heavy clustering hair upon one hand and sat staring into the glowing coals. Owen did not disturb his train of thought but patiently awaited his pleasure, and by and by he was rewarded. The hand dropped and the head was raised.

"And now, since you have shown an interest in my case, I shall tell you my story briefly. For years I have been the only support of a widowed mother, an only sister and a delicate younger brother. My father has been dead quite a number of years and sad as is the fact, it was rather a relief to be rid of him. The more pitiful because of the fact that he was a very intellectual man once, but hard luck during the early years of his married life, when it seemed that there was no work for him to do even though he offered his service for a mere pittance, had embittered him. He had loved the girl he married and bright were his visions of the future. But his misfortune made him desperate and he took to drink, which transformed the gentle-tempered, loving man into a veritable demon. Forgetting that unkind fate had already placed a much too heavy burden upon the slender shoulders of the delicate woman the demon of jealousy took possession of him. Discord dwelt where love and tenderness once held supreme sway.

"Only when at great intervals he let drink alone long enough to clear his befuddled brain, would the intelligent mind assert itself. But the realization of his wretched condition and surroundings would then drive him almost distracted and he would return to his cups with a wilder abandon than ever. When in a drunken brawl he was struck down and they brought the livid corpse to the wretched abode he had called home, the unhappy family were conscious of a feeling of relief rather than that of sorrow.

"I was then but fourteen years old, but tall for my age and on me fell the task of supporting my mother and younger brother and sister. It was little, indeed, that a lad of my age could earn; but we fared better than hitherto. And as I grew older and was able to earn more our condition improved.

"As my education had been sadly neglected in my childhood and I began to realize it, I determined yet to master it, so my evenings were now devoted to study. My sister, a very pretty and charming girl, when she became old enough also added her mite by becoming a factory girl. Her beauty made her position a difficult one, and her warm love nature, which had been starved into a craving hunger, caused her to fall an easy prey to the handsome, wealthy young scoundrel who was the son of the factory owner.

"Her condition soon became apparent and when I questioned her she broke down and confessed the whole pitiful story. She had not even the tender words and caresses of her lover, now, to support her. He had tired of his plaything and cast her aside. I understood what arts are employed to lure to her destruction a poor loving creature and could only pity her from the bottom of my heart. Not so, however, my mother. She had been reared within the narrow confines of the church. Her standard of virtue was, 'touch me not,' regardless of what the circumstances might have been. So the mother who should have been her stay and comfort only cast reproaches upon the head of the despairing girl, driving her almost insane. My brother, too, would not forgive her for the disgrace she had brought upon him. He would not speak to her. I have often seen him draw back at her approach that her clothing might not brush against him.

"Of course he was very young then, only a boy, not yet fifteen, but it would cut me to the heart to see the blood mount to her face. When it became unbearable she would fly to me and I would try all in my power to pacify her; drawing upon myself the condemnation of the others, who could not understand how I could countenance such shamelessness.

"But even my sympathy could not sustain the breaking heart, and when the trying hour came her strength failed, and with a little stillborn girl-baby folded in her arms my beautiful sister was laid out of sight.

"Although my mother wept bitter tears, I fear she felt much relieved that the matter ended as it did, for now grass would grow over the grave of Millie's shame. Robert, my brother, also seemed deeply affected. But her name was never mentioned now. I knew best what the poor girl had suffered, and it was a long time ere I could forgive either my mother or my brother. Robert was not very sweet-tempered at best. From his birth he had been delicate. A puny, fretful infant, he came at a time when the nightly debauches of my father set my mother almost wild, souring an otherwise gentle and loving nature.

"Notwithstanding his ailings, however, he was his mother's favorite. Though his advent had been dreaded, upon his arrival her heart went out to him with a spasmodic passion. She never refused him anything it was in her power to give, thereby showing a decided weakness of character.

"This was the worst thing she could have done, as it had the tendency to develop all the bad traits of Robert's weak character. As he was physically unfit for work the support of the family rested entirely upon my shoulders. But as the years sped by there came a change. A saucy black-eyed maiden crossed my path and my fate was sealed. I loved her with all the strength of my passionate nature. To me she seemed perfect and I had no greater desire than to make her my wife. First, however, I felt it my duty to tell her of the sad history of my early life. She gave the black curls a saucy toss and said she could not see how all this should possibly effect us any. I caught her in my arms and strained her to my breast, my heart filled with admiration of the grand nobility of character, which I thought was exhibited in those words; never once dreaming that it was her very lack of character which prompted that declaration."

CHAPTER XLI

"In a short time we were married. But my dream of happiness was short lived. My wife and my mother had little in common, and often the passionate red lips would utter words that wounded the elder woman to the very heart. I soon saw how matters stood but was unable to control them. I pleaded with Annie, I reasoned with my mother; but the two beings whom I loved better than any others in the world had no love for each other. Several times I spoke sharply to Annie and to my surprise Robert sided with my wife against me and the mother who worshiped him. This seemed to break her heart and it was not long until she closed her eyes in her last long sleep.

"When all was over I again sought to reason with my wife. I folded her to my heart whilst I could scarcely repress the sobs that would well up from its depths. It seemed to me that she at first shrank from me, but I thought it must be only imagination.

"She now often treated me to perfect storms of passionate caresses and I was as wax in her band. No request could I deny her, and I found myself rapidly sinking in debt. But I should not blame her. Poor child! she knew no better. She had been left an orphan at an early age; cuffed about from place to place, her heart always full of longings which were never satisfied. When she married me she believed all that would be at an end. What one man could do for his wife another should also do for his. That this was impossible she could not understand.

"Sometimes I felt like cursing her, then overwhelmed by a rush of tenderness I would almost crush her in my embrace and again she would win the victory. But the time came when I felt the waves closing over my head, and I surely must have been mad or I would never have done what I did."

The voice of the man broke and a suspicious moisture could be seen in his eyes. For a moment, he laid his hand over them ere he proceeded:

"I robbed my employer's safe of ten thousand dollars. I knew I would be received with a storm of kisses and caresses which would outweigh everything else. Let come what would, for once she should be perfectly happy.

"With the stolen treasure in my pocket I hurried home, a full hour earlier than usual, in a state of delirious excitement bordering upon insanity. I found the door locked, but having my latch key with me I did not ring but quietly let myself in.

"The little parlor was deserted; so was the dining room and kitchen. The soft carpet deadened the sound of my footsteps. I went from room to room and in Robert's room I heard voices. The door stood slightly ajar. Touching it lightly it opened several inches wider and the sight that met my eyes broke my heart. Clasped close in each other's arms; their heads pressing the same pillow, were Robert and my wife. A quick movement opened the door wide with a creaking sound; the two heard and both started up as if electrified. Annie screamed and clapped both hands to her face. Robert's face was a study. Hate and defiance were written in every line of it. With a sudden movement he took a revolver from his pocket and leveled it at my heart. But quick as was his action I forestalled him. With a single bound I gave his arm an upward blow sending the bullet into the ceiling and the revolver to the far end of the room.

"'Madman!' I cried. 'What would you do? Have you not enough upon your conscience that you would commit murder?'

"The sullen, defiant look upon his face deepened.

"'I hate you!' he almost hissed. 'You are a constant bar to my happiness.'

"Unjust as I knew this accusation to be I made no comment upon it but asked:

"'Tell me one thing, and without prevarication. Do you love Annie?'

"Quick as a flash came the answer,

"'I do!'

"'And you, Annie, do you love Robert?'

"But Annie sobbed and would not give an intelligible answer, until I sternly repeated the question, and then, between broken sobs:

"'O, I cannot help it. Indeed, indeed I cannot help it.'

"Staggering as beneath a blow I steadied myself for a moment against the table, then, with a mighty effort of will recovering myself, I took the stolen money from my pocket and threw it on the table.

"'Take it,' I said, 'and make the most of it. I have now no use for it. Be happy if you can, I shall no longer stand in the way. You are free in every sense of the word to do as you choose.'

"I turned to leave the room when Annie threw herself sobbing in my way. She clung to me in passion and despair, asserting again and again that she 'could not help it.' Almost forcibly I loosened her hold and pointing to the money on the table I said to Robert,

"'See to it, that you handle the money wisely, and remember that this girl now depends upon you for the comfort, of life. I have done with both of you!'

"Overcome by a sudden impulse I once more caught her in my arms, clasping her close to my breast. I pressed a last kiss upon her lips, then putting the half-fainting form from me I rushed out into the cold night air. I surely need say no more. You now can understand what drove me to the verge of desperation. To find the woman who had driven me to the verge of ruin, untrue, was more than I could bear. A day or two and I would stand before the world exposed. The shame, the disgrace and the walls of Sing Sing loomed up before my mind's eye. I had been a slave all my life to adverse conditions. And now to lose the one boon that I prized above all others—my liberty! No, I would die first! And yet I had it not in my heart to wish any ill to those two. True, I felt bitter towards my brother, but for some reason the fact of his actual helplessness was more clear in my mind than ever before. Have there not been countless cases wherein this very defect has appealed to the hearts of strong, healthy women?—and her pitiful 'I cannot help it' kept ringing in my ears. I knew I never loved her more dearly than in the moment I gave her up, or ever felt more tenderly towards him.

"Many conflicting thoughts surged through my brain; while constantly I questioned, 'Why? why?' And you may think me mad, sir, but the more I thought the more I blamed not them, the chief actors in this life tragedy, but the system from which such abnormal conditions could arise, and in one day make criminals of us all."

Owen listened as if entranced. The excited man had arisen and was pacing the room with hurried strides, wildly tossing the masses of dark curling locks. After a few moments he continued:

"Often and often I had gnashed my teeth in helpless fury when the few paltry dollars were laid in my hands that constituted the remuneration for work which I knew was worth more than fourfold that which I received. I knew if justice could be done I had only taken my own. But that was not law.

"Now my mind wandered in another direction. I knew Annie and Robert had been thrown long hours together in my absence. His weak, delicate condition first awoke her sympathy, and 'pity is akin to love.' The frequent squabbling during the life time of my mother helped develop these feelings in her heart. So the weakling, who all his life had been scorned and shunned by health-and-strength-loving maidens, suddenly found himself the object of tender and sympathetic glances, and what wonder that his starved heart became inflamed? I could see the whole proceeding was but natural. But oh, the shame of it. No one else in all New York would look at the matter as I did, when it became known. But then the thought struck me, 'Was it necessary?' and must I fill a convict's cell? I answered: 'No! No! No! Never!' Thus for many hours I walked the streets, thinking, thinking, thinking, until I found myself at the water's edge about to end all the maddening perplexities, when your hand stayed my movements. So now you are in possession of facts which I had expected to take with me into my watery grave."

The strange recital was at an end. Wearily the narrator flung himself into his chair and leaned back, white and exhausted. The bitter but musical voice was hushed while Owen Hunter sat with his head resting on his hand, lost in thought. Was the life of every good man a wreck? For that the man who sat before him was a good man he had not a single doubt. Aside from the bitter experience of his own life he had never thought of the struggling, suffering masses of humanity. Ten thousand dollars! He had no doubt that the sum seemed an enormous fortune to the man before him, while to Owen it seemed scarce worth mentioning.

"What salary," he asked, "did you receive?"

A bitter smile curved the lips of the other.

"Fifty dollars per month."

Fifty dollars! How often had Owen thoughtlessly squandered as much and more in a single evening; and here was a man who with his family had to live a whole month on it. For the first time in his life the question arose why it was that those who were the producers of all wealth should have so little of it to enjoy; for the first time he asked himself. "Have you a right to control so much money, while so many others are suffering for the actual necessaries of life?" What had he ever done to alleviate human suffering? In memory he saw large figures heading long lists of charity. "Charity!" Suddenly the word seemed to him the most cold and heartless in the English language. To offer charity where justice was due! In that instant he resolved that the sons and daughters of humanity, the many poverty stricken little children, should reap the benefit of the money he controlled. He did not yet see his way clear, and for the moment very wisely left the selection of methods to the future. The present hour belonged to the deeply stricken man who had permitted him to read the pages of his sad history.

"Will you not tell me your name?" he sympathetically inquired.

"My name?" With indescribable bitterness he spoke the words. "Why should I not give it you? All New York will be ringing with it in a few days when it will be known that the assistant bookkeeper of the firm of Hunter & Co. has proven false to his trust. My name is Milton Nesbit!"

As if electrified Owen turned upon the man before him.

"Repeat the name of the firm by which you were employed!"

"Hunter & Co."

With a gasping sound Owen sank back, pale to the very lips. Surprised, Milton Nesbit turned inquiringly to him.

"Why, what is wrong; are you ill?

Owen shook his head.

"No! no! It is not that, but——Well, why should I search for empty words? My name is Owen Hunter!"

It was now Milton Nesbit's turn to gasp with surprise. He had been holding his position some two years and in all that time had never seen the senior member of the firm. He had been told it had not always been thus; but for several years Owen Hunter no longer took an active part in the business, and most of the newcomers had never seen the man for whom they were coining and piling up money.

Milton Nesbit felt a strange thrill as his eyes rested upon the man who was to be his judge. An unspeakable bitterness vibrated through his voice when he again spoke.

"If you are the Owen Hunter of Hunter & Co. and if I were a good Christian I should say that the workings of an Almighty God could be traced in the events of this most fateful day; that he so willed it that it must be just the man whom I have robbed whose hand should stay the act which would have freed me from an accursed fate. But this just God who is said to be all love will not have it so. Earthly justice must first be satisfied; the almighty wrath must first be appeased by giving man a chance to avenge himself upon his fellow man. I simply call it cruel, relentless fate, which has pursued me so many years and which dates from the earliest recollections of my childhood. Very well! pass the sentence which I know lies in your power to enforce, for 'money rules the world,' you know. Hand me over to the guardians of the peace and let the law take its course. It matters little what becomes of me now. I may as well sleep behind prison bars as anywhere else. The sunshine of happiness has long since forsaken me; lost in the gloom and darkness of despair."

Oh, the bitterness, the hopeless misery in the strong man's voice. He had risen and walked back and forth the full length of the room, then with his elbow resting upon the mantel, his hand supporting his head, he stood glaring into the glowing coals, awaiting his sentence. But Owen now no longer calmly sat enjoying the comforts of the room. As the other ceased speaking he stepped to his side and gently laying his hand upon his shoulder, said:

"Will you look me in the face?"

Silently Nesbit turned and faced Owen. For some minutes they stood thus face to face; then Owen's hand was extended.

"May I ask you to give me your hand in friendship?"

Surprise was depicted upon Nesbit's face as he looked at the outstretched palm, and then inquiringly into the face of the man to whom it belonged.

"Friendship?" echoed Milton Nesbit, while he nervously passed his hand over his forehead as if he would dispel the mists which seemed to him to be gathering there.

"And why not? Am I selfish when I ask it? But with my millions a true friend is something which I have not, and now I am waiting to feel the clasp of genuine friendship. Do I ask in vain?"

Milton Nesbit's face was a study. Queer little quivers were stirring the muscles. Sinking once more into his chair he buried his face in both hands. For some time neither spoke, then the deeply moved man raised his head and looked the other searchingly in the eye.

"And how about the criminal?"

"Do you feel yourself one?"

The flash in the dark eye answered him even before the firmly spoken words:

"No, I do not!"

"Then once more I extend my hand and ask, will you be my friend and brother? I might be able to give you an insight into a life that would verify the words, 'All is not gold that glitters.'"

There was now no hesitation, and in that handclasp a life-long friendship was sealed. A Christmas morn it was to these two, that all their lives stood out clear and bright.

All that afternoon the two men sat in that quiet comfortable room, and as Owen had first listened to one of the saddest of life histories, so now, in turn, he opened his heart to his new friend, and in the first hour of his new-found friendship he proved it no idle phrase, for in this hour he claimed Nesbit's trust and full confidence. If Milton could not at first give his sanction to an affair like that of Owen, who having already a wife, however unworthy, could take to his heart another woman, and finding her as he had found her, should hold her above all other women—this certainly, should excite no surprise.

Remembering the woman who, though false to him, he still loved, Milton could not sit in judgment and condemn this other woman who had given the wealth of her love to Owen without first asking leave of some third person or persons. Just at present he could see nothing clearly. He could feel, but was in no condition to reason. Owen saw and understood, and knowing that in his present condition the best thing for Milton was change—change of scene and of mental occupation, he at once decided to put into execution a long-deferred plan of his own. He would travel; he would take Nesbit with him as traveling companion; and just then he remembered an old college mate whom he had not seen for many years. Why not begin the proposed journey by making a call upon the friend of his youth?

Accordingly a dispatch was at once sent to announce their coming and in a very few days the two friends, who had become such in a way so strange and unexpected, were comfortably seated in a luxurious Pullman car en route for the west.

CHAPTER XLII

And thus it is that the threads of our story once more unite. Again the figure of a man is pacing up and down the platform, awaiting the incoming train and, at last it comes thundering in and makes a brief halt, Norman's eyes rest upon the stalwart, manly figure of the companion of his earlier days, and the clasp of the hand that follows is almost painful. But even in that first quick meeting, when joy lights up the eyes of both, Norman sees the change in his old-time friend; sees the lines that the flight of years alone has not engraven on the handsome face.

"What is it Owen? There is that in your face which tells me all is not well. Have you been sick?"

"Heart-sick—yes! to the extent that life sometimes seems but a burden?"

"Why should a man of almost unlimited wealth, such as you possess, speak in such a strain?"

"Why, indeed! You speak as though wealth could buy happiness."

"And can it not? Do you not know what untold, what inconceivable misery could be turned to joy with the assistance of wealth?"

"In thousands of cases, yes. In my own instance, no! Wealth cannot heal a breaking heart, cannot buy the happiness which has fled."

"I believe I possess a panacea for an evil such as yours. The society of sweet women will restore you to life and love."

"Don't speak of woman and love to me. I have done with em!" Norman smiled.

"O, I have touched the right cord, have I? But that is a bold assertion which you have just made—that you have done with women forever. Yet I assert that you must—you must and you will be won."

"Don't you know that I am a married man?"

For a moment Norman looked him searchingly in the face; then, as if satisfied, replied,

"And what if you are? Are you sure that that fact should prove a barrier to future happiness?"

Owen Hunter in turn now looked Norman searchingly in the face —

"How am I to understand you? That the Norman I once knew, and who I know possessed such high-strung ideas of honor, should express himself thus?"

A slight flush rose to Norman's brow. Hastily he opened his lips to answer but as quickly checked himself — —

"No more, now! This is scarce a proper place to discuss the sort of topics we are drifting into. Without doubt ere we part there will be moments more opportune for thorough discussion. At present I am eager to introduce you into a most charmed and charming circle."

Owen shook his head.

"I have come to you for quiet, Norman. My heart is sore, and needs rest. I would rather not meet strangers. Besides I have with me a friend whom I wish to introduce to you; also to ask your forbearance for thus imposing on your hospitality as that is what I am about to do. Another storm-tossed soul in need of rest and quiet; one who has drained the bitter-cup of sorrow to its very dregs." Turning he approached a man who had hitherto stood motionless at some little distance. A man well worth looking at. Tall, well proportioned; dark, heavy beard and clustering hair; with an unspeakable sadness in the deep, gray eyes.

"I claim your hospitality for Milton Nesbit, as well as for myself, and promise that neither shall be too great a burden on your kindness, if you can secure us the welcome of your mother and sisters. I know it is much I ask of you, as our intimacy in the past years can scarcely be called by the name of friendship — but permit me, Mr. Nesbit, this is the friend of my college days, Norman Carlton, of whom I have been telling you."

Extending his hand and firmly grasping that of the stranger, Norman said:

"Permit me to welcome any friend that Owen Hunter may introduce. You are worthy, or he would not ask it: As for our friendship in the past, if we have not been intimate friends it has not been for lack of mutual attraction but rather that the ties that bound us were not close enough, and it is not too late to make them closer. I always felt the most profound admiration for the sunny tempered youth I knew as Owen Hunter.

"Thank you, for your generous welcome," replied a grave, musical voice. "I am but as an instrument in the hands of Mr. Hunter. I follow where he leads. Later I hope you will bid me welcome on my own account."

"Spoken like a man. I feel that already I may speak the words of welcome in your own behalf. But come, dinner will be waiting, and in a well regulated household, as you both understand, to the good housewife that is abomination, and my mother knows what good housekeeping is. But set your mind at rest; she will tender you the welcome I ask for my friends. Formal and precise she may be, but she is also a most gracious hostess. My sisters also you will find pleased to meet you. But they do not belong to the charmed circle to which I insist on introducing you. No protests! I will have my way. You are already announced, and in this instance I mean to be firm. You would scarcely be a man if our many charmers cannot succeed in dispelling the clouds, and a man must be of flinty hardness who could listen to our song-bird, sweet, winsome Cora, without being moved."

Owen started.

"Cora! did you say?—Cora? But pshaw! why should I excite myself over a name. There are hundreds of Coras in the world. But lead on. We are ready to follow."

So they piled into the cutter and as they dashed over the snow quite forgot their sorrows, and as events of their college years were gone over they soon felt better acquainted than they had ever felt in the olden days. But Milton Nesbit was quiet, very quiet. He only spoke when spoken to, and Owen now realized that it would be better for him to mingle more with others in order to awaken again in that crushed and bleeding heart an interest in life—to deaden the pain that was ever gnawing at his vitals, and though at first Nesbit refused to join the two friends when evening drew near, preferring to remain at home, and although Owen, too, would have much preferred to remain in the seclusion of his room, he feared to hurt the feelings of his kind host, and therefore sacrificed his own desire to that of Norman's. As for Milton, Owen believed it absolutely necessary that he should accompany them, and insisted on his doing so.

Unwilling to seem boorish, with a sigh Nesbit prepared to make a martyr of himself. So when Norman's cutter drew up to the Westcot mansion he brought two guests instead of the one expected, but both were made equally welcome. For some reason Norman had not mentioned the name of his intended guest. No intentional oversight, I ween. He had never heard the name of Cora's lover and therefore could not have known the link binding these two, so when the name of Owen Hunter was announced, each of the girls started. Owen must have thought, for an instant, that they acted strangely, but quickly recovering themselves they extended a hearty welcome. Soft white hands were clasped in the manly ones; rosy lips were wreathed in sweetest smiles. But as Norman's eyes went about the room he missed Cora, and he asked Imelda where her sister was.

"I believe she was telling baby Norma a story and when that was finished Meta wanted a song, so when she gets through entertaining the little folks she will no doubt make her appearance," she said.

Owen again started—upon being presented to Imelda Ellwood, and the two names kept forming themselves into one. "Cora, Ellwood; Cora, Ellwood!" Surely he must be going mad. It was only a coincidence, thought he. To find his own sweet girlie here would be too good to be true. So he devoted himself to Imelda and found himself admiring the intelligent, gravely sweet girl who was so well informed on whatever subject might be broached.

Milton Nesbit had been passed round, so to say, from one fair maid to another, and all were struck with the sad beauty of his manly face, but unable to elicit many words from him, as his thoughts were many miles away with the fair woman he had left behind him. But now it was Alice who was talking to him. That incessant little chatterbox did not give him much time to talk or to think, even if he had been so inclined,—she had so much herself to say. It was said in a way so quaint and sweet, and as she was mistress of the house and a married woman he felt himself more at ease and more free in her society, and ere long she managed to hold his attention, and soon he found himself admiring the dainty color in her cheeks, the pearly teeth gleaming from between rosy lips, the mischief sparkling in the clear blue eye, while her voice sounded like tinkling music. The large room was pretty well filled with ladies and gentlemen, but as she pointed each one out to him it was with a word of praise and love for some peculiar trait, attraction or accomplishment. Not one disparaging word, and as his eyes followed her indications he thought he had never found so much harmony.

While his eyes were roving from one to another they rested on Cora who had but just entered the room. Was it that he had not seen her before, or was it that she possessed some feature more attractive than the others? His eyes followed her every movement as she gracefully found her way to the piano and seating herself thereat began a prelude, and soon the rich, full voice filled the room with its rare music, while the sweet tones slightly trembled as the words dropped from her lips:

Across the sobbing sea of doom
The weary world is slowly drifting.
Eyes wet with tears peer through the gloom,
Yet see no sign of rest or rifting.
Still angels bright from some far height,

Repeat through hoots of weary waking—
"Hope's starlight shines through darkest night,
To keep the world's great heart from breaking!"

Listening to the words they all knew there was an undercurrent of meaning attached to the simple strain that a stranger would not be apt to detect. And yet Milton Nesbit understood, as well as if the story had been told him in so many words, that the gifted singer had known sorrow, and slowly his gaze sought Owen Hunter. What was it? Owen had risen from Imelda's side, evidently unconscious that he was acting strangely, that he was, to say the least, impolite. He had neither eyes nor ears for anything else but the fair singer. As if fascinated the song drew him to her side. He repeated the words:

"Hope's starlight shines through darkest night"—

whispering them close to the pink shell ear,

"O Cora, my own, is not the night over? May the morning now at last dawn?"

Quick as a flash Cora whirled about on her stool, and with the one glad cry, "Owen!" cast herself into his arms, regardless of the many eyes resting upon them, and was held by him in an embrace so close as if he meant never again to let her go.

As if in that one glad happy cry all her strength had been spent Cora lay back faint and white in her anxious lover's arms. Had the sudden joy killed her? He strained her close and kissed the white cold lips; then bearing her to a couch he began chafing her hands, helplessly looking about,

"She has fainted; can no one help me restore her?"

Quickly an anxious circle gathered about her, but Paul Arthurs soon reassured them.

"It is nothing—only the reaction. She will be herself in a few moments."

Taking a small vial from an inside pocket of his coat he forced a few drops between her lips and in a few moments had the satisfaction of seeing her open her eyes.

"Take her away where she can have rest and quiet for half an hour; then she will be quite herself again."

Winding her arm about her, Imelda was about to conduct her away when Owen laid his hand detainingly upon her arm,

"Will you not permit me?"

There was so much pleading in the manly voice and clear blue eyes that Imelda could not refuse him.

"You will take good care of her?" with a smile.

"Will I?—as of my life! May I, Cora?"

For answer Cora quietly laid her head against his shoulder, smiling into his eyes, and thus he led her from the room.

What if instead of the half hour they remained two long hours? and what if they thought it such a very little while and that they had not had a chance to say anything at all? Who would blame them? Doubtless it was true that they had said very little. Their hearts were too full to speak: too full of unutterable love and happiness, and certainly none in that room thought of blaming them. And when they returned Imelda and Norman were the first to greet them. Cora's arms wound themselves about her sister's neck while the men clasped hands with an undercurrent of feeling such as they had not felt before,

"So this is your charmed circle?" asked Owen Hunter in a husky voice, and smilingly Norman made answer:

"Don't you find it so?"

There was a suspicious moisture in Owen's eyes and his voice visibly trembled when he again asked,

"And no censure meets us here?"

"Why should there be?"

But the man of the world could not understand. His friend knew that he had left a wife, that his love for this girl was an illicit one; yet here he stood clasping his hand in a manner that seemed to indicate to the fortune-tossed Owen that Norman was proud to do so. So he drew him aside and asked the meaning of it all.

Nothing loath, Norman devoted himself for the next half hour to answering his eager queries, seeking to initiate him into the sweet love-laden theories of the new doctrine to which he himself only a few months ago had been a perfect stranger. Leaning against a pillar Owen stood half hidden in an alcove, lost in amaze and wonder; his eyes following every movement of the girl he so madly worshiped.

But still another was watching and waiting for a solution of this mystery. Milton's sad gray eyes saw the happiness of his friend; had seen him catch the fainting figure in his arms; had seen him press his face against hers and kiss the white lips. He could only guess that in some unlooked-for manner he had found the woman for whom he had so long been vainly seeking, and in the excitement which followed he for a time was overlooked and forgotten. But soon the merry peals of laughter, sweet music and soft strains of song again filled the room, and then, at the urgent request of Wilbur, Margaret read some strong dramatic scenes from various plays, holding her listeners spellbound with the purity of her voice, the strength and clearness of the rendition and the depth of feeling which she exhibited. So, as the evening passed, Milton Nesbit became more and more puzzled as to what it was that made this circle so charming—so delightfully entertaining that all his perplexities were for the time forgotten and that caused his sorrows to be dispelled as mist in the sunshine, and his heart to grow warm once more.

As he was one of the handsomest of the finely formed men in the room it did not take long for feminine eyes to detect that fact. Many were the admiring glances bestowed upon him. But there was something in the sad face which forbade intruding. Only Alice—airy, fairy Alice, was not backward. She again sought his side, showing him books, etchings, engravings, and albums filled with selections of art gems. Her sweet, airy manner, the soft tender voice, acted like a charm upon his overwrought nerves, and he soon found himself thoroughly enjoying her.

Lawrence, Wilbur, the young physician and the Wallace sisters had formed a little circle and were discussing economics. Imelda was devoting herself to her brother; making the evening pleasant for him; answering his questions as to the meaning of Cora's strange demeanor in connection with this handsome and refined looking stranger. Frank had already learned much, was learning every day, but all was not quite clear to him yet as to what it was that made these pure-minded women and men so different from others he had met and known in his reckless and checkered life. She told him that it was a lover of their sweet and lovable Cora, who, like himself, had once been reckless and wayward. Margaret, her mother and Osmond formed another group to which still another was attached. Homer had found a seat at Mrs. Leland's feet, resting his head against her knee, her hand gently toying with the clustering locks. The boy said scarcely a word, only listened. Mrs. Leland had also very little to say, only now and then a casual word. The brother and sister, however, who until a few days ago had been as strangers, had much to tell, and were opening their hearts, one to the other. Margaret was delighted with the gems she found stored away in this boy's mind.

While in this quieter mood they were surprised by a sudden burst of melody from the piano, evoked by the touch of a master hand. Nesbit having confessed to Alice that he was musically inclined, that bewitching morsel of humanity had so importuned him that, unable to resist, he soon found his heart swelling with emotion as he evoked the rich strains. This burst scattered the groups, and once more they formed into one whole circle. Nesbit's music was followed by singing and then by Margaret's selections, then in what seemed a very short space of time, Cora and Owen were again of their number, and finally, when the good nights were spoken it seemed there never had been quite such a feeling of content lodged in the innermost recesses of every heart then and there present.

The following day brought back the two newcomers at quite an early hour. They did not now protest against coming. They were there every day and evening, until the hour of Margaret's departure drew nigh. How brief the time allowed them had seemed. Wilbur drank in the glory of the blue wells, kissing the dewy lips again and again. Mrs. Leland folded her child close. It seemed almost harder to let her go now than it had been the first time. Osmond's eyes grew dim.

"I did not know how dear a sister might be. It will seem like a dream, if I must give you up so soon." And although Margaret's heart was sad she tried to hide it under a smiling exterior.

"Never mind," she said. "It will not be for long. A few short months will soon pass by, then a long summer will be ours to do with just as we see fit—a long delicious summer of enjoyment and planning. Listen! they are planning now. We are in that, and must hear all about it."

Slipping one hand through Osmond's arm, the other arm about the waist of her mother she drew them to where the others had drawn a circle about Hilda who, having been importuned, was trying to make plain that vague sweet dream of her future co-operative home, and none so attentive, or none more so than Owen. She spoke of the spacious halls where the ardent searchers after knowledge of any kind might find their teacher; of the library stocked with volumes from the ceiling to the floor; of the lecture hall and the theater; of the opportunities where every talent could be cultivated; of the liberty—the free life—where every fetter should be broken; of the dining hall where they would partake of their evening meal midst flowers and music; of the common parlor where every evening should be an entertainment for all wherein love and genuine sociability should always preside; of the sacred privacy of the rooms where each man or woman should reign king or queen—the sanctum of each, closed to all intruders, consecrated to the holiest and divinest of emotions and self-enfoldment. She spoke of the grand conservatories filled with choicest flowers—the sweet-scented blossoms, the trailing vines, the exotic plants; of the spacious gardens, the sparkling, ever-playing fountains; of the delicious, health-giving baths; of the life of unconventionality,—of the abandon; of the nursery rooms where baby lips were lisping their first words and little toddling feet taking their first uncertain steps; of the things of beauty surrounding the prospective mother; of the unutterably sweet welcome that awaited each coming child; of the full understanding that would be taught to woman of the responsibility of calling into a life a new being; of how man would revere her, how he would wait and abide her invitation; of the sweet co-operation and planning how all should be worked to keep up the financial part.

"O," said she, "it should, it would be paradise!—this my dream. But ah me! it is only a dream."

As a being transfixed Hilda stood among them, her eyes shining, her cheeks glowing, her bosom heaving, looking far beyond them into space. A feeling came over Lawrence Westcot as with bated breath his eyes rested on her, of how utterly unworthy he was of the love of a creature so grand, so superior. A still, small voice whispered, "Make yourself worthy!"—and then and there a high resolve was formed in his mind that he would surely do so. A solemn vow rose as a silent prayer from the depths of his heart that some day he would realize that sweet invitation. With him every man in the room became conscious of a feeling of inferiority, but not an impulse to bow in humility. Rather each head was crested higher with a feeling of lofty aspiration.

Owen Hunter answered the closing remarks of Hilda's dream picture:

"Why, my dreaming maiden, should your dream be but a dream?"

A sad smile played about her lips,

"You forget that it is such an expensive one. It would take a fortune, an almost limitless fortune, to build us such a home. Of course we could be very, very happy in our little circle, as it is, in a much smaller and less expensive home, but I would have it large, so that we might welcome all who possess the same lofty thought to our circle, so that we should be able to give to the world an object lesson in the art of making life worth living, so grand and so glorious that the whole world would want to imitate our example."

Owen smiled.

"What an enthusiast! Take my advice, little one, and until this grand, this glorious home can be ours, help us with your lofty aspirations, and help us not to despise our more limited advantages and privileges. In the meantime we will try to become more worthy of so perfect a home—as some years must of necessity elapse ere it can be completed."

"Have I not said it is only a dream? How can I dare to hope it could ever be realized; and when I come to this home, day after day, and realize what privileges are ours the feeling sometimes comes to me, how wrong-headed I am to be constantly sighing for still more."

Owen shook his head,

"You are mistaken, Miss Hilda. Your sentiments and aspirations are not wrong. Harmonious and beautiful as is the life that has been granted you through the mutual understanding and sympathy of our kind host and hostess, it is by no means complete. So dream on, plan on, and if there is an architect in our circle he shall transfer these plans to paper, and, as soon as practicable, we will look about us for a suitable site, and when the spring sunshine calls all nature again to life, work shall begin, and what has so long been only a vague dream shall, all in good time, bloom into a living reality."

All eyes hung on the lips of the speaker. All ears drank in his words. Could such a thing be possible? Only Cora seemed to understand. Pressing close to his side, she drew his hand with a caressing motion to her smiling lips. With a hasty movement he withdrew the hand to lay it on the head covered with the soft fluffy hair; he pressed it close to him. Hilda drew a step nearer and extending both hands,

"You mean— —O, Mr. Hunter! do you really mean that it can be done? that the home can and shall be ours? But how? how?"

Cora slipped down upon her knees at Hilda's side and caught both hands in hers.

"Did I not tell you long ago, when I told you that story of my heartaches and my noble lover, that he possessed almost limitless wealth? He could not be one of us did he not consecrate some of his millions to the happiness of others. It is in his power to lay the foundation stone for the future ideal society, giving to the world an example of how people should live. Don't you see, my Hilda? Owen is wealthy, and is going to build us our home."

CHAPTER XLIII

From that day forth a new life entered the charmed and charming circle. Lawrence proved to be the architect required, though he had never called his talent in this line to a practical account. Guided by Hilda's vivid imagination, inspired by her enthusiasm and aided by the practical suggestions of Owen, the plan grew, and by the time the first green of the young spring appeared upon the landscape they were ready for action. Margaret had left them at the call of duty, and could only from afar share in the excitement and enthusiasm. Every heart was beating high with hope, and with the advent of warmer weather, Owen, Wilbur, Lawrence and Norman kissed their loved ones good bye and started on a prospecting tour.

Mrs. Leland was importuned to remain with the girls. Why should she return all alone to her western home?—though the probability now was that the west would be where their new home would be located. Just at this time, too, came the change that caused the sisters' eyes to grow dim with tears and a feeling of sadness to pervade every heart. Frank was daily growing weaker, his cheek more hollow and white, his hands more waxy, and intuitively the girls clung to the more mature woman. On a bright sunny morning in the early part of May the tired lids closed, never to open again. Although almost every day brought a letter from some one of the absent ones yet they were still far-away when the death angel made his entrance into the midst of this happy circle, subduing their spirits with infinite sadness when they realized so well what had caused this painful result. So Frank's body was laid away to sleep beneath the daisies, and Imelda's and Cora's tears mingled as they knew that another bond was broken—only they two remained, united by ties of blood, but they also realized that it was better so. At best he had been to them but a wreck of what he might have been. Margaret had joined them just in time to lay a flower upon his pulseless breast and was now with them again for a brief time.

The young physician, Paul Arthurs, and Milton Nesbit had settled close by, and Paul was beginning to have quite a practice as he was fast becoming known. For some time however, something seemed to have been secretly gnawing at his heart, and when his manner had been warmest towards the stately Edith he would suddenly and abruptly leave her, until his conduct became quite an enigma to her. One morning he laid a pack of written papers in her hand and told her to read, and——ah, well! why dwell upon a sad story longer than absolutely necessary? He loved the queenly girl but was conscious of such a lack of worth on his own part that he felt it would be best to give her up. Somewhere under the green sod slept a woman whom he believed the poison of his own body had murdered. Having first made a wreck of himself, almost, by early transgressions, the meaning of which he had been ignorant of, he had later contracted the germs of a loathsome disease. In his unpardonable ignorance he married a sweet, confiding, loving girl whom he loved with all his heart but whom he irreparably wronged by permitting his poisoned manhood to mingle with her pure womanhood; and when her baby girl was laid in her arms her eyes closed in that sleep that knows no waking, and the baby slept with her— under the circumstances the very best, probably, that could have happened. He was quite young when all this occurred—in the early twenties, a period of his life he never liked to think of. It was after that experience that he gave himself up to the study of medicine, and then he underwent a most rigid course of treatment, including very stringent rules or habits of diet, bathing and open air exercise.

"I can now look a pure woman in the eyes and know of a certainty that no harm can come to her through me, but for all that, the past is a blur upon my life, a stain which nothing can ever wash away. One word from you, my heart's queen, will send me to my place and keep me there. I could not accept the sweet love shining in your eyes when I know my utter unworthiness, without laying bare the past, the memory of which follows me like a mocking fiend. Sweetheart, say but the word and I will never become an inmate of that home which now is being planned—if you deem me too impure, too unworthy to associate with the unsullied whiteness that will congregate there. But O, my darling! I love you as only a man can love when his manhood's strength is most fully developed; but I must abide the verdict you may render.

Yours suppliantly,

Paul."

And what had been sweet Edith's verdict? When next they met it was in the garden, under the blossom-laden trees. Paul was sitting with his head resting on his hand unaware of her approaching footsteps. From the rear she approached until she stood close to his side, when without a moment's warning two soft warm hands drew his head back, two warm, dewy clinging lips were touched to his bearded ones, and the next moment he was pressing his cherished Edith to his heart, pouring all the pent up love of a strong nature into her willing ears. His errors of the past belonged to the past. She saw only a noble manhood to which she felt it would be safe to trust her womanhood.

About this same time, also a strange restlessness took possession of Nesbit. A nightly visitor at Maple Lawn, he seemed to enjoy the society of the fair women there with the keenest relish. Alice's slight figure seemed perpetually dancing before his eyes and a great longing filled his heart. Alice, too, was restless. The color would rush in waves over her face at the sound of approaching footsteps. Although he saw and understood, yet he never said a word. With all the sweet possibilities the future so temptingly held out to him he kept his lips firmly closed while he knew full well that this fair little woman might be his for the asking.

One morning in early June Nesbit electrified them all by abruptly saying that he was going to New York. All looked their surprise. Margaret asked,

"Why?"

Alice nervously plucked the first full-blown rose to pieces as her color changed from red to white and white to red, but Margaret's question was evasively answered. Again she asked,

"When will you return?

To which she received a short, "I don't know."

Bidding them all good bye he turned to go, when his eye rested for a moment on the swaying form of Alice who found it difficult to stay the hot tears. He hesitated a moment then, approaching the spot where she stood, in a low voice said,

"Come with me down the maple walk."

Silently they walked until they reached the end, then,

"Do you know why I am going away?"

She shook her head.

"Because my heart yearns for you, and in that vast city dwells a woman whom I call wife. She has not been what the world calls true to me, yet I have treasured her long and faithfully. I feel I ought not to speak of love to another woman so long as she may have need of me. I know it was her own hand that cast the dice, yet I feel that I must know her fate ere I entirely cut loose from her. Oh, I loved her, Alice, in the days when she was mine, and still a latent tenderness lingers in my heart. Maybe she was not wholly to blame, but I have learned new lessons since. I feel a little woman here would prefer me to all others and my heart yearns to claim her. Will you kiss me just once ere I start on this journey which may bring me I know not what?"

Tenderly he raised the drooping head and forced the downcast eyes to look into his. It was too much. Two lips quivered pitifully, like those of some grieved baby, and two great tears rolled over her cheeks down upon the snowy whiteness of her gown. The sight robbed him of self-control. He gathered her in his arms, the tiny morsel, and held her there like some wee baby.

"I only want to see that she does not suffer; that she is taken care of, and then I will return. Indeed I will. Do not fear"—and then he was gone.

Thus Milton Nesbit left Maple Lawn and the charmed circle it contained, and another day brought him to old familiar scenes; brought him to the home where he had loved and suffered. It was Annie who opened the door in answer to his ring. Pale-faced, with a trace of tears about the eyes, with a gasp she caught her breath as she saw and recognized the man before her. He saw the effect of his appearance upon her and a great pity welled up his heart for her. Calmly he greeted her with,

"Will you not bid me enter?"

Hesitatingly she did so; speaking never a word, only stepping back she threw open the door of the well known little parlor. Within its cool shade he took both her hands in his,

"What is it, Annie? Trust me—tell me all. I have not come to censure you but to see that you are cared for. Has that scape-grace brother of mine——"

"Don't," she said, "Don't blame him. He may be faulty, but he loves me. Ah, yes, he loves me more than I deserve. I made him reckless with my foolish cravings. Every wish of mine was satisfied. I could not realize that ten thousand dollars was not a limitless fortune, and when Robert, always delicate, broke down altogether, we were almost penniless. I tried then to repay him. I nursed him and I worked for him. All the pretty things he gave me I again sold, but I am afraid I cannot retain him. He is slipping away from my grasp, and oh! I love him so, I love him so."

Almost choking, the words broke from her in a smothered sob. Her hands went up to her face and the tears trickled down through the thin, white fingers as the sobs shook her frame. A lump rose in Milton's throat,

"Take me to him!"

"You will say nothing harsh or unkind?"

She asked it with a fearful tremor in her voice. He took one trembling hand in one of his, the other with a gentle caressing motion he laid on the brown head,

"When was I ever so unkind to you that you should fear me now? Lead on, little girl. He is my brother, and he is sick."

With an effort she checked her sobs and dried her tears.

"Come," she said. He followed her up the stairway into what had once been their joint bedroom, and there reclining upon a lounge at the window, his eyes wandering wearily, lay Robert. Pain and care had made sad havoc with the delicate frame. Annie glided to him and knelt at his side laying her cheek to his hand.

"Robert," she said softly, "Robert, someone has come to see you!"

Turning from the open window his eyes fell upon the brother they both had so wronged; his face became ghastly,

"Milton, you here!"

Milton stepped forward,

"Softly, brother—no undue excitement. I bear you no ill will. I have learned to realize that it was not all your fault. It was all the outcome of circumstances over which none of us had any control. I have not come to censure you, but to look after your welfare. Without means, how can Annie give you the care you need?"

Robert scarcely could believe he heard aright,

"You do not hate me, then—me, the destroyer of your happiness? Oh, you mock me!"

"No! I do not mock you. True, you both have caused me suffering, but it was only the cleansing fire needed to purify the grosser part of my nature. I don't blame you now—it was only natural. What is it your doctor prescribes for you? I want to see you get well and strong, and you can not do so with the load of anxiety I know your heart is burdened with."

Annie bowed her head and wept, and Robert was too weak to restrain the tears that would start.

"O, Milton," said Annie, "you are good; you are noble; how can we ever repay your kindness?"

"Tush! tush! little woman; say no more about it, but answer my question. What is it the doctor prescribes?"

"Oh, he prescribes what is far beyond our means," sobbed Annie. "An ocean voyage may do wonders for him, the doctor says; and a tour in foreign lands. The sunny skies of Italy, the mountain breezes of Switzerland—a summer's sojourn there might give him such health as has never been his."

Milton stepped to the nearest window and gazed meditatively into— nothing. This would take more money than be had at his command, although he had quite a snug sum with which many necessities could be procured for the sick brother, but that was all. Should he call for aid upon the friend who had already been all too generous to him? Why not? Did he not know that his call would not be in vain? and was not the life of his brother at stake, and also the happiness of the woman who had once been all in all to him? These facts were now uppermost in his mind; all else was forgotten. Yes! he would ask Owen to aid him. So turning from the window he said:

"Cheer up, Annie, Robert shall have his voyage and tour, and you shall go with him. And when you return I hope to see the roses blooming in your cheeks. Possibly it may be wisest for you to remain abroad several years, spending your summers in the mountain air, your winters in the sunny south, in balmy Italy. In return I only wish to be kept posted as to all of your movements, I want regular reports as to the state of your health and when you are ready to return I may have something to tell you which I think will surprise you as much as you have been surprised today."

In this strain he went on leaving them neither time nor opportunity to say much. Preparations were immediately begun. A telegram was sent to Owen. In a few days the required amount in ready cash was at their disposal, and two weeks from the day Milton first appeared at the side of his brother he saw him and Annie safe on deck the steamer "Anchor," surrounded with every comfort money could buy.

"Be judicious with your supply of money," was his parting injunction. "Let past experience be a warning. It is to regain your health you are taking this voyage. Remember and be wise."

And Robert's answer had been,

"I will! so help me the memory of my noble brother."

As Milton bade Annie good bye, clasping her hand in his, he for a moment looked deep into the starry eyes, then bending he touched his lips tenderly to hers. Thus he left them. "Will it be for their good?" he asked himself. "Ah, well; time will tell!" Twenty-four hours later he held Alice in his arms, pressing burning kisses upon her sweet lips, while Lawrence saw and understood all. For Lawrence, in company with the others, had returned during Milton's absence, and could well afford to smile, for had not a pair of serious gray eyes smiled him a welcome which had the promise of heaven in it?

What had been the result of the prospecting tour? A rare, sweet spot of Mother Earth had been found, with just enough of rugged wildness to show to advantage nature's grandeur. Mountains in the distance; a rolling, undulating country; a winding river and the glassy bosom of the lake. Last, but not least, the towers and chimney pots of a distant city. All this could be seen from the rounded knoll gently sloped to its base, around which wound a merry rippling brooklet.

Thence a level meadow land which could be laid out in lovely lawns, parks and drives. Still farther on patches of woodland to the right and left; meadows with lowing cattle; a charming spot indeed, surrounded by nature's loveliest scenes. Only about ten minutes walk to the little station-house south of the knoll, where almost every hour of the day trains passed and stopped, and which in forty minutes would carry you to the heart of the city. But it was not until the early days of August that ground was broken and work begun upon the mansion that was to stand a pattern and a beacon for the generations to come. The winter months put an end to the work and the long stormy evenings were again spent as before. But again spring returned and again the work was resumed.

At the same time hot-houses were built; a vineyard laid out; orchards planted with rare fruit trees, and berry patches cultivated. Grounds were laid out; drives made; miniature lakes appeared; grassy knolls; groups of trees; charming arbors; inviting summer-houses; cozy retreats and lovers' nooks. To produce all this meant work—work to many willing hands; bread to hungry mouths. Owen paid the bills with generous hand, while each day at lunch time the workers enjoyed an hour or two of repose and shelter from the sun.

CHAPTER XLIV

Another winter came and still the home was not finished, but now the work on the buildings could still go on, as it was mainly within doors and under shelter. In the heated rooms the skilled workmen found their tasks easy, and under their hands the rooms were rapidly turned into bowers of beauty and use. The gardeners were kept busy during all the winter months and in the early springtime commenced their outdoor work of beautifying the place. Fountains, statues and other objects of beauty and use grew as if by magic. The hot-houses and conservatories were wonders of beauty and elegance. Then came the work of furnishing the building. Again money was not spared to make everything perfect. Every nook and arch contained some rare piece of art—of sculptured work. Exquisite paintings graced the walls. Breakfast and noonday meals were to be taken in what was called the breakfast room. This room was arranged simply for comfort—warm and cozy for the winter, cool and shaded for the summer. The furniture was covered with leather. The breakfast was to be simple, consisting principally of milk, grain foods and fruits. The mid-day meal to which it was expected few would gather was again simple—fruits and nuts playing a leading part.

But in the evening when all should be gathered together to enjoy as well as eat—but we are anticipating—too eager to lift the veil from the future. Let us wait, rather, until all our dear friends shall be gathered, to partake of their first evening meal here in the new home; for the present let us go on with our description of this glorious structure.

And yet, how shall we describe it? The most vivid fancy fails to do it justice. The corridors, whose floors are inlaid with tile; the marble staircases; the painted walls; the carved ceilings; the cozy private rooms—each in itself a gem; books and music to be found in them all; each a sanctum for the owner thereof. The library, the music room and the drawing room, each perfect as to form and dimensions; each flooded with brilliant light, or softly toned down as the fancy would demand or occasion call for, yet all arranged so as not to cause needless work.

It was the desire and expectation of this happy household to have such only move about the rooms as were fairly intelligent and cultured. "We don't want them to be servants, who do the work in this home." Owen had remarked, "but comrades and mates, each doing a share. No drones. Drones and idlers do not deserve to enjoy."

Among the details worthy of particular mention were the bath rooms. Not little tubs wherein one person could scarce recline, but a bath in which the bather could splash and swim and romp, not a bath in which false modesty would allow a single occupant only, but one in which a bevy of bathers could enjoy the luxury at the same time. Hot and cold water; steam baths and shower baths—O what a blessing in the cleansing, purifying element! bringing health and strength to all who are wise enough to rightly use it. Just watch the healthy babe in the bath, as it kicks and splashes and screams with delight. Was there ever a more beautiful sight?

Then we come to a wing of this grand building which as yet was, and for a little while would be, closed. Not that this wing was not furnished or completed in every little detail, but the use to which it had been dedicated was not yet here. One or more hearts were waiting and hoping for love's crown—in more than one breast the expectation was strong that at their knock the mystic door would open. What was this mysterious wing? The sanctum of the prospective mother!

Here she was to be surrounded by every beauty and comfort that art could supply and that money could buy. Wherever her eyes should turn they would rest upon representations of nature's most perfect work—the nude human form! From the little dimpled cupid to the graceful undulating curves of the perfect woman and the outlines of the strength and beauty of the perfect man. Here was the workshop of art. The expectant mother would here be taught to mold the clay, to use the pallet and brush or in the quiet and rest secured her here she could learn to wield the pen. Her gems of thought would thus influence and mold the mentality of her unborn child, and would leap like flashes of sunshine to the world without. Here the builder of the coming child could withdraw to perfect rest and quiet, and here she could steep her soul in music and poetry, and the child which was asked for, which was longed for and demanded, as a pledge of love— the child which was begotten under holiest influences and gestated under such perfect surroundings—could such a child be anything else than ideal? anything less than divine? Released from all the old superstitions of right and wrong; seeing absolutely no wrong in holy love, with a conscience that waits not for sanction of church or state for the consummation of love, but follows only nature's dictates,—who would dare to set the seal of impurity upon the product of such desires, such holy aspirations, such hopes and such longings! Gently, reverently, we close the door of this holy of holies until it opens again to the knock of the favored one.

Is there still more to tell? O yes much more, but space and language fail. We cannot tell you half there is to tell. There is the concert hall, the lecture hall, the dancing hall, the theater—all awaiting their turn to be unlocked, for hope is strong within the breasts of the little band that their number will not always be so small, but that in a few short years every room in the spacious building will have its occupant, every hall its throngs of visitors.

In still other rooms beyond, where baby-life is to thrive, the cooing, kicking, little mortals will not be wanting. Where the nurse, to whose care the little treasures are to be entrusted, fully understands the responsibility of her work. No gorging her little charges with sweets, souring their little stomachs; no dosing with soothing syrups and paregorics, sleeping potions, horrid teas and what not, dulling and stupefying their brains and destroying the natural brightness of the child's mentality. O no! This nurse understands better what is for the good of the dimpled, rollicking morsels of humanity entrusted to her care, and as a result she can sleep soundly the long night through. The babes do not disturb her. The perfectly healthy treatment they receive lulls them to sleep and they lie coiled up like downy balls, the chubby fists resting on the dimpled cheeks. What heart would not such a picture gladden?

Are we anticipating again? The picture is so alluring that we cannot help letting our imagination wander, sometimes, but we must return and bring our friends to the now finished home.

It was the close of a sultry summer day, late in August, when Owen, stepping abruptly into the midst of our friends at the Westcot mansion, said:

"Our home is finished! When will you be ready to start for the new quarters?"

This question, though long expected, was not readily answered. All were eager to start, yet much was still to be attended to. The Westcot home had been sold, as it stood, with all its handsome furnishings. The younger Wallace children had lived, during the past year, almost wholly at the Westcots, though Mrs. Wallace had at first demurred not a little. But as the change in them grew daily more apparent she had fully consented, and had left them almost entirely to the management of her stepdaughters. In the spacious grounds of the Westcot place they were taught to play and romp and enjoy themselves in a style they had never known. The plan of sending them to boarding school had been given up. A boarding school education was fashionable—yes, but horribly demoralizing. It was to be purchased at the expense of sparkling eyes and glowing cheeks. "Better not," Edith had said. "Mrs. Westcot's little girls are taught at home; why not give these girls home lessons also?"

Accordingly Edith taught them their grammar, their arithmetic and geography. Hilda heard their reading and spelling and superintended their writing. Imelda taught them music and drawing while Cora cultivated their voices.

They were now no longer overburdened with long hours of study, when body and brain were weary. There was now plenty of time for healthy romping games, long strolls in the shady woods where they became interested in the mysteries of botany, and when evening came, though the day had been so pleasant the curly heads scarce touched the pillows ere sleep had closed the tired lids, not to open again until the morning sun peeped in at the eastern windows.

The boys received similar treatment. As Paul's clear and experienced eye almost instantly detected the cause of the evil that was threatening to make a wreck of their young lives, the same methods had from the first been made use of to fill their unemployed hours.

Such had been the lives of our friends, and now came the task of moving, or of emigration. The old familiar scenes, the walks and drives, the groves and the cooling fountains, would know them no more. Mr. and Mrs. Wallace had long since known of this project and it was with sincere regret they saw the day approach when they should say good bye to these elder, and at one time considered burdensome children. But far worse than they had expected—their younger children refused to remain behind, but insisted on going along to the new home.

At first Mrs. Wallace would hear none of it, but as they begged so hard, and were seconded by all the members of the "colony," she finally gave her consent.

Of course it is not to be supposed that Mr. and Mrs. Wallace, especially the latter, fully understood the nature of the home to which her children were to be taken. She was too thorough a woman of the world to countenance a scheme so unconventional, so outlandish. She only knew that it was a co-operative home her children were going to; that they had become bright, healthy and strong since she had given them into the care of her stepdaughters, and as she knew she would now have to send them away again to complete their education she wisely concluded it was better to send them where she felt assured they would be properly cared for, and more so as it was just as easy for them to come home on a vacation from the co-operative home as from any other school. And—yes, she could go to see them. The invitation had been tendered her, so that matter was satisfactorily settled.

Osmond, too, had a severe battle to fight. His life for the past two years had been a series of battles. His father had soon discovered the presence of Osmond's mother, and knew of his visits to her. With a volley of oaths he had issued the command that Osmond should never go near her again. To his surprise the boy not only demurred to this but firmly declared that he would go to see his mother as often as he desired. Almost dumb-founded the father shouted:

"What! Court the society of that outcast! that shameless creature who knows not the meaning of the word decency? the woman who——"

"No more of that!"—came in firm, almost defiant tones from the lips of the boy. "You have slandered the best and purest of women long enough—the woman I am proud to own as my mother! An accident made me acquainted with her and with her friends, and never until then did I know what purity meant, what true manhood and womanhood meant. My mother and my sister are women with whom any man might well be proud to claim kinship. I will not give up their companionship. I would rather cut loose from you!"

Mr. Leland stormed, fumed and cursed, but to no avail. The boy was firm.

"I will disinherit you!" he exclaimed. "I will cut you off without a cent!"

"Do so!" was the calmly uttered reply. "Then I will find some work to do and will transfer my life altogether to the side of my mother."

At this point Mr. Leland wisely desisted. Somehow he hoped to circumvent the boy; hoped to regain full control, forgetting that Osmond's mind was daily developing, and that he was now able to think for himself. So when the son's intention of going away with his mother and sister became known another storm broke loose. But Osmond was firm, and on the morning that witnessed the departure of the colonists he appeared with the rest, equipped and ready for the journey. Meta's dark head appeared beside him. She was growing to be quite a big girl and all along the journey she was his especial care. His "little sweetheart"—she had been termed long since, and the grave-faced child was proud of the title.

CHAPTER XLV

At the close of a warm sunny day they alighted at "Willow Grove," the name of the station nearest their future home. Wagons were in waiting, upon which their effects were loaded.

"But we will walk!" said Owen, "only ten minutes. The exercise will do us good, after our long confinement with scarcely any movement."

And with an arm encircling Cora's waist he led the way. Many were the exclamations of delight as beauty after beauty unfolded itself before their eyes, but when a turn in the roadway brought in full view the imposing stone structure with its many arches and turrets, its profusion of vines and flowers, a long drawn "Oh!" escaped from each beholder.

Owen drew Cora aside so as to permit the next couple, Lawrence and Hilda, to be first. Silently every man bared his head. Lawrence kissed the little hand resting upon his arm,

"Our Hilda's Home!"

With hands clasped above her heart Hilda stood and gazed.

"My dream realized! Mine the dream, but yours," turning to Owen, "the realization. To you belongs the honor and greatness of this hour."

"Tut, tut, little one! How worthless my millions without the plan,—without the work of the mighty mind. Have you no wish reserved for the architect?"

With tears suffusing her sight she turned and extended both hands to Lawrence, who reverently knelt and bowed his head over them.

"Mine own! I may hope to win you now. To be worthy of your sweet love!" Edith and Paul saw, and a quick glance of comprehension flashed from eye to eye.

Owen's arm encircled his precious Cora and a mystical silence fell over this band of lovers. Who of them all could resist the supreme eloquence of the hour? Margaret leaned her head against Wilbur's shoulder and Wilbur's dark head was bowed over Margaret's fair one, reminding one of "Faust and Gretchen." Imelda's wine-brown eyes were drinking in the adoration of Norman's blue ones. Her hands went up to his face, taking it between them.

"You understand me now?"

"Long, long ago, my dear one."

And a kiss followed the words, a seal, the emblem of his love and trust.

Milton's hand pressed a blonde head to his breast and the bright, happy face that is turned up to him promises oblivion for the dark hours in his past life.

Our stately Edith must not be forgotten. A warm glow suffuses her cheeks as she also is drawn closer to a manly breast, and glancing up her dark lustrous eyes meet those of the young physician in unutterable love and trust.

Mrs. Leland is looking on; her eyes wander from the grand structure over the spacious grounds and thence from couple to couple, every face illumined with a commingling of love, hope and joy, as they stand knocking at the door of an unknown world. Will it fulfill all their expectations? Her eyes fill with tears. Unconsciously she folds her hands as she reads the love-lit faces and sees there the fond hopes that unite each lover couple. Presently an arm steals about her neck and a cherished voice says,

"I will be your lover, my own mother. You are too young, by far, to be thus left alone!"

She smiles as she answers:

"I know you are that, my boy, but in time you will be a true lover of a true and perfect woman."

Meanwhile the younger portion of our band make themselves more noisily heard. They feel the influence of the surrounding beauty, and, as is natural, give vent to exultant cries and shouts. Presently Elmer's voice is heard demanding:

"I say, why are we all standing out here? I am hungry and tired; a bath and supper will go good, I'll wager."

Thus admonished a forward movement was again made, and in a very few minutes the welcoming portals had opened and received them. Flowers! flowers! A profusion of flowers everywhere. Each room had been furnished and decorated with a view to being especially adapted to the tastes of its future inmate. Owen took delight in pointing out each room to its owner. When all had sufficiently admired their sanctums a half hour was spent in baths and other refreshments. Pretty, airy and comfortable dresses were donned. Some of the rare flowers that filled the vases were fastened in the hair and at the waists of our happy girls and on the coat lapels of those of the masculine gender. Then the way to the drawing room was found, or simply the "parlor," as was the term for this surpassingly beautiful room.

Soon all had gathered in. The lovely "salon" had been duly admired — such comfort and ease, so cosy and homelike. Everything beautiful. Rich, but not too grand for use. Dinner, supper, or whatever you might choose to call the evening meal, was then announced, and all repaired to the dining hall. Have we already described this room? No! Then we must enter with our dear friends and while noting the effect upon them we will try to describe, just a little, what kind of place it was that had been selected in which to partake of the main meal of the day.

An apartment ample in dimensions; high and arched; with walls of glass to permit the light of day to flood the place; for other life was here to thrive than that alone of our free love circle. Rare plants; palms and cactus; trailing vines; sweet-scented flowers in great profusion and under canopies as in an alcove, the dining table had been set, covered with snowy linen and decked with flowers. Flowers in all shapes and forms, and of all colors. Above the table suspended from the ceiling was hung a large bell, formed of white carnations, held in place by two cupids floating in the air. The center of the table held a huge basin of finest porcelain, forming a miniature pond containing a delicate fountain showering coolness into the sweet-scented air. The basin itself filled with the most perfect of water lilies, the golden centers gleaming in the snowy depths. Vases filled with rare roses; delicate green wreathings; the various dishes; while the air was filled with delicious music, — low and sweet. Luscious fruits, nuts and sweet new milk, and such simple fare, formed the chief part of the repast that had been prepared. Meats and rich pastries had been dispensed with. But when had the participants ever enjoyed a meal more keenly? The folding doors of those transparent walls had been thrown wide open and the pure refreshing evening air was wafted to them, bearing with it the promise of golden future; while jest and wit and mirth flashed and sparkled like costly jewels in the bright gas light.

But time was gliding by on tireless wings. The sun was nearing the horizon, casting its last golden rays aslant upon distant waters of the river, and farther on the lake, causing the waters to be resplendent with the reflection of the setting orb. Like a living, glowing, quivering mass of liquid fire were the dancing, rippling waves, and all looked on this display of nature's charms with a feeling of awe and veneration. Silently they stood grouped, loving forms were drawn closer and firmer together as they watched the grand and glorious sight. Slowly the glowing orb sank beyond the distant heights; slowly the waters changed their gleaming brilliance to a more somber quietness; and as daylight disappeared ushering in the twilight with its fantastic shadows, the coming night sent forth its heralds, the weird humming of the near insects and the occasional hoot of the distant owl. The rising moon cast its mellow rays on the peaceful landscape, causing the waters of the lake in the distance to gleam with a silvery sheen. All these brought with them a quiet peace that could never be felt in the heart of the busy city.

No music or song thrilled the air on this first evening in the new home. Hearts were too full for utterance; too full for mirthful joy. Tired with their journey, filled with grave and subtile musings our friends sought quiet rather than mirth. The new life had begun. Dreams were now to be tested, verified, and each and all looked anxiously to the future—a future filled with hope, with trust, with high anticipation, and yet never for one moment forgetting that this same future would bring grave duties and responsibilities—duties and responsibilities that would show whether or not this little band of reformers, of innovators, was composed of the right elements to achieve success in a comparatively untried field of human endeavor.

CHAPTER XLVI

Five years have passed since the dedication of that beautiful home; years that have brought their changes; as time invariably does. The mystic rooms—the sanctum of the expectant mother—have been occupied, again and yet again. Our royal Margaret was the first to come under the spell of its sweet and wonderful influence. Giving herself up to the delightful occupations provided for in these secluded rooms, keeping ever in mind the grand result which was to come of it, one morning after a night of pain and suspense Wilbur kissed a fine, beautiful, healthy boy that was laid in his arms. Kneeling at her side with his head resting on the same pillow with the fair white face of his peerless Margaret the whisper greeted his ear:

"I am blessed today beyond the measure of women."

Who shall say that his happiness did not equal her own.

Another had not been long in following her brave example. When Cora's baby girl was laid upon her breast Owen's measure of happiness was filled and tears blinded his eyes as he kissed the mother of his child.

The two sisters, Edith and Hilda, both brought joy and happiness to their lovers' hearts by presenting them with miniature reflections of themselves, and Norman had held Imelda's boy to his heart.

By this time the babies that first came to the new home were making glad the hearts of their mothers by their childish prattle; some of the mothers were watching the first trembling footsteps, and now Alice was waiting, watching for the coming hour. Milton watched with worshipful tenderness the little fairy whose love was life to him.

New faces also now greet us. New comers have helped to fill the precious home, who were just as good and worthy as those whose fortunes we have so long followed.

But to return to the young mothers. They did not devote all their time to their darling babies. O, no! Dearly as they loved them they found that they had other work to do while the little ones were left to the care of those who were perfectly trustworthy, Not to be petted, not to be pampered and spoiled, but left to those who understood how to get to the depths of each baby nature.

When it is remembered what preparation had been made for their advent it is not surprising that they were wonderfully good babies. When it is remembered with what joy they were welcomed—welcomed while still in the first stages of foetal growth; how carefully the prospective mothers had been kept under calm, sweet and pure influences; how their minds had been kept active without taxing their strength; how constantly their souls had been bathed in the luxury of sympathy and love; how every part of their natures had been kept teeming with life—overflowing life; how carefully undue excitement had been warded off; how they were given every opportunity for cultivating the higher instincts,—the spiritual nature;— when all this is remembered we cannot help seeing that, on the principle of natural causation, the children of such mothers and of such influences could not be other than exceptionally well endowed and exceptionally well behaved.

But when the months had passed, during which the mother should give her personal care and attention to her cherished babe, it was transferred to the sole care of the experienced nurse, and she herself returned to her usual work, whatever that work might happen to be. There were so many fields open, and each made her choice. The head gardener was glad to get help in the tending and nursing of his plants and flowers. Nimble, dextrous fingers were needed to fashion the garments to be worn by the occupants of the home, and this large and beautiful home needed many willing hands to keep it beautiful. All this however was work which could be entrusted to and performed by stronger hands, if other work should prove more attractive, work in which more than ordinary intelligence and skill were required. Among our band were teachers of music and song, as might be expected of the artist soul seeking expression. Margaret had kissed her lover and baby good bye and had given another season to her loved profession, and had returned again with, O, such longing and love for the home and the circle of loved ones it contained.

But there was other work. The forty minutes required to reach the heart of the city were used by quite a number, morning and evening. In the heart of the city rose a grand emporium many stories high, where many hundreds of young women and men were employed, and which was the property of the home circle; an emporium which had been built by Norman and Lawrence and fitted up by Owen, and which was one of the largest business places in the great city; an emporium where people of all ages and sizes could purchase for themselves an outfit from the crown of their heads to the soles of their feet. There was the tailor's department and that of the dressmaker. There the milliner fashioned pretty headgear, and there all the beautiful artificial flowers, of which countless numbers were used from week to week were made. There the visitor would go from floor to floor, from department to department, and would find every place to have its own attraction, its own work.

But the most beautiful department of them all was that of the florist, where nature's handiwork was heaped up in wild and charming confusion, and where these floral beauties, by deft and cunning fingers, were arranged into designs without number, and in this department it was that you could see our own fair girls moving about, giving orders here, lending aid there, and again seeing that patrons were promptly served. All was life, all were busy, yet none were overworked, as none worked longer than five hours here. At seven o'clock in the morning when the doors were opened, they admitted what was termed the morning "turn." And when twelve o'clock announced the noon hour the merry throng, laughing and singing arrayed themselves for the street and went trooping out like a merry flock of birds, for their day of work was over. It was a day's work, and thus they were paid. With the striking of the hour of one, the afternoon "turn" began, and others filled the places of the morning workers. So the faces of the saleswomen and salesmen were always fresh and smiling, with none of that tired, wornout appearance that is so often noticeable in the young faces you meet behind the counter.

Where were all these employes housed? Heretofore as these people generally are housed. Those who still had a father or mother or both living, lived with them; in most cases large families crowded into two or three rooms. Others who were not so fortunate, had to submit to all the discomforts of cheap boarding houses, or lived in some stuffy back room or bleak attic. But a change was about to take place. Today the large business building is closed. No one moves about its wide halls and its many departments. It is a grand "fete" and gala day. Today is to be dedicated the grand new home which has been erected for them.

After two years of life in their co-operative home its inmates were convinced of its success and felt almost like thieves that they should enjoy so many privileges which were beyond the reach of those to whom they gave employment, and then the plans were made for a new home, and again Owen's millions did service and now a beautiful and grand structure had been erected. But not so far-away from the place of work as their own. That would have been cruelty to the morning "turn" who were expected to be at their post at the hour of seven, and equally unpleasant for the afternoon "turn" as it would cause them to be late for their evening meal.

Right on the outskirts of the city, where fifteen minutes would be all that would be required to bring them back and forth, a site was bought upon the brink of the beautiful river, elevated just enough to be beyond the reach of any possible flood. A park had been laid out which in time would be one of the handsomest the city could boast of, with its miniature lakes, its splashing fountains, its dense shrubbery, its gleaming statuary and flowery banks. And right in the midst of these beautiful surroundings this monster home was built. For three long years the workmen toiled, until when finished it was the finest of its kind that fancy could depict. A place where home pleasures would be given the workers, such as they had never known; where every arrangement had been made to amuse, to instruct, to educate, to develop the inmates. It boasted of its school rooms, its college, its sculpture hall and artist's studio, its lecture hall and theater, for which the best of traveling troupes were to be engaged, with perfect arrangements for the accommodation of those troupes. Here the players would not have to undergo the extra fatigue, after their tiresome work, to again dress for the street, catch the last cold car which was to take them to their place of lodging. No, indeed! The theater of the workers' home was a marvel of its kind. Large, airy, comfortable and well furnished rooms were attached to it, a room to every player, so near and convenient to the stage that it was not necessary to dress in little boxes or holes for their work. Here they could dress in quiet and comfort and then rest until the signal to begin was given.

When through with their work, in the pleasant, comfortable dining room connected with the theater for the convenience of this hard-working class of people—how hard-working few, not of the profession, ever realize—a simple but refreshing repast was served, which repast was so restful and had so much of real comfort in it that the traveling bands invariably forgot that intoxicants were absent from it.

Then there was a library with its thousands of volumes containing reading matter of every kind, but always choice, always select, always instructive. A large billiard room was also there. Then came the gymnasium for the development of physical strength and where both sexes were expected to participate. There was to be a singing class and dancing school.

The baths were not forgotten. Larger, more complete than at the first home—so many more were to make use of them here.

All arrangements were complete. A large, airy hall where breakfast and the mid-day meal were to be served. But here, as in that other home, the evening meal, which would be the chief meal of the day, was to be taken amidst nature's beauties in a large and beautiful conservatory. Owen had spent a fortune in furnishing it with the required plants which were of the rarest kinds. A miniature lake was formed in its center, wherein the little golden speckled beauties were dashing and splashing about in their merry chase. A fountain was reared in its center composed of half a dozen nude mermaids holding their hands aloft, their finger tips forming a circle from which the water was flung aloft in showering spray. Sweet voiced songsters filled the air with their thrilling music. Flowers bloomed in wild profusion; huge vases were filled with their brilliant treasures wherever they could be suitably placed.

At several places small artificial hills had been erected, ferns and grasses growing amidst the rocks. Through a small rocky ravine the water came tumbling into a basin below, forming a small lake. Palms, cactus and other plants were grouped at convenient places. Nooks and alcoves without number had been arranged wherein the tables had been placed and were now spread and awaiting the hungry guests, each table seating about a dozen and through it all rare, sweet music, coming from some hidden source lulled the tired senses to rest and quiet.

The last preparations had been made. The last garlands had been hung. To every room its inmate had been assigned, which promised them all the same sweet privacy when privacy was desired, as in the first and smaller home. Every room was furnished cozily and comfortably, and every inmate, if so they desired, could claim some musical instrument for their private use, besides which there was a music hall where first class musical instruments of all kinds abounded. A number of the best teachers had been engaged to supervise the different departments, to teach and bring to light the hidden talents that none might be lost, but all shine in their full glory.

The grounds were something wonderful, or in time would be so, when the years would have done their work. The drives were beautiful, so wide and clean. Ponds covered with waterlilies. Fountains everywhere. Lover's nooks and cozy retreats. Plants, shrubbery and flowers in glorious profusion, and artistic designs wherever the eye might rest. Down the sloping banks of the river wide, spacious stairways of hewn stone had been made which led down beneath the laving waters. Skiffs, large and small were moored here, inviting and wooing lovers of the watery element to trust themselves to its glassy bosom, to be rocked on its silvery, rippling waves and be borne whithersoever they might wish.

Owen had made a deep hole in his millions. Lack of funds should not prevent success. And now the new inmates of this wonderful home were waiting the summons to their first evening meal. All the "salons" of the lower floors were swarming with gayly dressed maidens and with young men attired in their best. Instinctively they knew that henceforth they must always put their best efforts to the front, and the blending of youthful voices in merry laughter made the listener glad.

But not all were young that were assembled here tonight. Many there were who had seen the darker side of life and who in all probability would prefer the solitude and quiet of their own rooms to the noisy merry-making of a careless and care-free youth.

And among all those who found a home within the walls of this magnificent structure those had not been forgotten whose labor had produced it, had made it the thing of beauty it now stood. As might be expected the builders had grown to love it as they worked, and the knowledge that they should enjoy its beauties and comforts when finished had stimulated them to work more eagerly and with extra skill until the day of its completion.

But now all are ready. At last the signal is given, the doors are flung wide, and just as the music of a brass band clashes through the resounding halls, playing a march from one of the master composers, the workers, all the workers, pour into the monster conservatory.

They thought it was fairy land opened to their view, floating in a sea of light. Among the rest we see the members of our own circle, scattered about here and there, every face radiant with happiness reflected from within.

No waiters are in attendance. At every table one of the fresh young maidens plays the part of hostess. On a smaller table near at hand, all the side dishes have been arranged. Tanks with new sweet milk, ice water and hot water; nothing that is likely to be desired has been forgotten or omitted. The next evening another of the young ladies will be detailed to preside.

When supper is over the tables are let remain as they are. The day's work is over. In the morning many busy hands will restore order, and by noon everything will again shine with tasteful beauty; the tables reset, fresh flowers filling all the vases, and the dishes awaiting refilling.

After they have all steeped their senses in the beauties of the surroundings and have satisfied the cravings of appetite the evening's pleasures begin. Music, song and tableaux have been arranged with exquisite skill. Cora's voice has lost none of its richness, none of its charms. On the contrary it is more flexible, more sweet and full, more perfect in every respect, and well it may be. Has she not spent two years in hard study after they came to the home, in making herself perfect in her art? At many a concert, during these years, has her sweet, thrilling voice been heard, and tonight she almost outdoes herself. She is perfectly happy and throws her whole soul into her work; deafening applause rewards her.

Margaret's rendition of "Deborah" meets with equal favor. She never fails to please.

Then follows some renditions of music wherein Imelda and Milton both excel, for they too have been spending time in developing their precious talents.

The evening's entertainment then concludes with a series of tableaux, three in number, entitled "Progress," which are received with storms of applause. They represent "The Past, the Present and the Future."

There is one feature that has not been announced upon the program. One whom we have almost forgotten to mention has opened the evening's festivities with a short address, dwelling on the object, the aim, the hopes that are to follow the evening's work. That one is an old time friend, probably forgotten by most of our readers. It is an old, white-haired gentleman with a well preserved air about him. It is the Mr. Roland, of the lecture room of the olden days and the fatherly friend of our Margaret and Imelda, and who is followed by another almost forgotten friend, the lecturer "Althea Wood."

When the curtain has dropped on the last tableaux the assembled audience refuses to be satisfied. They well know whose money has erected the palatial building and "Owen Hunter! Owen Hunter!" is now the cry. In response to this call Owen steps upon the stage and in a slow, graceful manner saunters up to the footlights. Waiting for the stormy welcome to subside, then in slow even tones he begins:

"Friends and comrades! You do me far too great honor in thus calling me to the front. What you term an act of greatness is simply one of justice. No merit is due to me that I control millions of dollars while millions of my fellow human beings this night are starving. My early years were droned away in luxury, ease and pleasure hunting, and in all probability I would have gone on thus to the end had not circumstances given me a shaking up, thereby showing me something of the darker side of life.

"What these circumstances were, what the means by which the awakening was brought about I cannot here tell you. The story would be too long. But I awoke to a sense of the fact that I was of no use whatever in the world. With the aid of minds superior to mine a home was planned, one for a small number of congenial friends who wished to try co-operation, and having proved it a success, this one for the busy bees of our great industrial hive was next planned.

"You have, until now, been the employes of the 'Home Company.' From this day forth you are partners therein. You will receive your salaries just the same as heretofore. At the end of the year the accounts will be squared and a dividend declared with which you are to pay your rent, so-called, for your home, but which in reality you are buying. For when you have paid rent amounting to the sum it has cost to erect this building, you will be the owners of it, not I. Moreover, you shall not be taxed with a shameless interest, and when your home is paid for and the original capital again garnered in, there will be countless other employes who are in need of a home like this, and which it will devolve upon us to erect. Do you see?"

And see they do! Such deafening shouts of applause never before filled a hall. It is a perfect uproar and it takes some time ere quiet can again be restored. Owen smilingly shakes his head——

"You do me too much honor, as I have before remarked. Believe me, you have much more reason to thank the bright minds and gentle hearts of the ladies of the 'Home' than—

"Three cheers for the ladies!"—someone shouted, and three rousing cheers were given, and then three more, and yet again three.

Owen sees that they are getting excited, and that he will have but little chance to say more, so he determines to end it at once.

"That is all, comrades. With the best of wishes for the future well being of your home, and with the sincerest hopes for the happiness of each of you I bid you good night—as I see it written on many bright, young faces that their restless feet are anxious for the dance to begin."

Another deafening round of applause follows. They would recall him but Owen will not respond.

The crash of music is then heard, sending forth its inviting strains, and soon the light footsteps trip to the measured chimes and the hours speed in happy merriment.

With such surroundings, such inducements, it will not be difficult to keep the young maidens fresh, healthy and pure-minded, and to keep the young men away from the influence of drink, of vice, of demoralization. No danger that they will unsex themselves through starvation of their sex natures. The needed magnetism is theirs through their constant mingling, and while this is only the beginning, while they have so much yet to learn, there is every hope, every evidence that the home will develop fine, healthy and intelligent women, strong, brave and noble men.

Already Owen has another home planned, to be situated farther out into the open country. "Products of the soil" will furnish the chief employment of this group of workers. Not all men and women prefer the bustling city life. There are many who cannot live and enjoy life away from nature. They would pine for the open air, the green fields, the cool shade of the woods. Only under the blue vault of heaven can happiness come to them. And for such as these also it is the desire of our friends to secure the advantages that only the co-operative home can supply. Owen is determined to show that his millions have not been vainly entrusted to his care, and that the advantages that wealth can procure shall be theirs to whom the wealth justly belongs—the producers.

Here we must leave the inmates of the just completed and dedicated home, on the threshold of their new life, and take one more farewell word to our friends of the "F. L." home—the children of my fancy, who have grown under my care, and who have become inexpressibly dear to me.

CONCLUSION

The evening meal is over. All have gathered on the broad veranda to watch the golden sunset as it dips its slanting rays in the river beyond. They are unusually quiet, even for this serious band. Last night's merry-making has made them just a little tired, besides which their hearts are full of unuttered prayers for the future success of that new home.

Mrs. Leland is sitting in the comfortable depths of an easy chair. A sturdy little man of four summers perches upon her knee, patting grandma's cheek, tossing her hair in his efforts to smooth it, taking her face between both chubby hands and drawing her head forward so that he can kiss her happy, smiling lips and altogether making love in the most approved child fashion.

Margaret is sitting at her feet, her arm thrown across her mother's knee, while her eyes with a happy, tender light follow the movements of her boy, and her heart swells with fond tenderness and pride at the knowledge that he is her very own.

At grandma's back stands Wilbur whose eyes also follow the antics of the boy when they for a few moments lose sight of the glorious sunset.

Mr. Roland is a visitor at the home tonight, and sits a little to the right of this group, quietly drinking in the scene before him in the pauses of the animated conversation he is carrying on with the brilliant little lecturer, Althea Wood, who also is a guest at the home tonight.

Farther to the left are various groups. The two pairs of sisters—Imelda and Cora, Edith and Hilda—have formed a circle, their babies forming the center of their attention. There are little prattlers while one sweet little cooing innocent lies close to Imelda's breast.

O, the joys of young motherhood! And the group of men that were standing a little apart felt the influence of the spell and each thought his sweetheart had never looked more fair.

Alice in delicate health was reclining in an easy chair while Milton with adoring eyes stood over her chair ready to do her slightest bidding. O, if she were only safely tided over the coming hour of trial! And as the sigh escapes him his hand caressingly toys with the bright mass of shining hair.

Lawrence has his Norma perched upon his knee answering her many questions. She has grown to be quite a big girl now, but has never outgrown her early love for her papa, and ever with the old delight greets his coming. The two are so near to Alice that she can comfortably watch them, and while a smile of proud tenderness wreathes her lips, it is Milton's hand to which they are laid.

"My baby!" She whispered the tender words.

"A little longer patience," is Milton's whispered reply, "and your baby will be your own!"

Her hand went up to his face with a caressing touch.

"I know," she smilingly said, "but it was Norma I meant this time."

He drew the hand to his lips as with a knowing smile he answered,

"Ah, I see!"

Lawrence now and then let his eyes wander to the mother of his child, then they would turn to the group of fair young women where a pair of sweet gray eyes met his in a tender glance, then to rest on the little one reclining against his bosom. Which did he love most? His eyes lit up with a glad tenderness as they rested on the little one and then he drew the fair curly head so near him, close to his heart and hid his face in the fluffy masses; could he himself answer the question?

Many other faces we see which are all new to us, but they are all men and women worthy to be called by these names.

A group of the younger people have strayed down to the sweet-scented gardens gathering flowers as they go. Osmond and Homer are fast friends. Both are young men untouched by the rough hand of fate. Their young manhood, so perfect in its strength and beauty giving them the appearance of young kings, so proud, so lofty, was their bearing. Elmer, too, could scarcely be termed a boy any longer. His twenty years sat well on his broad shoulders and the eyes of the fifteen year old Meta shone bright as stars, her cheeks flushed as he chased her through the winding mazes of the park, and when he had caught her and kissed the rosy lips she submitted as a matter of course with the most natural grace.

Osmond had thrown himself at the feet of Hattie Wallace whose nineteen summers sat lightly on her shoulders. She was such a fairy and with rosy hued cheeks she listened to the soft, love-freighted words that fell in whispers from Osmond's lips.

Homer's companion was a dark, soft-eyed young girl timid and shy who had been an inmate of the home for one year, where she had come with her mother who had fled in the dead of night from her husband and sought refuge in this haven of rest, and Homer was teaching the sweet Katie her first experience in the mysteries of love.

Aleda, the youngest of the Wallace girls was also there, and seventeen years had developed a truly pretty and healthy girl from the delicate querulous child. Another new comer had engaged her attention. Reading from a volume of Tennyson, a boy scarce older than herself was reclining at her feet. He too had been brought there by a mother, not one who had fled the cruelties of an unappreciative husband, as she had never applied the title to any man. He had been a child of love.

His mother, in the wild sweet delirium of a first love, had abandoned herself to her artist lover without a thought of right or wrong. And he, pure and noble had no thought of wronging her. But disease had early marked him for its own, and ere the child of his Wilma had seen the light of day his own life had closed in that sleep that knows no waking, and she was left alone to buffet the storms of life as best she could, an orphan and without friends. With a babe in her arms, of "illegal" origin, the path of her life had not been strewn with roses. But amidst all her privations and trials she had kept her love pure for her child and had fostered only instincts pure and holy in the young mind, and when she heard of the home she applied at its gates, telling her story in pure, unvarnished words, never dreaming of an effort to hide any of her past. Only by the light of truth could the delicate fair woman thread her path through the world.

As might be expected, she had been received with open arms. Wilma, the mother of Horace, our young poet, and Honora, Katie's mother, could now be seen as they stand arm in arm watching the golden sunset and the children whose future promises to bring with it less of the pain that has so early drawn silver threads through their own brown locks.

The world at large knew not the full meaning of this home as yet. The world is yet too completely steeped in superstition and ignorance to have permitted its existence had the full meaning been known. The "Hunter Co-operative Home" it had been called, and thus it was known to the world. It was known that babes had made their advent therein, but none but the initiated knew that marriage as an institution was banished from its encircling walls.

Would you ask us if happiness was so unalloyed within those walls that no pangs of regret or of pain could enter there? Well, no! We are not so foolish as to make such claim. There are hours of temptation; there are moments of forgetfulness; there are sometimes swift, keen, torturing pangs that nothing earthly can completely shut out. Our heroes and heroines are not angels. They are—when the very best of them has been said—only intelligent, sensible and sensitive men and women—but men and women who are possessed of high ideals and who are striving hard to reach and practicalize them. They live in a world of thought. They do nothing blindly, inconsiderately; their every action is done with eyes wide open. In trying to gain the goal they have set themselves to reach, they strive not to think of self alone. The future of those who have been entrusted to their care, the young lives their love has called into existence, exacts from them much of self-denial. They are individualists, yet not so absolutely such that they do not realize that sometimes the ego must be held in check so as not to rob another of his, or her birthright.

You ask again, "Does this home life, as you have pictured insure against the possibility of the affections changing?"

And again we answer, No! Certainly not. Such changes will and must come. Yet it is not to be expected that where there is liberty, in the fullest sense of the word, life will be a constant wooing? Is it not the lack of liberty that deals the death blow to many a happy, many a once happy home? to many a home that was founded in the sweetest of hopes, the brightest of prospects, only to be shattered and wrecked in a few short years? aye, even a few short months or weeks? And when such a change does come, in spite of all efforts to prevent, how great a thing it must be to know yourself free! free to embrace the new love without the horrible stigma of "shame!" as our modern society now brands it, and which stigma causes such unspeakable misery, such endless suffering.

And if a woman desires to repeat the experience of motherhood, why should it be wrong when she selects another to be the father of her, instead of the one who has once performed this office for her? Why should the act be less pure when she bestows a second love, when the object of this second love is just as true, just as noble, just as pure-minded as was the first one? Why should an act be considered a crime with one partner which had been fully justified with another?

Reader, judge me not hastily. Judge not my ideas, my ideals, without having first made a careful study of life as you find it around you. My words are backed by personal experience and observation, experience as bitter as any that has been herein recorded. Indeed I doubt if I should, or could, ever have given birth to the thoughts expressed in these pages had it not been for that experience—which is one of a thousand—and when you have carefully weighed my words, think of the good that must result to future generations when unions are purely spontaneous, saying nothing of the increase of happiness to those who are permitted thus to choose, and to live.

When, O, when will the great mass of humanity learn and realize that in enforced motherhood, unwelcome motherhood, is to be found the chief cause of the degradation that gives birth to human woe. When will they see that unwelcome motherhood is the curse resting upon and crushing out the life energies of woman; while on the other hand, the consciousness of being the mother of a desired babe, a child conceived in a happy, a loving embrace, needs no other blessing, no other sanction, no other license, than such act itself bestows.